Dear Reader,

I love fast-paced stories where nothing is quite as it seems. That's one reason I enjoy writing amnesia stories. There is nothing more frightening than not being able to remember who you are—or worse, what has happened to you.

In *Deliverance at Cardwell Ranch*, Austin Cardwell gets caught in a blizzard just before Christmas and comes upon a car upside down in the middle of the highway. The sole occupant is a beautiful woman who is clearly terrified—and confused. She swears it isn't her car or her purse—or her child's baby seat!— inside the car. But if that's true, who is she? And maybe more important, who is after her?

In *A Woman with a Mystery*, one of my earlier books for Harlequin Intrigue, Holly Barrows stumbles out of a snowstorm and into the arms of Slade Rawlins. But is Holly's a case of amnesia, or is something more sinister at work here? Unfortunately, Holly vanishes before Slade can find out. But just over nine months later, Holly reappears claiming that someone has stolen her baby—a baby, if it existed, that could only be his.

I hope you enjoy these two stories set against the backdrop of the Montana I love at Christmastime.

Visit me at www.bjdaniels.com.

Happy reading!

B.J. Daniels

ABOUT THE AUTHOR

New York Times bestselling author B.J. Daniels wrote her first book after a career as an award-winning newspaper journalist and author of thirty-seven published short stories. That first book, *Odd Man Out*, received a four-and-a-half-star review from *RT Book Reviews* and went on to be nominated for Best Harlequin Intrigue that year. Since then, she has won numerous awards, including a career achievement award for romantic suspense and many nominations and awards for best book.

Daniels lives in Montana with her husband, Parker, and two springer spaniels, Spot and Jem. When she isn't writing, she snowboards, camps, boats and plays tennis. Daniels is a member of Mystery Writers of America, Sisters in Crime, International Thriller Writers, Kiss of Death and Romance Writers of America.

To contact her, write to B.J. Daniels, PO Box 1173, Malta, MT 59538, or email her at bjdaniels@mtintouch.net. Check out her website, www.bjdaniels.com.

Books by B.J. Daniels

HARLEQUIN INTRIGUE

*Whitehorse, Montana
§Whitehorse, Montana:
   The Corbetts
**Whitehorse, Montana:
   Winchester Ranch
^Whitehorse, Montana:
   Winchester Ranch Reloaded
‡Whitehorse, Montana:
   Chisholm Cattle Company
&Cardwell Cousins

Other titles by this author available in ebook format.

DELIVERANCE AT CARDWELL RANCH

&

A WOMAN WITH A MYSTERY

New York Times *and* USA Today *Bestselling Author*

B.J. DANIELS

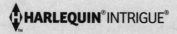

ISBN 13: 978-0-373-83802-8

Deliverance at Cardwell Ranch & A Woman with a Mystery

Copyright © 2014 by Harlequin Books S.A.

The publisher acknowledges the copyright holder of the individual works as follows:

Deliverance at Cardwell Ranch
Copyright © 2014 by Barbara Heinlein

A Woman with a Mystery
Copyright © 2001 by Barbara Heinlein

Recycling programs
for this product may
not exist in your area.

HARLEQUIN®
www.Harlequin.com

Printed in U.S.A.

CONTENTS

This book is for all my readers who enjoy coming back to Montana and visiting Cardwell Ranch! Happy Trails!

DELIVERANCE AT CARDWELL RANCH

Chapter One

Snow fell in a wall of white, giving Austin Cardwell only glimpses of the winding highway in front of him. He'd already slowed to a crawl as visibility worsened. Now on the radio, he heard that Highway 191 through the Gallatin Canyon—the very one he was on—was closed to all but emergency traffic.

"One-ninety-one from West Yellowstone to Bozeman is closed due to several accidents including a semi rollover that has blocked the highway near Big Sky. Another accident near West Yellowstone has also caused problems there. Travelers are advised to wait out the storm."

Great, Austin thought with a curse. *Wait out the storm where?* He hadn't seen any place to even pull over for miles let alone a gas station or café. He had no choice but to keep going. This was just what this Texas boy needed, he told himself with a curse. He'd be lucky if he reached Cardwell Ranch tonight.

The storm appeared to be getting worse. He couldn't see more than a few yards in front of the rented SUV's hood. Earlier he'd gotten a glimpse of the Gallatin River to his left. On his right were steep rock walls as the two-lane highway cut through the canyon. There was nothing but dark, snowcapped pine trees, steep mountain cliffs and the frozen river and snow-slick highway.

"Welcome to the frozen north," he said under his breath as he fought to see the road ahead—and stay on it. He blamed his brothers—not for the storm, but for his even being here. They had insisted he come to Montana for the grand opening of the first Texas Boys Barbecue joint in Montana. They had postponed the grand opening until he was well enough to come.

Although the opening was to be January 1, his cousin Dana had pleaded with him to spend Christmas at the ranch.

You need to be here, Austin, she'd said. *I promise you won't be sorry.*

He growled under his breath now. He hadn't been back to Montana since his parents divorced and his mother took him and his brothers to Texas to live. He'd been too young to remember much. But he'd found he couldn't say no to Dana. He'd heard too many good things about her from his brothers.

Also, what choice did he have after missing his brother Tag's wedding last July?

As he slowed for another tight curve, a gust of wind shook the rented SUV. Snow whirled past his windshield. For an instant, he couldn't see anything. Worse, he felt as if he was going too fast for the curve. But he was afraid to touch his brakes—the one thing his brother Tag had warned him not to do.

Don't do anything quickly, Tag had told him. *And whatever you do, don't hit your brakes. You'll end up in the ditch.*

He caught something in his headlights. It took him a

moment to realize what he was seeing before his heart took off at a gallop.

A car was upside down in the middle of the highway, its headlights shooting out through the falling snow toward the river, the taillights a dim red against the steep canyon wall. The overturned car had the highway completely blocked.

Chapter Two

Austin hit his brakes even though he doubted he stood a chance in hell of stopping. The SUV began to slide sideways toward the overturned car. He spun the wheel, realizing he'd done it too wildly when he began to slide toward the river. As he turned the wheel yet again, the SUV slid toward the canyon wall—and the overturned car.

He was within only a few feet of the car on the road, when his front tires went off the road into the narrow snow-filled ditch between him and the granite canyon wall. The deep snow seemed to grab the SUV and pull it in deeper.

Austin braced himself as snow rushed up over the hood, burying the windshield as the front of the SUV sunk. The ditch and the snow in it were much deeper than he'd thought. He closed his eyes and braced himself for when the SUV hit the steep rock canyon wall.

To his surprise, the SUV came to a sudden stop before it hit the sheer rock face.

He sat for a moment, too shaken to move. Then he remembered the car he'd seen upside down in the middle of the road. What if someone was hurt? He tried his door, but the snow was packed around it. Reaching across the seat, he tried the passenger side. Same problem.

As he sat back, he glanced in the rearview mirror. The rear of the SUV sat higher, the back wheels still partially up on the edge of the highway. He could see out a little of the back window where the snow hadn't blown up on it and realized his only exit would be the hatchback.

He hit the hatchback release then climbed over the seat. In the back, he dug through the clothing he'd brought on the advice of his now "Montana" brother and pulled out the flashlight, along with the winter coat and boots he'd brought. Hurrying, he pulled them on and climbed out through the back into the blinding snowstorm, anxious to see if he could be of any help to the passengers in the wrecked vehicle.

He'd waded through deep snow for a few steps before his feet almost slipped out from under him on the icy highway. No wonder there had been accidents and the highway had closed to all but emergency traffic. The pavement under the falling snow was covered with glare ice. He was amazed he hadn't gone off the road sooner.

Moving cautiously toward the overturned car, he snapped on his flashlight and shone it inside the vehicle, afraid of what he would find.

The driver's seat was empty. So was the passenger seat. The driver's air bag had activated then deflated. In the backseat, though, he saw something that made his pulse jump. A car seat was still strapped in. No baby, though.

He shined the light on the headliner, stopping when he spotted what looked like a woman's purse. Next to it was an empty baby bottle and a smear of blood.

"Hello?" he called out, terrified for the occupants of the car. The night, blanketed by the falling snow, felt too quiet. He was used to Texas traffic and the noise of big-city Houston.

No answer. He had no idea how long ago the accident had happened. Wouldn't the driver have had the good sense to stay nearby? Then again, maybe another vehicle had come from the other side of the highway and rescued the driver and baby. Strange, though, to just leave the car like this without trying to flag the accident.

"Hello?" He listened. He'd never heard such cold silence. It had a spooky quality that made him jumpy. Add to that this car being upside down in the middle of the highway. What if another vehicle came along right now going too fast to stop?

Walking around the car, he found the driver's side door hanging open and bent down to look inside. More blood on the headliner. His heart began to pound even as he told himself someone must have rescued the driver and baby. At least he hoped that was what had happened. But his instincts told him different. While in the barbecue business with his brothers, he worked as a deputy sheriff in a small town outside Houston.

He reached for his cell phone. No service. As he started to straighten, a hard, cold object struck him in the back of the head. Austin Cardwell staggered from the blow and grabbed the car frame to keep from going down. The second blow caught him in the back.

He swung around to ward off another blow.

To his shock, he came face-to-face with a woman wielding a tire iron. But it was the crazed expression on her bloody face that turned his own blood to ice.

Chapter Three

Austin's head swam for a moment as he watched the woman raise the tire iron again. He'd disarmed his fair share of drunks and drugged-up attackers. Now he only took special jobs on a part-time basis, usually the investigative jobs no one else wanted.

Even with his head and back aching from the earlier blows, he reacted instinctively from years of dealing with criminals. He stepped to the side as the woman brought the tire iron down a third time. It connected with the car frame, the sound ringing out an instant before he locked an arm around her neck. With his other hand, he broke her grip on the weapon. It dropped to the ground, disappearing in the falling snow as he dragged her back against him, lifting her off her feet.

Though she was small framed, she proved to be much stronger than he'd expected. She fought as if her life depended on it.

"Settle down," he ordered, his breath coming out as fog in the cold mountain air. "I'm trying to help you."

His words had little effect. He was forced to capture both her wrists in his hands to keep her from striking him as he brought her around to face him.

"Listen to me," he said, putting his face close to

hers. "I'm a deputy sheriff from Texas. I'm trying to help you."

She stared at him through the falling snow as if uncomprehending, and he wondered if the injury on her forehead, along with the trauma of the car accident, could be the problem.

"You hit your head when you wrecked your car—"

"It's not my car." She said the words through chattering teeth and he realized that she appeared to be on the verge of hypothermia—something else that could explain her strange behavior.

"Okay, it's not your car. Where is the owner?"

She glanced past him, a terrified expression coming over her face.

"Did you have your baby with you?" he asked.

"I don't have a baby."

The car seat in the back of the vehicle and the baby bottle lying on the headliner next to her purse would indicate otherwise. He hoped, though, that she was telling the truth. He couldn't bear the thought that the baby had come out of the car seat and was somewhere out in the snow.

He listened for a moment. He hadn't heard a baby crying when he'd gotten out of the SUV's hatchback. Nor had he heard one since. The falling snow blanketed everything, though, with that eerie stillness. But he had to assume even if there had been a baby, it wasn't still alive.

He considered what to do. His SUV wasn't coming out of that ditch without a tow truck hooked to it and her car certainly wasn't going anywhere.

"What's your name?" he asked her. She was shaking harder now. He had to get her to someplace warm.

Neither of their vehicles was an option. If another vehicle came down this highway from either direction, there was too much of a chance they would be hit. He recalled glimpsing an old boarded-up cabin back up the highway. It wasn't that far. "What's your name?" he asked again.

She looked confused and on the verge of passing out on him. He feared if she did, he wouldn't be able to carry her back to the cabin he'd seen. When he realized he wasn't going to be able to get any information out of her, he reached back into the overturned car and snagged the strap of her purse.

The moment he let go of one of her arms, she tried to run away again and began kicking and clawing at him when he reached for her. He restrained her again, more easily this time because she was losing her motor skills due to the cold.

"We have to get you to shelter. I'm not going to hurt you. Do you understand me?" Any other time, he would have put out some sort of warning sign in case another driver came along. But he couldn't let go of this woman for fear she would attack him again or worse, take off into the storm.

He had to get her to the cabin as quickly as possible. He wasn't sure how badly she was hurt—just that blood was still streaming down her face from the contusion on her forehead. Loss of blood or a concussion could be the cause for her odd behavior. He'd have to restrain her and come back to flag the wreck.

Fortunately, the road was now closed to all but emergency traffic. He figured the first vehicle to come upon the wreck would be highway patrol or possibly a snowplow driver.

Feeling he had no choice but to get her out of this storm, Austin grabbed his duffel out of the back of the SUV and started to lock it, still holding on to the woman. For the first time, he took a good look at her.

She wore designer jeans, dress boots, a sweater and no coat. He realized he hadn't seen a winter coat in the car or any snow boots. In her state of mind, she could have removed her coat and left it out in the snow.

Taking off his down coat, he put it on her even though she fought him. He put on the lighter-weight jacket he'd been wearing earlier when he'd gone off the road.

In his duffel bag, he found a pair of mittens he'd invested in before the trip and put them on her gloveless hands, then dug out a baseball cap, the only hat he had. He put it on her head of dark curly hair. The brown eyes staring out at him were wide with fear and confusion.

"You're going to have to walk for a ways," he said to her. She gave him a blank look. But while she appeared more subdued, he wasn't going to trust it. "The cabin I saw from the road isn't far."

It wasn't a long walk. The woman came along without a struggle. But she still seemed terrified of something. She kept looking behind her as they walked as if she feared someone was out there in the storm and would be coming after her. He could feel her body trembling through the grip he had on her arm.

Walking through the falling snow, down the middle of the deserted highway, felt surreal. The quiet, the empty highway, the two of them, strangers, at least one of them in some sort of trouble. It felt as if the world had come to an end and they were the last two people alive.

As they neared where he'd seen the cabin, he hoped

his eyes hadn't been deceiving him since he'd only gotten a glimpse through the falling snow. He quickly saw that it was probably only a summer cabin, if that. It didn't look as if it had been used in years. Tiny and rustic, it was set back in a narrow ravine off the highway. The windows had wooden shutters on them and the front door was secured with a padlock.

They slogged through the deep snow up the ravine to the cabin as flakes whirled around them. Austin couldn't remember ever being this cold. The woman had to be freezing since she'd been out in the cold longer than he had and her sweater had to be soaked beneath his coat.

Leading her around to the back, he found a shutterless window next to the door. Putting his elbow through the old, thin glass, he reached inside and unlocked the door. As he shoved it open, a gust of cold, musty air rushed out.

The woman balked for a moment before he pulled her inside. The room was small, and had apparently once been a porch but was now a storage area. He was relieved to see a stack of dry split wood piled by the door leading into the cabin proper.

Opening the next door, he stepped in, dragging the woman after him. It was pitch-black inside. He dropped his duffel bag and her purse, removed the flashlight from his coat pocket and shone it around the room. An old rock fireplace, the front sooty from years of fires, stood against one wall. A menagerie of ancient furniture formed a half circle around it.

Through a door, he saw one bedroom with a double bed. In another, there were two bunk beds. The bathroom was apparently an outhouse out back. The kitchen was so small he almost missed it.

"We won't have water or any lavatory facilities, but we'll make do since we will have heat as soon as I get a fire going." He looked at her, debating what to do. She couldn't go far inside the small cabin, but she could find a weapon easy enough. He wasn't going to chance it since his head still hurt like hell from the tire iron she'd used to try to cave in his skull. His back was sore, but that was all, fortunately.

Because of his work as a deputy sheriff, he always carried a gun and handcuffs. He put the duffel bag down on the table, unzipped it and pulled out the handcuffs.

The woman tried to pull free of him at the sight of them.

"Listen," he said gently. "I'm only going to handcuff one of your wrists just to restrain you. I can't trust that you won't hurt me or yourself if I don't." He said all of it apologetically.

Something in his voice must have assured her because she let him lead her over to a chair in front of the fireplace. He snapped one cuff on her right wrist and the other to the frame of the heaviest chair.

She looked around the small cabin, her gaze going to the back door. The terror in her eyes made the hair on the back of his neck spike. He'd once had a girlfriend whose cat used to suddenly look at a doorway as if there were something unearthly standing in it. Austin had the same creepy feeling now and feared that this woman was as haunted as that darned cat.

With the dried wood from the back porch and some matches he found in the kitchen, he got a fire going.

Just the sound of the wood crackling and the glow of the flames seemed to instantly warm the room.

He found a pan in the kitchen and, filling it with snow from outside, brought it in and placed it in front of the fire. It wasn't long before he could dampen one end of a dish towel from the kitchen.

"I'm going to wash the blood off your face so I can see how badly you've been hurt, all right?"

She held still as he gently applied the wet towel. The bleeding had stopped over her eye, but it was a nasty gash. It took some searching before he found a first aid kit in one of the bedrooms and bandaged the cut as best he could.

"Are you hurt anywhere else?"

She shook her head.

"Okay," he said with a nod. His head still ached, but the tire iron hadn't broken the skin—only because he had a thick head of dark hair like all of the Cardwells—and a hard head to boot.

The cabin was getting warmer, but he still found an old quilt and wrapped it around her. She had stopped shaking at least. Unfortunately, she still looked confused and scared. He was pretty sure she had a concussion. But there was little he could do. He still had no cell phone coverage. Not that anyone could get to them with the wrecks and the roads the way they were.

Picking up her purse, he sat down in a chair near her. He noticed her watching him closely as he dumped the contents out on the marred wood coffee table. Coins tinkled out, several spilling onto the floor. As he picked them up, he realized several interesting things about what was—and wasn't—in her purse.

There was a whole lot of makeup for someone who

didn't have any on. There was also no cell phone. But there *was* a baby's pacifier.

He looked up at her and realized he'd made a rooky mistake. He hadn't searched her. He'd just assumed she didn't have a weapon like a gun or knife because she'd used a tire iron back on the highway.

Getting up, he went over to her and checked her pockets. No cell phone. But he did find a set of car keys. He frowned. That was odd since he remembered that the keys had still been in the wrecked car. The engine had died, but the lights were still on.

So what were these keys for? They appeared to have at least one key for a vehicle and another like the kind used for house doors.

"Are these your keys?" he asked, but after staring at them for a moment, she frowned and looked away.

Maybe she had been telling the truth about the car not being hers.

Sitting back down, he opened her wallet. Three singles, a five—and less than a dollar in change. Not much money for a woman on the road. Not much money dressed like she was either. Also, there were no credit cards.

But there was a driver's license. He pulled it out and looked at the photo. The woman's dark hair in the snapshot was shorter and curlier, but she had the same intense brown eyes. There was enough of a resemblance that he would assume this woman was Rebecca Stewart. According to the ID, she was married, lived in Helena, Montana, and was an organ donor.

"It says here that your name is Rebecca Stewart."

"That's not my purse." She frowned at the bag as if she'd never seen it before.

"Then what was it doing in the car you were driving?"

She shook her head, looking more confused and scared.

"If you're not Rebecca Stewart, then who are you?"

He saw her lower lip quiver. One large tear rolled down her cheek. "I don't know." When she went to wipe her tears with her free hand, he saw the diamond watch.

Reaching over, he caught her wrist. She tried to pull away, but he was much stronger than she was, and more determined. Even at a glance, he could see that the watch was expensive.

"Where did you get this?" he asked, hating that he sounded so suspicious. But the woman had a car and a purse she swore weren't hers. It wasn't that much of a leap to think that the watch probably wasn't hers either.

She stared at the watch on her wrist as if she'd never seen it before. The gold band was encrusted with diamonds. Pulling it off her wrist, he turned the watch over. Just as he'd suspected, it was engraved:

To Gillian with all my love.

"Is your name Gillian?"

She remembered *something,* he saw it in her eyes.

"So your name *is* Gillian?"

She didn't answer, but now she looked more afraid than she had before.

Austin sighed. He wasn't going to get anything out of this woman. For all he knew, she could be lying about everything. But then again, the fear was real. It was almost palpable.

He had a sudden thought. "Why did you attack me on the highway?"

"I…I don't know."

A chill ran the length of his spine. He thought of how she'd kept looking back at the car as they walked to the cabin. She had thought someone was after her. "Was there someone else in the car when it rolled over?"

Her eyes widened in alarm. "In the trunk."

He gawked at her. *"There was someone in the trunk?"*

She looked confused again, and even more frightened. "No." Tears filled her eyes. "I don't know."

"Too bad you didn't mention that when we were down there," he grumbled under his breath. He couldn't take the chance that she was telling the truth. Why someone would be in the trunk was another concern, especially if she was telling the truth about the car, the purse and apparently the baby not being hers.

He had to go back down anyway and try to put up some kind of flags to warn other possible motorists. He just hated the idea of going back out into the storm. But if there was even a chance someone was in the trunk...

Austin stared at her and reminded himself that this was probably a figment of her imagination. A delusion from the knock on her head. But given the way things weren't adding up, he had to check.

"Don't leave me here," she cried as he headed for the door, her voice filled with terror.

"What are you so afraid of?" he asked, stepping back to her.

She swallowed, her gaze locked with his, and then she slowly shook her head and closed her eyes. "I don't know."

Austin swore under his breath. He didn't like leaving her alone, but he had no choice. He checked to make sure the handcuff attached to the chair would hold in case she tried to go somewhere. He thought it might be just like her, in her state of mind, to get loose and take off back out into the blizzard.

"Don't try to leave, okay? I'll be back shortly. I promise."

She didn't answer, didn't even open her eyes. Grabbing his coat, he hurried out the back door and down the steep slope to the highway. The snow lightened the dark enough that he didn't have to use his flashlight. It was still falling in huge lacy flakes that stuck to his clothing as he hurried down the highway. He wished he'd at least taken his heavier coat from her before he'd left.

His SUV was covered with snow and barely visible. He walked past it to the overturned car, trying to make sense of all this. Someone in the trunk? He mentally kicked himself for worrying about some crazy thing a delusional woman had said.

The car was exactly as he'd left it, although the lights were starting to dim, the battery no doubt running down. He thought about turning them off, but if a car came along, the driver would have a better chance of seeing it with the lights on.

He went around to the driver's side. The door was still open, just as he'd left it. He turned on the flashlight from his pocket and searched around for the latch on the trunk, hoping he wouldn't have to use the key, which was still in the ignition.

Maybe it was the deputy sheriff in him, but he had a bad feeling this car might be the scene of a crime and whoever's fingerprints were on the key might be important.

He found the latch. The trunk made a soft *thunk* and fell open.

Austin didn't know what he expected to find when he walked around to the back of the car and bent down to look in. A body? Or a woman and her baby?

What had fallen out, though, was only a suitcase.

He stared at it for a moment, then knelt down and unzipped it enough to see what was inside. Clothes. Women's clothing. No dead bodies. Nothing to be terrified of that he could see.

The bag, though, had been packed quickly, the clothes apparently just thrown in. That in itself was interesting. Nor did the clothing look expensive—unlike the diamond wristwatch the woman was wearing.

Checking the luggage tag on the bag, he saw that it was in the same name as the driver's license he'd found in her purse. Rebecca Stewart. So if Rebecca Stewart wasn't the woman in the cabin, then where was she? And where was the baby who went with the car seat?

He rezipped the bag and hoisted it up from the snow. Was the woman going to deny that this was her suitcase? He reminded himself that she'd thought there was *someone* in the trunk. The woman obviously wasn't in her right mind.

He shone the flashlight into the trunk. His pulse quickened. Blood. He removed a glove to touch a finger to it. Dried. What the hell? There wasn't much, but enough to cause even more concern.

Putting his glove back on, he closed the trunk and picked up the suitcase. He stopped at his rented SUV to look for something to flag the wreck, hurrying because he was worried about the woman, worried what he would find when he got back to the cabin. He was digging in the back of the SUV, when a set of headlights suddenly flashed over him.

He turned. Out of the storm came the flashing lights of a Montana highway patrol car.

Chapter Four

"Let me get this straight," the patrolman said as they stood in the waiting room at the hospital. "You handcuffed her to a chair to protect her from herself?"

"Some of it was definitely for my own protection, as well. She appeared confused and scared. I couldn't trust that she wouldn't go for a more efficient weapon than a tire iron."

The patrolman finished writing and closed his notebook. "Unless you want to press assault charges…that should cover it."

Austin shook his head. "How is she?"

"The doctor is giving her liquids and keeping her for observation until we can reach her husband."

"Her husband?" Austin thought of the hurriedly packed suitcase and recalled that she hadn't been wearing a wedding ring.

"We tracked him down through the car registration."

"So she *is* Rebecca Stewart? Her memory has returned?"

"Not yet. But I'm sure her husband will be able to clear things up." The patrolman stood. "I have your number if we need to reach you."

Austin stood, as well. He was clearly being dismissed

and yet something kept him from turning and walking away. "She seemed…terrified when I found her. Did she say where she was headed before the crash?"

"She still seems fuzzy on that part. But she is in good hands now." The highway patrolman turned as the doctor came down the hallway and joined them. "Mr. Cardwell is worried about your patient. I assured him she is out of danger," the patrolman said.

The doctor nodded and introduced himself to Austin. "If it makes you feel better, there is little doubt you saved her life."

He couldn't help but be relieved. "Then she remembers what happened?"

"She's still confused. That's fairly common in a case like hers."

The doctor didn't say, but Austin assumed she had a concussion. Austin couldn't explain why, but he needed to see her before he left. The highway patrolman had said they'd found her husband by way of the registration in the car, but she'd been so sure that wasn't her car.

Nor had the highway patrolman been concerned about the baby car seat or the blood in the trunk.

"Apparently the baby is with the father," the patrolman had told him. "As for the blood in the trunk, there was so little I'm sure there is an explanation her husband can provide."

So why couldn't Austin let it go? "I'd like to see her before I leave."

"I suppose it would be fine," the doctor said. "Her husband is expected at any time."

Austin hurried down the hallway to the room the doctor had only exited moments before, anxious to see her before her husband arrived. He pushed on the door slowly and peered in, half fearing that she might not want to see him.

He wasn't sure what he expected as he stepped into the room. He'd had a short sleepless night at a local motel. He had regretted not taking a straight flight to Bozeman this morning instead of flying into Idaho Falls the day before. Even as he thought it through, he reminded himself that the woman would have died last night if he hadn't come along when he did.

Austin told himself he'd been at the right place at the right time. So why couldn't he just let this go?

As the door closed behind him, she sat up in bed abruptly, pulling the covers up to her chin.

Her brown eyes were wide with fear. He was struck by how small she looked. Her unruly mane of curly dark hair billowed out around her pale face, making her look all the more vulnerable.

"My name's Austin. Austin Cardwell. We met late last night after I came upon your car upside down in the middle of Highway 191." He touched the wound on the back of his head where she'd nailed him. "You remember hitting me?"

She looked horrified at the thought, verifying what he already suspected. She didn't remember.

"Can you tell me your name?" He'd hoped that she would be more coherent this morning, but as he watched her face, it was clear she didn't know who she was any more than she had last night.

She seemed to search for an answer. He saw the moment when she realized she couldn't remember anything—even who she was. Panic filled her expression. She looked toward the door behind him as if she might bolt for it.

"Don't worry," he said quickly. "The doctor said memory loss is pretty common in your condition."

"My *condition?*"

"From the bump on your head, you hit it pretty hard in the accident." He pointed to a spot on his own temple. She raised her hand to touch the same spot on her temple and winced.

"I don't remember an accident." She had pulled her arms out from under the covers. He noticed the bruises on her upper arms. They were half-moon shaped, like fingerprints—as if someone had gripped her hard. There was also a cut on her arm that he didn't think had happened during her car accident.

She saw him staring at her arms. When she looked down and saw the bruises, she quickly put her arms under the covers again. If anything, she looked more frightened than she had earlier.

"You don't remember losing control of your car?"

She shook her head.

"I don't know if this helps, but the registration and proof of insurance I found in your car, along with the driver's license I found in the purse, says your name is Rebecca Stewart," he said, watching to see if there was any recognition in her expression.

"That isn't my name. I would know my own name when I heard it, wouldn't I?"

Maybe. Maybe not. "You were wearing a watch…"

"The doctor said they put it in the safe until I was ready to leave the hospital."

"It was engraved with: 'To Gillian with all my love.'" He saw that the words didn't ring any bells. "Are you Gillian?"

She looked again at the door, her expression one of panic.

"Don't worry. It will all come back to you," he said, trying to calm her even though he knew there might always be blanks that she could never fill in if he was right and she had a concussion. He wished there was something he could say to comfort her. She looked so frightened. "Fortunately a highway patrolman came along when he did last night."

"Patrolman?" Her words wavered and she looked even more terrified, making him wonder if he might be right and that she'd stolen the car, the purse and the watch. She'd said none of it belonged to her. Maybe she *was* telling the truth.

But why was she driving someone else's car? If so, where was the car's owner and her baby? This woman's fear of the law seemed to indicate that something was very off here. What if this woman wasn't who they thought she was?

"Where am I?" she asked, glancing around the hospital room.

"Didn't the doctor tell you? You're in the hospital."

"I meant, where am I…?" She waved a hand to encompass more than the room.

"Oh," he said and frowned. "Bozeman." When that didn't seem to register, he added, "Montana."

One eyebrow shot up. *"Montana?"*

It crossed his mind that a woman who lived in Helena, Montana, wouldn't be confused about what state she was in. Nor would she be surprised to find herself still in that state.

He reminded himself that the knock on her head

could have messed up some of the wiring. Or maybe she'd been that way before.

Her gaze came back to him. She was studying him intently, sizing him up. He wondered what she saw and couldn't help but think of his former girlfriend, Tanya, and the argument they'd had just before he'd left Texas.

"Haven't you ever wanted more?" Tanya hadn't looked at him. She'd been busy throwing her things into a large trash bag. When she'd moved in with him, she'd moved in gradually, bringing her belongings in piecemeal.

"I'm only going to be gone a week," he'd said, watching her clean out the drawers in his apartment, wondering if this was it. She'd threatened to leave him enough times, but she never had. Maybe this was the time.

He had been trying to figure out how he felt about that when she'd suddenly turned toward him.

"Did you hear what I said?"

Obviously not. *"What?"*

"This business with your brothers..." She did her eye roll. He really hated it when she did that and she knew it. *"If it isn't something to do with* Texas Boys Barbecue..."

He could have pointed out that the barbecue joint she was referring to was a multimillion-dollar business, with more than a dozen locations across Texas, and it paid for this apartment.

But he'd had a feeling that wasn't really what this particular argument was about, so he'd said, *"Your point?"* even though he'd already known it.

"You're too busy for a relationship. At least that is your excuse."

"You knew I was busy before you moved in."

"Ever ask yourself why your work is more important

than your love life?" She hadn't given him time to respond. *"You want to know what I think? I think Austin Cardwell goes through life saving people because he's afraid of letting himself fall in love."*

He wasn't afraid. He just hadn't fallen in love the way Tanya had wanted him to. *"Glad we got that figured out,"* he'd said.

Tanya had flared with anger. *"That's all you have to say?"*

And he'd made it worse by shrugging, something he knew *she* hated. He hadn't had the time or patience for this kind of talk at that moment. *"Maybe we should talk about this when I get back from Montana."*

She'd shaken her head in obvious disgust. *"That is so like you. Put things off and maybe the situation will right itself. You missed your own brother's wedding and you don't really care if they open a barbecue restaurant in Montana or not. But instead of being honest, you ignore the problem and hope it goes away until finally they force you to come to Montana. For once, I would love to see you just take a stand. Make a decision. Do something."*

"I missed my brother's wedding because I was on a case. One that almost got me killed, you might remember."

Tears welled in her eyes. *"I remember. I stayed by your bedside for three days."*

He sighed and raked a hand through his hair. *"What I do is important."*

"More important than me." She'd stood, hands on hips, waiting.

He'd known what she wanted. A commitment. The

problem was, he wasn't ready. And right then, he'd known he would never be with Tanya.

"This is probably for the best," he'd said, motioning to the bulging trash bag.

Tears flowing, she'd nodded. *"Don't bother to call me if and when you get back."* With that, she had grabbed up the bag and stormed to the door, stopping only long enough to hurl his apartment key at his head.

"Where are my clothes?"

Austin blinked, confused for a moment, he'd been so lost in his thoughts. He focused on the woman in the hospital bed. "You can't leave. Your husband is on his way."

Panic filled her expression. She tried to get out of the bed. As he moved to her bedside to stop her, he heard the door open behind him.

Chapter Five

Austin turned to see a large stocky man come into the room, followed by the doctor.

"Mrs. Stewart," the doctor said as he approached her bed. "Your husband is here."

The stocky man stopped a few feet into the room and stood frowning. For a moment, Austin thought there had been a mistake and that the man didn't recognize the woman.

But the man wasn't looking at his wife. He was frowning at Austin. As if the doctor's words finally jarred him into motion, the man strode to the other side of the bed and quickly took his wife's hand as he bent to kiss her forehead. "I was so worried about you."

Austin watched the woman's expression. She looked terrified, her gaze locking with his in a plea for help.

"Excuse me," Austin said as he stepped forward. He had no idea what he planned to say, let alone do. But something was wrong here.

"I beg your pardon?" said the alleged husband, turning to look at Austin before swinging his gaze to the doctor with a *who the hell is this?* expression.

"This is the man who saved your wife's life," the doctor said and introduced Austin before getting a page that he was needed elsewhere. He excused himself and hurried out, leaving the three of them alone.

"I'm sorry, I didn't catch your name," Austin said.

"Marc. Marc Stewart."

Stewart, Austin thought, remembering the name on the driver's license in the purse he'd found in the car. "And this woman's name is Rebecca Stewart?" he asked the husband.

"That's right," Marc Stewart answered in a way that dared Austin to challenge him.

As he looked to the woman in the bed, Austin noticed that she gave an almost imperceptible shake of her head. "I'm sorry, but how do we know you're her husband?"

"Are you serious?" the man demanded, glaring across the bed at him.

"She doesn't seem to recognize you," he said, even though what he'd noticed was that the woman seemed terrified of the man.

Marc Stewart gave him the once-over, clearly upset. "She's had a *concussion.*"

"Old habits are hard to break," Austin said as he displayed his badge and ID to the alleged Marc Stewart. "You wouldn't mind me asking for some identification from you, would you?"

The man looked as if he might have a coronary. At least he'd come to the right place, Austin thought, as the alleged Marc Stewart angrily pulled out his wallet and showed Austin his license.

Marc Andrew Stewart, Austin read. "There was a car seat in the back of the vehicle she was driving. Where is the baby?"

"With my mother." A blood vessel in the man's cheek began to throb. "Look Deputy…Cardwell, is it? I appreciate that you supposedly saved my wife's life, but it's time for you to butt out."

Austin told himself he should back off, but the fear in the woman's eyes wouldn't let him. "She doesn't seem to know you and she isn't wearing a wedding ring." He didn't add that the woman seemed terrified and had bruises on her upper arms where someone had gotten rough with her. Not to mention the fact that when he'd told her that her husband was on his way, she'd panicked and tried to leave. Concussion or not, something was wrong with all this.

"I think you should leave," the man said.

"If you really are her husband, it shouldn't be hard for you to prove it," Austin said, holding his ground— well, at least until Marc Stewart had hospital security throw him out, which wouldn't be long, from the look on the man's face. The woman in the bed still hadn't uttered a word.

For a moment, Marc Stewart looked as if he was about to tell him to go to hell. But instead, he dug into his pocket angrily and produced a plain gold band that caught the light as he reached for the woman's left hand.

"My wife left it by the sink yesterday," Marc Stewart said by way of explanation. "She always takes it off when she does the dishes. Sometimes she forgets to put it back on."

Austin thought, given the bruises on the woman's upper arms, that she had probably thrown the ring at him as she took off yesterday.

When she still didn't move to take the ring, the man snatched up her hand lying beside her on the bed and slipped the ring on her finger.

Austin watched her look down at the ring. He saw

recognition fill her expression just before she began to cry.

Even from where he stood, he could see that the ring, while a little loose, fit close enough. Just as the photo ID in Rebecca Stewart's purse looked enough like the woman on the bed. He told himself there was nothing more he could do. Clearly she was afraid of this man. But unless she spoke up…

"I guess I'll leave you with your husband, unless there is something I should know?" Austin asked her.

"Tell the man, Rebecca," Marc Stewart snapped. "Am I your husband?" He bent down to kiss her cheek. Austin saw him whisper something in her ear.

She closed her eyes, tears leaking from beneath dark lashes.

"We had a little argument and she took off and apparently almost got herself killed," Marc said. "We both said and did things we regret, isn't that right, Rebecca? Tell the man, sweetheart."

Her eyes opened slowly. She took a ragged breath and wiped away the tears with the backs of her hands, the way a little kid would.

"Is that all there is to this?" Austin asked, watching her face. Across from him, he could see Marc gritting his teeth in fury at this interference in his life.

She nodded her head slowly, her gaze going from her husband to Austin. "Thank you, but he's right. It was just a foolish disagreement. I will be fine now."

FEELING LIKE A fool for getting involved in a domestic dispute, Austin headed for Cardwell Ranch. Last night, a wrecker company had pulled his rental SUV out of the ditch and brought it to the motel where he was staying. Fortunately, his skid into the ditch hadn't done any damage.

Highway 191 was now open, the road sanded. As he drove, Austin got his first real look at the Gallatin Canyon or "the canyon" as his cousin Dana called it. From the mouth just south of Gallatin Gateway, fifty miles of winding road trailed the river in a deep cut through the mountains, almost all the way to West Yellowstone.

The drive along the Gallatin River was indeed breathtaking—a snaking strip of highway followed the Blue Ribbon trout stream up over the Continental Divide. This time of year, the Gallatin ran crystal clear under a thick cover of aquamarine ice. Dark, thick snowcapped pines grew at its edge, against a backdrop of the granite cliffs and towering pine-clad mountains.

Austin concentrated on his driving so he didn't end up in a snowbank again. Piles of deep snow had been plowed up on each side of the road, making the highway seem even narrower, but at least traffic was light. He had to admit, it was beautiful. The sun glistening off the new snow was almost blinding in its brilliance. Overhead, a cloudless robin's-egg-blue sky seemed vast and clearer than any air he'd ever breathed. The canyon looked like something out of a winter fairy tale.

Just before Big Sky, the canyon widened a little. He spotted a few older cabins, nothing like all the new construction he'd seen down by the mouth of the canyon. Tag had told him that the canyon had been mostly cattle and dude ranches, a few summer cabins and homes— that was, until Big Sky Resort and the small town that followed at the foot of Lone Mountain.

Luxury houses had sprouted up all around the resort.

Fortunately, some of the original cabins still remained and the majority of the canyon was national forest so it would always remain undeveloped. The "canyon" had remained its own little community, according to Tag.

Austin figured Tag had gotten most of his information from their cousin Dana. This was the only home she'd known and, like her stubborn relations, she apparently had no intention of ever leaving it.

While admiring the scenery on the drive, he did his best not to think about Rebecca Stewart and her husband. When he'd left her hospital room, he'd felt her gaze on him and turned at the door to look back. He'd seen her take off the ring her husband had put on her finger and grip it in her fist so tightly that her knuckles were white.

Trouble in paradise, he thought as he reached Big Sky, *and none of my business.* As a deputy sheriff, he'd dealt with his share of domestic disputes. Every law enforcement officer knew how dangerous they were. The best thing was to stay out of the middle of them since he'd seen both husbands and wives turn on the outsider stepping in to try to keep the peace.

Cardwell Ranch was only a few miles farther up the highway from Big Sky. But on impulse, he swung onto the road to Big Sky's Meadow Village, where he suspected he would find the marshal's department.

His cousin Dana's husband, Marshal Hud Savage, waved him into his office and shook his hand. "We missed you at the wedding." The wedding, of course, had been his brother Tag's, to Lily McCabe, on July 4. He knew he would never live it down.

"I was hoping to get up for it, but I was on a case..." He hated that he'd missed his own brother's wedding, but hoped at least Hud, being a lawman, would understand.

"That's right. Deputy sheriff, is it?"

"Part-time, yes. I take on special cases."

"As I recall, there were extenuating circumstances. You were wounded. You're fine now?"

He nodded. He didn't want to talk about the case that had almost gotten him killed. Nor did he want to admit that he might not still be physically a hundred percent.

"Well, have a seat," Hud said as he settled behind his desk. "And tell me what I can do for you. I suspect this isn't an extended family visit."

Austin nodded and, removing his hat, sat down, comfortable at once with the marshal. "You might have heard that I got into an accident last night. My rental SUV went into the ditch."

"I did know about that. I'm glad you weren't hurt. We couldn't assist because we had our hands full down here with a semi rollover."

"I was lucky I only ended up in the ditch. What made me hit my brakes was that I came upon a vehicle upside down in the middle of the highway last night."

Austin filled him in on the woman and everything that had happened up to leaving her about thirty minutes ago at the hospital in Bozeman.

"Sounds like she and her husband were having some marital issues," the marshal said.

Austin nodded. "The trouble is I think it's more than that. She had bruises on her arms."

"Couldn't the bruises have been caused by the accident?"

"No, these were definitely finger impressions. More than that, she seemed scared of her husband. Actually,

B.J. Daniels

she told me she wasn't Rebecca Stewart, which would mean this man wasn't her husband." He saw skepticism in the marshal's expression and admitted he would have felt the same way if someone had come to him with this story.

"Look," Austin said. "It's probably nothing, but I just have this gut feeling…"

Hud nodded, as if he understood gut feelings. "What would you like me to do?"

"First, could you run the name Marc Stewart. They're apparently from Helena."

"If it will relieve your mind, I'd be happy to." The marshal moved to his computer and began to peck at the keys. A moment later, he said, "No arrests or warrants. None on Rebecca Stewart either. Other than that…"

Austin nodded.

Hud studied him. "There's obviously something that's still worrying you."

He couldn't narrow it down to just one thing. It was the small things like the older-model car Rebecca had been driving, the baby seat in the back, the woman's adamant denial that she was Rebecca Stewart, the look of fear on her face when he'd told her that her husband was on his way to the hospital, the way she'd cried when he'd put that ring back on her finger.

Then there was that expensive diamond watch. *To Gillian with all my love.*

He mentioned all of this to the marshal and added, "I guess what's really bothering me is the inconsistencies. Also she just doesn't seem like the kind of woman who would leave her husband—let alone her baby— right before Christmas, no matter what the argument might have been about. This woman is a fighter. She wouldn't have left her son with a man who had just gotten physical with her."

Hud raised a brow as he leaned back in his chair. "You sure you didn't get a little too emotionally involved?"

He laughed. "Not hardly. Haven't you heard? I'm the Cardwell brother who never gets emotionally involved in anything. Just ask my brothers, or my former girlfriend, for that matter." He hesitated even though common sense told him to let it go. "There's no chance you're going into Bozeman today, is there?"

Hud smiled. "I'll stop by the hospital and give you a call after I talk to her and her husband."

"Thanks. It really would relieve my mind." Glancing at his watch, he saw he was late for a meeting with his brothers.

He swore as he hurried outside, climbed behind the wheel of his rental SUV and drove toward the small strip shopping mall in Meadow Village, all the time worrying about the woman he'd left in the hospital.

THE BUILDING WAS wood framed with stone across the front. It looked nothing like a Texas barbecue joint. As Austin climbed out of the SUV and walked through the snow toward the end unit with the Texas Boys Barbecue sign out front, he thought of their first barbecue joint.

It had been in an old small house. They'd done the barbecuing out back and packed diners in every afternoon and evening at mismatched tables and chairs to eat on paper plates. Just the smell of the wonderfully smoked meats brought people in. He and his brothers didn't even have to advertise. Their barbecue had kept people coming back for more.

Austin missed those days, sitting out back having a cold beer after the night was over and counting their money and laughing at what a fluke it had been. They'd grown up barbecuing so it hadn't felt like work at all.

As he pushed open the door to the building his brothers had bought, he saw by the way it was laid out that the space had started out as another restaurant. Whatever had been here, though, had been replaced with the Texas Boys Barbecue decor, a mix of rustic wood and galvanized aluminum. The fabric of the cushy red booths was the same as that on the chairs, and red-checked tablecloths covered the tables. The walls were covered with old photos of Texas family barbecues—just like in their other restaurants.

Through the pass-through he could see a gleaming kitchen at the back. Hearing his brothers—Tag, Jackson, Laramie and Hayes—visiting back there, he walked in that direction.

"Well, what do you think?" Tag asked excitedly.

Austin shrugged. "It looks fine."

"The equipment is all new," Jackson said. "We had to add a few things, but other than that, the remodel was mostly cosmetic."

Austin nodded. "What happened to the restaurant that was here?"

"It didn't serve the best barbecue in Texas," Tag said.

"We'd hoped for a little more enthusiasm," Laramie said.

"Sorry."

"What about the space?" Hayes asked.

"Looks good to me." He saw them share a glance at each other before they laughed and, almost in unison, said, "Same ol' Austin."

He didn't take offense. It was actually good to see his brothers. There was no mistaking they were related either since they'd all inherited the Cardwell dark good looks. A curse and a blessing. When they were teens they used to argue over who was the ugliest. He smiled at the memory.

"Okay, we're opening a Texas Boys Barbecue in Big Sky," he said to them. "So buy me some lunch. I'm starved."

They went to a small sandwich shop in the shadow of Lone Mountain in what was called Mountain Village. As hungry as he was, Austin still had trouble getting down even half of a sandwich and a bowl of soup.

During lunch, his brothers talked enthusiastically about the January 1 opening. They planned two grand openings, one on January 1 and another on July 4, since Big Sky had two distinct tourist seasons.

Apparently the entire canyon was excited about the Cardwell brothers' brand of barbecue. His brothers Tag, Hayes and Jackson now had all made their homes in Montana. Only he and Laramie still lived in Texas, but Laramie would be flying back up for the grand opening whenever that schedule was confirmed. None of them asked if Austin would be coming back for that one. They knew him too well.

Austin only half listened, too anxious for a call from the marshal. When his cell phone finally did ring, he quickly excused himself and went out to the closed-in deck. It was freezing out here, but he didn't want his brothers to hear. He could actually see his breath. He'd never admit it, but he couldn't imagine why they would want to live here, as cold and nasty as winter was. Sure, it was beautiful, but he'd take Texas and the heat any day.

"I just left her hospital room," the marshal said without preamble the moment Austin answered.

"So what do you think?"

"Apparently she has some loss of memory because of the concussion she suffered, according to her husband, which could explain some of your misgivings."

"Did you see the bruises on her arms?"

The marshal sighed. "I did. Her husband said they'd had a disagreement before she took off. He said he'd grabbed her a little too hard, trying to keep her from leaving, afraid in her state what might happen to her. As it was, she ended up in a car wreck."

"What does she say?"

"She doesn't seem to recall the twenty-four hours before ending up upside down in her car in the middle of the highway—and even that is fuzzy."

"You think she's lying?" Austin asked, hearing something in the marshal's voice.

Hud took his time in answering. "I think she might remember more than she's letting on. I had some misgivings as well until Marc Stewart showed me a photograph of the four of them on his cell phone."

"*Four* of them?"

"Rebecca and her sister, a woman named Gillian Cooper, Marc and the baby. In the photo, the woman in the hospital is holding the baby and Marc is standing next to her, his arm around her and her sister."

Austin sighed. Gillian Cooper. Her sister. That could explain the watch. Maybe her sister had lent it to her. Or even given it to her.

"The doctor is releasing her tomorrow. I asked her if she wanted to return home with her husband."

Austin figured he already knew the answer. "She said yes."

"I also asked him to step out of the room. I then asked her if she was afraid of him. She said she wasn't."

So that was that, Austin thought. "Thanks for going by the hospital for me."

"You realize there is nothing we can do if she doesn't want to leave him," Hud said.

Austin knew that from experience, even though he'd never understood why a woman stayed in an abusive marriage. Disconnecting, he went back into the restaurant, where his brothers were debating promotion for the new restaurant. He was in no mood for this.

"I really should get going," he said, not that he really had anywhere to go, though he'd agreed to stay until the opening.

Christmas was only a few days away, he realized. Normally, he didn't do much for Christmas. Since he didn't have his own family, he always volunteered to work.

"Where are you going?" Tag asked.

"I've got some Christmas shopping to do." That, at least, was true.

"Dana is planning for us all to be together on Christmas," Tag said as if he needed reminding. "She has all kinds of plans."

Jackson laughed. "She wants us all to try skiing or snowboarding."

"There's a sledding party planned on Christmas Eve behind the house on the ranch and, of course, ice-skating on an inlet of the Gallatin River," Hayes said with a laugh when he saw Austin's expression. "You really have to experience a Montana Christmas."

He tried to smile. Anything to make up for missing the wedding so everyone would quit bringing it up. "I can't wait."

They all laughed since they knew he was lying. He wasn't ready for a Montana Christmas. He'd already been freezing his butt off and figured he'd more than experienced Montana after crashing in a ditch and almost getting killed by a woman with a tire iron. However, never let it be said he was a Scrooge. He'd go Christmas shopping. He would be merry and bright. It was only for a few days.

"You know what your problem is, Austin?" his brother Jackson said as they walked out to their vehicles.

Austin shook his head although he knew what was coming. He'd already had this discussion with Tanya in Houston.

"You can't commit to anything," Jackson said. "When we decided to open more Texas Boys Barbecues in Texas—"

"Yes, I've been told I have a problem with commitment," he interrupted as he looked toward Lone Mountain. The peak was almost completely obscured by the falling snow. Huge lacy flakes drifted down around them. Texas barbecue in Montana? He'd thought his brothers had surely lost their minds when they had suggested it. Now he was all the more convinced.

But they'd been right about the other restaurants they'd opened across Texas. He wasn't going to stand in their way now. But he also couldn't get all that excited about it.

"Can you at least commit to this promotion schedule we have mapped out?" Hayes asked.

"Do what you think is best," he said, opening the SUV door. "I'll go along with whatever y'all decide." His brothers didn't look thrilled with his answer. "Isn't that what you wanted me to say?"

"We were hoping for some enthusiasm, *something,*" Jackson said and frowned. "You seem to have lost interest in the business."

"It's not that." It wasn't. It was his *life.* At thirty-two, he was successful, a healthy, wealthy American male who could do anything he wanted. Most men his age would have given anything to be in his boots.

"He needs a woman," Tag said and grinned.

"That's *all* I need," Austin said sarcastically under his breath and thought of Rebecca and the way she'd reacted to her husband. What kind of woman left her husband and child just before Christmas?

A terrified one, he thought. "I have to go."

"Where did you say you were going?" Hayes asked before Austin could close his SUV door.

"There's something I need to do."

"I told you he needed a woman," Tag joked.

"Dana is in Bozeman running errands, but she said to tell you that dinner is at her house tonight," Jackson said before Austin could escape.

All the way to the hospital in Bozeman, all Austin could think about was the woman he'd rescued last night. Rescued? And then turned her over to a man who terrified her.

Austin thought of that awful old expression: she'd made her bed and now she had to lie in it.

Like hell, he thought.

Chapter Six

When he reached the hospital, Austin was told at the nurses' station that Mrs. Stewart had checked out already. His heart began to pound harder at the news, all his instincts telling him he had been right to come back here.

"I thought the doctor wasn't going to release her until tomorrow?"

"Her husband talked to him and asked if she was well enough to be released. He was anxious to get her home before Christmas."

Austin just bet he was. "He was planning to take her straight home from the hospital?" he asked and quickly added, "I have her purse." He'd forgotten all about putting it into his duffel bag last night as the highway patrolman helped the woman down to his waiting patrol car.

"Oh, you must be the man who found her after the accident," the nurse said, instantly warming toward him. "Let me see. I know her husband stayed at a local motel last night. I believe they were going to go there first so she could rest for a while before they left for Helena."

"Her husband got in last night?" Austin asked in surprise. Helena was three hours away on Interstate 90.

"He arrived in the wee hours of the morning. When he came by the hospital to see his wife, he thought he'd be able to take her home then." She smiled at how anxious the husband had apparently been. "He left the name of the motel where he would stay if there was any change in her condition," the nurse said. "Here it is. The Pine Rest. I can call and see if they are still there."

"No, that's all right. I'll run by the motel." He realized Rebecca Stewart wouldn't have been allowed to walk out of the hospital. One of the nurses would have taken her down to the car by wheelchair. "You don't happen to know what Mr. Stewart was driving, do you?" She remembered the large black Suburban because it had looked brand-new.

The Pine Rest Motel sat on the east end of town on a hill. Austin spotted Marc Stewart's Suburban at once. Austin had to wonder why Marc's "wife" had been driving an older-model car.

That didn't surprise him as much as the lack of a baby car seat in the back of the Suburban. Marc had had the vehicle for almost a month according to the sticker in the back window. The lack of a car seat was just another one of those questions that nagged at him. Like the fact that Marc Stewart had gotten his wife out of the hospital early just to bring her to a motel in town. That made no sense unless he'd brought her there to threaten her. That Austin could believe.

The black Suburban was parked in front of motel unit number seven—the last unit at the small motel.

Austin didn't go anywhere without his weapon. But he knew better than to go into the motel armed—let alone without a plan. He tended to wing things, following his instincts. It had gotten him this far. But it had also nearly gotten him killed last summer. He had both the physical and mental scars to prove it.

Glancing at the purse lying on the seat next to him, he wondered if all this wasn't an overreaction on his part. Maybe it had only been an argument between husband and wife that had gotten out of control. Maybe once Rebecca Stewart's memory returned, she wouldn't be afraid of her husband.

Maybe.

He picked up the purse. It was imitation leather, a knockoff of a famous designer's. He pulled out the wallet and went through it again, this time noticing the discount coupons for diapers and groceries.

He studied the woman in the photo a second time. It wasn't a great snapshot of her, but then most driver's license mug shots weren't. Montana only required a driver to get a license every eight years so this photo was almost seven years old.

If it hadn't been for the slight resemblance… He put everything back into the purse, opened the car door and stepped out into the falling snow.

Every cop knew not to get in the middle of a domestic dispute. This wasn't like him, he thought as he walked through the storm to the door of unit number seven and knocked.

At his knock, Austin heard a scurrying sound. He knocked again. A few moments later, Marc Stewart opened the door a crack.

He frowned when he saw Austin. "Yes?"

"I'm Austin Cardwell—"

"I know who you are." Behind the man, Austin heard a sound.

"I forgot to give Rebecca her purse," he said.

Marc reached for it.

All his training told him to just hand the man the damned purse and walk away. It wasn't like him to butt into someone else's business—let alone a married couple's, even if they had some obvious problems—when he wasn't asked.

"If you don't mind, I'd like to give it to her myself," he heard himself say. Behind the man, Austin caught a rustling sound.

"Look," Marc Stewart said from between gritted teeth. "I appreciate that you found…my wife and kept her safe until I could get here, but your job is done, cowboy. So you need to back the hell off."

Rebecca suddenly appeared at the man's side. "Excuse my husband. He's just upset." She met Austin's gaze. He tried to read it, afraid she was desperately trying to tell him something. "But Marc's right. We're fine now. It was very thoughtful of you to bring my purse, though."

"Yes, thoughtful," Marc said sarcastically and shot his wife a warning look. "You shouldn't be up," he snapped.

She was pale and a little unsteady on her feet, but she had a determined look on her face. Behind her, he saw her open suitcase—the same one he'd found in the overturned car's trunk. The scene looked like any other married couple's motel room.

Even before Marc spoke, Austin realized they were about to pack up and leave.

"We were just heading out," Marc said.

"I won't keep you, then," Austin said, still holding the purse. Rebecca Stewart looked weak as she leaned into the door frame. He feared her husband had gotten her out of the hospital too soon. But that, too, was none of his business. "I didn't want you leaving without your purse."

"Great," Marc said and turned to close her suitcase. "We have a long drive ahead of us, so if you'll excuse us…" Austin stepped aside to let him pass with the suitcase. "You should tell him our good news," he called over his shoulder.

"Good news?" Austin asked, studying the woman in the doorway. He realized that even though her suitcase had been open, she was still wearing the same clothing she'd had on last night. That realization gave him a start since there was a spot of blood on her sweater from her head injury the night before.

"We're pregnant again," Marc called from the side of the Suburban, where he was loading the suitcase.

Austin was watching her face. She suddenly went paler. He thought for a moment that she might faint.

"Marc, don't—" The words came out like a plea.

"Andrew Marc, our son, is going to have a baby sister," Marc said as if he hadn't heard her or was ignoring her. "Isn't that right, Rebecca? I think we'll call her Becky."

Austin met her gaze. "Congratulations." He couldn't have felt more like a fool as he handed her the purse.

She took it with trembling fingers, her eyes filling with tears. "Thank you for bringing my purse all this way." Her fingers kneaded the cheap fabric of the bag. He saw she was again wearing the wedding band that her husband had put on her finger at the hospital. That alone should have told him how things were.

"No problem. Good luck." He meant it since he knew in his heart she was going to need it. He started to step away when she suddenly grabbed his arm.

"Wait, I think this must be your coat," she said and turned back into the room.

"That's okay, you should keep it," he said.

She returned a few moments later with the coat.

"Seriously, keep it. You need it more than I do."

"Take the damned coat," Marc called to him before slamming the Suburban door.

Austin shook his head at her. "Keep it. Please," he said quietly.

Tears filled her eyes. "Thank you." She quickly reached for his hand and pressed what felt like a scrap of paper into his palm. "For everything." She then quickly pulled down her shirtsleeve, which had ridden up. He only got a glimpse of the fresh red mark around her wrist.

Austin sensed Marc behind him as he helped her into his coat. It swallowed her, but the December day was cold, another snowstorm threatening.

"Well, if we've all wished each other enough luck, it's time to hit the road," Marc said, joining them. "Hormones." He sounded disgusted as he looked at his wife. "The woman is in tears half the time." He put one arm around her roughly and reached into his pocket with the other. "Forgive my manners," he said, pulling out a crinkled twenty. "Here, this is for your trouble."

Austin stared down at the twenty.

Marc thrust the money at him. "Take it." There was

an underlying threatening sound in his voice. The man's blue eyes were ice-cold.

"Please," Rebecca said. Austin still couldn't think of her as this man's wife. There was pleading in her voice, in her gaze.

"Thanks," he said as he took the money. "You really didn't have to, though."

Marc chuckled at that.

"Have a nice trip, then. Drive carefully." Austin turned and walked toward his rental SUV.

Behind him, he heard Marc say, "Get in the car."

When he turned back, she was pulling herself up into the large rig. He climbed into his own vehicle, but waited until the Suburban drove away. He caught only a glimpse of her wan face in the side window as they left. Her brown eyes were wide with more than tears. The woman seemed even more terrified.

His heart was already pounding like a war drum. That red mark around her right wrist. All his instincts told him that this was more than a bossy husband.

He tossed down the twenty and, reaching in his pocket, took out the scrap of paper she'd pressed into his palm. It appeared to be a corner of a page torn from a motel Bible. There were only four words, written in a hurried scrawl with an eyeliner pencil: "Help me. No law."

Chapter Seven

Austin looked down the main street where the black Suburban had gone. If Marc Stewart was headed for Helena, he was going the wrong way.

He hesitated only a moment before he started the engine, backed up and turned onto the street.

Bozeman was one of those Western towns that had continued to grow—unlike a lot of Montana towns. In part, its popularity was because of its vibrant and busy downtown as well as being the home of Montana State University.

Austin cursed the traffic that had him stopped at every light while the black Suburban kept getting farther away. What he couldn't understand was why Marc Stewart was headed southwest if he was anxious to get his wife home. Maybe they were going out for breakfast first.

He caught another stoplight and swore. The Suburban was way ahead and unfortunately a lot of people in Bozeman drove large rigs, which made it nearly impossible to keep the vehicle in sight. He was getting more nervous by the moment. All his instincts told him the woman hadn't been delusional. She was in trouble.

From the beginning, she'd said the car wasn't hers,

the purse wasn't hers and that her name wasn't Rebecca Stewart. What if she had been telling the truth?

It was that thought that had him hitting the gas the moment the light changed. Determined not to have to stop at the next one, he sped through the yellow light and kept going. He sped through another yellow light, barely making it. But ahead, he could see the Suburban. It was headed southwest out of town.

That alone proved something, didn't it?

But what? That Marc Stewart had lied about wanting to get his wife home to Helena as quickly as possible. What else might he be lying about? The pregnancy?

Austin used the hands-free system in the SUV to put in a call to the doctor at the hospital who'd handled the case. He knew he couldn't ask outright about the patient's condition. But…

Dr. Mayfield came on the line.

"Doctor, it's Austin Cardwell. I'm the man who found Rebecca Stewart—"

"Yes, I remember you, Mr. Cardwell. What can I do for you?"

"I ended up with Mrs. Stewart's purse after last night's emergency." He was counting on the doctor not knowing he'd already stopped by the hospital earlier. "I wanted to drop it by if Mrs. Stewart is up to it."

"I'm sorry, but her husband checked her out earlier today."

"I noticed she has prenatal vitamins in her purse when I was looking for her identification."

A few beats of silence stretched out a little too long. "Mr. Cardwell, I'm not sure what Mrs. Stewart told you, but I'm not at liberty to discuss her condition."

"Understood." He'd heard the surprise in the silence

before the doctor had spoken. "Oh, one more thing. I just wanted to be sure she got her watch before she left the hospital. She was worried about it."

"Just a moment." The doctor left the line. When he came back, he said, "Yes, her husband picked it up for her."

Her husband picked up the watch with the name Gillian on it?

"Thank you, Doctor." He disconnected. Ahead, he could see the black Suburban still headed west on Highway 191. Marc had lied about her being pregnant, but why?

Austin thought about calling Marshal Hud Savage, but what would he tell him? That Marc Stewart was a liar. That wasn't illegal. Even if he told the marshal about the note the woman had passed him or about the diamond watch with the wrong name on it, Austin doubted Hud would be able to do more than he already had. Not to mention Rebecca had specified, *No law.*

Her name isn't Rebecca, just as she'd said, he realized with a jolt.

It's Gillian. Gillian Cooper. Rebecca's sister? The thought hit him like a sledgehammer. That was the only thing she had reacted to last night other than the man who was pretending to be her husband. It was the name on the expensive watch. It was proof—

Austin groaned as he realized it proved nothing. If she was Rebecca, she could have a reason for wearing her sister's watch. He thought of a woman he knew who wore her brother's St. Christopher medal. Her brother had died of cancer a few years before.

So maybe there was no mystery to the watch. But the woman in that black Suburban was in trouble. She'd asked for his help. Even if she was Rebecca and Marc Stewart was her husband, she was terrified of him. Terrified enough to leave her child and run.

That was the part that just didn't add up. Maybe Marc wouldn't let her take the child. All this speculation was giving him a headache.

Austin saw the four-way stop ahead. The black Suburban was in the left-hand turn lane. Marc Stewart was turning south—back up the Gallatin Canyon where Austin had found her the night before. So where was he going if not taking her home?

Instead of taking the highway south, though, the Suburban pulled into the gas station at the corner. Austin slowed, hanging back as far as he could as he saw Marc pull up to a gas pump and get out. The woman climbed out as well, said something to Marc and then went inside.

Austin saw his chance and pulled behind the station. He knew he didn't have much time since he wasn't sure why the woman had gone into the convenience store. If he was right, the man would be watching her, afraid to let her out of his sight. All he could hope was that the Suburban's gas tank was running low. He knew from experience that it took a long while to fill one.

Once inside the store, he looked around for the woman, anxious to find her since this might be his only chance to talk to her. There were several women in the store. None was the one he'd rescued last night.

It had only taken a few minutes for him to park. Surely she hadn't already gone back out to her vehicle. He glanced toward the Suburban from behind a tall rack of chips. Its front seats were both empty. Marc was still pumping gas into the tank, his gaze on the front of the store. The glare on the glass seemed to keep him from seeing inside. The woman was in here. Austin could think of only one other place she might be.

He found the restrooms down a short hallway. As she came out of the ladies' room, she saw him and froze. Eyes wide with fear, she looked as if she might turn and run. Except there was nowhere to run. He was blocking her way out.

He rushed to her. "Talk to me. Tell me who you are and what is going on."

She shook her head, glancing past him as if terrified Marc Stewart would appear at any moment.

"You gave me the note. You obviously are in trouble. Let me help you."

"I'm sorry. I shouldn't have involved you," she said. "Please forget I did. You can't help me." She tried to step past him, but he grabbed her arm. She flinched.

"He hurt you again, didn't he?"

"You don't understand. He has my sister."

"Your *sister?*"

Tears welled in her eyes. "Rebecca. If I don't go with him—" Her eyes widened in alarm again and he realized a buzzer had announced that someone had entered the store. Fortunately he and the woman couldn't be seen where they were standing, though. At least not yet.

"Your name is Gillian, isn't it? The watch—"

"Where are your restrooms?" he heard Marc ask the clerk.

Gillian gripped his arm, her fingers digging into his flesh. "If you tell anyone, he'll kill her."

There wasn't time to reassure her. "Where's he taking you?"

"A cabin in Island Park."

"Here, take this. If you get a chance, call me." He pressed one of his business cards into her palm and then pushed into the men's restroom an instant before he heard Marc's voice outside the door.

"It took you long enough," Marc snapped. "Come on."

Austin waited until he was sure they were gone before he opened the door and headed for his SUV. He had no idea what Island Park was or how to get there. All he knew was that he had no choice but to go after her.

Chapter Eight

As Gillian climbed into the Suburban, she could feel Marc watching her, his eyes narrowed.

"It took you long enough in there," he said, studying her. "You didn't try to make any calls while you were in there, did you?" he asked, his voice low. She knew how close he was to hitting her when his voice got like that.

"How would I have made a call? You have my cell phone, I have no money and, in case you haven't noticed, there aren't pay phones around anymore."

He narrowed his eyes in warning. She knew she was treading on thin ice with him, but kowtowing to him only seemed to make him more violent.

Marc was still staring at her as if searching for even a hint of a lie. "I figure if anyone could find a way, it would be you. I've learned the hard way what you're capable of, sister-in-law. Let's not forget that you've managed to get some local marshal sniffing around—not to mention a deputy from *Texas*."

"I told you that wasn't my doing. The deputy was merely worried about me." She looked away, wishing he would start the engine. He was looking for any excuse to hurt her again.

"*Worried about you?* That Texas cowboy took a

shine to you after you told him you weren't my wife. You take a shine to him, too? The patrolman said the cowboy had you in some cabin handcuffed to a chair. He have his way with you?"

"You disgust me," she said and turned to look out the side window. A pickup had pulled up behind them, the driver now waiting for the gas pump.

"Gave you his coat. How gallant is that?" he said, his voice a sneer. "You must have done something to keep him coming back."

She wished he would just start the engine. "You know I didn't know what I was saying. I have a concussion. Or don't you believe that either?" She turned to face him, knowing it was a daring thing to do. He was just looking for an excuse. He hated everything about her and her sister.

"Right, your head injury from an accident that would never have happened if you hadn't—"

"Been running for my life?"

His face twisted into a mask of fury. "You—"

She braced herself for the smack she knew was coming. The only thing that saved her was the driver behind them honking loudly.

Marc swore and flipped the man off, but started the engine and pulled away from the pump and onto the highway headed south toward West Yellowstone.

Gillian breathed a small sigh of relief. All she'd done was buy herself a little time. She'd be lucky if Marc didn't kill her. Right now, she was more worried about what he'd already done to Rebecca.

"What are you looking at?" Marc snapped.

"Nothing," she said as she turned toward him.

"You were looking in your side mirror." He hurriedly checked his rearview. "Is that cowboy following us?"

She realized her mistake. "What cowboy?"

"Don't give me that what cowboy bull. You know damned well. That *Texas* cowboy. Did you see him back there?"

"In the ladies' room?" She scoffed at his paranoia. "I was only looking out the window." It was a lie and she feared he knew it.

He kept watching behind them as he drove. "If you said something to him back at the motel—"

"You were there. You know I didn't say anything. Why did you say Rebecca was pregnant with a baby girl?" She held her breath for his answer.

Marc let out a snort. "I figured it would just get the guy off my back once he thought you were pregnant." He chuckled as if pleased with himself and seemed to relax a little, although he kept watching his mirror.

She hated that she'd involved Austin Cardwell in all this, but she'd been so desperate... Now she prayed that if he really was following them, that he didn't let Marc see him. There was no telling what Marc would do.

"What did you tell him last night?"

Gillian didn't need to ask whom he was talking about. "I didn't even know who I was last night, so how was I going to tell him anything?"

"That was convenient. But you recognized *me* when you saw me, didn't you?"

She'd been so confused, so terrified and yet she hadn't known of what or whom. But once Marc had come into her hospital room, she'd remembered, even before he'd whispered in her ear, "I'll kill your sister if you don't go along with what I say."

It had all come back in a wave of misery that threatened to overwhelm her. When Marc had slipped her sister's wedding band onto her finger... She hadn't been able to hold back the tears. She'd made matching rings for her sister and Marc when they'd married. Marc had lost his almost at once, but Rebecca... She felt a sob try to work its way up out of her chest. If Marc was carrying Rebecca's wedding ring in his pocket, was she even still alive?

AUSTIN STAYED BACK, letting the black Suburban disappear down Highway 191 toward Big Sky, while he called Hud.

"I need a favor," he said. "Does Marc Stewart own a cabin in a place called Island Park?"

Silence, then, "I'm sure you have a good reason to ask."

"I do."

"Want to tell me what's going on?"

"I wish I could."

"I hope you know what you're doing," the marshal said.

Austin hoped so, as well.

More silence, then the steady clack of computer keys.

"Funny you should ask," Hud said when he came back on the line. "Marc Stewart has been paying taxes on a place in Island Park."

Austin leaned back, relieved, as he drove out of the valley and into the canyon. The traffic wasn't bad compared to Houston. Most every vehicle, other than semis, had a full ski rack on top. The roads had become more packed with snow, but at least he had some idea now where Marc Stewart might be heading.

"Where and what is Island Park?"

Hud rattled off an address that didn't sound like any he'd ever heard. "How do I find this place?" he asked frowning. "It doesn't sound like a street address in a town."

"Finding it could be tricky. Island Park is a thirty-three-mile-long town just over the Montana border from West Yellowstone. Basically, it follows the highway. The so-called town is no more than five hundred feet wide in places. They call it the longest main street in the world."

"Seriously?"

Austin was used to tiny Texas towns or sprawling urban cities.

"Owners of the lodges along the highway incorporated back in 1947 to circumvent Idaho's liquor laws, which prohibited the sale of liquor outside city limits."

"So how do I find this cabin?"

"In the middle of winter? I'd suggest by snowmobile unless it is right off a plowed road, which will be doubtful. Have you ever driven a snowmobile?"

"No, but I'll manage." He'd deal with all that once he knew where to look for the cabin.

"I don't know Island Park at all so I can't help you beyond the address I gave you. I should warn you that you're really on your own once you cross the border into Idaho. I would imagine any help you might need from law enforcement would have to come out of Ashton, a good fifty miles to the south. Where you're headed is very isolated, with cabins back in heavily wooded areas. They get a lot of snow over there."

"Great." He'd already known that he was on his own. But now it was clear there would be no backup should he get himself in a bind. He almost laughed at that. He couldn't be in a worse situation right now, headed into country he didn't know and into a possible violent domestic dispute between Marc Stewart and his real wife.

"I suppose you won't be able to join us for dinner tonight?"

Austin had forgotten about dinner. "I'll try my best, but if things go south with this..."

"Not to worry. Dana is used to having a marshal for a husband. Just watch your back. And keep in touch," Hud said.

Austin didn't see the black Suburban again on the drive through the canyon. When the road finally opened up, he found himself on what apparently was called Fir Ridge. Off to his left was a small cemetery in the aspens and pines. Then the highway dropped down into a wooded area before crossing the Madison River Bridge and entering the small tourist town of West Yellowstone.

Had Marc stopped here to get Gillian something to eat? Buy gas? Or was he just anxious to get to wherever he was going?

Austin had no way of knowing. He only knew that he couldn't cross paths with him if he hoped to keep Gillian alive. All his training told him to bring the law into this now. Going in like the Lone Ranger was always a bad idea—especially when you weren't sure what you were getting into.

And yet, he couldn't make himself do it. Gillian did not want the law involved. She was terrified of Marc Stewart, and with her sister in danger, Austin couldn't chance that calling in law enforcement would push Marc into killing not only her, but also her sister, as well.

Not that he wasn't worried about getting her killed himself. If only he'd had more time with Gillian at the convenience store. There was so much he needed to know. Such as where was Rebecca's young son, Andrew Marc? Was he really with his grandmother? Or was that, too, a lie?

West Yellowstone was a tourist town of gas stations, curio shops, motels and cafés. Austin took the first turn out and headed for the Idaho border. He still hadn't seen the black Suburban. He could only hope that Gillian was right about where Marc was taking her.

Last night, Gillian had been driving her sister's car. He suspected the registration, the purse, the baby car seat, even the suitcase in the back belonged to her sister, Rebecca.

From the way the clothes had been thrown into the suitcase, he was assuming Rebecca had tried to leave her husband. So how had Gillian ended up in her sister's car?

He had many more questions than he had answers. No wonder he felt anxious. Even if he hadn't been shot and almost died just months ago when a case had gone wrong, he would have been leery of walking into this mess. No law officer in his right mind wanted to go in blind.

His cell phone rang. He snatched it up with the crazy thought that somehow Gillian Cooper had gotten away from Marc and was now calling.

"Where the hell are you?" his brother Tag demanded. "You did remember that we're supposed to have dinner with Dana, didn't you?"

Austin swore under his breath. "Something has come up."

"*Something?* Like something came up and you couldn't make my wedding?"

"Do we have to go through this again? I'm sorry. If it wasn't important—"

"More important obviously than your family."

"Tag, I'll explain everything when I get back. I'm sure you can go ahead with…" He realized his brother had hung up on him.

NOT THAT HE could blame his brother. He disconnected, feeling like a heel. He had a bad habit of letting down the people he cared about. He blamed his job, but the truth was he felt more comfortable as a deputy than he did in any other relationship.

"*Maybe I'm like my dad,*" he'd said to his mother when she'd asked him why of the five brothers, he was the one who was often at odds with the others. "*Look how great Dad is with* his *sons,*" he'd pointed out.

His parents had divorced years ago when Austin was still in diapers. His mother had taken her five boys to live in Texas while their father had stayed in Big Sky. Austin had hardly seen his father over the years. He knew that his brothers had now reconciled with him, but Austin didn't see that happening as far as he was concerned. He wouldn't be in Montana long enough, and the way things were going…

It amazed him that his mother always stood up for the man she'd divorced, the man who had fathered her boys. "*I won't have you talk about your father like that,*" his mother had said the last time they discussed it. "*Harlan and I did the best we could.*"

Austin had softened his words. "*You did great, Mom.*

But let's face it, I could be more like Harlan Cardwell than even you want to admit."

"Tell me, is there anything you care about, Austin?" she'd asked, looking disappointed in him.

"I care about my family, my friends, my town, my state."

"But not enough to make your own brother's wedding."

"I was on a case."

"And there was no one else who could handle it?"

"I needed to see it through. I might not be great at relationships, but I'm damned good at my job."

"Watch your language," she'd reprimanded. *"A job won't keep you warm at night, son. Someday you're going to realize that these relationships you treat so trivially are more important than anything else in life. I thought almost losing your life might have taught you something."*

As he dropped over the Idaho border headed for Island Park, he thought no one would ever understand him since he didn't even understand himself. He just knew that right now Gillian Cooper needed him more than his brothers or cousin Dana did. Just as the woman he'd tried to save in Texas had needed him more than Tag had needed another attendant at his wedding.

He'd failed his family as well as that woman in Texas, though, and it had almost cost him his life. He couldn't fail this one.

"You look like hell."

Gillian didn't bother to react to Marc's snide comment as they drove into West Yellowstone. He wanted to argue with her, to have an excuse to hit her. His anger was palpable in the interior of the Suburban. She'd out-witted him—at least for a while before she'd lost con-trol of Rebecca's car and crashed.

Her head ached and she felt sick to her stomach. How much of it was from the accident? The doctor had dis-cussed her staying another night, but Marc had told her that her sister would be dead if she did. She wasn't sure if her ailments were from her concussion solely or not. She'd often felt sick to her stomach when she thought of the man her sister had married.

"I'll get you something to eat," Marc said. "I don't want you dying on me. At least not yet." He pulled into a drive-through. "What do you want?"

She wasn't hungry, but she knew she needed to eat. She would need all her strength once they reached the cabin.

Marc didn't give her a chance to answer, though. "Give us four burgers, a couple of large fries and two big colas." As he dug his wallet out, she felt him look-ing at her. "You're just lucky you didn't kill yourself last night. As it is, you owe me for a car."

Just like Marc to make it about the money.

"I'm sure my insurance will pay for it," she said drily. "If I get to make the claim."

He snorted as he pulled up to the next window and paid. A few moments later, he handed her a large bag of greasy-smelling food.

Just the odor alone made her stomach turn. She thought she might throw up. "I need to go to the bath-room." The business card Austin Cardwell had given her was hidden in her jeans pocket. She knew she should have thrown it away back at the convenience store, but Marc hadn't given her a chance.

He shook his head. "You just went back at Four Corners."

"I have to go again." She had to get rid of the business card. If Marc found it on her—

She regretted telling Austin where they were headed. Not only had she put him in danger and possibly made things even worse, but she wasn't sure he would be able to find the cabin anyway. She'd stolen glances in the side mirror and hadn't seen his SUV. He was a deputy sheriff in Texas. What if he contacted law enforcement here?

No, she couldn't see him doing that. Just as she couldn't see him giving up. He was back there somewhere. He'd saved her life last night. But she wasn't so sure he could pull it off again. Worse, she couldn't bear the thought that she might get him killed.

If she could get to a phone, she could call the number on the card and plead with him not to get involved. Even as she thought it, she knew he wouldn't be able to turn back now. She'd seen how determined he was at the hospital and later at the motel room. Her heart went out to him. Why couldn't her sister have married someone like Austin Cardwell?

"You'll just have to hold it," Marc was saying. "Hand me one of the burgers and some fries," he said as he drove onto the highway again.

She dug in the bag and handed him a sandwich. The last thing she wanted was food, but she made herself gag down one of the burgers and a little of the cola. Marc ended up devouring everything else. She prayed her sister was still alive, but in truth she feared what was waiting for her at the cabin.

As they drove up over the mountain and dropped

down into Idaho, she stared out the window at the tall banks of plowed snow on each side of the road. Island Park was famous for its snow—close to nine feet of it in an average winter. And where there was snow…

Three snowmobiles buzzed by like angry bees on the trail beside the highway and sped off, the colorful sleds catching the sunlight.

She stole a glance in the side mirror. The highway behind them was empty. Her stomach roiled at the thought that Austin was ahead of them because of their food stop, that he might be waiting at the cabin, not realizing just how dangerous Marc was.

Gillian closed her eyes, fighting tears. She'd been so afraid for her sister she'd been desperate when she'd asked for his help. If only she could undo what she'd done. The man had saved her life last night and this was how she repaid him, by getting him involved in this?

There was no saving any of them, she thought as more snowmobiles zoomed past, kicking up snow crystals into the bright blue winter sky. It wasn't until they passed a cabin with a brightly decorated tree in the front yard that she remembered with a start that Christmas was only a few days away.

Chapter Nine

Not long after the Idaho border, the terrain closed in with pines and more towering snowbanks. Austin started seeing snowmobilers everywhere he looked. They buzzed past on brightly colored machines, the drivers clad in heavy-duty cold-weather gear and helmets, which hid their faces behind the black plastic.

Even inside the SUV, he could hear the roar of the machines as they sped by—all going faster on the snow track next to him than he was on the snow-slick highway.

Just as Hud had told him, he began to see cabins stuck back in the pines. He would need directions. He figured he was also going to need a snowmobile, just as Hud had suggested, if the cabin was far off the road.

When he reached the Henry's Fork of the Snake River, he pulled into a place alongside the highway called Pond's Lodge. The temperature seemed to be dropping, and tiny snowflakes hung around him as if suspended in the air as he got out of the SUV. He shivered, amazed that people lived this far north.

Inside, he asked for a map of the area.

"You'll want a snowmobile map, too," the older woman behind the counter said.

He thought she might be right as he stepped back outside. Snow had begun falling in huge lacy flakes. He wasn't all that anxious to get out in it on a snowmobile for the first time. But after a quick perusal of the map, he knew a snowmobile was his best bet.

As the marshal had told him he would, he could see the problem of finding the cabin—especially in winter. He figured a lot of the dwellings would be boarded up this time of year. Some even inaccessible.

He had to assume that Marc Stewart's family cabin would be open—but possibly not the road to it. What few actual roads there were seemed to be banked in deep snow. Clearly most everyone traveled by snowmobile. He could hear them buzzing around among the trees in a haze of gray smoke.

Back in his rented SUV, he drove down to a small out-of-the-way snowmobile rental. The moment he walked in the door, he caught the scent of a two-stroke engine and the high whine of several others as two snowmobiles roared out of the back of the shop. Even the music playing loudly from overhead speakers behind the counter couldn't drown them out. Beneath the speakers, a man in his late twenties with dozens of tattoos and piercings glanced up. The name stitched on his shirt read "Awesome."

"My man!" he called. "Looking for the ultimate machine, right? Are we talking steep and deep action or outrageous hill banging to do some high marking today?"

The man could have been speaking Greek. "Sorry, I just need one that runs."

Awesome laughed. "If it's boondocking you're looking for, chutes, ridges, big bowls, I got just the baby for you." He shoved a map at him. "We have an end-less supply of cornices to jump, untouched powder and more coming down, mountainsides just waiting for you to put some fresh tracks on them."

"Do you have one for flat ground?"

Awesome looked a little disappointed. "You seri-ously want to pass up Two Top, Mount Jefferson and Lion's Head?"

He seriously did. "I see on your brochure that you have GPS tours. It says here I can pinpoint an area I want to go to with the specific coordinates and you can get me there?"

"I can." Awesome didn't seem all that enthusiastic about it, though. "We have about a thousand miles of backwoods trails."

"Great. Here is where I need to go. You have a ma-chine that can get me there?"

He looked at the map, his enthusiasm waning even faster. "This address isn't far from here. I suppose you need gear? Helmet, boots, bibs, coat and gloves? They're an extra twenty. I can put you in a machine that will run you a hundred a day."

"How fast do these things go," Austin asked as one sped by in a blur.

"The fastest? A hundred and sixty miles an hour. The ones we have? You can clock in at a hundred."

Austin had no desire to clock in at a hundred. Even the price tag shocked him. The one sitting on the show-room floor was on sale for fourteen thousand dollars and everyone around here seemed to have one. He fig-ured Marc Stewart would have at least one of the fast-est snowmobiles around. He tagged the guy as someone who had done his share of high marking. "What is high marking, by the way?"

Awesome laughed and pointed at a poster on the wall. "You try to make the highest mark on the side of a mountain." On the poster, the rider had made it all the way up under an overhanging wall of snow.

"It looks dangerous."

Awesome shrugged. "Only if you get caught in an avalanche."

Austin didn't have to worry about avalanches, but what he was doing was definitely dangerous. Gillian was terrified for her sister. Austin wouldn't be trying to find them if he didn't believe she had good reason for concern.

But he was smart enough to know that a man like Marc Stewart, when trapped, might do something stupid like kill an off-duty state deputy sheriff who was sticking his nose where it didn't belong.

GILLIAN LOOKED OUT through the snow-filled pines as Marc drove. She couldn't see the cabin from the road. She'd been here once before, but it had been in summer. The cabin sat on Island Park Reservoir just off Centennial Loop Trail. While old, it was charming and picturesque. At least that's what she'd thought that summer she and her sister had spent a week here without Marc.

That had been before Rebecca and Marc had married, back when her sister had been happy and foolishly naive about the man she'd fallen in love with.

Gillian hugged herself as she remembered her sister's text message just days before.

On way to your house. I've left Marc.

She'd tried her sister's number, but the call went

straight to voice mail. She'd texted back. Are you and Andy all right?

No answer. Helena was a good two hours away from Gillian's home in Big Sky. Even the way her sister drove, Rebecca wouldn't have arrived until after dark. Gillian had paced, checking the window anxiously and asking herself, "What would Marc do?" She feared the answer.

It was night by the time she finally saw her sister's car pull up out front. Relieved to tears, she'd run outside without even a coat on. But it hadn't been Rebecca in the car.

By the time she'd realized it was Marc alone and furious, it was too late. He'd grabbed her and thrown her into the trunk. She'd fought him, but he'd been so much stronger and he'd taken her by surprise. He'd slammed the trunk lid and the next thing she'd known the car was moving.

"Did you really forget your name?" Marc asked, dragging her out of her thoughts. He sounded amused at the idea. "Sometimes I'd like to forget my name. Hell, I'd like to forget my life."

She didn't tell him that pieces of memory had her even more confused. She'd remembered there was someone in the trunk of the car she'd been driving, but she hadn't remembered it was her.

When Austin had returned to the cabin with the patrolman, he'd told her that the only thing he'd found in the trunk of the car was a suitcase. She'd been more confused.

It wasn't until she'd laid eyes on her alleged *husband* that she'd remembered Marc forcing her into the trunk.

When he'd stopped at a convenience mart in the canyon, she'd shoved her way out by kicking aside the backseat.

She hadn't known where they were when she'd crawled out. He'd left the car running because of the freezing cold night. Not knowing where she was, she'd just taken off driving, afraid that he would get a ride or steal a car and come after her.

The next thing she remembered was waking up in a hospital with vague memories of the night before and a tall Texas cowboy.

"I'm curious. Where was it you thought you were going?" Marc asked. He sounded casual enough, but she could hear the underlying fury behind his words.

"I have no idea." She'd been running scared. All she'd been able to think about was getting to a phone so she could call the police. Her cell phone had been in her pocket when she'd rushed out of her house, but Marc had taken it.

"You should have waited and run me down with the car." Marc glanced over at her. "Short of killing me, you should have known you wouldn't get away."

She shuddered at the thought, but knew he was right. She had managed to get away from him, but not long enough to help herself or her sister. Maybe that had been a godsend. He'd told her at the hospital that if they didn't get back to her sister soon, she would be dead.

Gillian hadn't known then where he'd left Rebecca. But she'd believed him. He'd had her sister's wedding band in his pocket. It wasn't until Marc headed out of Bozeman that she'd figured out where he was taking her.

Now Marc slowed the Suburban as he turned down a narrow road with high snowbanks on each side. He drove only a short distance, though, before the road ended in a huge pile of snow. She glanced around as he pulled into a wide spot where the snow had been plowed to make a parking area. Other vehicles were parked there, most of them with snowmobile trailers.

"Here." He tossed her a pair of gloves. A snowmobile buzzed past, kicking up a cloud of snow. "If you want to see your sister alive, you will do what I say. Try to make another run for it—"

"I get it." As angry and out of control as he was, she feared what kind of shape her sister was in. Marc had told Austin that their son, Andrew Marc, was with his grandmother. That had been a lie since Marc's parents were both dead and he had no other family that she knew of.

So where was Andy? Was he with his mother at the cabin? She didn't dare hope that they were both safe.

Marc backed up to where he'd left his snowmobile trailer. Both machines were on it, Gillian noticed, and any hope she'd had that her sister might have escaped evaporated at the sight of them. Even if Rebecca was able to leave the cabin, she had no way to get out. The snow would be too deep. One step off the snowmobile and she would be up to her thigh in snow. As she glanced in the direction of the cabin, Gillian could see the fresh tracks that Marc had made in and back out again from the cabin on the deep snow. Neither trip had packed down the trail enough to walk on.

Marc cut the engine. She could hear the whine of snowmobiles in the distance, then an eerie quiet fell over the Suburban.

"Come on," he said as he reached behind the seat for his coat. "Your sister is waiting."

Was she? Gillian could only pray it was true as she pulled on the coat Austin had given her and climbed out into the falling snow. Even as she breathed in the frosty air, she prayed they hadn't arrived too late. Marc had told her last night that if Rebecca was dead, it was her fault for taking off in the car and causing him even more problems.

The only thing that made her climb onto the back of the snowmobile behind her brother-in-law was the thought of her sister and nephew. Whatever was going on, Marc had brought her here for a reason. She couldn't imagine what. But if she could save Rebecca and Andy...

Even as she thought it, Gillian wondered how she would do that against a man like Marc Stewart.

Austin was pleased to find that driving a snowmobile wasn't much different from driving a dirt bike. Actually, it was easier because you didn't have to worry as much about balance. You could just sit down, hit the throttle and go.

With the GPS in his pocket, along with a map of the area, and his weapon strapped on beneath his coat, he headed for Marc Stewart's cabin. The area was a web of narrow snow-filled roads that wove through the dense pines. From what he could gather, the Stewart cabin was on the reservoir.

He followed Box Canyon Trail until it connected with another trail at Elk Creek. Then he took Centennial Loop Trail.

He passed trees with names on boards tacked to them. Dozens of names indicating dozens of cabins back in the woods. But he had a feeling that the Stewart cabin wasn't near a lot of others or at least not near an occupied cabin.

Snowmobiles sped past, throwing up new snow, leaving behind blue exhaust. It was snowing harder by the time he reached the spot on the GPS where he was supposed to turn.

He slowed. The tree next to the road had only four signs nailed on it. Three of them were Stewarts. Off to his right, Austin saw a half dozen vehicles parked at what appeared to be the entrance to another trailhead that went off in the opposite direction from the Stewart family cabins.

The black Suburban was parked in front of a snowmobile trailer with one machine on it. There were fresh snow tracks around the spot where a second one must have recently been unloaded.

Austin double-checked the GPS. It appeared the cabin at the address the marshal had given him was a half mile down a narrow road.

As he turned toward the road, he saw that there were several sets of snowmobile tracks, but only one in the new snow—and it wasn't very old based on how little of the falling snow had filled it.

Marc and Gillian weren't that far ahead of him.

Chapter Ten

The road Austin had taken this far was packed down from vehicles driving on it. But the one that went back into the cabins hadn't been plowed since winter had begun so the snow was a good five or six feet deep.

Austin had to get a run at it, throttling up the snowmobile to barrel up the slope onto the snow.

Fortunately, the snowmobile ahead of him had packed down the new snow so once he got up on top of it, the track was fairly smooth. Still, visibility was bad with the falling snow and the dense trees. He couldn't see anything ahead but the track he was on. According to the map, the road went past the Stewart cabins for another quarter mile before it ended beside the lake.

His plan was to go past the cabin where the snowmobile had gone, then work his way back. As loud as the snowmobile motor was, it would be heard by anyone inside the cabin. His only hope for a surprise visit would be if those inside thought he was merely some snowmobiler riding around.

A corner of a log cabin suddenly appeared from out of the falling snow. Austin caught glimpses of more weathered dark log structures as he continued on past. The shingled roofs seemed to squat under the layers of snow, the smaller cabins practically disappearing in the drifts.

No smoke curled out of any of the rock chimneys. In fact as he passed, he saw no signs of life at all. Wooden shutters covered all the windows. No light came from within.

He would have thought that the cabins were empty, still closed up waiting for spring—if not for the distinct new snowmobile track that cut off from the road he was on and headed directly for the larger of the three cabins.

Austin kept the throttle down, the whine of his snowmobile cutting through the cold silence of the forest as he zoomed past the cabins huddled in the pines and snow. He stole only a couple of glances, trying hard not to look in their direction for fear of who might be looking back.

MARC PULLED AROUND the back of the cabin and shut off the snowmobile engine.

Gillian could barely hear over the thunder of her heart. Her legs felt weak as she slipped off the back of the machine and looked toward the door of the cabin. The place was big and rambling, dated in a way that she'd found quaint the first time her sister had invited her here.

"Isn't this place something?" Rebecca had said, clearly proud of what she called Stewart Hall.

The main cabin reminded Gillian of the summer lodges she'd seen on television. All of it told of another time: the log and antler decor, furniture with Western print fabric, the bookshelves filled with thick tomes and board games, and the wide screened-in front porch with its wicker rockers that looked out over a marble-smooth green lake surrounded by towering pines.

"It is *picturesque,"* Gillian had said, not mentioning that it smelled a little musty. *"How often does Marc's family get up here?"*

"There isn't much family left. Just Marc and me." Rebecca's hand had gone to her stomach. Her eyes brightened. *"That's why he wanted to start our family as soon as possible."*

"You're pregnant?*"* Her sister and Marc had only been married a few months at that time. But Gillian had seen how happy her sister was. *"Congratulations,"* she'd said and hugged Rebecca tightly as she remembered how she'd tried to talk her out of marrying Marc and her sister had accused her of being jealous.

Now as she watched Marc pocket the snowmobile key, she wished she'd fought harder. Even when they were only dating, Gillian had seen a selfishness in Marc, a need to always be the center of attention, a need to have everything his way. He was a poor sport, too, often leaving games in anger. They'd been small things that Rebecca had ignored, saying no man was perfect.

Gillian wished she had fought harder. Maybe she could have saved Rebecca from a lot of pain. But then there would be no baby. No little Andy...

"You know what you have to do," Marc said as he reached in another pocket for the key to the door.

She nodded.

"Do I have to remind you what happens if you don't?" he asked.

Gillian looked into his eyes. It was like looking into the fires of hell. "No," she said. "You were quite clear back at the motel."

AUSTIN RODE FARTHER up the road until he could see another cabin in the distance. He found a spot to turn the snowmobile around. The one thing he hadn't considered was how hard it would be to hike back to the Stewart cabins.

The moment he stepped off the machine, his leg sunk to his thighs in the soft snow. His only hope was to walk in the snowmobile track—not that he didn't sink a good foot with each step.

He checked his gun and extra ammunition and then headed down the track. The falling snow made him feel as if he were in a snow globe. Had he not been following the snowmobile track, he might have become disoriented and gotten lost in what seemed an endless forest of snow-covered trees that all looked the same.

An eerie quiet had fallen around him, broken only by the sound of his own breathing. He was breathing harder than he should have been he realized. It had been months now since he'd been shot. That had been down on the Mexico border with heat and cacti and the scent of dust in the air, nothing like this. And yet, he had that same feeling that he was walking into something he wouldn't be walking back out of—and all because of a woman.

A bird suddenly cried out from a nearby tree. Austin started. He couldn't remember ever feeling more alone. When he finally picked up the irritating buzz of snowmobiles in the distance, he was thankful for a reminder of other life. The snow had an insulating effect that rattled his nerves with its cold silence. That and the memory of lying in the Texas dust, dying.

It seemed he'd been wrong. He hadn't put it behind him, he realized with a self-deprecating chuckle. And now here he was again. Only this time, he didn't know the area, let alone what was waiting for him inside that cabin, and he wasn't even a deputy doing his job.

The structure appeared out of the falling snow. He realized he couldn't stay on the track. But when he stepped off into the deep snow, he found himself laboring to move. It was worse under the trees, where it formed deep wells. If you got too close… He stepped into one and dropped, finding himself instantly buried. He fought his way to the surface like a swimmer and finally was able to climb out. The snow had chilled him. He'd never been in snow, let alone anything this deep and cold.

But his biggest concern was what awaited him ahead. He had no idea what he was going to do when he reached the main cabin. He needed to know what was going on inside. Unfortunately, with the shutters on all the windows, he wasn't sure how to accomplish that.

As he neared the side, he saw an old wooden ladder hanging on an outbuilding and had an idea. It was a crazy one, but any idea seemed good right now. The snow was deep enough where it had drifted in on this side of the cabin that it ran from the roof to the ground. If he could lay the ladder against the snowdrift, it was possible he could climb up onto the roof. The chimney stuck up out of the snow only a few feet. With luck, he might be able to hear something.

The snowmobile that had made the recent tracks to the cabin was parked out back—just as he'd suspected. Steam was still coming off the engine, indicating that whoever had ridden it hadn't been at the cabin long.

Austin took the ladder and, working his way through the snow, leaned it against the house and began to climb.

IT WAS LIKE a tomb inside the cabin with the shutters closed and no lights or heat on. Gillian stood in the large living room waiting for Marc to turn on a lamp. When he did, she blinked, blinded for a moment.

In that instant, she saw the cabin the way it had been the first time she'd seen it. The Native American rugs, the pottery and the old paintings and photographs on the walls. The vintage furniture and the gleam of the wood floors.

She'd felt back then that she'd been transported to another time, one that felt grander. One she wished she'd had as a child. She'd envied Marc his childhood here on this lake. How she'd longed to have been the little girl who curled up in the hammock out on the porch and read books on a long, hot summer day while her little sister played with dolls kept in one of the old trunks.

If only they could have been two little girls who swam in the lake and learned to water-ski behind the boat with her two loving parents. And lay in bed at night listening to the adults, the lodge alive with laughter and summer people.

For just an instant, Gillian had heard the happy clink of crystal from that other time. Then Marc stepped on a piece of broken glass that splintered under his snowmobile boot with the sound of a shot. He kicked it away and Gillian saw the room how it was now, cold, dark and as broken as the lonely only child Marc Stewart had been.

Most of the lighter-weight furniture now looked like kindling. Anything that could be broken was. Jigsaw pieces of ceramic vases, lamps and knickknacks littered the floor, along with the glass from the picture frames.

The room attested to the extent of Marc Stewart's rage—not that Gillian needed a reminder.

She looked toward the large old farmhouse-style kitchen. The floor was deep in broken dishes and thrown cutlery.

Past it down the hall, she saw drops of blood on the worn wood floor.

"Where's my sister? Rebecca!" Her voice came out too high. It sounded weak and scared and without hope. *"Rebecca?"*

"She's not up here," Marc said as he kicked aside what was left of a spindle rocking chair.

The weight of the fear on her chest made it hard to even say the words. *"Where is she?"*

"Down there." He pointed toward the old root cellar door off the kitchen.

Gillian felt her heart drop like a stone. She couldn't get her legs to move. Just as she couldn't get her lungs to fill. "You left her down there all this time?"

"We would have been here sooner if it wasn't for you." Marc looked as if he wanted to hit her, as if it took everything in him not to break her as he had everything else in this cabin. "Are you coming?"

Austin climbed across the roof to the chimney. The snow silenced his footfalls, but also threatened to slide in an avalanche that would take him with it should he misstep. He knelt next to the chimney to listen just as he heard Gillian call out her sister's name.

He waited for an answer.

He heard none.

"Can't you bring her up here?" Austin heard the fear in Gillian's voice. Bring her up? Was there a basement under the cabin? He didn't think so. A root cellar possibly? Then he felt his skin crawl as he remembered a root cellar one of his friends had found at an old abandoned house. He was instantly reminded of the musky smell, the cobwebs, the dust-coated canning jars with unidentifiable contents and the scurry of the rats as they'd opened the door.

"I thought you understood that we were doing this my way," Marc said, his tone as threatening as the smack that followed his words and Gillian's small cry of pain. "Come on."

Austin heard what sounded like the crunch of boot heels over gravel, then nothing for a few moments.

Chapter Eleven

Gillian peered down the steep wooden stairs into the dim darkness and felt her stomach roil. Only one small light burned in a black corner of the root cellar. The musty, damp smell hit her first.

"Rebecca?" she called and felt Marc shove her hard between her shoulder blades. She would have tumbled headlong down the stairs if she hadn't grabbed the door frame.

"Move," Marc snapped behind her.

Gillian thought she heard a muffled sound down in the blackness, but it could have been pack rats. What if Marc had lied? What if Rebecca was dead? Then the only reason Marc had come after her and brought her back here was to kill her, too.

She took one step, then another. There was no railing so she clung to the rough rock wall that ran down one side of the stairs. With each step, she expected Marc to push her again. All her instincts told her this was a trap. She wouldn't have been surprised to hear him slam and lock the door at the top of the steps behind her. Leaving her to die down here would be the kind of cruel thing he would do.

To her surprise, she heard the steps behind her groan

with his weight as he followed her down. It gave her little relief, though. The moment she reached the bottom, she turned on him. "Where is she? Marc, where is my sister?"

Gillian heard another moan and turned in the direction the sound had come from. Something moved deep in the darkest part of the root cellar. "Oh, God, what have you done to her?"

Marc pushed her aside. An instant later, a bare overhead bulb turned on blinding her. Gillian blinked, shielding her eyes from the glare as she tried to see—all the time terrified of what Marc had done to her sister.

In the far reaches of the root cellar, Gillian saw her. Rebecca was shackled to a chair. He'd left her water and a bucket along with at least a little food. But there was dried blood on her face and clothes. Her face was also bruised and raw, but her eyes were open.

What Gillian saw in her sister's eyes, though, sent her heart plummeting. Regret when she saw her sister, but when her gaze turned to her husband, it was nothing but defiance. Gillian tried to swallow, but her mouth felt as if filled with cotton balls.

"You're her last hope, big sister," Marc said as he looked from his wife to her. "Get her to tell you what she did with my ledger, my money and my son…" He met her gaze. "Or I will kill her and then I will beat it out of you since I know she tells you everything."

Not everything, Gillian thought. She swallowed again, her throat working. "I already told you that I don't know."

He nodded, his facial features distorted under the harsh glare of the single bulb hanging over his head. How could such a handsome man look so evil…?

"Either you get it out of her or I will beat her until her last scream." He handed her a key to the lock on the shackles.

Gillian moved to her sister, falling on her knees in front of her. She worked to free her, her hands shaking so hard she had trouble with the lock. "She needs water and food and help out of this chair." She turned to glare back at him. "It's too cold and damp down here. I think she is already suffering from hypothermia. She's going to die before you can kill her."

He took a step toward her. "Who the hell do you think you are, telling me what I *have* to do?"

It took all of her courage to stand up to him knowing the kind of man he was. But if she and Rebecca had any chance, they had to get out of this root cellar.

"If she dies, then what she knows dies with her," Gillian said quickly. "I told you. I don't know. She didn't tell me because she knows I'm not as strong as she is. I would tell you."

He seemed to mull that over for a moment, his gaze going to his wife. Marc looked livid. He raised his hand and Gillian tried not to cower from his fist.

To her surprise, he didn't strike her. "Fine," he said with a curse.

Rebecca didn't move, didn't seem to breathe. If it weren't for the movement of her eyes, Gillian would have sworn she was already dead.

"I hope you don't think you're going to get away again," Marc said, meeting her gaze. "I have nothing to lose and I'm sick of both of you."

AUSTIN HEARD THE sound of footfalls and murmured voices. He froze, listening, and was relieved when he heard Gillian's voice. He hadn't been able to hear anything for a while.

"We need to get her warm." Her voice was louder. So were the footfalls. They'd come up from the root cellar. He also heard another sound, a slow shuffling, almost dragging, gait.

"Maybe you could build a fire or turn on the furnace."

Marc swore at Gillian's suggestion. The footfalls stopped abruptly. Gillian let out a small cry. Austin cringed in anger, knowing that Marc had hit her.

"Enough wasting time," Marc snapped.

"You want her to talk? Then give me a chance. But first we need to warm her up. Can you get some quilts from the bedroom?"

Marc swore loudly, but Austin heard what sounded like him storming away into another room. "Move and I'll—" he said over his shoulder.

"I'm not going to move," Gillian snapped. "My sister can barely stand, let alone run away. I'm going to put her in the living room in front of the fireplace. Maybe you could build a fire?"

Austin didn't catch what Marc said. He could guess, though. Marc was an abusive SOB. But Austin still had no idea why he'd brought Gillian and her sister here, nor where the child was. From what he had surmised, Marc thought Gillian could get her sister to talk, but talk about what?

Austin decided it didn't matter. Marc had forced Gillian to come here against her will. He had abused her and her sister and had apparently held Rebecca captive here. It was time to put a stop to this.

Working his way back off the roof, he walked around

to where Marc had left the snowmobile. All Austin's instincts warned him not to go busting in. He couldn't chance what Marc would do.

He moved carefully back the way he'd come until he was at the far side of the cabin complex. He found an old door with a single lock and waited until he heard the sound of several snowmobiles nearby. Hoping they would drown out the noise, he busted the lock and carefully shoved open the door.

GILLIAN HELPED HER SISTER into a straight-backed chair from the dining room and gently wiped her sister's face with the hem of her sweater. "Oh, Becky."

Rebecca's gaze locked with hers, her voice a hoarse whisper. "I thought I could do this without getting you involved."

Marc returned with the quilts and dropped them next to the chair.

"We're going to need a fire," Gillian said, not looking at him as she rubbed life back into her sister's hands and arms.

After a moment, she glanced over her shoulder to see what Marc was doing. He was busy building a fire in the rock fireplace using some of the furniture he'd destroyed. He struck a match to the wadded up newspaper under the stack of wood. The paper caught fire. The dried old wood of the furniture burst into flames and began to crackle warmly.

"She needs something to drink. Is there any water in the kitchen?"

"What do you think?" Marc snapped. "It's winter. Everything is shut off."

"Maybe you could melt some snow." She motioned

with her head for him to go as if the two of them were in collaboration. The thought made her sick.

He glanced from her to her sister and back again. "Don't do anything stupid," he said as he walked into the kitchen and came back out with a pot in one hand.

Marc had both women in an old cabin in the woods, far enough from the rest of the world that they would never be found if he killed them and buried them in the root cellar. So what was the stupid thing he thought she might do?

He gave her a warning look anyway and left, going out the back door where he'd left the snowmobile. She let go of her sister's arms and to her surprise Rebecca fell over in the chair, catching herself before she fell on the littered floor.

Gillian helped her sit up straighter, shocked at how weak her sister was and terrified she wasn't going to survive this.

Marc came back in, shot them a look, but said nothing as he headed for the kitchen with the cooking pot full of fresh snow. She heard him turn on the stove. She could feel time slipping through her fingers.

"Becky, what's going on?" she whispered. "What is this about some ledger of Marc's? And where is Andy?"

Her sister shook her head in answer as she glanced toward the kitchen, where Marc was cussing and banging around.

"Tell him what he wants to know—otherwise he is going to kill you," Gillian pleaded.

"So sorry to get you—" her sister said from between cracked and cut lips.

"Becky—"

"Remember when we were kids and that big old tree blew over?"

Gillian stared at her. Had her brain been injured as a result of Marc's beating? Gillian's heartbreak rose in a sob from her throat as she looked at what that bastard had done to her sister.

Rebecca suddenly gripped her arm, digging in her fingernails. "Tell me you remember," her sister said.

"I remember."

Her sister's eyes filled with tears. "Love you." She licked her lips, her words coming out hoarse and hurried. "Save Andy. Make Marc pay." Pain filled her sister's eyes. "Can't save me."

"Stop talking like that. I'm not leaving here without you."

Her sister smiled, even though her lips were cut and bleeding, and then shook her head. "Get away. Run. He'll hurt you." She stopped talking at the sound of heavy footfalls headed back in their direction.

Gillian stared at her sister. "What are you going to do?" she whispered frantically. She could feel Marc closing the distance.

"Get ready to run," her sister said under her breath as Marc's shadow fell over them.

"What's all the whispering about?" Marc demanded as he handed Gillian a cup of melted snow.

She held it up to her sister's swollen lips. Her gaze met Rebecca's in a pleading gesture. Her sister was talking crazy. Worse, she seemed about to do something that could get them both killed.

Without warning, her sister knocked the cup out of her hand. It hit the floor, spilling the water as it rolled across the floor.

"You stupid—" Marc shoved Gillian out of the way. She fell backward and hit the floor hard. From where she was sprawled, she saw him pull his gun and crouch down in front of Rebecca. He put the end of the barrel against his wife's forehead. "Last chance, Rebecca."

With horror, Gillian saw Becky's expression—and what she had picked up from the floor and hidden in her hand. "No!" she screamed as her sister swung her arm toward Marc's face. The shard of sharp broken glass clutched in her fingers momentarily flashed as it caught the dim light.

Blood sprouted across Marc's cheek and neck as Rebecca raked the glass down his face. He bucked back and then shoved the barrel of the gun toward Rebecca's head as Gillian scrambled to her feet and launched herself at him.

The sound of the gunshot boomed, drowning out Gillian's scream as she careened into him, knocking them both to the floor.

THE DOORKNOB TURNED in Austin's hand as he heard the scream. He charged into the cabin, running toward the echoing sound of the scream and the gunshot, his heart hammering in his chest.

His lungs ached with the freezing-cold musty smell of the cabin. He had his gun drawn, his senses on alert, as he burst into the room and tried to take in everything at once. He saw it all in those few crucial seconds. The large wrecked living room; the small glowing fire crackling in the huge stone fireplace; snowy, melting footprints on the worn wood floor; and three people— all on the floor.

"Drop the gun!" Austin ordered as he saw Gillian

and Marc struggling for the weapon. The other figure—Rebecca Stewart, he assumed—lay in a pool of blood next to them.

There was no way he could get a clear shot. He rushed forward an instant before the sound of the second gunshot ripped through the room. The bullet whistled past him. Marc wrestled the gun from Gillian and scrambled to his feet, dragging her up with him as a shield, the barrel of his gun against her temple.

"You drop *your* gun or so help me I will put a bullet in her head," Marc said, sounding in pain. Austin saw that he was bleeding from a cut down his cheek and neck.

"You can't get away," Austin said his weapon aimed at Marc's head.

Marc chuckled at that as he lifted Gillian off her feet and backed toward the door where he'd left his snowmobile. "Drop your gun or I swear I will kill her!" Marc bellowed. His eyes were wide, blood streaming down his face, but the gun in his hand was steady and sure.

"The police are on their way. Let her go!" Austin doubted the bluff would work and it was too risky to try a shot since Marc was making himself as small a target as possible behind Gillian.

Marc kept backing toward the door. His snowmobile was just outside. If he could manage to get to it… Austin couldn't stand the thought of the man getting away, but his first priority had to be the safety of the women. Austin knew Marc wouldn't try to take Gillian with him. He needed to get away quickly. If he could make him let her go… He wouldn't be surprised, though, if at the last moment Marc put a bullet in her head.

Gillian was crying, the look on her face one of horror

more than terror. She was looking at her sister crumpled on the floor in front of the fireplace. Rebecca wasn't moving.

Marc dragged Gillian another step back. He would have to let Gillian go to open the door. Austin waited as the seconds ticked by.

As Marc reached behind him to open the door, Austin knew he would have only an instant to take his shot. Moving fast, Marc shoved Gillian away, turned the gun and fired as Austin dove to the side for cover—and took his own shot.

He heard a howl of pain and then a loud crash, looking in time to see Marc grab a large old wooden hutch by the door and pull it down after him. The hutch crashed down on its side, blocking the door as Marc made his escape.

Austin raced toward the door but couldn't see Marc or the snowmobile to get off a shot. As he started to scramble over the downed hutch, he heard the engine, smelled the smoke as the man roared away.

Behind him, Gillian, sobbing hysterically, pushed herself up from the littered floor and rushed to her sister.

His need to go after Marc blinded him for a moment. He'd wounded Marc, but it hadn't been enough to stop him. He couldn't bear the thought of Marc getting away after what he'd done. He swore under his breath. But as badly as he wanted the man, he couldn't leave Gillian and her sister to chase after him.

"Help her," she pleaded from where she was kneeling on the floor. "My sister—"

He holstered his gun and knelt down next to Rebecca

to feel for a pulse. "She's alive." Just barely. He checked his phone. Still no service.

"Go for help. I'll stay here with her," Gillian said. "Go."

Chapter Twelve

Marc couldn't believe this. He was bleeding like a stuck pig. Reaching the road and his Suburban, he stumbled off the snowmobile and lurched toward his vehicle. He couldn't tell how badly he was wounded, but his movements felt too slow, which he figured indicated that he was losing blood fast.

He thumbed the key fob, opened the Suburban's door and pulled himself inside. The last thing he wanted to do was take the time to check his wounds for fear the cowboy would be coming after him, but something told him if he didn't stop the bleeding, he was a dead man either way.

The Texas deputy had said he'd already called the cops. Marc couldn't risk that the man was telling the truth. His hand shook as he turned the rearview mirror toward him and first inspected the cut.

"Son of a bitch!" He couldn't believe what Rebecca had done to him. The cut ran from just under his eye, down his cheek to under his chin and into his throat. He took off his gloves and pressed one to the spot that seemed to be bleeding the most.

After a few moments, the bleeding slowed—at least on his face. He could feel blood running down his side, chilling him as it soaked into his clothing. He became aware of the pain. His shoulder felt as if it were on fire. Unzipping his coat, then unbuttoning his shirt, he inspected the damage.

Again, he'd been lucky. The bullet had only grazed his shoulder. He stuck the other glove on the wound and zipped his coat back up. He would have to get more clothes. He couldn't wear a coat drenched in blood with a bullet hole in it—especially given the way his face looked.

He swore again, furious with Rebecca but even more furious with himself. She'd purposely pushed him so he would pull the trigger. Now he was no closer to finding his ledger and his money—or his son—than he had been at first.

Starting the Suburban, he pulled away. He would have to ditch this rig and pick up another. That was the least of his problems. He knew someone who could stitch up his wounds and get him another vehicle.

But now he was a man on the run from the law.

GILLIAN WAS CRADLING her sister's head in her arms when Austin returned with local law enforcement. Rebecca was breathing, but she hadn't regained consciousness. Gillian had wanted to go in the ambulance with her sister, but the officer had needed her to answer questions about what had happened.

"I'll take you to the Bozeman hospital to see your sister," Austin said when the interrogation had finally ended and they were allowed to go.

Gillian was still shaken and worried about her sister as she climbed into Austin's SUV. The officers who'd questioned them had taken them to a local station to talk. She'd been grateful to get out of the cold cabin.

"We have to make sure Marc doesn't get to Becky," she said as Austin pulled onto Highway 191, headed north.

"That isn't going to happen. There will be a guard outside her room at the hospital, not that I suspect Marc will try to see her. There is a BOLO out on your brother-in-law. He can't get far in that large black Suburban. Also, he's wounded and needs medical attention. Law enforcement has thrown a net over the area. When he shows his face, they will arrest him."

She glanced at the Texas cowboy. "You don't know Marc. He has access to other vehicles. He's resourceful. He'll slip through the net. He has nothing to lose at this point. He will be even more dangerous."

"You don't have any idea where your brother-in-law might go?"

She shook her head, then winced in pain. "The man is crazy. Who knows what he'll do now."

"Whatever information he was trying to get out of your sister...he didn't get it, right?"

"No," she said, her eyes filling with tears. "Apparently Rebecca would rather die than tell him."

"I'm trying to understand all of this. Marc Stewart brought you to the cabin to make your sister talk, right? He thought she would tell you. Did she?"

Gillian wiped her tears. "No. Rebecca knew the moment I saw what he'd done to her that I would have told him anything he wanted to know. She didn't tell me *anything*. I didn't know about any ledger or about Andy being gone until Marc told me. I'm just praying she regains consciousness soon and tells us where we can find Andy. My nephew is only ten months old...."

"Maybe Marc will turn himself in given that he's wounded and now wanted by the law."

She scoffed at that. "I highly doubt that since whatever is in this ledger Rebecca took would apparently put Marc behind bars for years. He'd never go down without a fight."

"A lot of criminals say that—until it comes time to die and then they find they prefer to turn state's evidence," Austin said. "Your sister never even hinted what Marc might be up to?"

"No. I knew they were having trouble. I couldn't understand why she stayed with the man. He was domineering and tight with the money, and treated Rebecca as if she was his property. But I never dreamed something like this would happen. When Rebecca texted me that she had left Marc, I was shocked since there had been no warning."

AUSTIN GLANCED OVER at her as he drove. Gillian looked numb. Her face was still pale, her eyes red from crying. He hated to ask, but he needed to know what they were up against. "Would you mind telling me how all this began?"

She sat up a little straighter, drawing on some inner strength that impressed him. He knew, given what she'd been through, she must be exhausted let alone physically injured and emotionally spent.

"I had no idea what was going on. Rebecca and Andy had been at my house just a week before and everything seemed to be fine. Then I got the text. When I saw her car pull up to my house last night, I ran out thinking it was her."

He listened to her explain that instead of it being her sister in the car, it had been Marc. She told him how Marc had thrown her into the trunk and she'd escaped partway down the canyon.

"So there *had* been someone in the trunk," he said. It all made sense now. Even as confused as she'd been after her car accident, she'd recalled someone in the trunk.

"I wasn't thinking clearly when I took off. I just knew I had to get away from Marc and find my sister."

"You did everything you could to save her without any thought to your own life," Austin said. "This is on Marc, not you. But there is one thing I don't understand. Why did your sister choose now to leave him? I mean, had something happened between them?"

Gillian sighed. "I don't know. All I can figure is that Rebecca got her hands on Marc's business ledger, saw what was inside and realized she was married to a criminal—as well as an abuser. Apparently there was a reference to all the money Marc had stashed in the ledger and that's why she went to the Island Park cabin and he followed her there." She shook her head. "I don't know what she was thinking. How could she not know what Marc would do?"

"It sounds as if she was just trying to keep her son safe from him," Austin said. "She was also trying to protect you by not telling you anything." He felt Gillian's gaze on him.

"I'm sorry I dragged you into this."

"We're past that. As I told you before, I'm a deputy sheriff down in Texas. I'm glad I can help."

"I wish you could help, but I have no idea where my sister hid her son, let alone this ledger that Marc is losing his mind over. Marc will only be worse now. He's dangerous and desperate. I'm afraid of what he will do—especially if he finds his son."

Austin hated the truth he heard in her words. He'd known men like Marc Stewart. "Which is another reason I don't want to let you out of my sight. It won't make any difference if he believes your sister told you anything or not. He'll blame you."

"He already does for involving you in this. I'm so sorry. But I can't ask you—"

"I'm in this with you," he said, reaching over to take her hand. He gave it a squeeze and let go.

Gillian met his gaze. Her eyes shimmered with tears. "If you hadn't shown up when you did…" She looked away. He could tell she was fighting tears, worried about her sister and her nephew, and maybe finally realizing how close she had come to dying back there. "I have to find Andy and this notebook, ledger, whatever it is, before Marc does. If he finds it first, he'll skip the country with Andy. I know him. I wouldn't be surprised if he doesn't have a new identity all set up."

MARC AVOIDED LOOKING in the mirror as he drove. His friend had fixed him up. But when he saw his bandaged face in the mirror, it made him furious all over again. And when he was furious, he couldn't think straight.

He'd just assumed that Rebecca would cave at some point and tell him what he wanted to know. Frankly, he'd never thought her a strong woman. Boy, had she proven him wrong, he thought as he silently cursed her to hell. If she had just told him what he wanted to know all this would be over by now. She might even still be alive. Or not. But at least he would have made her death look like an accident.

Word was going to get out about Rebecca's murder. His DNA would be found at the scene. Not to mention he'd shot at a Texas deputy. Gillian would swear he'd kidnapped her... How had things gotten so out of hand? He had a target on his back now. Even with an old pickup and a change of identity, he couldn't risk getting stopped even for a broken taillight—not with this bandage down the side of his face.

His cell phone rang. "What?"

"You don't have to bite off my head."

Marc rolled his eyes, but bit his tongue. He needed his friend's help. "Sorry, Leo. What did you find out?"

"They took your wife to the hospital in Bozeman. I couldn't get any information, though, on her condition."

Rebecca was *alive?*

"As for your sister-in-law? She and some cowboy left together after spending a whole lot of time talking to the cops. I suspect they're headed to Bozeman and the hospital. You want me to keep following them?"

"The man with her? He's a sheriff's deputy from Texas. He'll know if he is being followed, so no. I'll call you if I need you."

He disconnected, not sure what to do next. When his cell rang, he thought it was Leo again. Instead it was his...so-called partner. In truth, Victor Ramsey ran the show and always had. Marc began to sweat instantly as he picked up.

"What the hell is going on, Marc? Why are there cops after you?"

AT THE HOSPITAL in Bozeman, Gillian was told that her sister was stable and resting. She hadn't regained consciousness, but the doctor promised he would call when she did.

Gillian tried not to let the tidal wave of relief drown out the news. Becky was alive and stable. Once she woke up, she could tell them what they needed to know. But in the meantime...

Down the hallway, she saw Austin on his cell phone and overheard the last of what he was saying as she approached. She felt awful as she realized that he'd come to Montana to see his family and Christmas was just days away.... She didn't know what she would have done without him, though, but she couldn't have him missing a family Christmas because of her.

"Hey," he said, smiling when he saw her. "Good news?"

She nodded. "Becky's still unconscious but stable. Listen, Austin, I already owe you my life and my sister's. Aside from almost getting you killed, now I'm keeping you away from your family who you came all the way to Montana to see and it's almost Christmas."

"I came up for the grand opening of our first Texas Boys Barbecue restaurant in Montana."

"Barbecue?"

He nodded at her surprise. "My brothers and I own a few barbecue joints."

"I thought you said you were a deputy sheriff?"

"I am. My brother Laramie runs the company so the rest of us can do whatever we want." He gave a shrug.

"Cardwell?" Why hadn't she realized who he was? "You're related to Dana Savage?"

"She's my cousin. She and her husband own Cardwell

Ranch. My brothers came up to visit her, fell in love with Montana and all but one of them has fallen in love with more than the state and moved here."

"You can't miss this grand opening...."

"Believe me, my family can manage without me. Actually, they're used to it. I'm not good at these family events and I'm not leaving you until Marc is behind bars. You're stuck with me." He smiled. He had an amazing smile that lit up his handsome face and made his dark eyes shine.

She hadn't realized how handsome he was. Maybe because she hadn't taken the time to really look at him. "Are you trying to tell me that you're the black sheep of the family?" she asked as they took the elevator down to the hospital parking area.

He laughed at that. "And then some. I missed my brother Tag's wedding last summer. I was on a case. I'm often on a case. I'm only here now because they all ganged up on me and made me feel guilty."

"When is the grand opening?"

"The first of January. See? Nothing to worry about."

"You're that confident Marc will be caught by then?" she asked.

He turned that smile on her. "With my luck, he will and I won't have any excuse not to attend not only the grand opening but also Christmas at my cousin's house with the whole family."

"You aren't serious."

"On the contrary. I usually volunteer to work the holidays so deputies with families can spend them at home. I'm the worst Scrooge ever when it comes to Christmas. So trust me when I say my family won't be surprised I'm not there, nor will they mind all that much."

"I think you're exaggerating," she said as they reached his SUV.

He shook his head. "Nope. It's the truth. What do you suggest we do now?"

She turned to look at him. "I can't ask you—"

"You aren't asking. I already told you. I'm not leaving you alone until Marc is behind bars."

Tears filled her eyes. She bit down on her lower lip for a moment. "Thank you. I need to go to my house."

"Where is that?"

"I have a studio at Big Sky."

"A studio?"

"I'm a jeweler."

"The watch." He frowned and she could see he was wondering who'd made it for her.

"My father was the one who taught me the craft. I lost him five years ago. Before that, my mother. I can't lose my sister."

He put an arm around her and pulled her close. "You won't. The doctor said she is stable, right? She's a strong woman and she has every reason to pull through."

Gillian nodded against his strong chest. He smelled of the outdoors, a wonderful masculine scent that reminded her how long it had been since a man had held her. She reminded herself why Austin Cardwell was here with her and stepped away from his arm.

"I need to figure out what my sister was thinking," she said as Austin opened the door to the SUV. "It was one thing to hide the ledger, but another to hide my nephew."

As he slid behind the wheel, he asked, "Those few moments you had with your sister before Marc returned, did she say anything that might have been a clue where either might be?"

"I'm not even sure she was in her right mind at the end. Marc told me she was taking some kind of pills for stress before all this happened."

Austin shook his head as he started the engine. "She got her son away from Marc and she hid a book that can possibly get her husband put away for a long time. On top of that, she wounded Marc in a way that makes him easy to spot. That doesn't sound like a woman who wasn't thinking straight."

Gillian's eyes filled with tears. "But why didn't she tell me where to find Andy and the ledger?"

"Maybe she mailed you something. Or said something that didn't make sense at the time, but will later. You've been through so much, not to mention Marc taking you out of the hospital too soon after a head injury. You say you live at Big Sky?"

"Before you get to Meadow Village. I have an apartment over my studio and shop." She rubbed her temples with her fingers.

"Headache?"

Gillian nodded. "Maybe Becky *did* send me something in the mail. If that's the case…" She turned to look at him. "Then we need to get to my house before Marc does."

THEY WERE ONLY a few miles out of Big Sky when Gillian fell into an exhausted sleep. Austin's heart went out to her. He couldn't imagine what the past forty-eight hours had been like for her. He worried about her even though she was holding up better than he would have expected. The woman was strong. Or maybe it hadn't really hit her yet.

What drove him was the thought of Marc Stewart not just getting away with kidnapping and attempted murder, but possibly finding his son and taking him out of the country. If that happened, Austin doubted either Rebecca or her sister would ever see the child again.

The man had to be stopped, and Austin was determined to do what he could to make that happen.

When Gillian woke near the outskirts of Big Sky, she looked better, definitely more determined. There was so much more he needed to know about the situation he'd found himself in and he was anxious to ask. But first they had to reach her studio. There was the chance that Marc Stewart had been there—was even still there.

Chapter Thirteen

Marc held the phone away from his ear for a moment as he considered how much to tell Victor. The first time Marc had met Victor Ramsey, he'd been amused by the man's clean-cut appearance that belied the true man underneath. That was five years ago. Victor still had one of those trustworthy faces, bright blue eyes and a winning smile. But if you looked deeper into those blue eyes, as Marc had done too many times, you would see a cold-blooded psychopath.

"What's going on, Marc?" Victor asked now as if he'd just called to catch up.

The two had met through a mutual friend, something Marc later suspected had been a setup from the start.

Want to make more money than you've ever dreamed possible? his friend had said one night after they'd consumed too much alcohol.

His answer had been, *Hell yes.* The auto body shop he'd taken over from his father was a lot of work and for average income, not to mention he hated it.

His friend, now deceased under suspicious circumstances, had made the introduction. At first Marc had been in awe of Victor, a self-made man with a lot of charm and ambition. It wasn't until he was in too deep that he'd begun to regret all of it.

"Just having a little domestic trouble," Marc answered now.

"Attempted murder is a little more than domestic trouble. I want to see you. Where are you?"

He'd been expecting this, but the last person he wanted to see him like this was Victor. "Right now isn't a great time."

"I'm staying at my place in Canyon Creek. I'll give you two hours. Don't be late. You know how I hate anyone who wastes my time." Victor hung up.

Marc swore. After Victor saw his face—and found out everything else—Marc knew he would be lucky to walk out of that meeting alive.

With a curse, he realized he had really only one choice. Get out of the country—or at least try. But it would mean leaving without his son—or settling the score with his wife, his sister-in-law and the Texas deputy who'd stuck his nose in where it didn't belong.

He would prefer to find the ledger and his son, take care of all of them and then get out of the country. Rebecca had discovered some of his money, but he had more hidden.

Unfortunately the clock was ticking and if he hoped to live long enough to do what had to be done, he would have to meet with Victor and try to talk his way out of this mess.

AUSTIN PARKED BEHIND a three-story building with a sign that read Gillian Cooper Designs. As she led the way up the back steps, Austin kept an eye out for Marc Stewart.

There was no sign of his black Suburban, but Austin figured he would have gotten rid of it by now.

There were no other buildings around Gillian's. The studio and apartment sat against the mountainside with only one parking spot in back. The building was unique in design. When he asked her about it, he wasn't surprised to find out that she'd designed it herself.

As she led him into the living area, he saw that the inside was as uniquely designed as the outside with shiny bamboo floors, vaulted wood ceilings, arches and tall windows. He could see that she had more than just a talent for jewelry. The decor was a mixture of old and new, each room bright with color and texture.

Remembering how Marc had torn up the Island Park cabin, he was relieved to see that the man hadn't been in Gillian's apartment. From what he could gather, nothing had been disturbed. Maybe Marc had been wounded badly enough that he'd been forced to get medical attention before anything else. Once an emergency room doctor saw the bullet wound, the law would be called and Marc would be arrested. At least Austin could hope.

He stood in the living area, taking in the place. He found himself becoming more intrigued by Gillian Cooper as he watched her scoop up the mail that had been dropped through the old-fashioned slot in the antique front door.

"I love your house," he said, hoping he got a chance to see the jewelry she made.

"Thanks," she said as she sorted through the mail. He could tell by her disappointed expression that there was nothing from her sister. She looked up at him. "Nothing." Her voice broke as she shook her head.

"Why don't you get a hot shower and a change of clothes," he suggested.

She nodded. "There is a shower in the guest room if you…"

"Thank you." They stood like that for a moment, strangers who knew too much about each other, bound together by happenstance.

He moved first, picking up his duffel bag, which he'd brought up from the car. She pointed toward an open door as if no longer capable of speech. He'd seen it often in people who were thrown into extraordinary circumstances. They often found an inner strength that made it possible for them to do extraordinary things. But at some point that strength ebbed away, leaving them an empty shell.

The shower was hot, the water pressure strong. Austin stood under it, spent. He'd had little sleep last night and then today… He was just thankful he'd burst into the cabin when he had. He didn't want to think what would have happened otherwise. Nor did he want to think about what he'd gotten himself into and where it would end.

CLEAN AND WARM and dressed in clean jeans and a long-sleeved T-shirt, Austin went back out into the living room. Where was Marc now? Austin could only imagine. Hopefully he'd been arrested, but if that were the case, Austin would have received a call by now. The officer who'd responded to his call had promised to let him know when Marc Stewart was in custody.

Which meant Marc Stewart was still out there.

A few minutes later, Gillian emerged from the other side of the house. Her face was flushed from her shower.

She wore a white fluffy sweater and leggings. Her long dark hair was still damp and framed the face of a model.

For a moment, she looked nervous, as if realizing she was now alone with a complete stranger.

"If you don't mind talking about it, could you tell me more about this ledger Marc is looking for?" he said, finding ground he knew would ease the sudden tension between them.

"I only know what Marc told me," she said as she walked to the refrigerator, opened it and held up a bottle of wine. He nodded and she poured two glasses, which they took into the living room.

Gillian curled up at one end of the couch, tucking her feet under her. Austin took a chair some distance away. He watched her take a sip of her wine and she seemed to relax a little.

"I gathered Marc wrote down some sort of illegal business dealings in a black ledger that he never let out of his sight," she said after a moment. "Marc is dyslexic so he has trouble remembering numbers, apparently. He wrote everything down. According to him, my sister drugged him and took the book."

"What do you know about your brother-in-law's business?"

"Nothing really. He owns an auto body shop, repairs cars."

"That doesn't sound like something that would force him to go to the extremes he has to recover some ledger he kept figures in."

"I'm not sure what's in it other than where he hid large amounts of money, but I gathered, from Marc's terror at the ledger landing in the wrong hands, that there is enough in it to send him to prison."

"I don't understand why she didn't take it to the police or the FBI. Marc would be in jail now and none of this would have happened."

Gillian shook her head. "Apparently she thought she could force him into giving her a divorce and custody of Andrew Marc in exchange for the ledger. She also needed money. I guess she didn't realize just how dangerous that would be."

"Or she didn't get a chance to before Marc realized the ledger was missing. He figured out she was headed for the Island Park cabin fairly quickly."

She nodded. "He'd stashed money there." She grew quiet for a moment. "Apparently she hid the ledger. I know it's not at their house. He said he tore the place apart looking for it."

"You and your sister were close. Any ideas where she could have hidden it?"

"None. Becky and I…" She hesitated, turning to glance out the side window. "We weren't that close recently. Marc thought I was a bad influence on her. I didn't want to make things worse for her but I couldn't stand being around him. He kept her on a short leash. The last time we were together before this, I begged her to leave Marc. She kept thinking he was going to change."

Austin heard the worry in her voice. "A lot of women have trouble leaving."

"I always thought my sister was smarter than that," she said as she got up to refill their glasses.

"Intelligence doesn't seem to have much to do with it." He doubted this helped at the moment. Marc Stewart was out there somewhere, wounded and still obsessed with finding not only the ledger, but also his son. Which meant Gillian wasn't safe until Marc was behind bars and maybe not even then, depending on just what Marc Stewart was involved in.

She met his gaze as she filled his glass. "You saw what Marc's like. Just out of spite, he might do something to Andy if he finds him." Her voice cracked, and for a moment, she looked as if she might break down.

Austin rose to take her in his arms. She felt small but strong. It was he who felt vulnerable. He'd never met anyone like her, and that scared him. Not to mention the fact that Gillian felt too good in his arms.

He let go of her and she stepped away to wipe her tears.

"We'll find your nephew," he said to her back. He had no idea how, but he agreed with her. Marc was a loose cannon now. Anyone in his path was in danger. "Your sister was living in Helena? Where would she stash her son that she thought he would be safe? Marc said the boy was with his grandmother."

Gillian shook her head. "No grandparents are still alive."

"Maybe a babysitter? A friend she trusted?"

Again Gillian shook her head. "Marc didn't allow her to leave Andy with anyone, not that she had need of a babysitter because he would check on her during the day to make sure she hadn't gone anywhere."

Austin hated the picture she was painting of her sister's life. "Then how did your sister manage to not only get possession of Marc's ledger, but hide their son?"

Gillian shook her head again. "I suspect she'd been planning it for weeks, maybe even months. Rebecca did tell me when I was trying to get her to leave him that time in Helena that Marc had threatened to kill her and Andy if she did."

He guessed that Rebecca had believed her husband. But then she'd taken the ledger and thought she had leverage. "You said your sister visited a while back. Is there a chance she left you a note that you might have missed?"

Gillian shook her head and stepped to one of the windows to look out. Past her, he caught glimpses of the Gallatin River and the dense snowcapped pines. It was snowing again, huge flakes drifting down past the window. How could his brothers live in a place where it snowed like this?

"Apparently my sister found quite a bit of money that Marc kept hidden in his locked gun cabinet." She turned toward him. "It is missing, as well."

He thought of the ransacked Island Park cabin. "Your sister had gone to the cabin to get more money he had stashed there?"

She nodded. "So foolish. I guess she wanted to keep him from skipping the country and taking his money, and she thought that would work. She apparently didn't think she could keep him in jail long enough to do whatever she had planned."

He watched her look around the room as if remembering her sister's last visit. She frowned. "If Becky was well into her plan when she came to see me, why didn't she say something? Why didn't she tell me so I would know what to do now?" She sounded close to tears again.

"While she was here, where did she stay?"

"In the spare bedroom. You don't think she might have hidden the ledger in there?"

He followed her, thinking there was a remote chance at best. Still, they had to look. Like the rest of the place, it was nicely furnished in an array of colors. The wall behind the bed was exposed brick. Several pieces of artwork hung from it.

Gillian searched the room from the drawers in the bedside tables to under the mattress and even under the bed. Austin went into the bathroom and looked in the only cabinet there. No note or a ledger of any kind.

As Gillian finished, she sat down on the end of the bed. She looked pale and exhausted, like a woman who should be in the hospital.

"Are you sure you shouldn't have seen a doctor while we were at the hospital? I don't mind taking you back."

"I'm fine," she said with a sigh. "Just disappointed. I knew it was doubtful that Becky left anything. She would have been afraid I would find it and try to stop her. Rebecca never wanted to be a bother to anyone, especially me, her older sister. She hid a lot of things from me, like just how bad it was living with Marc."

"Why don't you get some rest? We can talk more in the morning and figure out what to do next."

She nodded. "I can't even think straight right now."

He reached out and took her hand to pull her up from the bed. "You still have that headache?"

She smiled at him. "It's nothing to be alarmed about. I'm fine. Really." Suddenly she froze. "Becky *did* leave something." Her voice rose with excitement. "I didn't think anything about it at the time. Since Andy had been playing with an old key ring of hers that had a dozen keys on it. She left a key on the night table beside the bed. I thought it must have come off Andy's key ring so I just tossed it in the drawer for when he came back."

She opened the drawer beside the bed and took out the key.

Austin had hoped for a safety deposit key. Instead, it appeared to be an ordinary house key. He realized that Gillian's first instinct on finding it was probably right.

"You didn't find anything else?"

She shook her head, her excitement fading. "It's probably nothing, huh?"

"Probably," he said, taking the key. "But we'll hang on to it just in case." He pocketed it as Gillian started to leave the room.

"You can have this room," she said over her shoulder. She stopped in the doorway and turned to look back at him. "That is, if you're staying."

"As I told you, I'm not going anywhere until Marc is behind bars. I'm a man of my word, Gillian."

She met his gaze. "Somehow I knew that."

"No matter how long it takes, I'm not leaving you." Austin knew even as he made the promise that there would be hell to pay with his family. But they were used to him letting them down. She started to turn away.

"One more thing," he said. "Did your sister have a key to this house?"

"No." Realization dawned on her expression. She shivered.

"Then there is nothing to worry about," he said. "Try to get some sleep."

"You, too."

He knew that wouldn't be easy. An electricity seemed to spark in the air between them. They'd been through so much together already. He didn't dare imagine what tomorrow would bring.

She hesitated in the doorway. "If you need anything…"

"Don't worry about me." As he removed his jacket, her gaze went to the weapon in his shoulder holster. He saw her swallow before she turned away. "Sweet dreams," he said to her retreating back.

Chapter Fourteen

It had begun to snow. Large lacy flakes fell in a flurry of white as Marc pulled up to Victor's so-called cabin in the mountains overlooking Helena, Montana. The "cabin" was at least five thousand square feet of luxury including an indoor pool, a media center and a game room. At his knock, one of Victor's minions answered the door, a big man who went by only Jumbo.

"Mr. Ramsey is in the garden room." Oh, yeah, and the house had a garden room, too.

There was no garden in the glassed-in room, but there was an amazing view of the valley below and there was a bar. Victor was standing at the bar pouring himself a drink. Marc got the feeling he'd seen him drive up and had been waiting. Today he wore a velour pullover in the same blue as his eyes.

"What would you like to drink?" he asked as he motioned to one of the chairs at the bar. Victor seemed to take in his bandaged face and neck, but said nothing.

Marc took one of the chairs. "Whatever you're having."

"Wise man," Victor said with a disarming smile. "I only drink the best. Isn't that the reason you and I became friends to begin with?"

Friends? What a joke. Marc didn't need him to spell things out. "I like the best things in life like anyone else."

"But you aren't like anyone else," Victor said as he pushed what looked like three fingers of bourbon in a crystal glass over to him.

"No, I'm unique because I know you." He knew it was what the man wanted to hear, and right now he was fine with saying anything that could get him out of here. He took a gulp of the drink. It burned all the way down. As he set the glass down, he said, "Okay, I screwed up, but I'm trying to fix it."

Victor lifted a brow. "You think? And how is it you hope to do that?"

He wasn't surprised that his mess was no secret to the man. Victor had someone inside law enforcement. There was little he didn't know about.

"I didn't mean to almost kill her."

"The her you're referring to being your *wife?*"

"Who else?"

"Who else indeed. With you I never know." Victor took a sip of his drink, studying him over the rim of the glass. "Attempted murder, kidnapping, assault?" Victor leaned on the bar like one friend confiding in another. "Tell me, Marc. What's going on with you?"

He knew this tone of voice. He'd seen it used on other men who'd messed up in their little…organization. He also knew what had happened to those men. Victor was most dangerous when he was being congenial.

"The bitch drugged me and took my ledger—you know, where I kept track of the business."

Victor leaned back, his expression making it clear that his concern had shifted to himself rather than

Marc's future. "By the business, you mean your automotive business."

Marc didn't answer.

"You wrote down *our* business transactions?"

"It was a lot of names and numbers, and I do better if I can write it down."

"You mean like names of our associates and their phone numbers." His voice had dropped even further.

"Yeah, that and a few transactions just so I could remember whom I'd dealt with. You have a lot of associates."

Victor looked as if he might have a coronary. "This... ledger? I'm assuming you got it back. Tell me you got it back."

"Why do you think I tried to kill her? She hid it *and* my kid. I was trying to get the information out of her...."

"That's why you involved her sister." Victor closed his eyes for a moment. He was breathing hard. Marc had never seen him lose his cool. Victor was the kind of man who didn't do his own dirty work. He prided himself on never losing control, but he seemed close right now.

"So you don't have the information and you don't know where it is," Victor said.

That about sized it up. "But I'm going to find it."

"She could have mailed it to the FBI."

Marc hadn't thought of that. Probably because he was still caught up in his old belief that Rebecca wasn't all that smart. "I don't think she'd do that."

Victor looked at him, aghast. "You don't *think* so?"

"She's just trying to use the ledger to get a divorce and custody of my kid."

"Let me guess." Victor didn't look at him. Instead,

he turned his glass in his hands as if admiring the cut crystal. "You refused to give her what she wanted."

"She isn't taking my kid." The blow took him by surprise. The heavy crystal glass smashed into the side of his face, knocking him off his stool. The crystal shattered, prisms flying across the Italian rock flooring of the garden room an instant before Marc joined them.

Jumbo appeared, as if he had been waiting in the wings, expecting trouble. "You all right, Mr. Ramsey?"

Marc swore. Victor wasn't the one on the floor surrounded by glass. As he rose, he saw Victor picking glass out of his hand. Jumbo rushed around the bar to get a rag.

"No harm done. Isn't that right, Marc?" Victor said.

Blood was running down into his eye. He reached up and pulled a shard of glass from his temple.

"Get Marc a bandage to go with his other bandages, will you, Jumbo?" their boss said. "Sorry about that," he said after Jumbo had left. "I seldom lose my temper."

Marc said nothing. His head hurt like hell and this was the second time in twenty-four hours that he'd been cut. The blow had opened his other cut, and it, too, was now bleeding. First his wife had tried to kill him, now this.

Jumbo returned with a first aid kit. "Let him see to it," Victor ordered when Marc tried to take the kit from the man. It was all he could do to sit still and let an oaf like Jumbo work on him. "Here, be sure there isn't any glass in the cut first." Victor handed the man a bottle of Scotch. "Pour some of the good stuff on it."

Marc gritted his teeth as Jumbo shoved his head to the side and poured the alcohol into the wound. The Scotch ran into Rebecca's handiwork as well, sending fiery pain roaring through him. He swore, the pain so intense he thought he might black out. Jumbo patted the spot on his temple dry with surprising tenderness before carefully applying something to stop the bleeding.

"There, all better," Victor said. "Thank Jumbo. He did a great job."

"Thanks, Jumbo," Marc mumbled.

After Jumbo had cleaned up the mess and left, his boss refilled Marc's glass and got himself a new one. "Now," he said, "I don't need to tell you what needs to be done, do I?"

"No. I'm going to get the ledger." He knew better than to mention his son. Victor didn't give a crap about Andy.

The man frowned. "The sister, is she going to be a problem?"

"Naw." He tried to keep his gaze locked with Victor's, but he broke away first even though he knew it was a mistake.

"The sister isn't the only problem, is she? Who is this Texas deputy who got involved?"

Marc swore under his breath. It amazed him how Victor got his information and so quickly. He must have "associates" everywhere. The thought did nothing to make him feel better.

"I'll take care of them."

Victor shook his head. "You just get this…ledger you lost back. And what are you going to do with it?"

"Destroy it."

Victor looked pained. "Wrong, you're going to bring it to me. I'll take care of it. There are no copies, right?"

"No, I'm not a fool." From Victor's expression, it was clear he thought differently. Marc should have been relieved. What Victor was saying was that they were finished. No more money. It was over. Their relationship was terminated.

Marc searched his emotions for the relief he should have been feeling. Instead, all he could think was that he would kill them. First Rebecca. Then her sister and the cowboy. "I'll fix everything."

Victor didn't look convinced. "Just find the ledger. That's all I ask."

But Marc knew nothing in his life had ever been that simple. He downed his drink, stood up and left.

GILLIAN WENT TO her bedroom, but she doubted she would be able to sleep. Her mind was racing. She kept going over the few conversations she'd had with her sister in the months, weeks and days before all this.

What had Rebecca been thinking? Why hadn't she taken the incriminating evidence to the police? Had she really thought Marc would just agree to a divorce?

No, she thought. That's why Rebecca had hidden not only the ledger, but also her son.

As she pulled on a nightgown and climbed into bed, she was reminded that she wasn't alone in the house. That should have given her more comfort than it did. She was very…aware of Austin Cardwell. It surprised her that she could feel anything, as exhausted and distraught as she was. Mostly, she felt…off balance.

She closed her eyes, praying for the oblivion of sleep.

"I might need your help."

Gillian's eyes came open as she recalled something her sister had said. The conversation came back to her slowly.

"You know I will do anything for you."

"I don't like involving you, but if things go wrong..."

"Becky, what's going on?"

"I keep thinking about when we were kids."

"You're scaring me."

"I'm sorry. I was just being sentimental."

"Is everything okay, Becky?"

"Yes," her sister said, laughing. *"I was just remembering how much fun it was growing up. I love you, Gillian. Always remember that."*

Oh, Becky, she thought now as tears filled her eyes. Things had gone very wrong. Unfortunately, Gillian had no idea what to do about it and now she had a Texas cowboy in her spare bedroom.

She wasn't going to get a wink of sleep tonight.

MARC SCRATCHED THE back of his neck and glanced in the rearview mirror. He caught sight of a large gray SUV two cars behind him. Without slowing, he drove from Victor's toward downtown Helena. At the very last minute, he swung off the interstate and glanced back in time to see the gray SUV cross two lanes to make the exit.

He sped up, wanting to lose the tail. That damned Victor. He'd put a man on him. Marc shouldn't have been surprised. Had he been Victor, he wouldn't have trusted him either. Victor had to know that with the ledger and his testimony, his "friend" Marc could walk away from this mess a free man while Victor rotted in prison.

Not that Victor would let him live long enough for that to happen.

Swearing, he slowed down and pulled into a gas station. He saw the gray SUV go past to stop a few doors down in front of a fast-food restaurant. Getting out, he filled his tank and considered what to do next.

His throat felt dry. He would kill for a beer. The problem was stopping at just one beer. It would be too easy to get falling-down drunk. Still, he headed for one of the bars he frequented. Behind him, the gray SUV followed.

Victor's going to have me killed.

Not until I find the ledger.

The thought turned Marc's blood to ice.

But it was quickly followed by another thought.

In the meantime, Victor couldn't chance that the ledger would turn up and fall into the wrong hands. *Checkmate,* he thought with relief until he had another thought.

Unless Victor decided he could do a better job of getting the whereabouts of the book from Rebecca.

That thought echoed in his head, making his heart thump harder against his chest. Marc felt the truth of those words racing through his bloodstream. What if Victor decided to take things into his own hands?

He thought of Rebecca lying in her hospital bed. If Victor paid her one of his famous visits…

Marc reminded himself that Victor never got his own hands dirty even if he could find a way to get near Rebecca in the hospital.

What if Rebecca really had mailed the ledger to the FBI? His pulse jumped, heart hammering like a sledge in his chest. He wouldn't let himself go there. No, she'd hidden the book thinking she was smarter than he was, thinking she could force him into the divorce and take Andy from him. Stupid woman.

He tried to concentrate on what to do now. Because if she hadn't sent the book to the FBI, he had to assume she didn't know what she had in her possession. That was the good news, right?

The bad news was that no matter the outcome, he and Victor were finished. Even if he found the book and turned it over, Victor would never trust him again. Not that he could blame him. The information in that book could bring them all down. Victor would have him killed.

If he didn't find the ledger and the cops did, he was going to prison for a good part of the rest of his life. Of course that life wouldn't be long since Victor and his buddies would be in prison with him.

He still couldn't believe the mess he was in. He realized there was only one way out of this. He had to get to Rebecca before Victor did. Once she understood the consequences if she didn't turn over the ledger…he'd give her the divorce and custody. She would hand over his ledger and then when she thought she was safe, he would kidnap his kid and skip the country.

Why hadn't he thought of that in the first place? Because the woman had made him so furious. Also, he'd thought she would tell him where the ledger was with only minor persuasion.

He parked beside the bar in a dark spot away from the streetlamp and put in a call to the hospital. Rebecca was still unconscious. Swearing, he hung up.

The clock was ticking.

Inside the bar, Marc Stewart took a stool away from everyone else and ordered a beer. The bartender gave him a raised eyebrow at his bandaged face and the black eye that was almost swollen shut, but was smart enough not to comment.

The first beer went down easy. The second took a

little longer. He was doing a lot of thinking. Mostly about Rebecca and how he'd underestimated her. He kept mentally kicking himself. He had to get over her betrayal and think about what to do.

"Another beer?" the bartender asked as he cleared away his second empty bottle.

Marc focused on an old moose head hanging on the wall behind the bartender that could have used a good dusting. It reminded him of something. "No, I'm good," he told the bartender. Something about the moose head still nagged at him, but his head hurt too badly to make sense of it.

He slid off the bar stool, picked up most of his change from the bar and pocketed it. But as he looked toward the door, he told himself he had to ditch the tail that he knew would be parked outside waiting.

Marc smiled to himself even though it hurt his face to do so and put in the call. It was time to take care of business.

Chapter Fifteen

Gillian thought she would never be able to sleep again.
At the very least she'd expected to have horrible night-
mares.

She must have fallen into a death-like sleep. She
couldn't remember anything. Now, though, it all came
back in a rush, including the Texas cowboy in her spare
bedroom.

What did she really know about Austin Cardwell?
Nothing. Nothing except he'd saved her life twice and
made her feel... She wasn't even sure how to describe
it other than she felt too aware of the man.

She caught the smell of bacon cooking. *Austin?*
Grabbing her robe, she opened her door to find him
standing in her kitchen with a pancake flipper in his
hand. He was wearing one of her aprons, which actually made her smile.

"You didn't find bacon in my refrigerator," she said.

He turned to smile back at her. "Nope. Apparently
you exist on wine."

"I haven't gotten to the store in a while."

"I noticed." He flipped over what she saw were pancakes sizzling on her griddle. "Hungry?"

She started to say she wasn't. Just as she'd thought

she'd never be able to sleep again, she thought the same of eating. But her stomach growled loudly at the smell of bacon and pancakes.

Austin chuckle. "I'll take that as a yes." He motioned for her to have a seat at the breakfast bar.

"I should change," she said, pulling the collar of her robe tighter.

"No need. Eat them while they're hot." He slid a tall three-inch stack of pancakes onto her plate along with two slices of bacon. "This is my mother's recipe for corn cakes. It's the Texan in me. Wait until you taste the eggs. I hope you like hot peppers."

She felt her eyes widen in surprise. "You made eggs, as well? I really can't—"

"Insult me by not trying some?"

She couldn't help but smile at him in all his eagerness. "Are you trying to fatten me up?"

"You could use a little Texas cooking—not that you aren't beautiful just as you are."

"Good catch," she said, knowing it wasn't true. She hadn't been taking good care of herself because she'd been so worried about her sister. "Thank you."

"My pleasure." He joined her, loading his plate with pancakes, bacon and eggs before putting a spoonful of the eggs onto her plate. "Just try them. Some people aren't tough enough to handle my cooking."

It sounded like a dare—just as he'd meant it to. She studied him for a moment. What would she have done without him? Died night before last in the snowstorm beside the road and no doubt yesterday in Island Park.

Austin handed her the peach jam he'd bought. "Try some of this on your pancakes. Much better than maple syrup."

"Why not?" she said, doing as he said.

"Now take a bite of the pancake and one of the egg. Sweet and hot."

She did and felt her eyes widen in alarm for a moment at the heat. But he was right. The sweet cooled it right down. "Delicious."

"Now add a bite of bacon for saltiness and you've got an Austin Cardwell Texas breakfast." He laughed as he took a bite, chewed and, closing his eyes, moaned in obvious contentment.

Gillian was caught up in his enjoyment of breakfast and her own, as well. She couldn't remember the last time she'd eaten like this and was shocked when she realized that she'd cleaned her plate.

"Well?" he said, studying her openly. "Feeling better?"

She was. Earlier when she'd awakened, she'd felt light-headed and sick to her stomach. Now she was ready to do whatever had to be done to save her nephew, and she was pretty sure that had been Austin's plan.

"Don't you dare tell me you lost him," Victor said when he saw who was calling that morning.

"Sorry, boss. He let me think he knew he was being tailed and had accepted it."

He swore, but quickly calmed back down. He hadn't gotten where he was by losing control. True, Marc had already pushed him to the point of losing his temper. Marc Stewart had been a mistake. When he'd first met him, Marc had impressed him. He'd seemed like a man who had all his ducks in a row. That, added to the man's hunger for the finer things in life, and his charm and willingness to bend the rules, had made him a perfect associate.

Even when he'd realized the man had his flaws, he'd told himself that most men did. Unfortunately, the flaw Victor hadn't seen in Marc Stewart was about to bring them all down.

"Marc won't get far from home," Victor said. "John, I need you to watch his auto shop. Get Ray to keep an eye on the Friendly Bar over on the south side of town. It's Marc's go-to bar when things aren't going well. If either of you spot him again, stay on him. Trade off. Don't lose him again."

He hung up, hating that he hadn't put Jumbo on him. Jumbo wouldn't have lost him. Victor had realized last night after talking to Marc that he couldn't trust anyone with this, especially Marc. He'd already bungled things.

Changing into a clean sport shirt and a pair of jeans, Victor pulled on his lucky buffalo-skin boots and checked himself in the mirror. His unthreatening good looks had always served him well. He hoped they didn't let him down when he went to visit Rebecca Stewart at the hospital in Bozeman.

IT WAS GOOD to see some color in Gillian's face as they finished cleaning up the breakfast dishes together and she excused herself. Last night Austin had been worried he was going to have to take her back to the hospital. He was surprised she'd even been on her feet after the car wreck, the concussion and yesterday's events, not to mention Marc knocking her around before that. Her strength and endurance surprised him and filled him with admiration. If he had almost lost one of his brothers…

The thought was a punch to the gut and a wake-up call. He realized that he'd taken his four brothers for granted, assuming they would always be there.

He pulled out his cell phone and dialed his cousin Dana. He didn't want to have a long discussion with any one of his brothers. He knew it was cowardice on his part, but at the same time, he wanted to let them know he was all right and that he would try to make Christmas and the grand opening.

Actually, he didn't want to have to explain himself to anyone, even his cousin Dana. He'd hoped he would get her answering machine and he groaned inwardly when she answered on the third ring.

"Hey, Dana. It's Austin, your cousin?"

"The elusive Austin Cardwell? Hud said he met you, but I haven't had that opportunity yet."

"Sorry, but I'm afraid it could be a while yet."

She chuckled. "Hud said not to expect you for dinner until I saw the whites of your eyes."

"Your husband is one smart man."

"Yes, he is. I suppose you're calling me with a message for your brothers."

"Hud's wife is pretty sharp, as well."

She laughed. "What would you like me to tell them?"

Austin thought about that for a moment. "I'll try to make Christmas, but if I don't…"

"They're determined you will be at the grand opening. They're going to put it off until you're here. Don't see any way out for you."

"I guess it's too much to hope they'll go ahead without me if I don't show."

"Yep. Should I tell them you'll be getting back to them?"

"Tell them…I'll see them as soon as I can. You, too. If I can make Christmas, I will be there with bells on."

"Your cabin will be ready."

"EVERYTHING ALL RIGHT?" Gillian asked as she saw him pocket his cell phone.

"Fine. I talked to my cousin. She'll let my brothers know that I've been…detained."

She hated that he already had problems with his brothers and now she was making it worse. He followed her into the living room, the two of them sitting as they had the night before. "Are your parents still alive?"

He nodded. "Divorced. I was born in Montana, but my mother took all five of us boys to Texas when we were very young. My father stayed in Montana. Now my mother has remarried, and she and her new husband just bought a place near here where three of my brothers are living." He shrugged.

"You're lucky to have such a large family. After we lost our parents, it was just Becky and me. With her…" She fought the stark emotion that had her praying one moment and wanting to just sit down and bawl the next.

"I'm sure you already called the hospital. How is she doing?"

"There's been no change, but the doctor did say she is stable and he is hopeful. Have you ever lost anyone close to you?"

"A friend and fellow deputy." Austin hadn't gone a day in years without thinking about Mitch. "He was like a brother." He'd been even closer to Mitch than he was to his brothers. "He was killed in the line of duty. I wasn't there that day." And he'd never forgiven himself for it. He'd been away on barbecue company business.

"I'm sure it gets better," she said hopefully.

He nodded. "It does and it doesn't. You can never fill that hole in your life. Or your heart. But you put one foot in front of the other and you go on. Your sister, though, is going to come back."

"I hope you're right." She cleared her throat. "Right now I can't imagine how to go on. I'd hoped Becky had left me a letter, some kind of message...." Her voice broke.

"Tell me what you remember she said in what time you did have with her yesterday. It might help."

Shaking her head, she got up and walked to the opening into the living room. The December day glistened with fresh snow and sunshine. The bright sunlight poured through the leaded glass windows. Prisms of color sparkled in almost blinding light. She'd always loved this room because of the morning sunlight, but not even the sun's rays could warm her right now.

"Becky talked about our childhood."

"Where did you grow up?"

"In Helena. But we spent our summers at our grandfather's cabin. My sister mentioned the time the wind blew down an old pine tree in a thunderstorm. Becky and I loved thunderstorms and used to huddle together on Grandpa's porch and watch the lightning and the waves crashing on the shore." A lump formed in her throat. She couldn't lose her sister.

"Where is your grandfather's cabin?"

"Outside of Townsend on Canyon Ferry Lake."

"You think your nephew is at your grandfather's cabin?"

She shook her head. "The cabin's been boarded up

for years. That's why what she said doesn't make any sense."

"Maybe she left you a message there," Austin suggested. "The only place she mentioned was the cabin, right?"

Gillian nodded.

"If your sister was in her right mind enough to hide her son and try to get Marc Stewart out of his life, then anything she said might have value. Can we get to the cabin this time of year?"

"The road should be open. They get a lot less snow up there than we do down here."

"What is the chance Marc knows about the cabin and will go there?" Austin asked.

She felt a start. "If he remembers it… I think Becky took him there once when they were dating. Since it was nothing like his family's place in Island Park, I don't think he was impressed."

"I suspect there is a reason your sister reminded you of the downed tree and your grandfather's cabin. How soon can you be ready to leave?"

Chapter Sixteen

Marc watched his side mirror as he drove toward Townsend, Montana. His mind seemed sharper this morning. His face still hurt like hell, though. He'd changed the bandage himself, shocked at the damage his wife had done and all the more determined to kill her.

Last night, he'd managed to lose his tail and find a cheap motel at the edge of town, where he'd fallen asleep the instant his head hit the pillow.

It was this morning after a shower that he'd thought of that old moose head he'd seen at the bar and remembered his wife's family's cabin. Rebecca had taken him to see it when they were dating. As far as he knew, though, Rebecca and her sister still owned the place.

She'd been all weepy and sentimental because the cabin had belonged to her grandfather who'd died. Apparently she and her sister had spent summers there with the old man. He didn't get the weepy, emotional significance of the small old place in the pines. That was probably why he'd forgotten about it. That and the fact that they'd never returned to the place.

But he was good at getting back to a place he'd only been to once. He paid attention even when someone else was driving. Given how his wife felt about the old cabin, wasn't it possible she might return there when she had something to stash?

He drove toward the lake. The sleep had helped. He felt more confident that he could pull himself out of this mess. Ahead, he saw a sign that looked familiar and began to slow. If Rebecca had hidden the ledger at the cabin—which he was betting was a real possibility—then he would know soon enough.

Marc hoped his instincts were right as he turned off the main highway and headed down the dirt road back into the mountains along the lake. It had snowed so there was a fine dusting on the road, but nothing to worry about. This area never got as much snow as those closer to the mountains.

The road was the least of his worries anyway. He thought of Gillian and the cowboy deputy. Would Gillian think of the cabin?

Swearing under his breath, he realized that if he had, then she would, too. Maybe she was already there. Maybe she already had her hands on the ledger. The thought sent his pulse into overdrive.

But as he turned onto the narrow road that led up to the cabin, he saw that there were no other tracks in the new dusting of snow. His spirits buoyed. Maybe he would just wait around and see if Gillian showed up. It was a great place to hide out, especially this time of year.

He knew her. If she thought the ledger might be hidden at the cabin, she wouldn't tell the police. She would come for it herself. This cabin meant too much to her to have the police tearing the place apart looking for the ledger and any other evidence they thought they might find.

Even if the Texas deputy was still with Gillian this morning, it would just be the two of them. Marc hoped he was right. He'd brought several guns, including a rifle. This cabin that meant so much to his wife would be the perfect place to dispose of Gillian and the cowboy.

THE CABIN WAS back in the mountains that overlooked Canyon Ferry Lake. Huge green ponderosa pines glistened in the midday sun among large rock formations. It had snowed the night before but had now melted in all but the shade of the pines.

"Turn here," Gillian said when the road became little more than a Jeep trail.

Austin noticed tracks where someone had been up the road. He figured Gillian had noticed them, too. It could have been anyone. But he was guessing it was Marc Stewart. As the structure came into view, he saw that the windows were shuttered. At first glance, it didn't appear anyone had been inside for a very long time.

But as he parked, Austin saw that the front door was open a few inches and there were fresh gouges in the wood where whoever had been here had broken in. The old cabin looked like the perfect place for a wounded fugitive to lay low for a while and heal. Even though there was no sign of a vehicle and the tracks indicated that whoever had been here had left, he wasn't taking any chances.

"Stay here," Austin said as he opened his door and pulled his weapon. Long dried pine needles covered the steps up to the worn wood of the small porch. There were footprints in the wet dirt, large, man-sized soles.

Austin moved cautiously as he pushed open the door. It groaned open.

A stale, musty scent rushed out. Weapon ready, Austin stepped into the dim darkness. The cabin was small so it didn't take long to make sure it was empty. As he looked around the ransacked room, it was clear that Marc had been here. From the destruction, Austin was betting the man hadn't found what he was looking for, though.

In a small trash container in the bathroom, he found some bloody bandages. From the amount of blood, it appeared Marc had been wounded enough to warrant medical attention. But no doubt not by anyone at a hospital, where the gunshot wound would have had to be reported.

When he returned to the porch, he found Gillian sitting on the front step looking out at the lake in the distance.

"He was here, wasn't he?" she said. "Did he—"

"I don't think he found anything."

Gillian nodded.

"You don't use the cabin?" Austin asked as he looked at the amazing view.

"No. It stayed in the family, but after my grandfather died…well, it just wasn't the same."

He watched her take a deep breath of mountain air before letting it out slowly. "I haven't been here in nine years. I doubt my sister has either, but I continue to pay the taxes on it."

Austin didn't want to believe that Rebecca Stewart had just been babbling when she'd mentioned the cabin. She had to be passing on a message.

"Would you mind taking a look around and see if

your sister might have left you anything inside that
Marc missed? He made a mess."

She nodded and pushed to her feet. There were tears
in her eyes as she entered the cabin and stopped just
inside the door.

Austin gave her a moment. He tried to imagine what
it must have been like to visit here when Gillian's grandfather was alive. He and his brothers would have loved
this place. Even at his age, he loved the smell of the
pine trees, the crunch of the dried needles beneath his
boot heels, the feeling of being a boy again in a place
where there were huge rocks and trees to climb, forts
to build and fish to catch out of the small stream that
ran beside the cabin.

At the sound of her footfalls deeper in the cabin, he
went inside to find her standing in the small kitchen.
"My grandfather liked to cook. He made us pancakes."
She looked over at Austin. "You remind me of him."

He couldn't help being touched by that. "Thank you."

Dust motes danced in the sunlight that streamed in
through the cracks of the shutters. The interior of the
cabin looked as if it might have been decorated in the
1950s or early 1960s. While rustic, it was cozy from
the worn quilts on the couch and chairs to the soot-
covered fireplace.

"There's nothing here." She shook her head. "Becky
hasn't been here. She would have left at least a glass or
two in the sink and an unmade bed. Everything is just
as it was the last time I was here—except for the mess
Marc made searching the place."

Austin couldn't help his disappointment. He'd hoped
Rebecca had mentioned the cabin for a reason. Maybe
she *had* been out of her head. As much as he wanted

to find this ledger that would nail Marc Stewart to the wall, his greatest fear was for the boy. With whom would a woman possibly not in her right mind have stashed her ten-month-old son?

MARC HAD WAITED after he'd searched the cabin looking for the ledger. It wasn't there. He'd looked everywhere. He'd thought that maybe if Gillian really hadn't known what her sister had done with it that she and the cowboy might show up at the cabin.

But he'd never been good at waiting. Still, even as he was leaving, he hadn't been able to shake the feeling that Rebecca *had* been there. Had she left some message that he hadn't recognized? Frankly, he'd never thought his wife as that clever. But then again, he'd been wrong about how strong she was.

Belatedly, he was realizing that he might not have really known his wife at all.

RAW WITH EMOTIONS, Gillian looked around the cabin for a moment longer before turning toward the front door to escape even more painful memories.

She stumbled down the porch steps, breathing hard. Even the pine-scented air seemed to hurt her lungs. It, too, filled her with bittersweet memories.

Behind her, she heard Austin locking up the cabin. She felt as if she was going to be sick and stumbled down to the fallen tree her sister had reminded her about. Why hadn't Becky left her a clue? She'd wanted Gillian to find the ledger, get Marc put away and take care of Andy. But how did she expect her to do that without some idea of where to start? What had Becky been thinking?

She prayed that her sister had left Andy somewhere safe until she could find him.

"Is this the tree that blew over?" Austin said behind her, startling her.

Gillian stood leaning against it. The pine was old and huge. It had fallen during a summer thunderstorm, landing on a large boulder instead of falling all the way to the ground. Because of that, it laid at a slight slant a good three to six feet off the ground. She and her sister used to walk the length of it, pretending they were high-wire artists. Gillian had a scar on her arm from a fall she'd taken.

She told Austin about the night the tree fell and how she and Becky had played on it, needing to share the memories, fearing they would vanish otherwise. "It made a tremendous sound when it crashed," she said, her voice breaking.

"I was thinking earlier how my brothers and I would have loved this place."

She watched Austin walk around the root end of the tree. Most of the dirt that had once clung to the roots had washed off over the years in other storms. But because of its size, when the tree had become uprooted, it had left a large hole in the earth that she and Becky used to hide in.

"Gillian."

Something in the way he said her name made her start. She looked at his expression and felt a jolt. He was staring down into the hole.

"I think you'd better see this."

Chapter Seventeen

Austin stood back as Gillian hurried around the tree to the exposed roots and looked down into the deep cave of a hole. "What is that?"

She made a sound, half laugh, half sob. "That's Edgar."

"Edgar?" he repeated as she clambered down into the hole. She picked up what appeared to be a taxidermy-type stuffed crow on a small wooden stand and handed it up to him before he helped her out.

The bird had seen better days, but its dark eyes still glittered eerily. She took the mounted crow from him and began to cry as she held the bird to her as if it were a baby. "Edgar Allan Poe. Becky and I made friends with Edgar when he was young and orphaned. We fed him and kept him alive and he never left. He would fly in the moment we arrived at the cabin and caw at us from the porch railing. He followed us everywhere," she said excitedly and then sobered. "One time we came up and we didn't see him. We looked around for him...and found him dead. It was our grandfather's idea to have him mounted. Edgar had always looked out for us, Grandpa said. No reason he couldn't continue doing that."

Austin thought of the odd pets he and his brothers

had accumulated and lost over the years and the attachment they'd had with them. "Your grandfather was a wise man."

She nodded through her tears. "Becky and I took Edgar to our tree house so he could keep an eye out for trespassers."

"Your tree house? Is that where you left him?"

Gillian met his gaze, hers widening. "Becky put Edgar here. That's what she was trying to tell me…" She pushed to her feet. "She *did* leave a message, since the last time I saw Edgar he was still in the tree house standing guard."

"Did Marc know about it?"

Gillian frowned. "I doubt it. He didn't like the outdoors much and his family's cabin was so much nicer on the lake in Idaho. Also I'm not sure how much of the tree house is even still there. It's been years."

Austin followed Gillian into the woods. They wound through the tall thick ponderosa pines. The December day was cold but clear. Sunlight slanted in through the trees but did little to warm them. The skiff of snow that had fallen overnight still hung to the pine boughs back here, making it feel even colder.

As they walked, he watched the ground for any sign that Marc had come this way. It was hard to tell since the ground was covered with pine needles.

They had gone quite a ways when Gillian stopped abruptly. He looked past her and saw what was left of the tree house. It was now little more than a few boards tacked up between trees. The years hadn't been kind to it. What boards had remained were weathered, several hanging by a nail.

He could feel Gillian's disappointment as they moved

closer, stepping over the boards that had blown down. A makeshift ladder had been tacked to a tree at the base of what was left of the tree house. Austin tested the bottom step.

"I don't think it's safe for you to go up there," Gillian said.

"Your sister must have climbed up there." But he knew Rebecca weighed a lot less than he did as he tried the second step. The board held so he began the ascent, hoping for the best. It had been years since he'd climbed a tree. He'd forgotten the exhilaration of being high above the ground.

When he reached what was left of the tree house, he poked his head through the opening and felt a start much like he had when he'd seen Edgar down in the roots of the fallen tree.

"Do you see anything?" Gillian called up.

A fabric doll with curly dark hair sat in the corner of the remaining tree house floor, its back against the tree. It had huge dark eyes much like Gillian's and it was looking right at him. As he reached for it, he felt the soft material of the doll's yellow dress and knew it hadn't been in this tree long.

Other than the doll, there was nothing else in what had once been Gillian and Rebecca's tree house. He stuck the doll inside his coat and began the careful descent to the ground.

GILLIAN SET EDGAR down next to the base of a tree, thinking about her sister. Rebecca had always liked puzzles and scavenger hunts. This was definitely feeling like a combination of both.

As Austin pulled the doll from his coat, she stared

at it in surprise for only a moment before taking it and crushing it to her chest in a hug.

"The doll looks like you," Austin said.

She nodded, afraid if she spoke she would burst into tears again. Her emotions were dangerously close to the surface as it was. Being here had brought back so many memories of the summers she and Becky had spent here with their grandfather.

After a moment, she held the doll at arm's length. The dolls had been a gift from their parents, she told Austin. "Mother had a woman make them so they resembled Becky and me. We never told her, but I found them to be a little creepy and used to turn mine against the wall when I slept. I half expected the doll to be turned around watching me when I woke up. But Becky loved hers so much she even took it when she went to college." That memory caused a hitch in her chest.

"The doll has to be a clue," Austin said.

"If it is, I have no idea what that clue might be." She studied the doll. Its dress was yellow, Gillian's favorite color, so she knew it was hers. The dress had tiny white rickrack around the collar and hem and puffy sleeves. She looked under the hem, thinking Becky might have left a note. Nothing. She felt all over the doll, praying for a scrap of paper, something sewn inside the stuffing, anything that would provide her with the information she desperately needed. Nothing.

When she looked at Austin, she felt her eyes tear up again. "I have no idea what this means, if anything."

"The doll wasn't in the tree long. Since it seems likely your sister left it there, it has to mean something."

She almost laughed. "If my sister was thinking

clearly she wouldn't have climbed up into that tree to put my doll there without a note or some message…"

"Your sister was terrified that Marc would find not only the ledger but their son, right?" Austin asked.

She nodded.

"I know all this seems…illogical, but I think she knew she had to use clues that only you would understand, like Edgar."

"I hope you're right," she said, smiling at this man who'd been there for her since that first horrible night in the blizzard.

"Are you leaving Edgar here?" he asked.

Gillian nodded. "Becky always said this was his favorite spot. He used to fly around, landing on limbs near the tree house, watching over us as we played. I know it sounds silly—"

"No, it doesn't. I get it."

She saw that he did and felt her heart lift a little.

"So there were two dolls?" he asked. "Where is your sister's?"

VICTOR STRAIGHTENED THE white clerical collar and checked himself in the mirror before picking up his Bible and exiting the car in the hospital parking lot.

He couldn't be sure how much security the cops had on Rebecca Stewart. He suspected it would be minimal. Most police departments were stretched thin as it was. This was Montana. Security at the hospital was seldom needed. Victor was counting on the uniform outside her room being some mall-type security cop that the hospital had brought in.

The security guard would have been given Marc Stewart's description, so the man would be on the lookout for him—not a pastor. The guard would have been on the job long enough that he would be bored and sick of hospital food.

As he walked into the lower entrance to the hospital, he saw that his "assistant" was already here sitting in one of the chairs in the lobby thumbing through a magazine. He gave Candy only a cursory glance before he walked past the volunteer working at the desk.

While some hospitals were strict about visitors, this wasn't one of them. That's what he loved about small Montana communities. People felt safe.

He already knew the floor and room number and had asked about visiting hours, so he merely tipped his head at her and said, "Hope you're having a blessed day."

She smiled at him. "You, too, Reverend."

At the elevator, he punched in the floor number. A man and woman in lab coats hurried in. Victor gave them both a solemn nod and looked down at the Bible in his hands. Before the doors could close, a freshly manicured hand slipped between them. He caught the flash of bright red nail polish and the sweet scent of perfume.

As the doors were forced open, Candy stepped in, turning her back to the three of them.

He had told her to dress provocatively but not over the top. She'd chosen a conservative white blouse and slim navy skirt with a pair of strappy high heeled winter boots. The white blouse was unbuttoned enough that anyone looking got teasing glimpses of the tops of her full breasts. She smelled good, that, too, not overdone. Her blond hair was pulled up, a few strands curling around her pretty face.

Victor was pleased as the elevator stopped and the doors opened. They all stepped off, the man and woman in the lab coats scurrying down one hallway while he and Candy took the other. He let her get a few yards ahead before following. The way she moved reminded him of something from his childhood.

If I had a swing like that, I'd paint it red and put it in my backyard.

It was a silly thing to come to mind right now. He worried that he was nervous and that it would tip off even the worst of security guards. So much was riding on this. If he could just get into Marc's wife's room…

At the end of the hallway, he spotted the rent-a-cop sitting in a plastic chair outside Rebecca Stewart's room.

The security guard spotted Candy and got to his feet as she approached.

Chapter Eighteen

Austin found himself watching his rearview mirror. If he was right, Rebecca Stewart had left a series of clues that only her sister could decipher. She'd used items from their past, the shared memories of sisters and things that even if she had mentioned to Marc, he wouldn't have recalled. It told Austin that she'd been terrified of her husband finding their son.

He could see that it was breaking Gillian's heart, these trips down memory lane with her sister. Had Rebecca worried that she could be dead by the time Gillian uncovered them? He figured she must have known her husband well enough that it had definitely been a consideration.

No wonder she hadn't told her sister a thing. Gillian would have done anything to save her sister and Marc would have known that. He must have realized Gillian didn't know the truth. Not that he hadn't planned to use her to try to get her sister to talk. There was no doubt in Austin's mind that, in an attempt to save her sister, Rebecca had pushed Marc and his rotten temper so he would lose control and kill her. If Gillian hadn't thrown herself at Marc when she had...

The drive north to Chinook took the rest of the day.

They traveled from the Little Belt Mountains to the edge of the Rockies, before turning east across the wild prairie of Montana. It was dark by the time they reached the small Western town on what was known as the Hi-Line.

Chinook, like most of the towns along Highway 2, had sprung up with the introduction of the railroad. Both freight and passenger trains still blew their whistles as they passed through town.

A freight train rumbled past as Austin parked in front of a motor inn. Gillian had called ahead but had gotten no answer at the Baker house. Austin could tell that made her as nervous as it did him. Was it possible that as careful as Rebecca had been, Marc had been one step ahead of them?

"I can't believe Rebecca would have confided in anyone," Gillian said. "But if there is even a chance Nancy knows where Becky left Andy…"

Gillian had explained about her sister's doll on the drive north. Nancy Rexroth Baker and her sister had been roommates at college. Becky had been Nancy's maid of honor when she'd married Claude. While as far as Gillian knew the two hadn't stayed in touch, when Nancy had a baby girl last year they'd named her Rebecca Jane. That's the name Nancy and Becky used to call her doll at college. Touched by this, her sister had mailed Nancy her doll.

"She told you this?" Austin had asked. "Wouldn't Marc have known?"

She shook her head. "Since my sister has apparently had this plot of hers in the works for some time, I wouldn't think so. But Marc is anything if not clever. He could have known a whole lot more than Becky suspected."

Gillian tried the Baker home number again. The line went to voice mail after four rings. "Maybe we should drive by the house."

Austin didn't think it would do much good, but he agreed. She gave him the address, which turned out to be in the older section of the town just four blocks from the motel. The houses were large with wide front porches, a lot of columns and arches.

The Baker house sat up on the side of a hill with a flight of stairs that ended at the wide white front porch. There were no lights on behind the large windows at the front, no Christmas decorations on the outside, and the drapes were drawn.

"Let's see if there is an alley," Austin said and drove around the corner. Just as he'd suspected, there was. He took it, driving down three houses before stopping in front of a garage. "I'll take a look." He hopped out to check the garage. As he peered in the window, he saw that it was empty.

It came as somewhat of a relief. As he climbed back into the SUV, he said, "It looks like they've gone somewhere for Christmas."

"Christmas." The way she said it made him think that she'd forgotten about it, just as he had, even with all the red and green lights strung around town.

He thought of his brothers all gathered in Big Sky for the holidays, no doubt wondering where he was. He quickly pushed the thought away. They should be used to him by now. Anyway, his cousin Dana would have told them he was tied up. Her husband, Hud, the marshal, would have a pretty good idea why he was tied up since he would have heard about Marc Stewart's attempted murder of his wife, the kidnapping of his sister-in-law, Gillian, and the BOLO out on Marc.

As Austin drove them back to the motel, he said, "We need to get into that house because if I'm right, then this family has your nephew and he's safe. The doll brought us this far. There has to be another clue that we're missing."

"The key," Gillian said on an excited breath. "The one I found at the house after Rebecca and Andy left. Do you still have it?"

"I'm GOING TO walk back and get into the house," Austin said after they returned to the motel. He'd gotten them adjoining rooms, no doubt so he could keep an eye on her, Gillian thought.

She was grateful for everything he'd done. But she was going with him. She came out of her room and stood in front of him, her hands on her hips. "You're not going alone."

He shook his head. "Maybe you don't understand the fine line between snooping and jail. Breaking and entering is—"

"I'm going with you."

He looked like he wanted to argue, but saw that she meant what she said. "Wear something dark and warm. It's cold out."

She was already one step ahead of him as she reached for a black fleece jacket she'd grabbed as they were leaving her apartment. Donning a hat and gloves, she turned to look at him.

He was smiling at her as if amused.

"What?" she said, suddenly feeling uncomfortable

under his scrutiny. She knew it was silly. He'd seen her at her absolute worst.

"You just look so…cute," he said. "Clearly breaking the law excites you."

She smiled in spite of herself. It had been a while since a man had complimented her. Actually, way too long. But it wasn't breaking the law that excited her, she thought and felt her face heat with the thought.

The night was clear and cold, the sky ablaze with stars. She breathed in the freezing air. It stung her lungs, but made her feel more alive than she had in years. Fear drove her steps along with hope. The bird, the doll, all of it had led them here. She couldn't be wrong about this. And yet at the back of her mind, she worried that none of this made any sense because Rebecca hadn't known what she was doing.

At the dark alley, Austin slowed. It was late enough that there were lights on in the houses. Most of the drapes were open. She saw women in the kitchen cooking and families moving around inside the warm-looking homes. The scenes pulled at her, making her wish she and her sister were those women.

A few doors down, a dog barked, a door slammed and she heard someone calling, "Zoey!" The dog barked a couple more times; then the door slammed again and the alley grew quiet.

"Come on," Austin said and they started to turn down the alley.

A vehicle came around the corner, moving slowly. Gillian felt the headlights wash over them and let out a worried sound as she froze in midstep. Her first thought was Marc. Her heart began to pound even though she knew Austin had his shoulder holster on and the gun inside it was loaded.

Her moment of panic didn't subside when she saw that it was a sheriff's department vehicle.

"Austin?" she whispered, not sure what to do.

He turned to her and pulled her into his arms. Her mouth opened in surprise and the next thing she knew, he was kissing her. His mouth was warm against hers. At first, she was too stunned to react. But after a moment, she put her arms around his neck and lost herself in the kiss.

As the headlights of the sheriff's car washed over them, the golden glow seemed to warm the night because she no longer felt cold. She let out a small helpless moan as Austin deepened the kiss, drawing her even closer.

As the sheriff's car went on past, she felt a pang of regret. Slowly, Austin drew back a little. His gaze locked with hers, and for a moment they stood like that, their quickened warm breaths coming out in white clouds.

"Sorry."

She shook her head. She wasn't sorry. She felt... light-headed, happy, as if helium filled. She thought she might drift off into the night if he let go of her.

"Are you okay?" he asked, looking worried.

She unconsciously touched the tip of her tongue to her lower lip, then bit down on it to stop herself. "Great. Never better."

That made him smile. For a moment, he stood merely smiling at her, his gaze on hers, his dark eyes as warm as a crackling fire. Then he sighed. "Let's get this over with," he said and took her gloved hand as they started up the alley.

There was only an inch of snow on the ground, but it crunched under their feet. If anyone heard them and looked out their window, she doubted they would think anything of it. They would appear to be what they were, a thirtysomething couple out walking on an early December night.

She looked over at Austin. Light from one of the yards shone on his handsome face, catching her off guard. He wasn't just handsome. He was caring and kind and capable, as well. She warned herself not to let one kiss go to her head. Of course she felt something for this man who'd saved her life twice and probably would have to again before this was over.

But her pulse was still pounding hard from the kiss. It had been the best kiss she'd ever had. Not that it meant anything.

She reminded herself that this was what Austin Cardwell did for a living. Not kiss women he was trying to save, but definitely doing whatever it took to save those same women.

She'd bet there was a long line of women he'd saved and all of them had gone giddy if he'd kissed them like that. That was a sobering thought. He could have ended up kissing all of them. Or even something more intimate.

That thought settled her down. She was behaving like a teenager on a date with the adorable quarterback of the football team. She told herself it was only because she hadn't dated all that much, especially since she'd started her business. True, she hadn't met anyone she cared to date. But she wasn't the kind of woman who fell head over heels at the drop of a kiss. Even one amazing kiss on a cold winter night.

But any woman in her place would be feeling like this, she told herself. She'd never believed that knights on white horses really existed before Austin Cardwell. It was one reason she was still single. That and she liked her independence. But mostly, it was because she'd never met a man who had ever made her even consider marriage.

Becky's marriage to Marc certainly hadn't changed her mind about men in general. She'd known Marc was domineering. She just hadn't known what the man was capable of. She doubted Becky had either.

Just the thought of her sister brought tears to her eyes. She wiped at them with her free gloved hand, determined not to break down, especially now. Austin hadn't wanted to bring her along as it was.

She needed to be strong. She concentrated on finding Andy. Becky had hidden him somewhere safe. Gillian had to believe that. What better place than with someone she could trust, like her former college roommate, Nancy Baker?

Gillian hated that she'd let Marc keep her from her sister. But the few times she'd visited he'd made her so uncomfortable that she hadn't gone back. And Marc had put Becky on a leash that didn't allow her to come up to Big Sky to visit often. It wasn't that he forbade it, he just made sure Becky was too busy to go anywhere.

Rubbing a hand over her face, she tried to concentrate on what lay ahead rather than wallowing in regret. Becky was stable. Gillian couldn't count on her regaining consciousness. It was why she had to find Andy—and that damned ledger—before Marc did.

Austin slowed as they reached the back of the Baker house. She saw him look down the alley both ways before he drew her into the shadows along the side of the garage. The yard stretched before them. Huge pines grew along the sides against a tall wooden fence.

They walked toward the back of the house staying in the deep cold shadows of the pines. At the back door, Austin hesitated for a moment. She could tell he was listening. She heard voices but in the distance. Someone was calling a child into the house for dinner. Closer, that same dog barked.

Austin headed up the steps to the back door. She followed, trying to be as quiet as possible. The houses weren't particularly close, but this was a small town. Neighbors kept an eye on each other's homes, especially when they knew a family was away for Christmas.

That was where the Bakers had gone, wasn't it?

Gillian took a deep breath as she saw Austin pull out the key. It was such a long shot, she realized now, that she felt silly even mentioning it. But it didn't matter if the key worked or not. She knew Austin would get them into the house. She was praying once they got in the house that they wouldn't find evidence of Marc having been there—and especially not of any kind of struggle.

She held her breath as he tried the key. It slipped right in. Austin shot her a look, then turned the key. She felt her eyes widen as the door opened.

"Rebecca left the key," she said more to herself than to Austin. She knew she sounded as disbelieving as he must have felt. Her heart lifted with the first feeling of real hope she'd felt since Marc had abducted her. "It has to mean that Nancy has my nephew, that Andy is safe."

As CANDY APPROACHED, the security guard ran a hand down the front of his uniform as if to get out any wrinkles and remind himself to suck in his stomach. He stood a little straighter as well, puffing up a bit, without even realizing he was doing it, Victor thought amused.

"May I help you?" the guard asked her.

Candy gave him one of her disarming smiles.

Victor saw that it was working like a charm. He looked into one of the rooms, before moving down the hall to Rebecca's. He could hear Candy asking for directions, explaining that her best friend had just had her third baby.

"Ten pounds, eleven ounces! I can't even imagine."

Victor smiled and gave a somber nod to the guard as he pushed open the door to Rebecca's room. He was so close, he could almost taste it.

"Just a minute," the guard said, stopping him.

"I told the family I would look in on Mrs. Stewart," Victor said.

"Did you say first floor like down by the cafeteria?" Candy asked the guard, then dropped her purse. It fell open. Coins tinkled on the floor. A lipstick rolled to the guard's feet.

The guard began to stoop down to help pick it up, but shot Victor another look before waving him in.

"I'm so sorry," Candy was saying as the door closed behind Victor. "I'm so clumsy. How did you say I get to my friend's room? I would have sworn she said it was on this floor."

Victor approached the bed. He'd met Marc's wife only once and that had been by accident. He liked to keep his business and personal lives entirely separate. But there'd been a foul-up in a shipment so he'd stopped by Marc's auto shop one night after hours. Marc had told him he would be there so he hadn't been surprised to see a light burning in the rear office.

As he'd pushed open the side door, though, he'd come face-to-face with a very pregnant and pretty dark-haired woman. She'd had a scowl on her face and he could see that she'd been crying. It hadn't taken much of a leap to know she must be Marc's wife. Or mistress.

"Sorry," she'd said, sounding breathless.

He'd realized that he'd startled her. *"I'm the one who's sorry."*

"Are you here to see Marc?"

"I left my car earlier," Victor had ad-libbed. *"The owner said he might have it finished later tonight. I saw the light on...."*

She'd nodded, clearly no longer interested. *"He's in his office,"* she'd said and he'd moved aside to let her leave.

As the door closed behind her, Marc had come out of his office looking sheepish. *"I didn't know she was stopping by."* He'd shrugged. *"My wife. She's pregnant and impossible. I'll be so glad when this baby is finally born. Maybe she will get off my ass."*

Victor hadn't cared about Marc's marital problems. He'd never guessed that night that Rebecca Stewart might someday try to take them all down in one fell swoop.

As he stepped to the side of the bed and looked down at the woman lying there, he could see the brutality Marc had unleashed on her. His hands balled into fists at his side. He'd known this kind of violence firsthand and had spent a lifetime trying to overcome it in himself.

"Rebecca?"

Not even the flicker of an eyelid.

"Rebecca?" he said, leaning closer. "How are you doing today?"

Still nothing. Glancing toward the door, he could hear Candy just outside the room, still monopolizing the guard's attention.

Victor pulled the syringe from his pocket. He couldn't let this woman wake up and tell the police where they could find the ledger. He uncapped the syringe and reached for the IV tube.

Rebecca's eyes flew open before he could administer the drug. She let out a sound just a moment before the alarm on the machine next to her went off.

Chapter Nineteen

Marc could feel time slipping through his fingers like water. He tried to remain calm, to think. With a start, he realized something. If Gillian knew where the ledger and Andy were, then she would go to both. Once she had the ledger in her hot little hands, she would turn it over to the cops. Victor would be on his private jet, winging his way out of the country—after he had Marc killed.

Which meant Gillian really didn't know where either item was. It was the only thing that made any sense because otherwise, by now, the ledger would be in the hands of the police.

But she would be looking for it. Was she stumbling around in the dark like he was? Or had her sister given her a hint where it was? Unlike her, he had cops after him. He felt as if he was waiting for the other shoe to drop. Once that ledger surfaced... He didn't want to think about how much worse things could get for him.

For a moment, he almost wished that Rebecca had cut his throat and he'd died right there at her feet—after he'd pulled the trigger and put the both of them out of their misery.

Marc shook himself out of those dark thoughts. If

he was right and Gillian didn't have a clue where the ledger was any more than he did…well, then there was still hope. He dug out his cell phone.

When the hospital answered, he asked about Rebecca's condition.

"I'm sorry," the nurse said. "I can't give out that information."

"There must be someone I can talk to. I'm her brother. I can't fly out until later in the week. I'm afraid it will be too late."

"Let me connect you to her floor."

He waited. A male nurse came on the line. He could hear noise in the background. Something was happening. Was it Rebecca?

When he asked about his "sister's" condition, the nurse started to say he couldn't give out that information over the phone. "How about her doctor? Surely I can talk to someone there." He gave him his hard-luck pitch about not being able to get there right away.

"Perhaps you'd like to talk to the pastor who just went into her room," the nurse said.

Pastor? Marc stifled a curse. *Victor.* That son of a…

"I'm sorry, I don't see him," the nurse said. "Why don't I have the doctor call you?"

Marc slammed down the phone and let out a string of oaths. How dare Victor. Marc had told him he'd handle this. Not only that, he wanted to be the person who killed her—after he found out where she'd hidden the ledger and his son.

So was Rebecca dead? The last person Victor had paid a visit to while dressed as a pastor…well, needless to say, that person had taken a turn for the worse.

ONCE THE DOOR of the Baker house closed behind them, Austin snapped on his small penlight and handed a second one to Gillian. The silence inside the house gave him the impression that no one had been home for some time.

They were standing in the kitchen. He swung the light over the counter. Empty. Everything was immaculate. No dishes in the sink. Stepping to the refrigerator, he opened it. There was nothing but condiments. No leftovers that would spoil while the family was gone. As he closed the door, he noticed the photographs tacked to it and the children's artwork. There was no photo of Gillian's sister.

"They're gone, aren't they?" Gillian said from the doorway to the living room. "But they must have Andy. My sister wouldn't have left me the key unless…" She stopped to look at him in the dim light.

He agreed, but he knew they both wanted proof. "Let's check the kid's room upstairs." It made sense that if this family had Andy they might have left something behind to assure Gillian that her nephew was fine, or, better yet, another clue as to where Gillian could find the ledger and put Marc away for a long time.

As they moved through the living room, Gillian whispered, "No Christmas tree. No presents. They aren't coming back until after Christmas."

Or until they hear that it's safe, he thought. Had Rebecca told them she would call them when it was safe? But what if she couldn't call?

They climbed the stairs to the bedrooms. It didn't take long to find the child's room. It was bright colored with stuffed animals piled on the bed. Gillian stepped to the bed. He knew she must be looking for her sister's doll. It wasn't there.

"Do you see anything of Andy's?" he asked.

She sighed and shook her head. "His favorite toy is a plush owl, but it's not here. Then again, it wouldn't be. He'd want it with him, especially if he wasn't with his mother." Her voice broke.

They checked the other rooms but found nothing. Going back downstairs, Austin looked more closely in the living room. Rebecca had been scared of her husband. But her clues for Gillian did make him wonder about the state of her mind. He reminded himself that she'd been terrified of Marc. The clues had to be vague, things only Gillian would understand.

They searched the house, but found nothing that would indicate that Andy Stewart had been here. Like Gillian, he kept telling himself that Rebecca had left them a key to this house. Didn't that mean that the Bakers had Andy and all were safe since there was no sign of a struggle in the house?

He'd stopped to go through a desk in the study when he heard Gillian go into the kitchen. She had looked as despondent as he felt. He'd been so sure they would find—

Gillian let out a cry. Austin rushed into the kitchen to find her standing in front of the refrigerator. Her hand was covering her mouth and her eyes were full of tears as her penlight glared off the refrigerator door.

He'd checked the kitchen first thing and hadn't seen anything. As he moved closer, she pointed at what he'd assumed had been artwork done by the daughter. What he hadn't seen was a note of any kind.

"What?" he asked, looking from Gillian to the front of the refrigerator in confusion.

She carefully plucked one of the pieces of artwork from the door. "Andy."

He looked down at the sheet of paper in her hand. It was a drawing of an owl with huge round eyes. Someone had taken a crayon to it. The owl was almost indistinguishable under the purple scribbles.

"Andy?" he repeated confused.

"I told you. He loves owls."

That seemed a leap even to him.

Gillian began to laugh. "Rebecca drew this at my house when she and Andy came up to visit. Andy's favorite color is purple."

"You're sure this is the same drawing?" he asked. He couldn't help being skeptical.

"Positive. Look at this." She pointed to a spot on the owl. The artist had drawn in feathers before they had been scribbled over. In the feathers he saw what appeared to be numbers. "It's a phone number. I'm betting it is Nancy Baker's cell phone number."

VICTOR POCKETED THE syringe as he stepped back from the hospital bed. Rebecca Stewart's eyes were open. She was staring right at him, a wild, frightened look in her dark eyes.

As a doctor and two nurses rushed in, the security guard at their heels, Victor clutched his Bible and moved aside.

"What happened?" the doctor demanded.

"Nothing," he said. "That is, I was saying a prayer over her when she suddenly opened her eyes and that alarm went off."

The doctor began barking orders to the nurses. "If you don't mind stepping out, Pastor."

"I have other patients I promised to see, but I will check back before I leave," Victor said, but the doctor was busy and didn't seem to care.

On the overhead intercom, a nurse was calling a code blue as he walked toward the door. He felt the security guard's gaze on him as he stepped aside to let a crash cart be wheeled into the room. Without looking at the man, Victor started down the hallway away from all the noise and commotion in Rebecca's hospital room.

He half expected the security guard to call after him, but when he glanced back as he ducked into the first restroom he came to he saw that the guard was more interested in what was going on in Rebecca's room.

Reaching into his pocket he put on the latex gloves, then carefully removed the syringe from his other pocket and stuffed it down into the trash. Removing the gloves, he discarded them, as well. After washing his hands, he left.

The security guard didn't look his way as Victor turned and walked down the hallway, stopping at one of the empty rooms for a moment as if visiting a patient.

The guard hadn't asked his name. No one had. As he left the empty room, he saw a nurse coming out of Rebecca's room with the crash cart. He couldn't tell by the woman's face what the outcome had been for the patient.

Nor did he dare wait to find out. Turning, he walked out of the hospital.

Chapter Twenty

Marc felt sick to his stomach. His fingers shook as he dialed the hospital. Again, he pretended to be her brother.

"I have to know her condition. I can't get a flight out because of the weather right now. Tell me I'm not going to get there too late."

"Just a moment. Let me check," the nurse finally said, relenting.

He waited, his heart pounding. As long as Rebecca was alive, he stood a chance of fixing this mess. He would do anything she wanted. He would convince her to give up the ledger to save not just her own life but his and their son's. She had no idea the kind of people who would be after her and Andy.

But if Victor had killed her... *Hell,* he thought. The cops would think he'd done it! Or paid someone to do it. What had Victor been thinking?

The answer came to him like another blow, this one more painful than the crystal tumbler. Victor planned to kill everyone who knew about the ledger and what was in it. He would take his chances that wherever Rebecca had hidden it, the incriminating book wouldn't turn up. Or if it did, the finder wouldn't have a clue what it was and wouldn't take it to the authorities. Or...it was this third option that made his pulse jump. Or...Victor was tying up loose ends before he skipped the country.

The nurse came back on the line. Marc held his breath.

"Good news. Your sister's condition has been upgraded. She had an episode earlier, but the doctor is cautiously optimistic about her complete recovery."

He tried to breathe. Victor had failed? His relief was real. "Can I talk to her?"

"I'm afraid not. The doctor wants her to rest. She is drifting in and out of consciousness. Perhaps by tomorrow..."

GILLIAN COULDN'T BEAR to wait until they returned to the motel to make the call, but Austin was anxious to get out of the house. She tried the number she'd found on Rebecca and Andy's artwork on the walk back to the motel.

The phone was answered on the second ring. "Gillian?"

"Nancy." She began to cry.

"Is everything all right?" Nancy asked, sounding as anxious as Gillian felt.

"I'm sorry, I'm just so relieved. Tell me you have Andy."

Several heartbeats of unbearable silence before Nancy said, "He's safe."

"Thank God."

"He keeps asking about his mother, though. Rebecca said she would join us before Christmas."

Gillian didn't know how to tell her. "Rebecca's in the hospital. The last I heard, she's unconscious."

"Oh, no. And Marc?"

"He's on the loose. Tell me you have Andy somewhere Marc wouldn't dream of looking."

"We do."

"A deputy sheriff from Texas is helping me try to find a ledger that will send Marc to prison. Do you know anything about it?"

"No. Rebecca only told me that Marc was dangerous and she needed Andy to be safe until she could come get him. She doesn't even know where we are. I was to tell her only when she called."

"Good. I don't need to know either. I can't tell you how relieved I am that Andy is with you and safe. But did Rebecca give you a message to pass on to me if I called?"

"She did mention that it was possible you would call."

So her sister had feared she wouldn't be able to call herself. Gillian felt sick.

"Becky said that if you called to tell you she forgives you for the birthday present you gave her when she turned fourteen and that she is overcoming her fears, just as you suggested. Does that make any sense to you?"

Gillian tried hard not to burst into uncontrollable sobs. "Yes, it does," she managed to say. "That's all?"

"That's it. Whatever is going on, it reminded me of how much your sister always loved puzzles."

"Yes. I'm just grateful that Andy is with you and safe. Give him my love."

She disconnected, still fighting tears. "Andy's safe."

"I heard. Your sister left you another clue?" he asked.

Before she could answer, she saw that she had a message. "The hospital called." She hurriedly returned the call, praying that it would be good news. *Please let Becky be all right. Please.*

"Yes," the floor nurse said when he finally came on the line. "We called you to let you know that your sister is doing much better. She has regained consciousness."

"Can I talk to her?"

"I'm sorry. The doctor gave her something for the pain. She's asleep. Maybe in the morning."

Gillian smiled through fresh tears as she disconnected. "Rebecca is better." She gulped the cold night air. "And I think I know where she hid the ledger."

MARC HUNG UP from his call to the hospital, still shocked that Victor had failed. Rebecca was alive. Didn't that mean he had a chance to reason with her? He knew it was a long shot that he could persuade Rebecca of anything at this point. But if she realized the magnitude of what she'd done, given the criminal nature of his associates, maybe she would do it for Andy's sake…

He wished he'd explained things in the first place instead of losing his temper. He thought of Victor, Mr. Cool, and began to laugh. Victor must be beside himself. He was a man who didn't like to fail.

Would he try to kill Rebecca again? Marc didn't think so. It would be too dangerous. He was surprised that Victor had decided to do the job himself. That, he realized, showed how concerned the man was about cleaning up this mess—and how little confidence Victor had in him.

I'm toast.

If he'd had any doubt that Victor wouldn't let him survive, he no longer did. Now he had only one choice. Save himself. To do that, it meant going to the feds.

But without the ledger…he couldn't remember names and numbers. He'd been told he was dyslexic. But he knew that wasn't right because he'd heard dyslexics had trouble writing words and numbers correctly. He thought it had more to do with not being able to remember. He could write just fine. That's what had him in this trouble.

When Victor had asked him why he'd done something so stupid as to write everything down, Marc hadn't wanted to admit that there was anything wrong with him. He'd hired someone else to handle the details at his auto shop.

But he couldn't very well do that with the criminal side of his work, could he? He told himself it was too late to second-guess that decision. He had to get his hands on the ledger. He realized there was a second option besides turning it over to the feds. He could skip the country with it. The ledger would be his insurance against Victor dusting him.

Without the ledger, though, he had no bargaining power.

Sure he knew some things about Victor's operation, but not enough without the ledger. It contained the names and dates, names he knew the feds would love to get their hands on.

Rebecca! What did you do with that damned book?

It wasn't as if he hadn't been suspicious that she was up to something in the weeks before. He'd actually thought she might be having an affair. But he'd realized that was crazy. What would she have done with Andy? It wasn't like she had a friend to watch their son. No, he'd known it had to be something else.

He'd wondered if she'd taken up gambling. He didn't

give her much money, but she had a way of stretching what he did… No, he'd ruled out gambling. Unless she won all the time, that didn't explain her disappearances.

He had started making a habit of calling home at different hours to check on her. She was never there. Oh, sure, she made excuses.

Andy and I were outside in the yard. I didn't hear the phone. Or she didn't have her cell phone on her. Other times she was at the park or the mall. She would say it must have been too noisy to hear her phone. He told her to put it on vibrate and stick the thing in her pocket.

"Was there something you wanted?" she'd asked.

He hadn't liked the tone of her voice. She'd seemed pretty uppity. Like a woman who knew something he didn't. He'd said, "I was just making sure you and Andy were all right. That's what husbands do."

"Really." She'd actually scoffed at that.

Not only had he resented her attitude, he'd also hated that she acted as if she was smarter than him. Or worse, that she thought for a moment that she could outwit him.

That's why he'd started writing down the mileage on her car.

He had checked it each night after that since he usually got in after she and the kid were asleep, and then he would compare it the next night. It had been a head-scratcher, though. She had never gone far, so while he'd continued to write it down, he hadn't paid any attention lately.

He fished out the scrap of paper he'd been writing it down on from his wallet and did a little math. At first he thought he'd read it wrong. She'd gone over a hundred miles four days ago. The day before she'd drugged him with his own drugs, stolen his ledger and hidden his son, she'd driven more than fifty miles that morning alone.

What the hell? Marc realized that he hadn't seen his son that day. Had she already hidden him away somewhere the day before? He tried to remember. He'd gotten home late that night. He glanced into his son's room. He hadn't actually seen the boy in his bed. It could have been the kid's pillow under the covers.

He let out a string of curses. Where had she gone? Not to her family cabin, he'd already checked it. Then where? He refused to let her outsmart him. He pulled a map of Montana from the glove box. It was old, but it would do. Suddenly excited, he drew a circle encompassing twenty to twenty-five miles out from Helena. Rebecca thought she was so smart. He'd show her.

Chapter Twenty-One

"What do you want to do?" Laramie asked his brothers. They were all sitting around the large kitchen table at their cousin Dana Savage's house on Cardwell Ranch. They'd just finished a breakfast of flapjacks, ham, fried potatoes and eggs. Hud had motioned his wife to stay where she was as he got up to refill all of their mugs with coffee.

"I hate to put off the grand opening of the restaurant," Tag said.

"Can't it wait until Austin can be here?" Dana asked.

Jackson got up to check on the kids, who were eating at a small table in the dining room. "We might never have a grand opening if we do that."

"Jackson's right," his brother Hayes said. "We know how Austin is and now apparently he's gotten involved with some woman who's in trouble." He looked toward Hud for confirmation.

The marshal finished filling their cups and said, "He got involved in a situation where he was needed. That's all I can tell you."

"A dangerous situation?" Dana asked.

Hud didn't answer. He didn't have to. His brothers

knew Austin, and Dana was married to a marshal. She knew how dangerous his line of work could be.

"This is the woman he met in the middle of the highway, right?" Laramie shook his head. "This is his M.O. He'd much rather be working than be with his family."

"I don't think that's true," Dana said in her cousin's defense. "I talked to him. He can't just abandon this woman. You should be proud that he's so dedicated. And as I recall, there are several of you who are into saving women in need." She grinned. "I believe it is why some of you are now married and others are involved in wedding planning."

There were some chuckles around the table.

Laramie sighed. "Some of us are still interested in the business that keeps us all fed, though. Fortunately," he added. "Let's go ahead with the January first grand opening. I, for one, will be glad to get back to Texas. I am freezing up here."

His brothers laughed, but agreed.

"Maybe Austin will surprise you," Dana said.

Laramie saw a look pass between Dana and her marshal husband. He was worried about Austin. Last July, Austin had been shot and had almost died trying to get some woman out of a bad situation. He just hoped this wouldn't prove to be as dangerous.

MARC WENT TO an out-of-the-way bar. He hadn't seen a tail, but that didn't mean there wasn't one again. In a quiet corner of the bar, he studied the map and tried to remember any places Rebecca might have mentioned. He had a habit of tuning her out. Now he wished he'd paid more attention.

They'd gone to a few places while they were dating,

but he doubted she would be sentimental about any of them, the way things had turned out. He had never understood women, though, so maybe she would hide the ledger in one of those places because she thought it was a place he would never look.

Just trying to think like her gave him a headache. He wanted to choke the life out of the woman for putting him through this. He realized he hadn't heard from Victor demanding an update. Which he figured meant he was right about one of Victor's men tailing him again.

He'd lost the tail the first time, but maybe Victor had put someone like Jumbo on him. Jumbo was a more refined criminal, not all muscle and no brains, which made him very dangerous.

Marc folded the map and put it away. He couldn't do anything until daylight. Between songs on the jukebox, he put in another call to the hospital with his brother story. He knew he was whistling in the dark. He'd be lucky if he even got to talk to Rebecca, let alone convince her he was sorry. But it was a small hospital and he doubted the cops had done more than put security outside her room, if that, since Victor had circumvented whatever safety guards they'd taken.

Still to his amazement, he was put through to Rebecca's room.

"Hello?" she sounded weak but alive. "Hello?"

"Becky, listen," he said once he got past his initial shock. "Don't hang up. I have to tell you something."

Silence.

"Are you still there?" He hated that his voice broke and even more that she'd heard it.

"What could you possibly want, Marc?"

Humor. He bit back a nasty retort. "That book you

took, it doesn't just implicate me. The people I work for… Rebecca they won't let you live if I don't get that book back."

"Don't you mean they won't let you live?"

"Not just me. They'll go after your sister, too." He could hear her breathing. "And Andy." His voice broke at the thought.

"You bastard, what have you gotten us all into?"

"Hey, if you had left well enough alone—"

"What is it? Drugs?"

"It doesn't matter what it is. I was only trying to make some money for Andy. I wanted him to have a better life than I had."

"Money for Andy? You are such a liar, Marc." She laughed. It was a weak laugh, but still it made his teeth hurt. "You hid that money for yourself."

And now she had a large portion of it. She'd hidden that, too, he reminded himself. He felt his blood pressure go through the roof. He still couldn't believe she'd done this to him. If he could have gotten his hands on her… He took a breath, trying to regain control, as he reminded himself that he needed her help.

"Rebecca, honey, you just didn't realize what you were getting in to. But we can fix this. I can save you and your sister and our son. These people…sweetie, I need to know what you did with the ledger. Did you mail it to the police?" Her hesitation gave him hope. "I know I reacted…badly. But, honey, I knew what would happen if that ledger got into the wrong hands. These people aren't going to stop. They will kill you. I suspect one of them has already tried. You didn't happen to see a man dressed as a pastor, did you?"

Her quick intake of breath told him she had "A blond guy, good-looking. He was there to kill you."

She started to say something, but began coughing. He could hear how weak and sick she was.

"He isn't going to give up. The only way out of this is the ledger. I can save us both. Honey, I'm begging you."

"Begging me?" She sounded like she was crying. "You mean like I begged you for a divorce?"

"I'm sorry. I'll give you a divorce. I'll even give you custody of Andy. I'll give you whatever you want. Just tell me where the ledger is so I can make this right."

"I don't think so," she said, her voice stronger. "It's over, Marc. I never want to see you again. Once the police arrest you…"

He swore under his breath. "I'll get out of jail at some point, Rebecca."

"Not if I have my way." The line went dead. As dead as they were both going to be, because if he went, she was going with him one way or another.

"So she told you where we could find the ledger?" Austin asked as he and Gillian walked back to the motel. She'd grown quiet after the call. He wondered if this last clue was one she didn't want to share. Was she worried she couldn't trust him?

When she said nothing, he asked, "Is something wrong?"

She looked over at him, her dark eyes bright. "I'm glad you're here with me."

Her words touched him more than they should have. There was something about this woman… He smiled, his heart beating a little faster. "So am I," he said, taking her gloved hand.

As if the touch of her had done it, snow began to fall in thick, lacy flakes that instantly clung to their clothing.

Gillian laughed. It was a wonderful sound in the snowy night. "Andy is safe, my sister is going to be all right and Marc Stewart is going to get what's coming to him." She moved closer to him as they walked. "How do you feel about caves?"

"Caves?" he said, looking over at her in surprise.

"Assuming my sister was in her right mind, she hid the ledger in a cave." She repeated the so-called clue Nancy Baker had given her.

"And from that you've decided the ledger is in some cave?"

"Not just some cave. One up Miners Gulch near Canyon Ferry Lake. Rebecca is terrified of close places, especially caves. It's a boy's fault we ended up in one on her fourteenth birthday. I had this horrible crush on a boy named Luke Snider. He was a roughneck, wild and unruly, and adorable. I was sixteen and dreamed of the two of us on outrageous adventures. I thought I would see the world with him, live in exotic places, eat strange food and make love under a different moon every night."

They had almost reached the motel. He hated to go inside. The night had taken on a magical quality. Or maybe it was just sharing it with Gillian that made him feel that way.

"You were quite the romantic at sixteen."

She laughed. "I was, wasn't I? It didn't last any longer than my crush. Luke graduated from high school, went to work at his father's tire shop. He still works there. I bought a tire from him once." She smiled at that. "I definitely dodged a bullet with Luke."

He laughed as he let go of her hand and reached for the room key.

Gillian turned her face out toward the snow. He watched her breathe in the freezing air and let it out in a sigh. "If I'm right about this clue then my sister is getting even with me for being such a brat on her birthday that year." She seemed as reluctant as he did to leave the snow and the night behind, but stepped inside.

"I suspect caves have something to do with Luke and your sister's birthday," he said.

Gillian shook snowflakes from her coat. As she slipped out of it, he took it and hung her coat, along with his own, up to dry when she made no move to go into her adjoining room.

"I overheard Luke and his friends say they were going to these caves in the gulch. I knew they wouldn't let me go along, but if I just happened to run into them in the caves... I didn't want to go alone to look for them, and my friends could not imagine what I saw in Luke and his friends. You know how it is when you're sixteen. Just seeing him, saying hi in the hall, could make my day. I wanted him to really notice me. I figured if he saw how adventurous I was in the caves... So I told my sister I had a surprise birthday present for her."

He shook his head, smiling, remembering being sixteen and impulsive. He'd also had his share of teenage crushes. He hated to think of some of the things he'd done to impress a girl. He offered her the motel chair, anxious to hear her story, but she motioned it away and sat down on the end of his bed.

"Rebecca is claustrophobic so the last place she

wanted to go was into a cave. I told her she needed to overcome her fears. Her message she left with Nancy was that she was now overcoming her fears."

"She mentioned this birthday present, so you think she put the ledger somewhere in these caves?"

"If I'm right, I know the exact spot." Gillian gave him a sad smile. "The spot where Rebecca totally freaked that day." Tears filled her eyes.

Austin reached across to take her hand. "Ah, childhood memories. I can't even begin to tell you about all the terrible things my brothers and I did to each other. It's just what siblings do."

She shook her head. "I hate that I did that to her."

"And yet, when the chips were down, she went back into those caves with you."

She smiled. "If I'm right."

His voice softened. "You've been right so far about everything."

GILLIAN FELT A lump form in her throat. Her pulse buzzed at the look in his eyes. If he kissed her again… "I should—"

"Yes," he said, letting go of her. "We should get some sleep. Sounds like we have a big day ahead of us tomorrow." He rose and stepped back, looking uncertain as if he didn't seem to know what to do with his hands.

She thought of being in his arms and how easy it would be to find herself in his bed. She told herself she was feeling like this about him because he'd saved her life, but a part of her knew it was more than that. It was…chemistry? She almost laughed at the thought. It sounded so…high school.

But she couldn't deny how powerful it had felt when

he'd kissed her. Or now, the way he'd looked at her with those dark eyes. She marveled at the feeling since it was something she hadn't felt in a long time. Nor had she ever experienced anything this intense. The air around them seemed to buzz with it.

He'd felt it, too. She'd seen it in his expression. What made her laugh was that she could tell he was even more afraid of whatever was happening between them than she was.

"Something funny?" he asked.

Gillian shook her head and took a step back in the direction of her room. She realized she loved feeling like this. It didn't matter that it couldn't last. "Thank you again for *everything.*"

He smiled at that and almost looked bashful.

"Everything," she repeated and stepped through the doorway, closing the adjoining door to lean against it. Her heart was pounding, her skin tingling and there was an ache inside her that made her feel silly and happy at the unexpected longing.

Chapter Twenty-Two

Marc spent the night in a crummy old motel. He couldn't go home. Not only were the cops looking for him but also he had Victor's enforcers on his tail. Victor had failed yesterday at the hospital. That meant he'd be in an even fouler mood. Marc hoped he wouldn't have to see him for a while. Never would be even better.

He'd fallen asleep after staring at the map for hours. His face hurt like hell, not to mention his shoulder. He'd drunk a pint of whiskey he'd picked up at the bar. It hadn't helped. He thought about changing the bandage, but wasn't up to looking at the damage this morning in the mirror.

Picking up the map, he stared again at the circle he'd drawn around Helena. Maybe he should expand it. That one day, she'd driven a hundred miles. He made another circle, this one fifty miles out around the city.

Where the hell did she go? He had no idea since he couldn't conceive of a place she might think to hide the ledger. She knew him and he'd thought he'd known her. She would have had to up her game to beat him, and she would have known that.

He thought back to the days before he'd awakened

still half drugged and found her note telling him how things were going to be now.

Marc started to shake his head in frustration when he recalled coming home early one day to find Andy crying and Rebecca looking…looking guilty, he thought now. She'd been standing in the kitchen.

He'd told her to shut the kid up, which she had. Then she'd disappeared into the bedroom to change her clothes. He frowned now. Why had she needed to change her clothes? At the time, he couldn't have cared less. They hardly ever had sex except when he forced the issue. He hadn't been in the mood that day or he might have followed her into the bedroom and taken advantage of the situation.

What had she been wearing that she'd had to change? His pulse jumped and he sat up straighter as he imagined her standing *before* him—before she'd changed her clothing. She was wearing the pair of canvas pants he'd bought her for hunting. She'd only worn them once when she'd tagged along. It had been early in their marriage. He'd made the trip as miserable as he could since he had been hoping she wouldn't ask to come along again.

Why would she have been wearing such heavy-duty pants? He recalled that their knees had been soiled. And Rebecca's hair had been a mess. She'd looked as if she'd been working out in the yard. But there'd been snow on the ground. Where had she been that she'd gotten what had looked like mud on the pant knees?

He realized with a start that it must have been the same day she'd put so many miles on her car.

He looked at the map again.

THE NO-TRESPASSING sign was large, the letters crude, but the meaning clear enough. Austin looked from it to Gillian.

The climb up the steep mountain reminded him of the difference in altitude between Montana and Texas. Add to that a sleepless night in the motel knowing Gillian was just yards away and he found himself out of breath from the climb.

They'd wound up a trail of sorts from the creek bottom through boulders and brush to reach this dark hole in the cliff. It looked like rattlesnake country to him. He was glad it was winter and cold even though there were only patches of snow in the shade—just as there had been near her family's cabin.

It amazed him how different the weather could be within the state. "It's the mountains," Gillian had said when he'd mentioned it. "Always more snow near the higher mountains."

"This isn't a mountain?" he'd asked with a laugh as he looked out into the distance. He could see the lake, the frozen surface glinting in the winter sunlight.

"Have these caves always been posted like this?" he asked as he looked again at the sign.

"It's always been closed to the public," she said with a shrug.

Great, he thought. They would probably end up in jail. But if they found the ledger, they would at least have a bargaining chip to get out.

"Would your sister really come up here alone?" he asked. He couldn't help being skeptical. Rebecca was desperate, and desperate people often did extraordinary things. Still… "What about her son? She couldn't have brought him."

"It definitely isn't like Becky, I'll admit. She must have trusted someone with Andy, someone none of us knew about. The more I'm learning about my sister, the more secrets I realize she kept from me."

They were wasting time, but he wasn't that anxious about going into the caves. He didn't think Gillian was either, now that they were here. The adorable young Luke Snider wasn't in there with his friends to entice her.

They'd stopped at an outdoor shop on the way and bought rope and headlamps, along with a first aid kit, hiking boots and a backpack. He'd brought water and a few energy bars. He hoped they wouldn't need anything else.

"I'm assuming you remember the way?" he asked.

Gillian nodded but not with as much enthusiasm as he would have liked. "It's been a while."

"Your sister remembered," he reminded her.

"Yes, that's assuming I'm right about her message. Also, this was probably the most traumatic thing that happened to my sister until she married Marc Stewart."

"You're not reassuring me," Austin said as he stepped into the cool shade of the overhanging rock. The cave opening was large. They climbed over several large boulders at the entrance before the cave narrowed and grew dark. They turned on their lamps. A few candy wrappers, water bottles and soda cans were littered on the path back into the cave. Apparently he and Gillian weren't the only ones who'd ignored the no-trespassing sign.

They hadn't gone far before the cave narrowed even more. Gillian sat down on a rock that had been worn smooth and slithered through the hole feetfirst. He followed to find the cave opened up a little more once they were inside.

Austin could feel them going deeper into the mountain. They hadn't gone far when they came to a room of sorts. Water dripped from the rocks over their heads. The air suddenly felt much colder.

"You doing all right?" he asked, his voice echoing a little.

"It was easier when I was sixteen," she said, but gave him a smile.

"That was because you were in love and chasing some cute boy."

Their gazes met for a moment and he felt as he had last night after he'd kissed her. He tamped down the feeling, not about to explore it right now. Probably never. "We should keep moving."

She nodded and led the way through a slit in the rocks that curved back into a tunnel of sorts. They climbed deeper and deeper into the mountain.

MARC STEWART HAD shared one shameful secret with his wife. He was claustrophobic. He hated being in tight spaces. When he was a kid, a neighbor boy had locked him in a large trunk. He'd thought his heart was going to beat its way out of his chest before the idiot kid let him out.

As he parked next to the white SUV below the mountain, he'd told himself if he hadn't already been in a foul mood, this would have definitely put him in one. Even when he'd seen the gulch on the map, he hadn't wanted to believe it.

But at the back of his mind, he remembered bits and pieces of stories he'd overheard between his wife and her sister. Being trapped in some cave had been one of the worst experiences of Rebecca's life. Somehow her sister Gillian was to blame.

That he knew about the caves was no mystery. He'd grown up in Helena. Every kid knew about them. Most kids had explored them. Marc Stewart was the exception.

The last thing he wanted to believe was that his wife had gone back into the cave where she'd experienced the "then" worst thing in her life. He could imagine she'd experienced worse things since then, him being one of them.

The moment he'd seen the rig the deputy had been driving parked next to the creek below the caves, he'd sworn, hating that his hunch had been right. As he cut the engine on the old pickup, he told himself that he didn't have to go *in* the caves. He could just sit right here and wait for them to come out with the ledger.

That made him feel a little better before he realized that once they saw another vehicle, even a strange one, parked down here, they might hide the ledger. Add to that, the cowboy was a sheriff's deputy. He would probably be armed.

No, Marc realized he was going to have to go up there. He wouldn't have to go inside, though. He could wait and ambush them when they came out.

Getting out, he locked the pickup and looked around. He didn't think he'd been followed, but he couldn't be sure. Not that it mattered. He should have the ledger in his possession within the hour.

Then what?

Turn it over to Victor? Make a deal with the feds? Or make a run with it?

He didn't kid himself. He would be damned lucky to get out of this alive.

He thought of Rebecca and felt his stomach churn as he climbed the mountain. The steepness of the slope forced him to stop a half dozen times on the way up. He was trying to hurry, but he couldn't seem to catch his breath. If he didn't get to the top before they came out…

What difference would it make if some Texas deputy shot him? Really, in the grand scheme of things, wouldn't that be better than what Victor probably had planned for him? he thought as he stopped to rest a dozen yards from the cave opening. Maybe that would be the kindest ending to all of this.

The thought spurred him on. He reached the opening and slipped behind a rock to wait. The winter sun was bright but not warm. He'd never been good at waiting. His mind mulled over his predicament until his head ached.

He glanced toward the opening. Still no sound. He couldn't wait any longer. He was going to have to go in. Why hadn't he realized the cave was the perfect place to dispose of the bodies? The last thing he wanted to do was kill them outside the cave where the deed would be discovered much quicker. But if he killed them in the cave, hell, maybe he could make it look like an accident. Drop some rocks on them or something.

Warmed by that idea, he pulled his gun and headed into the cave.

DEEP IN THE CAVE, Gillian stopped to get her bearings. Her headlamp flashed across the cold, dark rock. "It's just a little farther," she said. "I remember it being… easier, though, at sixteen."

"Everything is easier when you're sixteen and think you're in love."

She smiled at that. "Was there a girl when you were sixteen?"

"Nope. I was still into snakes, frogs and fishin'. It took me another year or two before I would give up a day fishing to chase a girl."

Gillian chuckled as they moved on, climbing and slipping over rocks, as they went deeper and deeper into the mountain. She thought of Becky and how she'd forced her to come along that day—on her birthday. A wave of guilt nearly swamped her when she thought of how scared Becky had been.

Then she was reminded that if she was right, Becky had come in here alone. Gillian smiled to herself, proud of her sister. She'd always felt that she needed to protect her. She realized that she'd never thought of Becky as being strong. As it turned out, Becky was a lot tougher than any of them had thought.

She saw the opening around the next bend. Rebecca hadn't been stuck exactly at this point in the cave. The opening was plenty wide. It was just that the trail dropped a good four feet as you slipped through the hole. Unable to see where she was going to land, Rebecca had frozen.

Gillian remembered a high shelf in the rocks. She scrambled up the side of the cave wall to run her hand over it, positive that would be where her sister had hidden the ledger. Nothing.

No, don't tell me all of this has been for nothing.

As she started to climb down, she saw it. A worn, thick notebook with a faded leather cover, the edges of the pages as discolored and weathered as the jacket. She grabbed it and almost lost her balance.

As usual, Austin was there to keep her from falling. He caught her, lifting her down. She clutched the ledger to her chest, tears of relief brimming in her eyes. Finally, they could stop Marc.

"Are you sure that's it?" he asked.

She held it out to him. He glanced at the contents for a moment from the light of his headlamp before handing it back.

"No, you hang on to it," she said.

He smiled and stuck it inside his jacket.

She started to move past him on the trail they'd just come down when he grabbed her arm. "Shh," he whispered next to her ear.

Gillian froze as she heard someone coming.

AUSTIN HEARD WHAT sounded like a boot sole scrapping across a rock as the person stumbled. He motioned for her to turn off her headlamp as he did the same.

It pitched them both into total darkness. "You don't think…?" Gillian whispered.

That Marc had followed them? He wasn't about to underestimate the man. A whole lot was riding on this ledger. Marc had already proven how far he would go to get his hands on it. Austin hoped it was only kids coming into the cave, but he wasn't taking any chances.

He touched Gillian's hand. She flinched in surprise before he took her hand and led her back a few yards in the cave. He remembered a recessed area they'd passed. If they could wedge themselves into it… Otherwise, if they stayed where they were, they would be sitting ducks.

He found the opening by brushing his free hand along the rocks. Stopping, he drew her closer and whispered, "There's a gap in the rocks where we can hide. Can you slip in there?" He led her to it, still holding her hand. As she slipped in, he moved back into the crevice with her, trying to make as little noise as possible. From there, with luck, they would be able to see who passed without being noticed—if they stayed quiet. If it was Marc, then he would have recognized Austin's rental SUV. If it was kids…or cops…

The footfalls on the rocks grew louder. Austin pulled his weapon, but kept it at his side, hidden, in case it was the authorities or kids.

It didn't sound like kids, though. It sounded like a single individual moving stealthily toward them.

A beam of light flickered off the walls of the cave. Austin pressed himself against Gillian as the light splashed over the rock next to him.

MARC FELT THE cave walls closing in on him. He swung his flashlight, the beam flickering off the close confines of the walls as he moved deeper into the cavern. He was having trouble breathing.

His chest hurt, his breathing a wheeze. He stumbled again and almost fell. When he caught himself on the rock wall, he lost his grip on the flashlight. It hit, rolled, smacked a rock and went out. For a few terrifying moments, he was plunged into blackness before it flickered back on.

He lurched to the flashlight, the beam dimmer than before. Picking it up, he stood, listening. Earlier when he'd entered the cave, he'd thought he heard noises. Now he heard nothing. Was it possible he'd taken the wrong turn? The thought made his heart pound so hard it hurt. He tried to settle down. There hadn't been a fork or even a tunnel through the rocks other than the one he was on large enough to move through. He couldn't have taken a wrong turn.

More to the point, Gillian and the cowboy were in here. He'd recognized the SUV. If only he could be patient enough to find them. What if they had heard him coming? What if it was a trap and the cowboy was waiting for him around the next corner of the cave?

He shone the light into the dark hole ahead of him. His breath came out in rasps. Suddenly, there didn't seem to be enough air. If he didn't get out of here now…

He spun around, banged his head on a low-hanging ledge of rock and almost blacked out as he tried not to run back the way he'd come. To hell with the ledger. To hell with Gillian and her cowboy. To hell with all of it. He was getting out of here.

Chapter Twenty-Three

Victor believed in playing the odds. He'd always known the day could come when this life he'd built might come falling down around him. He would have been a fool not to have made arrangements for that possibility. He was no fool. He had a jet at the airport and money put away in numerous accounts around the world, as well as passports in various names.

So what was he waiting for?

He looked around his mountain home. He'd grown fond of this house and Montana. He didn't want to leave. But there was a world out there and really little keeping him here.

So why wasn't he already gone? He didn't really believe that Marc was going to save the day, did he? Wasn't that why he'd gone to Rebecca Stewart's hospital room himself? It had been foolish, but he'd hoped to get the information from her and then take care of the problem. That's what he did, take care of problems. He'd especially wanted to take care of her.

He hated that he'd made this personal. He'd always said it was just business. But a few times it had felt personal enough that he'd taken things into his own hands. Killing came easy to him when it was someone he felt had wronged him. In those instances, he liked to do it himself.

But he'd failed and he was stupid enough to try to kill her again.

Victor glanced at the clock on the wall. Was he going to wait until the FBI SWAT team arrived? Or was he going to get out while he could?

He pulled out his phone. "Take care of Marc."

Jumbo made a sound as if he'd been eagerly awaiting this particular order. "One thing you probably want to know, though—he's gone into a cave apparently looking for his missing ledger."

"A cave?"

"He's not alone. There's a white SUV here." He read off the plate number. It was the same one Victor's informant had given him.

"The Texas deputy and Marc's sister-in-law." Victor swore. "Where is this cave?"

Jumbo described the isolated gulch.

"Make sure none of them come out of the cave."

"What about the ledger?"

Victor considered. "If he has it on him, get it. Otherwise..."

Austin held his breath. The footfalls had been close. He'd almost taken advantage of the few moments when the person had dropped his flashlight. But he hadn't wanted to chance it, not with Gillian deep in this cave with him.

What surprised him was when the footfalls suddenly retreated. The person sounded as if he were trying to run. What the—

"What happened?" Gillian whispered.

"I don't know." He kept listening, telling himself it could be a trick. Why would the person turn back like that? The only occasional sound he heard was some distance away and growing dimmer by the minute.

"I think he left," he whispered. "Stay here and let me take a look."

He eased out of the crevice a little, his weapon ready. In the blackness of the cave, he felt weightless. That kind of darkness got to a person quickly. He listened, thought he heard retreating footfalls, and turned on his light for a split second. He'd half expected to hear the explosion of a gunshot, but to his surprise, he heard nothing. He turned his light back on and shone it the way they'd come. Whoever it had been had turned around and gone back.

The cave, as far as he could see, was empty.

He had no idea who it might have been.

Austin felt Gillian squeeze his arm a moment before she whispered, "Are they gone?"

"It appears so, but stay behind me," he whispered.

She turned on her headlamp and they headed back the way they'd come.

"You think someone will be able to make sense of this?" Gillian asked as she watched Austin thumb through the ledger. They'd stopped to catch their breaths and make sure they were still alone.

"Yeah, I do." He looked up at her. "This is big, much bigger than some guy who owns an auto shop."

She heard the worry in his voice. "If you're going to tell me that there are people who would kill to keep this book from surfacing—"

He smiled at her attempt at humor, but quickly sobered. "I'm afraid the people your brother-in-law associated with would make him look like a choirboy."

"So we need to get this to the authorities as quickly as possible," she said and looked down toward the way out of the cave. "You think that was Marc earlier?"

"Maybe. Or one of his associates."

"Why did he turn around and go back?" she asked with new concern.

"Good question." He tucked the ledger back into his jacket. "When we get to the opening, if anything happens, you hightail it back into the cave and hide."

"You think he's waiting for us outside?"

"That's what I would do," Austin said.

"That day with my sister? I never did see Luke. I saw him go into the cave, but I never saw them come out. There must be another way out of the caves. But I have no idea where."

Austin seemed to take in the information. "Let's hope we don't need it."

Gillian followed him as they wound their way back the route they had come. The cave seemed colder now and definitely darker. She turned off her headlamp at Austin's suggestion to save on the battery, should they need it. She could see well enough with him ahead of her lighting the way.

But just the fact that he thought they might need that extra headlamp made it clear that he didn't think they would get out of here without trouble.

As Marc stumbled headlong out of the cave, he gulped air frantically. His whole body was shaking and instantly chilled as the December air swept across his sweat-soaked skin. He bent over, hands on his thighs, and tried to catch his breath. So intent on catching his breath, he didn't even notice Jumbo at first.

When Jumbo cleared his voice, he looked up with a start to see the big man resting against a large boulder just outside the cave.

"Where is the ledger?" Jumbo asked.

"Inside the cave."

Jumbo lifted a heavy brow. "Why don't you have it? You were just in there."

Marc shook his head as he straightened. His gun bit into his back where he'd stuffed it in the waistband of his jeans. "My wife's sister has it." Jumbo's expression didn't change. "If you are so anxious to have it, then go into the cave and get it yourself."

Jumbo acted as if he was considering that. At the same time the thought dawned on Marc, Jumbo voiced it. "If I go in for the ledger, then what do I need you for?"

Marc's mind spun in circles. Why hadn't Jumbo just come into the cave? Something told him the big man didn't like caves any better than he did. "Good point. I guess I'd better go get it."

Jumbo smiled and stood. "Or I can simply wait until she comes out of the cave and take it from her."

Marc shook his head. "You don't want to kill her and the deputy out here where their bodies will be found too soon. Anyway, the cowboy's armed and expecting trouble. Give me a minute and I'll go back in so I can take care of them."

Jumbo's smile broadened. "You're smarter than Victor thinks you are."

He wasn't sure that was a compliment, but he

didn't take the time to consider the big man's meaning. He drew his gun and fired.

AUSTIN HEARD THE gunfire outside the cave. It sounded like fireworks in the distance, but he knew it wasn't that.

"Stay here," he said to Gillian. "I'll come back for you."

She grabbed his jacket sleeve. He turned toward her, pushing back his headlamp so as not to blind her. In the ambient light, her face was etched in worry.

He drew her to him. She was trembling. "You'll be all right. I'll make sure of that."

"I'm not worried about me."

He leaned back a little to meet her eyes. "Trust me?"

She nodded. "With my life."

"I will be back." He kissed her, holding her as if he never wanted to let her go. Then he quickly broke it off. "Here." He leaned down and pulled a small pistol from his ankle holster. "All you have to do is point and shoot. Just make sure it isn't me you're shooting at."

She smiled at that. "I've shot a gun before."

"Good." He didn't want to leave her, but he hadn't heard any more shots. He had to get to the cave entrance now. "Gillian—"

"I know. Just come back."

He turned and rushed as fast as he could through the corkscrew tunnel of the cave until he could see daylight ahead. Slowing, he listened for any sound outside and heard nothing but his own breathing and the scrape of his footfalls inside the cave.

Finally, when he was almost to the cave entrance, he stopped. No sound came from outside. A trap? It was definitely a possibility. He eased his way toward the growing daylight of the world outside as he heard the roar of a vehicle engine.

He rushed forward, almost tripping over a body. The man was large. Austin didn't recognize him. It appeared he'd been shot numerous times.

Below him on the mountain, an old pickup took off in a cloud of dust and gravel. He spun around at a sound behind him to find Gillian standing in the mouth of the cave. She had the gun he'd given her in her hand.

"I thought you might need me," she said as she lowered the gun.

"MARC'S NOT DONE," Gillian said as she watched Austin try to get cell phone coverage to call the police. She realized she still had the gun he'd given her. She slipped it into her pocket without thinking. Her mind was on Marc and what he would do now. "He gave up too easily. Why didn't he wait to kill us, as well?"

"He's wounded," Austin said and swore under his breath. "There is no cell phone coverage up here."

"How do you know that?"

Austin pointed to several large drops of blood a few yards from the dead man. "Right now he's headed to a doctor. Hopefully at a hospital. This is almost over."

Gillian shook her head. "I hope you're right."

He stopped trying to get bars on his phone and looked at her. "Then where is it you think he's gone?"

"If he is headed for a hospital it's my sister's. If he thinks we have the ledger and it's over… I have to get to the hospital. Now!" She could tell that Austin thought she was overreacting. "Please. I just have this bad feeling.…"

"Okay. As soon as we can get cell service I'll call

the hospital and make sure there is still a guard outside your sister's room and that she is safe, and then I'll call the police."

"Thank you." She couldn't tell him how relieved she was as they hurried down the mountain. Austin seemed to think that the reason Marc had left was because of his wound. The one thing she knew for sure was that Marc wasn't done.

If he'd given up on getting the ledger, then he had something else in mind. She feared that meant her sister was in danger.

VICTOR EXITED HIS car and started across the tarmac to his plane. A bright winter sun hung on the edge of the horizon, but to him it was more like a dark cloud. Jumbo hadn't gotten back to him to tell him that all his problems had been handled up at the gulch. He'd been right in not waiting to see how it all sorted itself out.

He squinted and slowed his steps as he saw a figure standing next to his plane. Jumbo?

Marc Stewart stepped out of the shadow of the plane. He had his hands in the pockets of his oversize coat. "Going somewhere?"

Victor smiled, accepting that Marc wouldn't be here if Jumbo was alive. "Taking a short trip."

Marc nodded and returned his smile. "I told you I would take care of everything."

He cocked his head. "I assume you have, then."

Anger radiated off him like heat waves. "I thought you had more faith in me. Sending Jumbo to kill me? That hurts my feelings."

Victor didn't bother to answer. He'd noticed that

Marc seemed to be favoring his right side. Was it possible Jumbo had wounded him?

"I can't let you get on that plane," Marc said, his hands still in his pockets. "Not without me."

"I doubt you want to go where I'm going. Nor do I suspect you're in good enough shape to travel. I'm guessing that you're wounded and that if you don't seek medical attention—"

Marc swore. "Give me the briefcase."

Victor had almost forgotten he was carrying it. He glanced down at the metal case in his right hand. "There's nothing in there but documents. You've forced me to buy myself the same kind of protection you would have had if you'd been able to get your ledger back."

"Jumbo said I'm smarter than you think I am. Actually that was the last thing he said. Now give me the briefcase. I know it's full of money."

Before Victor could say, "Over my dead body," Marc pulled the gun from his pocket.

He glanced toward the cockpit but saw no one. Nor was there any chance of anyone appearing to turn things around. Realizing it *would* be over his dead body, Victor relented. Marc might have killed his pilot, but Victor was more than capable of flying his own plane. A flight plan had already been filed.

All he had to do was settle up with Marc. It was just money and as they say, he couldn't take it with him if Marc pulled that trigger.

Stepping toward him, Victor said, "It's all yours. A couple million in large untraceable bills." He started to hold the case out to him. At the last minute, as if his arm had a mind of its own, he swung the heavy metal case. It was just money, true enough, but it was *his* money.

He'd never thought Marc particularly fast on his feet. Nor had he thought Marc had the killer instinct. But circumstances could change a man. In retrospect he should have considered that somehow Marc had bested Jumbo. He should have considered a lot of things.

The first bullet tore through his left shoulder just above his heart. The impact made him flinch and stagger. As the second bullet punctured his chest at heart level, Marc wrenched the briefcase out of his hand.

Victor dropped to his knees and looked up at the man as his life's blood spilled out on the small airstrip's tarmac.

"I made you," he said. "You were nothing before I took you under my wing."

"Yes, you made me into the man I am now." Marc Stewart stepped to him, placed the barrel of the gun against his forehead. "You shouldn't have told Jumbo to kill me." He pulled the trigger.

Chapter Twenty-Four

Marc stood over the dead man. He wiped sweat out of his eyes, chilled to the skin and at the same time sweating profusely from the pain and the adrenaline rush.

It made him angry that Victor had put him in this position. None of this should have happened. If Rebecca hadn't— He stopped himself before he let his thoughts take him down that old road again.

What was done was done. Jumbo was dead and so was Victor. He stared down into that boy-next-door face. Victor looked good, even dead. The man's words still hung in the air. Yes, Victor had made him. He'd turned him into a killer.

Marc had been happy enough running his own body shop. Hell, he'd been proud of himself. He'd made a decent living. He hadn't needed Victor coming into his life.

But there was no going back now. *That* Marc Stewart was dead. He was now a man *he* didn't even recognize. But he felt stronger, more confident, more in control than he ever had before. Rebecca hadn't understood his frustration, his feelings of inadequacy. He'd struck out because he hadn't felt in control.

But now…he knew who he was and what he was capable of doing. He hefted the briefcase as he walked to his pickup filled with a sense of freedom. He had more money than he could spend in a lifetime. He could just take off like Victor was planning to do. He wouldn't be flying off in a jet, but he could disappear if he wanted to.

Without his son.

That thought dug in like the bullet from Jumbo's weapon that had torn through his side.

Or he could finish what he started. He thought of Rebecca. It galled him that she might win. He thought of his son. *My son,* he said under his breath with a growl.

Then there was Gillian and the cowboy deputy. He tucked the gun back into his jacket pocket as he climbed into his truck and started the engine. Once he got bandaged up… Well, the people who had tried to bring him down had no idea who they were dealing with now.

Austin put in the call as soon as they neared Townsend and he was able to get cell phone coverage. As he hung up, he looked over at Gillian. "The guard is outside your sister's room. Rebecca is fine. I told the doctor we are on our way."

She nodded, but he could tell she was no less worried.

He called the police, knowing there would be hell to pay for leaving the scene. Right now his main concern was Gillian, though. He'd always followed his instincts so how could he deny hers?

The drive to Bozeman took just over an hour since he was pushing it. Gillian said little on the trip. He could see how worried she was.

When his cell phone rang, he saw it was Marshal Hud

Savage, his cousin-in-law. Had Hud already heard about what had happened back up at the gulch?

"I was worried about you," Hud said.

With good reason, Austin thought. "I'm fine. Gillian Cooper is with me. We have Marc Stewart's ledger. We're pulling into the hospital now so Gillian can see her sister. Rebecca has regained consciousness, the doctor said. Gillian's worried that Marc is also headed there and not for medical attention. He's wounded after killing a man neither of us recognized. I spoke with the nurse earlier and all was fine, but—"

"I'll meet you there," Hud said and hung up.

THE FIRST THING Gillian saw as they started down the hallway toward Rebecca's room was the empty chair outside her door where the guard should have been. Austin had seen it first. He took off at a sprint. She wasn't far behind him, running down the hallway toward her sister's room.

Out of the corner of her eye, she saw that there was no nurse at the nurses' station. In fact, she didn't see anyone in the hallway.

The hospital felt too quiet. Her heart dropped at the thought that they'd arrived too late.

Austin crashed through the door into the room, weapon drawn, yelling, "Call security!" to her. But it was too late for that. She'd been right behind him and was now standing next to him in the center of Rebecca's room. Even if she had called security, it would have been too late.

"I wouldn't do that if I were you," Marc Stewart said. He stood shielded by Rebecca, his gun to her temple. The security guard who'd been posted at the door lay on the floor next to a nurse. Neither was moving. "Drop your gun or I will kill her and everyone else I can in this hospital."

Austin didn't hesitate, telling Gillian that he'd realized the same thing she had. Marc Stewart was no longer just an abusive bastard. He'd become a killer.

"Now kick it to me." After Austin did as he was told, Marc turned his attention to her. "Now, you. Lock the door."

Gillian stepped to the door and locked it before turning back to the scene unfolding before her. Rebecca was conscious, her condition obviously improved, but she still looked weak. What she didn't look was scared.

"You found the ledger in the cave, didn't you?" Marc said, although he didn't sound all that interested anymore.

"I have it right here," Austin said and started to reach inside his coat.

"I wouldn't do that if I were you," Marc warned.

She could hear voices on the other side of the door. But if she turned to unlock the door, she feared Marc would shoot her sister.

"You can have it," Austin said and took a step toward Marc. "You can make a deal with it."

Marc shook his head and motioned for him to stay back. "Too late for that. Could have saved a lot of bloodshed if I had gotten the ledger back when I asked for it." Her sister made a pained sound as Marc tightened his hold on her for emphasis. "Now a lot of people are going to die because of it. Starting with you, cowboy!" He turned the gun an instant before the shot boomed.

Gillian screamed as Austin went down. She dropped to the floor next to him. She felt something heavy in her jacket pocket thud against her side. The gun. She'd forgotten about it. She reached for Austin. He'd fallen on his side. She'd expected to find him in a pool of blood, but as she knelt next to him she saw none. She could hear him gasping for breath.

"Any last words for your sister, Rebecca?" Marc demanded over the sudden pounding on the hospital room door.

Rebecca was crying. She'd dropped to the floor at Marc's feet when he'd let go of her to fire on Austin.

"Come on, don't you want to tell her how sorry you are for what you did?" Marc demanded. "I'd like to hear it. But make it quick. We don't have much time left."

Seeing that Marc's attention was on his wife, Gillian started to stick her hand in her pocket for the gun. In that instant, she saw Marc's thick leather ledger lying next to Austin, a bullet lodged somewhere in the pages. Austin's hand snaked up and took the gun from her.

"Stand up, Gillian," Marc ordered. "Rebecca, I want you to see this." He reached down to take a handful of his wife's hair and pulled her to her feet. As he did, Rebecca grabbed Austin's weapon up from the floor where he'd kicked it. She pressed the barrel into Marc's belly.

Suddenly aware of the mistake he'd made, Marc swung to hit his wife. The gunshots seemed to go off simultaneously in what sounded like cannon fire in the hospital room.

Gillian saw Marc's reaction when both Austin and Rebecca fired. He took both bullets, seeming surprised and at the same time almost relieved, she thought. Before he hit the floor, she thought she saw him smile. But he could have been grimacing with pain. It was something she didn't intend to think about as Austin got to his feet and she rushed to her sister.

In that instant, the door to the hospital room banged open as it was broken down. Marshal Hud Savage burst into the room, gun drawn. Within minutes the room was filled with uniformed officers of the law.

Chapter Twenty-Five

Christmas lights twinkled to the sound of holiday music and voices. Suddenly, a hush fell over the Cardwell Ranch living room. The only sound was the crackle of the fire. Dana saw the children all look toward the door. She had heard it, as well.

"Are those sleigh bells?" she asked in a surprised whisper.

The Cardwell brothers all exchanged a look.

Dana glanced over at Hud. "Did you—?"

"Not my doing," he said, but Dana was suspicious. She knew her husband was keeping something from all of them.

She felt a shiver of concern as she heard the sound of heavy boots on the wooden porch. A moment later, the front door flew open, bringing with it a gust of icy air and the smell of winter pine.

A man she'd never seen before stomped his boots just outside the doorway before stepping in. Because he looked so much like his brothers, though, she knew he had to be Austin Cardwell.

He carried a huge sack that appeared to be filled with presents. The children began to scream, all running to him.

"I told you Austin would be here for Christmas," she said as she got to her feet with more relief than she wanted to admit. "I'm your cousin Dana," she said. "Come on in."

It was then that she saw the woman with Austin. She was dark haired and pretty. Dana thought she recognized her as the jeweler who lived up the road, although they'd never officially met.

She knew at once, though, that this was the woman Austin had met in the middle of the highway and the reason he'd been missing the past few days.

"This is Gillian Cooper," Austin said as he set down the large bag and put an arm around the woman.

Dana knew love when she saw it. There was intimacy between the two as well as something electric. She smiled to herself. "Come on in where it's warm. We have plenty of hot apple cider."

She ushered them into the large old farmhouse and then stood hugging herself as she looked around the room at her wonderful extended family. Having lost her family for a while years ago, she couldn't bear not having them around her now.

Her sister Stacy took their coats as Austin's brothers pulled up more chairs for them to sit in.

The children were huddled around the large bag with the presents spilling out of it.

Mugs of hot cider were poured, Christmas cookies eaten. An excited bunch of children was ushered to bed though Dana doubted any of them would be able to sleep.

"They think you're Santa Claus," she told Austin.

"Not hardly," he said.

"I'm amazed that you remembered it was Christmas," Tag teased him. "At least you didn't miss the grand opening."

"Wouldn't have missed it for the world," Austin said and they all laughed.

"Gillian," Laramie said. "Please stay safe until after New Year's. We want all five brothers together."

Austin looked over at Gillian. They'd just busted a huge drug ring. Arrests were still being made from the names in Marc's book. Rebecca and her son were finally safe. It was over, and yet something else was just beginning.

"We'll be there."

SNOW HAD BEGUN to fall as Gillian left the ranch house later that Christmas Eve night with Austin. They walked through the falling snow a short way up to a cabin on the mountainside. Austin had talked her into staying, saying it was late and Dana had a big early breakfast planned.

"It should just be you and your family," Gillian had protested.

But Dana had refused to hear it. "Do you have other plans?" Before Gillian could answer, Austin's cousin had said, "I didn't think so. Great. Austin is staying in a cabin on the hill. There is one right next to it you can stay in."

Gillian had looked into the woman's eyes and known she was playing matchmaker and this wasn't the first time. Three of Austin's brothers had come to Montana and were now either married or headed that way. She suspected Dana Cardwell Savage had had a hand in it.

Gillian was touched by Dana's matchmaking, not that it was needed. Fate had thrown her and Austin together. In a few days, they had lived what felt like a lifetime together. But they lived in different worlds, and while maybe Austin's other brothers could leave their beloved Texas, Austin was a true Texan with a job that was his life.

"Did you have fun?" Austin asked, interrupting her thoughts as they walked toward the cabins up on the mountainside.

"I can't remember the last time I had that much fun," Gillian answered honestly.

He smiled over at her as he took her hand. "I'm glad you like my family."

"They're amazing. I don't know what makes you think you're the black sheep. Clearly, they all adore you. I think several of them are jealous of your exciting life."

Austin laughed. "They were just being polite in front of you. That's why I begged you to come with me. They couldn't be mad at me on Christmas Eve—not with you there."

"Is that why you wanted me here?"

He put his arm around her. "You know why I wanted you with me. Making my brothers behave in front of you was just icing on the cake. You're okay staying here?"

"Your cousin does know I won't be staying in that cabin by myself, doesn't she?"

"Of course. I saw the look in her eyes. She knows how I feel about you."

"She does, does she?" Gillian felt her heart beat a little faster.

Austin stopped walking. Snow fell around them in a cold white curtain. "I'm crazy about you."

"You're crazy, that much I know."

He pulled off his gloves and cupped her face in his hands. His gaze locked with hers. "I love you, Gillian."

"We have only known each other—"

He kissed her, cutting off the rest of her words. When the kiss ended, he drew back to look at her. "Tell me you don't know me."

She knew him, probably better than he knew himself. "I know you," she whispered and he pulled her close as they climbed the rest of the way to his cabin. To neither of their surprise, a fire had been lit in the stone fireplace. There was a bottle of wine and some more Christmas cookies on the hearth nearby.

"It looks as if your cousin has thought of everything," Gillian said, feeling an ache at heart level. She was falling in love with his family. She'd already fallen for Austin. Both, she knew, would end up breaking her heart when Austin returned to Texas.

She should never have let him talk her into coming here tonight. Hadn't she known it would only make things harder when the two of them went their separate ways?

She looked around the wonderfully cozy cabin, before settling her gaze on Austin. It was Christmas Eve. She couldn't spoil this night for either of them. He'd promised to stay until the grand opening of the restaurant. In the meantime, she would enjoy this. She would pretend that Austin was her Christmas present, one she could keep forever. Not one that would have to be returned once the magic of the season was over.

Because naked in Austin's arms in front of the roaring fire, it *was* pure magic. In his touch, his gaze, his softly spoken words, she felt the depth of his love and returned it with both body and heart.

THE NIGHT OF the grand opening, Austin was surprised by the sense of pride he felt as Laramie turned on the sign in front of the first Texas Boys Barbecue restaurant in Montana.

He felt a lump form in his throat as the doors were opened and people began to stream in. The welcoming crowd was huge. A lot of that he knew was Dana's doing. She was a one-woman promotion team.

"This barbecue is amazing," Gillian said as Austin joined her and her sister and nephew. He ruffled the boy's thick dark hair and met Gillian's gaze across the table. Andy had made it through the holidays unscathed.

As soon as Rebecca was strong enough, the Bakers had brought him down to Big Sky, where the two were staying with Gillian. Rebecca had healed. Just being around her son and sister had made her get well faster, he thought. Marc was dead and gone. That had to give her a sense of peace—maybe more so because she'd had a hand in seeing that he never hurt anyone again. She was one strong woman—not unlike her sister.

"Everything is delicious," Rebecca agreed. "And what a great turnout."

Austin looked around the room, but his gaze quickly came back to Gillian. He felt her sister watching him and was sure Rebecca knew how he felt. He was in love. It still bowled him over since he'd never felt like this before. It made him want to laugh, probably because he'd given his brothers Hayes, Jackson and Tag such a hard time for going to Montana and falling in love with not only a woman but the state. He had wondered what had happened to those Texas boys.

Now he knew.

DANA THREW A New Year's party at the ranch for family and friends. Austin got to meet them all, including his cousin Jordan and his wife, Liza, Stacy's daughter, Ella, as well as cousin Clay, who'd flown up from California. The house was filled with kids and their laughter. His nephew Ford was in seventh heaven and had become quite the horseman, along with his new sister, Natalie.

As Austin looked at all of them, he felt a warmth inside him that had nothing to do with the holidays. He'd spent way too many holidays away from his family, he realized. What had changed?

He looked over to where Gillian was visiting with Stacy. Love had changed him—something he would never admit to his brothers. He would never be able to live it down if he did.

Suddenly, Dana announced that it was almost midnight. Everyone began the countdown. Ten. Nine. Eight. Austin worked his way to Gillian. Seven. Six. Five. She smiled up at him as he pulled her close. Four. Three. Two. One.

Glitter shot into the air as noisemakers shrieked. Wrapping his arms around her, he looked at the woman he was about to promise his heart to. Just the thought should have made his boots head for the door.

Instead, he kissed her. "Marry me," he whispered against her lips.

Gillian drew back, tears filled her eyes.

"I'm in love with you."

She shook her head. "I've heard all the stories your brothers tell about you. *All Austin needs is a woman in distress and it's the last we see of him.* Austin, you've spent your life rescuing people, especially women. I'm just one in a long list. I bet you fell in love with all of them."

"You're wrong about that," he said as he cupped her

face in his hands. "And don't listen to my brothers," he said with a laugh. "You can't believe anything they tell you, especially about me."

"I suspect your brothers are just as bad as you. After listening to how they met their wives, I'd say saving damsels in distress runs in this family."

He grinned. "You're the one who saved me."

Her eyes filled with tears.

"Remember our first kiss?" he asked.

"Of course I do."

"I knew right then you were the one. Come on, you felt it, didn't you?"

Gillian hated to admit it. "I felt…*something*."

He laughed as he drew her closer and dropped his mouth to hers for another slow, tantalizing kiss. It would have been so easy to lose herself in his kiss.

She pushed him back. True, the holidays had been wonderful beyond imagination. She'd fallen more deeply in love with Austin. But her life was here in Big Sky, especially since she couldn't leave her sister and Andy. Not now.

She said as much to him, adding, "You love being a sheriff's deputy and you know it."

He dragged off his Stetson and raked a hand through his thick dark hair. Those dark eyes grew black with emotion. "I did love it. It was my life. Then I fell in love with you."

She shook her head. "What about the next woman in distress? You'll jump on your white horse and—"

"Laramie needs someone to keep an eye on the restaurant up here. I've volunteered."

She stared at him in shock. "You wouldn't last a

week. You'd miss being where the action is. I can't let you—"

"I've been where the action is. For so long, it was all I've had. Then I met you. I'm through with risking my life. I have something more important to do now." He dropped to one knee. "Marry me and have my children."

"*Our* children," she said.

"I'm thinking four, but if you want more…"

She looked into his handsome face. "You're serious?"

"Dead serious. You may not know this, but I was the driving force originally behind my brothers and I opening the first barbecue joint. I can oversee the restaurant—and take care of you and kids and maybe a small ranch with horses and pigs and chickens—"

Just then, they both realized that the huge room had grown deathly quiet. As they turned, they saw that everyone was watching.

Austin shook his head at his brothers not even caring about the ribbing he would get. He turned his attention back to Gillian. "Say you'll marry me or my brothers will never let me live this down," he joked, then turned serious. "I don't want to spend another day without you. Even if it isn't your life's dream to become a Cardwell—"

"I can't wait to be a Cardwell," she said and pulled him to his feet. "Yes!" she cried, throwing herself into his arms. He kissed her as the crowd burst into applause.

From in the crowd, Dana Cardwell Savage looked to where her cousin Laramie was standing. "One more cousin to go," she said under her breath and then smiled to herself.

* * * * *

A WOMAN
WITH A
MYSTERY

Thanks to Randy Harrington, RPh, for his advice on hypnotic drugs; Marcia Proctor, CHt, RBT, for her technical input on hypnosis; Carmen R. Lassiter for her computer expertise and moral support; and as always, the Bozeman Writers Group for keeping me honest.

Prologue

Halloween

The pain. It dragged her up from the feverish blackness, doubling her over in a scream of anguish. Her eyelids fluttered, a flickering screen of light and dark. Three shadows moved at the end of the bed, silhouetted against a shaft of blinding light. They wavered in a whisper of dark clothing and low voices, hovering at her feet, waiting.

"Help me," she tried to say, but her mouth was cotton, her words lost in their whispers.

The shadows moved, blocking the blinding light. She blinked, focused. A scream tore from her throat as she saw them, really saw them. Her eyes locked open, her heart clamoring in her chest at the sight of their grotesque faces as they huddled around her. The three made no move to stop her from screaming and she knew from some place deep inside her that she couldn't be heard outside this room or they would have.

She tried to get up. Another pain shot through her. She pushed herself up on her elbows, suddenly lightheaded and sick to her stomach. She could feel the agony again, coming like a speeding train toward her. She had to get away before it was too late.

One of them stepped from the bright light, face hidden behind a hideous mask, voice muffled. "It will be over soon."

Her eyes widened, blood thundered in her ears. She knew that voice! Oh, my God!

Hands held her down as the pain accelerated, the macabre shadows a frenzied flicker of movement and whispers, the horrible whispers, suddenly rising in alarm.

She tried to see what was wrong, but her view was blocked, the hands strong holding her down. She squeezed her eyes shut against the horrifying images, against the paralyzing fear and the unimaginable pain. Gasping for each breath, she fought not to scream, fought not to lose her mind. But she knew it was already too late. The moment she'd seen their masked faces, she'd known. The moment she'd heard the familiar voice. The monsters had come to take her baby.

Chapter One

Christmas Eve

Aware only of the letter in his pocket, Slade Rawlins didn't feel the thick wet snowflakes spiraling down from the growing darkness or take notice of the straggling shoppers scurrying to their cars.

He strode down the street toward his office, oblivious to everything but the weight of the letter pressed against his heart, heavy as a stone.

"Ho! Ho! Ho!" A department-store Santa suddenly stepped from a doorway onto the sidewalk in front of him, a blur of red in the densely falling snow. "Merry Christmas!"

Startled, Slade jerked back in alarm as the Santa, his suit flocked with snow, thrust a collection pot at him with one hand and clanged his bell with the other.

Hurriedly digging in his pants pocket, Slade withdrew a handful of coins and dropped them into the pot, then sidestepped the man to get to his office door.

The stairs to the second floor were dimly lit, one of the bulbs out. But that was the least of his troubles. He took the steps two at a time, the sound of Christmas music, traffic and the incessant jangle of the Santa bell-ringer following him like one of Ebenezer Scrooge's ghosts.

"Bah, humbug!" he muttered under his breath as he opened the door to Rawlins Investigations and, without turning on the light, went straight to the small fridge by the window. He pulled out a longneck bottle of beer, unscrewed the cap and took a drink as he looked down on the small town from his little hole of darkness.

Outside, snowflakes floated down from a pewter sky, the cold frosting the edges of his window. Inside, the office was hotter than usual, the ancient radiator churning out musty-scented heat.

He could afford an office in the new complex at the edge of town. But he couldn't imagine himself there any more than he could imagine leaving this town. He felt rooted here, as if some powerful force held him.

And he knew exactly what that force was.

He shook off a chill in the hot room as the phone rang. He'd been expecting the call. "Rawlins."

"I heard you were down here a few minutes ago giving my people a hard time," snapped Police Chief L. T. Curtis.

Slade relaxed at the familiar rumble of the cop's voice. He'd heard it all his life. It had been as much a part of his childhood as the smell of his mother's bread baking. The thought gave him a twinge. Had nothing really been as it seemed?

"Did anyone tell you it's Christmas Eve?" Curtis asked sarcastically. "Why aren't you home decorating a damn tree or something?" Slade's father and Curtis had both been cops and best friends.

"I found new evidence in mom's case," Slade said, cutting to the chase. It was all he'd been able to think about since he'd discovered the letter. "I think I know who really killed her."

Curtis groaned. "Slade, how many times have we been down this road? I don't for the life of me understand why you keep pursuing this. The case is closed. It has been for twenty damned years. Her killer confessed."

"Roy Vogel didn't kill her," Slade said, rushing on before the chief could interrupt him. "I found a letter my mother wrote my aunt Ethel before she died."

"Aunt Ethel? The one who passed away in Townsend a couple weeks ago?" Curtis said. "I was sorry to hear about it."

Aunt Ethel had been a cantankerous spinster a good ten years older than Slade's mother. Because of some family disagreement years before the marriage, Ethel had never liked Slade's father, so had hardly ever come around.

"Yeah, well, she left everything to me, which amounted to several boxes of old letters," Slade said as he leaned against the radiator, needing the warmth right now. "Did you know my mother was seeing another man?" Even as he said the words, he had trouble believing them.

"Where the hell did you get an idea like that?"

"She as much as admits it in the letter."

"Bull," Curtis said. "Not your mother. She worshiped the ground your father walked on and you know it."

"I thought I did. But it seems my mother had a secret life none of us knew about."

"In a town like Dry Creek, Montana? Not a chance."

While relieved that Curtis was having trouble believing it too, Slade couldn't disregard what he'd found.

His mother's murder was one of the reasons he'd become a private investigator. He'd been the one who'd found her. Twelve years old, Slade had come home early from school and had to call his father at the police station to tell him. That day, he'd promised himself—and her—that he'd find her killer—no matter what his father said. Joe Rawlins had been afraid that Marcella's killer might come after his kids next and had told Slade to let him handle it.

Later that evening, the troubled young man who lived down the street was found hung in his garage. Roy Vogel had left a suicide note confessing to Marcella Rawlins's murder. All these years, Slade had never believed it. He'd always been suspicious of anything that wrapped up that neatly. But there had been no other leads. Until now.

"I just have a feeling about this," Slade said.

"Well, I'm telling you, you're all wrong, feeling or no feeling," Curtis said. "I wish to hell you'd just get on with your life and let your mother rest in peace."

"That's not going to happen until her murderer is brought to justice."

Curtis swore. "Damn, but you're a pain in the—"

"But you'll take a look at the letter tonight at Shelley's?" They'd all spent every Christmas Eve together as far back as Slade could remember. L. T. and Norma Curtis had been his parents' best friends and had finished raising Slade and his sister Shelley. But they'd been like family long before that.

"You haven't told Shelley?" Curtis asked.

"Nor do I intend to unless I have to."

"It will never come to that," the chief said. "Because you're dead wrong."

Slade hoped Curtis was right about that. But then there was the letter. The chief would know who had been friends with Marcella Rawlins twenty years ago. And if he didn't, his wife, Norma, would.

"Go Christmas shopping. Buy some eggnog. Give this a rest until after the holidays," Curtis advised, surely knowing his words were falling on deaf ears.

Once Slade got something in his head, nothing could stop him. "I'll see you tonight at Shelley's. I want you to see the letter. This can't wait until after the holidays."

"Merry damn Christmas then." Curtis hung up.

Slade replaced the receiver and turned again to the window. The snow fell in a silent white cloak, obliterating the buildings across the street. But he knew this town and everyone in it by heart.

Did that mean he'd known the man his mother had been seeing? Still knew him? *He's still here,* Slade thought. *And he thinks he got away with murder. He doesn't know I'm coming for him. Yet.*

He thought of what the chief had once told him about people trapped in their own lives, in their own illusions of reality, unable to get out, and wondered if he wasn't one of them. Well, then, so was his mother's killer, he thought, as he raised his bottle, the snow falling so hard now he could barely see the Santa below his window, although he could still hear the bell.

It had been snowing the day he'd found his mother's body. He hadn't seen her at first—just the Christmas tree. It had fallen over on the floor. As he'd moved toward it, he was thinking the cat must have pulled it over. Then he saw her. Marcella Rawlins lay under a portion of the tree, a bright red scarf knotted tightly around her neck, one of the Christmas ornaments clutched in her hand. On the radio, Christmas music played and, as tonight, somewhere off in the distance, a seasonal Santa jangled his bell.

Behind him, the soft scuff of a heel on the hardwood floor jerked him from his thoughts. He remembered belatedly that he'd failed to shut and lock his office door. Damn.

"We're closed!" he called out, not bothering to turn around. He took another drink and watched the snow fall, waiting for the footsteps to retreat.

When they didn't, he turned, a curse on his lips.

She stood silhouetted against the dim light from the stairs, her body as sleek and curved as the longneck in his hand and just as pleasing as the cold beer. She didn't move. Nor did she speak. And that was just fine with him.

He ran his hand down the neck of the sweating bottle, enjoying the slick wet feel of it as much as he liked looking at her. Something about her reminded him of another woman he'd known and with the lights off he could almost pretend—

The bell suddenly stopped, the snow silencing everything down on the street. Slade could hear the quickened beat of his heart, the radiator thumping out heat and the faint sound of Christmas music drifting from the apartment next door.

"Mr. Rawlins?" Her voice was as seductive as her silhouette and almost…familiar.

He frowned and tipped the bottle toward her in answer, telling himself he was letting his imagination run away with him.

"Do you mind if I turn on a light?" she asked.

He did. He was tired and all the holiday cheer and

the letter had left him on edge. Why couldn't she just stand there? Or leave? He'd bet his pickup she wouldn't look half as good in the light. And once he'd seen her, he wouldn't be able to pretend anymore.

She flicked the light switch.

He blinked, too shocked to speak. He'd been wrong about the light. She looked even better than she had in silhouette. Dangerous curves ran the length of her, from the full, rounded breasts straining against the thin silk of her blouse beneath the open wool coat to the long, shapely legs that peeked between her skirt and her snow boots, all the way back up to her face. And, oh, what a face it was. Framed in a wild mane of curly dark hair. Lips lush. Baby blues dark-lashed and wide.

It was a face and body he'd spent months trying to forget.

He swore under his breath, more in shock than anger, although he'd spent most of the last year looking for her, worrying that she was dead—and blaming himself for letting it happen.

"I need your help," she said, a slight catch in her voice. "I know it's Christmas Eve…"

He shook his head in disbelief. A thousand questions leapt into his mind, all having to do with where she'd been, what she was doing here now and why she'd left him. Oh, yes, especially why she'd left him, he thought bitterly.

"What the hell do you think you—" He took a tentative step toward her, then stopped as he saw her expression. Blank as a wall. No recognition. She didn't know him!

He let out a colorful curse.

"I really shouldn't have bothered you." She turned to leave.

He knew if he had any sense at all, he'd just let her go. If only he'd done that the first time.

"Just a minute." He reached for her, afraid the moment he touched her, she would disappear again. Another one of Scrooge's ghosts.

His hand brushed hers. She turned back to him, her blue eyes glistening with tears. She didn't evaporate into thin air. Didn't disappear like a mirage before him. And after touching her, he knew she was most definitely flesh and blood. But not the woman he'd known.

This woman was a walking shell of that woman, and he couldn't help but wonder what had happened since to make her that way.

"I'm sorry, you just caught me by surprise," he said, looking into all that blue again. Just as he had a year ago, when she'd come running out of the snowstorm and into the street. He'd tried to stop his pickup in time, but the snow and ice— He'd jumped from his truck and run to her. She'd lain sprawled in the snow just inches from his bumper. When she'd opened her eyes in the headlights, they were that incredible blue—and blank. Not as blank as they were now. There'd been something in her expression…something that had hooked him from the moment his gaze had met hers.

"Here," he said, offering her a chair as he closed his office door, afraid she'd change her mind and leave. "What can I do for you?"

She seemed to hesitate, but accepted the chair he offered her, sitting on the edge of the seat, her handbag in her lap, her fingers clutching it nervously.

He leaned against the edge of his desk and stared

down at her. Easy on the eyes, but hard on the heart, he thought. He knew better than to get involved with her again. But curse his curiosity, he had to know.

Last year when she'd come to in the street, he'd picked her up and put her in the cab of his pickup, planning to take her to the hospital. But she'd pleaded with him to just take her somewhere safe. She had no memory. No name. No past. But she'd been convinced someone was trying to kill her and had pleaded with him not to involve the police.

"I need your help," she said now.

"*My* help?" he asked, still looking for some recognition in her gaze. But it appeared she didn't know him from Adam! Either he wasn't that memorable or the woman had a tendency to forget a lot of things. "Why me?"

She shook her head and clutched her purse tighter. "I'm afraid this was a mistake." She started to get up.

He was on his feet, moving toward her. "No," he said a little more strongly than he'd meant to. "At least give me a chance."

She lowered herself back into the chair, but seemed apprehensive of him. Certainly not as trusting as last time, he thought with no small amount of resentment.

He'd taken her in and tried to unravel her past, believing she must be suffering from some sort of trauma.

But two months later, he was the one who'd gotten taken in. Just when he thought he might be making some progress into her past, she'd disappeared without a trace, along with a couple hundred dollars of his money and a half dozen of his case files. He'd spent months looking for her, fearing someone *had* killed her. Wanting to wring her neck himself.

And now she was back. Alive. And in trouble. Again.

"I'm afraid you're going to think I've lost my mind," she said, her voice as soft as her skin, something he wasn't apt ever to forget. She shivered as if her words were too close to the truth.

"Why would I think that?" he asked, wondering if she could just be playing him. It was too much of a coincidence that she'd come into his life twice—both times in trouble, on Christmas Eve and supposedly with no memory. At least, this time, no memory of him, it seemed.

"The help I need is rather unusual."

He pulled up a chair and sat down. "Try me."

She seemed to relax a little now that he wasn't towering over her, but she still clutched her handbag, still looked as if she might take off at a moment's notice. Is that what had happened last time? She'd gotten scared? Scared of what he was going to find out about her? Or had she just planned to rip him off the whole time? And all these months he'd been telling himself that she'd just gotten cold feet about what was happening between the two of them.

"I think someone stole my baby."

He stared at her. She had a child? "Wouldn't you *know* if someone had taken your child?"

"I know it sounds…crazy, but, you see, that's just it, I'm not sure."

Déjà vu. This would have been a good time to tell her he couldn't help her. Wasn't about to get involved in her life again. But he had to know who she was and where she'd been all this time. And why. Why she'd conned him. Why she'd stolen from him. Mostly, how much of it had been a lie.

"Why don't you start at the beginning," he suggested. "Like with your name."

"Oh, I'm sorry," she said with obvious embarrassment. She kneaded nervously at her purse and he could tell she was having more than second thoughts about coming here.

He gave her a smile. "Take your time."

Her answering smile was like bright sunlight on snow. Dazzling. And it had the same effect on him it had had a year ago.

"My name is Holly Barrows. I'm an artist. I live in Pinedale."

Pinedale? Just fifty miles over a mountain pass from here. Had she really been that close all these months? "How long have you lived there?" he had to ask.

"All my life."

So is that what had happened? Her memory had returned last year and she'd just gone home? It seemed a little too simple given that she'd been so convinced someone was trying to kill her. Not to mention that she'd stolen his money and case files—then apparently forgotten him. And Christmas past.

"Please go on," he encouraged.

"When I gave birth…" she said, the words seeming to come hard. "I have little memory of the delivery. I think I was drugged."

"You gave birth in Pinedale?" he asked.

She shook her head. "I don't know where it was, just that it wasn't a normal hospital. I think the room was soundproofed and the doctors…" She looked away. Her hands trembled. "When I woke, I was in County Hospital. I was told that my baby was stillborn. I don't know how I got there. But I keep remembering hearing my baby cry. When I asked to see my baby at the hospital—" she stopped, seeming to be fighting to compose herself "—I knew the infant they gave me wasn't mine."

He stared at her in shock. "The hospital let you see your stillborn baby?"

"See it, hold it, name it," she said in that same blank, distant voice. "So the mother knows it's really gone."

Sweet heaven. He couldn't imagine. "What made you think the baby wasn't yours if you never saw it right after the birth?"

She shook her head. "A mother knows her own baby."

He wondered if that was true. "What is it you think happened to *your* baby, presuming you're right and the baby was born alive at this other place?" Then replaced with a dead one? How plausible was that?

"I know how insane it sounds, but I keep having these flashes of memory. My baby was alive. Someone stole it."

Someone? The same someone she'd thought was trying to kill her a year ago?

She was wasting his time. It was obvious he wasn't going to get his money—or his case files—back. Nor any explanation, let alone satisfaction, for the heartache she'd caused him. She was a nutcase. A beautiful, desirable nutcase.

She fumbled to open her purse.

The movement should have concerned him. She might be going for a weapon. As crazy as she was, she might shoot him. But the way her hands shook, she wouldn't have been able to hit the broad side of a barn even if she pulled a howitzer from the bag.

She tugged out a tissue and wiped her eyes.

He'd heard enough, but still, he had to ask, "Why would someone want to take your baby?"

She glanced up, tears in her eyes. "I don't know. I just have this feeling that this isn't the first time they've done this. That there have been other babies they've stolen."

She was worse than he'd thought.

He rubbed a hand over his face, remembering something she'd said. "During the delivery, you mentioned the doctors. You saw them then?"

She shook her head, one glistening tear making a path down her perfectly rounded cheek. "Not their faces." She seemed to hesitate as if what she was about to say could be any worse than what she'd already told him. "They wore masks."

"Masks? You mean surgical masks?"

"Halloween masks with hideous monster faces." She avoided his gaze as she rooted around in her purse again. "I will pay you whatever you want to prove that I'm not crazy and to get my baby back."

He closed his eyes for a moment, taking a deep breath. And to think he used to fantasize about finding her. "When was this anyway?"

"Five weeks ago."

He nodded distractedly, wondering why it had taken her five weeks.

When he opened his eyes, she had the checkbook in her hand, her expression filled with hopefulness as she looked up at him again.

Sweet heaven. He couldn't believe that a part of him would gladly leap on his noble steed and ride off to battle evil for this damsel in distress yet again. Except that she'd punctured a hell of a hole in his armor the last time around. She'd gone straight for his heart, and he wasn't apt to forget it, no matter how desirable, how beautiful or how crazy and in need of help she was this time around.

"I'm sorry, but I'm afraid I can't help you," he said, getting to his feet.

Slowly, she lowered her gaze to her lap. He watched her put the checkbook back into her purse and rise from the chair.

"I'm sorry to have wasted your time," she said without looking at him.

He watched her walk to the door and thought he should at least suggest she seek medical help. Did she know a good psychiatrist?

But he let her go. She was either a crackpot, or a con artist. Her name probably wasn't even Holly Barrows.

He listened as her boot heels tapped down the stairs, and he waited for the sound of the door closing on the street below, before he picked up his beer bottle and went to the window again.

It had stopped snowing, the sky dark, the air cold against the glass. He watched her hurry to a newer SUV parked at the curb. Out of habit, he jotted down her license-plate number when her brake lights flashed on.

Why had she come to him with this latest ludicrous story? Hadn't she gotten what she'd come for the last time?

She pulled out into the street, and he had to fight the urge to run after her.

As he started to turn from the window, he caught a movement on the sidewalk below and looked down. The Santa bell-ringer no longer had his pot. Or his bell.

He was looking after the retreating Holly Barrows and talking hurriedly into a cell phone.

Slade felt a jolt as the Santa glanced up toward his office window. The look was brief, but enough. Slade swore and scrambled around his desk and out of the office. He launched himself down the stairs, nearly falling on the wet steps, his mind racing faster than his feet, and burst through the door to the sidewalk.

The Santa was gone—except for his red hat and white fake beard lying on the pavement.

The quiet snowy darkness settled over Slade as he stared down the now-empty street. He'd seen the Santa's alarmed expression when he'd looked up and spotted Slade at the window, recalled the agitated way the man had been talking into the cell phone.

Worry clutched at him the way Holly Barrows had clutched at her purse. Sweet heaven, could she have been telling the truth this time? More important, had she been telling the truth a year ago when she'd thought someone was trying to kill her?

Suddenly a thought lodged like a stake in his heart. If she wasn't crazy, if Holly Barrows really had been pregnant and had delivered a baby five weeks ago, then— If nothing else, he'd always been good at math.

He stumbled back against the side of the building as he stared down the street in the direction her car had disappeared. If there really had been a baby, there was a damned good chance it was his.

Chapter Two

"Are you all right?" Shelley asked him as she sliced a loaf of homemade cranberry bread. Her kitchen smelled the way their mother's used to. Something was always cooking.

"Fine, why?" He leaned against the counter to watch her, trying to put on his best holiday face.

It was obvious to anyone who saw them together that Slade and Shelley were siblings. Shelley's hair was the same thick, dark blond as his, her eyes a little paler hazel. They'd both taken after their father's side of the family. Like him, she had the Rawlinses' deep dimples. They were, in fact, fraternal twins.

"You think I can't tell when something is bothering you?" she asked. "Something *more* than Christmas."

Christmases were always hard on him. This one was especially tough after what he'd found in his mother's letter, but he wasn't going to tell her that.

"Remember that woman? The one I met last year about this time?"

She kept cutting the bread. "The one who couldn't remember who she was. You called her Janie Doe." She frowned. "I remember how worried you were about her when she disappeared."

"Yeah, well, she waltzed into my office late this afternoon."

Shelley stopped slicing to look over at him, and he wondered if she realized just how involved he'd gotten with Janie Doe. "Then she's all right?"

He shrugged. He wouldn't exactly say that. "The case is complicated." That was putting it mildly. "But I can't get it off my mind."

"It? Or her?"

"Both," he admitted with a sheepish grin. That seemed to satisfy her.

"Would you carry this into the living room? Norma called to say they were running a little late."

"I hope they come," Slade said, wondering how badly the chief didn't want to read the letter he'd found.

"Of course they'll come," Shelley said in surprise. "It wouldn't be Christmas without them. Well, Norma anyway," she added with a laugh. Chief Curtis seemed as fond of Christmas as Slade was.

Shelley put out a tray of snack food while Slade poured them each a glass of wine. With Christmas music playing on the stereo, he helped her decorate the tree. It had become their tradition, since being on their own, to decorate the tree on Christmas Eve, then take it down right after the new year, and always at Shelley's.

The first Christmas after their mother's murder had been the worst, with both parents gone. But the chief and Norma Curtis had helped them start new traditions and Slade had gone along with it for his sister. As far as he was concerned, he could skip the holiday all together and never miss it.

"This is one of my favorites," she said, stopping to

admire a small porcelain Santa. "I remember it from pictures of when we were just babies."

Their mother had loved collecting Christmas ornaments. She could recount where she'd gotten each, many from friends or family, and what year. Each one had special meaning for her.

He watched his sister cradle the Santa in her palm and couldn't help but think about the Santa bell-ringer below his office window earlier. It kept him from thinking about other Christmases—and his mother.

After he'd missed catching the Santa bell-ringer, he'd returned to his office and tried to call Holly Barrows in Pinedale. Of course there was no listing. Why wasn't he surprised? She'd probably made up the name.

Not that he knew what he'd have said even if he'd found a number for her. *I think Santa Claus had my building staked out and I think he was looking for you?* He would sound as crazy as she had.

But he couldn't quit worrying about her. Or worse, worrying that she might be in real trouble—and he hadn't taken her seriously. Between that, and worrying about his mother's letter—and the possible implications of her words—the last thing he wanted to be doing tonight was decorating a Christmas tree. He felt antsy and anxious. Both incidents had shaken him—and during a season when he didn't feel all that grounded anyway.

He and Shelley had just finished decorating the tree when the chief and his wife arrived.

"Slade, get them some wine," Shelley said as she took their coats and shook off the snow. "You must be freezing."

"Nothing like a white Christmas!" Norma exclaimed and moved to the fireplace. "Oh, your tree is just lovely!"

"Want to help me with the wine?" Slade asked the police chief pointedly.

Curtis sighed but followed him into the kitchen. Chief Curtis was built like a battering ram, neckless and balding, with a florid complexion, a reputation for being outspoken to the point of being rude and as tough as a rabid pit bull off his chain. Slade knew the chief's bark was worse than his bite, but he still had a healthy respect for the man.

He handed him the letter, then proceeded to fill two glasses with wine, knowing Shelley would get suspicious if they took too long.

"Do we have to do this now?" Curtis asked, looking down at the yellowed envelope in his hand. "Damn, Slade, it's Christmas Eve."

"Roy Vogel didn't kill her. Now I know there was someone else. A man. A secret lover who wanted to remain secret. Maybe at all costs."

Curtis shook his head. "You just aren't going to let this go, are you?"

"No. I can't. And considering how my parents felt about you, I wouldn't think you could either."

Curtis shot him a withering look, then slowly opened the flap and withdrew the handwritten pages. They crackled in his thick fingers as he unfolded them with obvious hesitancy.

"Well?" Slade demanded when Curtis had finished reading.

"It's vague as hell," the cop said with his usual conviction. But Slade noticed that the older man's hands shook a little as he folded the paper, forced the pages back into the envelope and handed it to him. The letter had obviously upset him as much as it had Slade.

"She admitted she'd been secretly meeting someone she didn't want Joe to know about, and she pleaded with Ethel not to give away her secret," Slade said as he put the letter back into his pocket. "What's vague about that?"

"She didn't say she was having an affair," Curtis pointed out, keeping his voice down so the women couldn't hear in the next room.

"I'm going to find out who she'd been meeting," Slade told him as he handed the chief a glass of wine. "Are you going to help me? Someone had to know. Maybe one of her friends. Or her hairdresser. Or the damned meter reader. Someone."

"You're going off half-cocked," Curtis warned. "Even if there was someone, it doesn't mean he killed her."

"There *was* someone. The letter makes that clear. And if Roy Vogel didn't kill her—"

With an oath, Curtis shook his head. "Why did he confess then?"

"Who knows? The guy was always weird and not quite right in the head. But for that very reason, Mom would never have let him into the house, let alone offered him a drink. You do remember the second, half-empty glass on the coffee table?"

"Both glasses had only your mother's fingerprints on them," Curtis pointed out as if he'd said it a million times to Slade. He probably had.

"So the killer wore gloves. It was December. Right before Christmas. It was cold that year. Or he never touched his drink."

Curtis shook his head. "I should never have allowed you to have a copy of the file. What do you do, dig it out and reread it every night before bed?"

"Don't have to. I know it by heart." He didn't tell the chief that he no longer had the file. It was one of the cases the mysterious Holly Barrows, if that was really her name, had stolen, along with a half dozen other older cases. There was no rhyme or reason to the ones she'd taken. None of the cases current—or interesting enough to steal. Probably because the woman was unstable.

"Your father went over that case with a fine-tooth comb. If he'd thought for a moment that Roy Vogel hadn't been guilty—"

"What if he knew about her affair, maybe even knew who it was?" Slade interrupted. Joe Rawlins had died of a heart attack not six months after his wife's murder. But Joe had never had a bad heart. That's why Slade had always believed it had been heartbreak that had killed him.

Curtis let out an oath. "You think a cop like your father would let Marcella's murderer go free?"

"Maybe there was a reason Dad didn't go after the real killer. Or couldn't." All Slade had was a gut instinct, one that had told him years ago that the wrong man had died for the crime.

Curtis shook his head. "You're opening up a can of worms here. Have you thought at all about Shelley and what this is going to do to her?"

"I always think of Shelley," Slade snapped.

Curtis raised a brow as Shelley called from the other room.

"What's keeping you two? No work! It's Christmas Eve!"

Curtis reached for the glass of wine Slade had poured for Norma. "Isn't it bad enough that your mother was murdered? You want to murder her reputation as well? And for what? Roy Vogel killed her."

"Then you think she *was* having an affair," Slade said.

Curtis swore. "If she was, I for one don't want to know about it."

Slade fell silent, thinking about what Curtis had said as he followed the chief back into the living room. The conversation turned to the holidays and food and parties.

He stared at the fire, the bright hot flames licking up from the logs, and tried to follow the conversation. But he couldn't quit thinking. About his mother's murder. About the young woman who'd come up to his office. He wondered what she was doing tonight and if she was all right. If she'd ever been all right. And if it was possible she'd given birth to his baby.

He couldn't help but remember in detail how it had been between them and wonder…what if her memory of him were to come back—

He reminded himself that she was a thief and, more than likely, a liar. She'd stolen more than his money and his files. She'd stolen his heart.

Maybe that's why he couldn't get her or the Santa bell-ringer out of his head. Or completely forget about the damned letter in his pocket—and its possible ramifications.

"Don't you think so, Slade?"

He jerked his head up. "What?"

"I asked if you thought this was our best tree yet?"

Shelley turned to the others. "Slade and I went out and cut this one ourselves."

He nodded. "The best ever." But he could feel his sister's worried gaze on him. She knew him too well. It would be hard to keep his concerns from her, let alone the letter. Especially once he started asking around town about their mother.

When Chief Curtis got up to clear the snack dishes, Slade offered to help, following the cop into the kitchen.

"Now what?" Curtis asked, only half as put out as he pretended, Slade suspected.

"Any chance you could get a license plate run for me tonight?"

"Tonight?" the chief asked in disbelief.

"It's for a missing-person case I'm working on." He gave Curtis the license number from the SUV the alleged Holly Barrows had left his office in. "I need a name and address. It's important and I have a feeling it can't wait until after Christmas."

The chief grumbled but stuffed the number in his pocket. "I'll have someone at the DMV call you. *I'm* trying to enjoy the holiday." As annoyed as he sounded, the cop seemed glad that Slade had given up on his investigation into Marcella Rawlins's possible infidelity. At least temporarily.

After all these years, Slade thought, his mother's murder could wait another day. Maybe the woman who called herself Holly Barrows couldn't.

Chapter Three

Christmas Day

The next morning, after opening presents and eating Shelley's famous cranberry waffles with orange syrup, Slade followed the snowplow over the pass to Pinedale. It had snowed off and on throughout the night, leaving the sky a clear crystalline blue and everything else flocked in white with a good foot of new snow on the highway.

Pinedale was a small mountain town, forgotten by the interstate, too far from either Yellowstone or Glacier Parks and not unique enough to be a true tourist trap.

He wondered what Holly Barrows was doing here—if indeed the woman he'd met yesterday in his office really was the same Holly Barrows the Department of Motor Vehicles reported lived at 413 Mountain View and drove a blue Ford Explorer.

Pinedale was smaller than Dry Creek, set against a mountainside and surrounded by dense pines. The entire town felt snowed-in and deserted, caught in another time. It had once been a mining camp, some of the scars of its past life still visible on the bluffs around it.

He found Mountain View and drove up to 413. The

sign on the lower level of the building read: Impressions Art Gallery. He got out of his truck and glanced in the gallery window, not surprised to see a typical Montana gallery with bronze cowboys and horses, oils and acrylics of Native Americans, and watercolor scenics. He spotted a nice acrylic of a sunny summer scene along a riverbank. The name in the right-hand corner was H. Barrows.

Off to the left of the gallery was an old garage and tracks in the snow where a vehicle had been driven in within the past twenty-four hours.

He stepped back to look up at what he assumed was an apartment on the second floor. The sun glinted on the large upstairs window but not before he'd glimpsed the dark image of a woman there, not before he'd felt a chill.

Rounding the corner of the building, he found a stairway that led up to the apartment. He stopped at the foot of the stairs and glanced around the neighborhood. A handful of kids were dragging shiny new sleds up the side of the mountain a few doors down. A dog barked incessantly at one of the boys. A mother called from a doorway to either the dog or the boy, Slade couldn't tell which. Neither paid any attention.

He didn't see a Santa bell-ringer, but then he hadn't expected to. He figured the man in the Santa suit already knew where to find Holly Barrows. The Santa had been waiting for Holly to show up at Rawlins Investigations as if he'd either feared she would—or had been expecting her. Why was that?

He realized as he glanced up the stairs that he had more questions than answers. And one big question he needed answered above all the rest. Had Holly given birth to a baby—his baby?

He noticed fresh footprints in the snow on the steps to the apartment. The boot print looked small, like a woman's, and since this was the address Holly Barrows had given as her home on her car registration, he figured the tracks were probably hers and was relieved to see that there was only one set of prints and they ended at the bottom of the stairs.

Someone had come down, it appeared, to get the newspaper and had then gone back up. The newspaper box was empty, the snow on top dislodged. With any luck, Santa hadn't been here and Holly Barrows was home. But was the person he'd glimpsed in the window the woman he was looking for?

He climbed the stairs, finding himself watching the street. The dog was still barking. One of the kids squealed as he and his bright-colored sled careened down the hill and into the street. Kids.

Slade knocked at the door at the top of the stairs and waited, more anxious and apprehensive than he wanted to admit. He expected a complete stranger to open the door, figuring the woman in his office yesterday had lied about everything, although he had no idea why. Maybe she'd borrowed the car. Or even stolen it.

So, when she opened the door, it took him a moment. He stared at her in surprise. And only a little relief. She hadn't lied about her name. Or her occupation. But did that mean she hadn't lied about the rest of it either?

She stood in the doorway, a paintbrush in her hand and a variety of acrylic colors on her denim smock. She wore a sweatshirt and jeans under the smock, but she looked as good in them as she had in the skirt and blouse last night.

"You're the last person I expected to see," she said, not sounding all that enthused about the prospect.

"Yeah." He glanced to the street again, then back at her. "Mind if I come in?"

She opened the door farther, motioning him inside. The place was small, but tastefully furnished, the colors warm and bright, the furniture comfortable-looking. Homey. Except there was no tree. No sign at all that it was Christmas Day.

"Don't you celebrate Christmas?" he asked, curious.

"Not this year."

He followed her through the living area to her studio on the north side of the building. The room, bathed in light, was neat and orderly. He watched her, wondering if the woman he'd come to know this time last year was the true Holly Barrows or if this woman, who seemed to be as dazed as a sleepwalker, was the real one.

She moved around an easel in front of a huge picture window and stopped, seeming startled by what she'd painted.

Not half as startled as he was as he stepped around the easel and saw what she'd been working on. He'd expected something like the idyllic summer scene he'd seen in the gallery downstairs. The two paintings were so different no one would have believed they were done by the same artist.

He stared at the disturbing scene on the canvas, feeling ice-cold inside. He didn't need to ask what the painting depicted. It could have been the birth of Satan, it was so foreboding and sinister. Three horrible creatures with misshapen grotesque faces and dark gowns huddled at the end of a bed waiting expectantly for the birth.

While he couldn't see the patient's face in the painting, he could feel her pain and confusion—and fear in the angle of her body, the disarray of her wild dark curly hair and the grasping fingers of the one hand reaching toward the ghouls at the end of the bed, toward her baby.

The painting was powerful and compelling, and seized at something deep inside him. Sweet heaven.

"We need to talk," he said, even more convinced of that after seeing what she'd been painting.

She nodded and washed her paintbrush, the liquid in the jar turning dark and murky as she worked. He watched her methodically put the brush away, wipe her hands on the smock, then take it off.

"Why did you wait so long to start looking for your baby?" he asked.

She looked up, her eyes the same color as the Montana winter sky behind her. "Mr. Rawlins—"

"Slade."

"Slade." She seemed to savor his name in her mouth for a moment as if she'd tasted it before, then, frowning, continued as she led him into the living room. "I believed that my baby had been stillborn. I had no reason not to." She waited for him to sit, then perched on the edge of a chair, her hands in her lap. "I woke in a hospital. The nurse told me. I thought at first that my belief that the stillborn wasn't my baby was nothing more than denial. It wasn't until I started having these memories—if that's really what they are—" She shook her head. "Before that, I just assumed my sister-in-law was right. That my grief over losing the baby was causing my…confusion about the birth."

Sister-in-law? "You're married?" he asked, unable to hide his surprise—or dismay.

She shook her head. "Widowed. My husband died a

year ago." She looked away. "Are you going to take my case, Mr. Rawlins?"

He didn't correct her. He was still mulling over the fact that she'd had a husband. And the man had died a year ago. Just before Slade had met her? He felt as if she'd sucker punched him. "There are a few things I need to know." That was putting it mildly.

"I will tell you everything I can."

An odd answer, he thought, all things considered. "I'll need you to agree to an examination by a doctor."

"To prove that I recently delivered a baby."

He nodded.

She didn't seem offended. "What else?"

"I'll need the name of your doctor during your pregnancy, and I'll want to talk to the doctor at the hospital who allegedly delivered your baby."

"I didn't have a doctor during my pregnancy. I was seeing a midwife."

He lifted a brow at her. She didn't seem like the midwife type. "Was that your idea?"

She flushed. "Actually, my sister-in-law suggested her. The woman is highly regarded as one of the top midwives in the country. Her name is Maria Perez. She just happened to have bought a place near here and was on a sabbatical. I was very lucky to get her."

He stared at her. Something in the way she said it caught his attention. It almost sounded rehearsed. And too convenient. "You have her number then?"

Holly came up with the number from memory. He wasn't sure why that surprised him either.

"Something else. Why did you drive fifty miles over a mountain pass in a blizzard on Christmas Eve to hire a private investigator?"

"I went to Dry Creek to the last-minute-shoppers art festival at the fairgrounds to look for promising new artists for my gallery. I go every year."

Again, the lines sounded rehearsed. Or as if they weren't her own. Was the art festival where she'd been last year before she'd come stumbling out of the snow and into his headlights?

"Although, this year I almost didn't go," she added with a frown, a clear afterthought.

"So why did you?"

She shook her head. "My sister-in-law thought it would be the best thing for me."

He wondered about this sister-in-law who knew so much. "And do you hire a private investigator every year?" he asked, the sarcasm wasted on her.

"Of course not. I never intended to hire anyone. I was driving by and I saw your sign through the snow and—" She looked up at him and shook her head. "I don't know why I came to you. I just had this sudden need to know the truth and there you were."

"No matter what that truth is?" he had to ask.

"No matter what you discover," she said, but he heard a slight hesitation in her words. She sounded scared and unsure. He couldn't blame her. He felt the same way.

He went for the big one. "What about the father of your baby?"

"I don't see what that has to do—"

"If your baby really was stolen, the father of the baby seems the prime suspect."

It was clear she'd already thought of this. She nodded. "I..." She licked her lips and swallowed. "I don't..."

"You don't know who the father of your baby is?"

"I know what you must be thinking."

He doubted that. "Surely, you have some idea or can at least narrow it down."

"Are you familiar with alcoholic blackouts?"

He stared at her. "You're an alcoholic?" The only thing he'd ever seen her drink was cola.

"Let's just say I don't remember getting pregnant and leave it at that for now."

He studied her for a long moment. Was it possible he knew more about the conception of their baby than she did? "When can you see a doctor?"

Relief washed over her features at his change of subject. "The sooner the better," she said.

"No problem. I think I can get you an appointment this afternoon." Dr. Fred Delaney had delivered both Slade and Shelley and had been a friend of the family for years. He would make time for this, Slade knew. Dr. Delaney was also on his list of people to talk to about his mother. "Is that too soon?"

"No." She rose as he got to his feet.

He considered telling her about the two of them. That after doing the math, he figured the baby had to be his. But first he had to know if there really had been a baby.

He started to leave and stopped. "Last night, when you came to see me at my office…"

"Christmas Eve," she said, then waited for him to go on.

"There was a Santa bell-ringer in front of my building. Maybe you saw him?"

She shook her head, frowning as if wondering what that had to do with anything.

"I think he had my office staked out. I saw him on a cell phone as you were leaving. I think he'd been waiting for you." He saw her pale, her hand trembling as she grasped the back of the chair he'd been sitting in for support.

"Then they know I've come to you," she said, fear making her blue eyes darken.

"They?" he asked, just to clarify.

"The people who took my baby."

The monsters in the painting.

If "they" existed outside this woman's mind.

The Santa bell-ringer, on the other hand, had been real. He described the Santa as best he could, hoping she'd recognize the guy as someone she knew. But while the man hadn't been hiding behind a monster mask— he *had* been hiding under a beard and hat and possibly a whole lot of padding. Like the monsters in her painting, real or not, Santa hadn't wanted to be recognized either, it seemed.

"I can't place him from your description," she said.

He nodded, not surprised. "You just might want to be…careful." He wanted to warn her, but he didn't have any idea against what—or whom. The bottom line was: if those monsters in her painting existed, then Holly Barrows was in danger.

"You don't have a phone?" he asked, remembering that he hadn't found a listing.

"I have it listed under the gallery." She rattled off the number.

He memorized it. "I'll call you with a time. We can meet at the doctor's office."

He glanced back at the painting as he left and almost wished she really *was* crazy. The alternative scared the hell out of him.

DR. FRED DELANEY had grayed in the years since he'd delivered Slade and Shelley. He'd come to Dry Creek right out of medical school and ended up staying. Now in his sixties, he was semiretired.

"You know my office is closed the week of Christmas," he said when Slade called him.

"That's why I'd like you to see this woman. I'd just as soon have this done…quietly."

Dr. Delaney didn't ask. "Three o'clock."

Holly Barrows arrived a few minutes before her appointment. Slade had half expected her not to show and realized he was going to have to start believing at least some of what she said.

The checkup didn't take long. Dr. Delaney came out of the examining room and motioned for Slade to follow him into his office.

"Close the door," he said as he went around behind his desk.

Slade didn't like the look on the older man's face.

"She delivered a baby in the last month or so. Is that what you wanted to know?"

Sweet heaven. Slade felt light-headed. His baby. Holly had been telling the truth.

"There was quite a lot of tearing," Dr. Delaney continued. "The baby could have been overly large. Either there wasn't time for an episiotomy or…one just wasn't done. I would imagine she was in a lot of pain during the delivery."

Slade felt a cold anger fill him. "You're saying the delivery wasn't handled properly?"

Dr. Delaney blinked. "I would have no way of knowing that. The baby could have come too quickly for anything to be done."

"Or the doctor could have bungled it." Slade knew

how doctors hung together. Especially when the word *malpractice* started floating around.

"Do you know who delivered this baby?" Dr. Delaney asked in answer.

He shook his head. Maybe a midwife. Maybe monsters. "But believe me, I intend to find out."

It wasn't until he and Holly left the office that Slade realized he'd forgotten to ask Dr. Delaney about the man in Marcella Rawlins's life.

"Are you all right?" he asked Holly once they were outside.

She looked over at him and he sensed something different about her. She didn't look as much like a sleepwalker. "Did you get the proof you needed?"

"Yes. I'm sorry you had to go through all of that." All of it, including the pregnancy and delivery without him.

"Where to next?" she asked, her eyes glinting with what appeared to be a combination of anger and stubborn resolve. This wasn't easy for her, he could see that. But she wasn't backing down. It reminded him of the Holly Barrows he'd known. And that was something he didn't need to be reminded of.

He hadn't planned to take her with him, but he changed his mind. "The hospital. I want to find out who supposedly delivered your baby."

Dr. Eric Wiltse didn't look anything like a doctor. He wore jeans, a T-shirt and a Carhartt jacket. His face was tanned and his sun-bleached hair hadn't even started to gray at the temples. It was pulled back in a ponytail. How he'd ended up in Dry Creek, Slade could only wonder. His office was in the new building at the edge of town but this morning he was making rounds at County Hospital, a small fifteen-bed hospital with an even smaller staff because of the holiday.

"Dr. Wiltse?" Slade inquired, although he'd already seen the man's name tag. He stepped in front of Wiltse, blocking his way.

The doctor, not much older than Slade, seemed more annoyed than surprised as he glanced from Slade to Holly. He didn't seem to recognize her.

"We just need a moment of your time," Slade said, pushing open a supply-room door and shoving the good doctor in.

"Hey, what the—" That was all Dr. Wiltse got out before Slade grabbed a handful of the man's shirt and shoved him against a shelf full of towels.

"I understand you were the emergency-room doctor the night Holly Barrows delivered her baby," Slade said. "I don't have a lot of time and even less patience."

The doctor's eyes widened as he took in Holly again. "This is against all hospital pol—"

"The delivery. Were you assisted? Did you deliver the baby by yourself? If you want, Ms. Barrows here will sign whatever papers you need to release you from any oaths you might have taken, Doctor."

"And who will keep me from filing assault charges against you?" the doctor asked, jerking free of Slade's grasp. But he didn't try to leave the supply room. Nor did he look like he was going to put up a fuss.

"I'm sorry, but I don't remember you," he said to Holly. Memory loss seemed to be going around. "When did you deliver?"

"Halloween night. I was told my baby was stillborn."

His eyes narrowed and he nodded, recollection sparking in his expression. "Yes. You look…different."

His gaze came back to Slade's, a hardness to it. "I assume you're the father?"

Slade assumed the same thing, but said nothing.

The doctor continued. "Yes, I remember now. The male infant was stillborn."

A son. Slade felt sick, filled with a terrible sense of loss. The baby had been stillborn. His baby. His baby and Holly's. And, as much as he didn't want to admit it, the sister-in-law had been right. In her grief, Holly had come up with this crazy story about monsters, a secret room and a baby who had lived and was stolen and replaced with a stillborn.

"Then you delivered the baby," Slade said, feeling sick.

The doctor looked surprised as he glanced from Slade to Holly and back again. "She had already given birth when she was brought in, more than likely without any help, from her condition." His look said he thought Slade would have known that. "She was unconscious and suffering from hypothermia. I stitched her up and tried to make her comfortable the best I could."

Slade stared at him. "She didn't give birth here? Then where?"

"I have no idea. I was told that both mother and infant had been found in that condition and some Good Samaritan got them to the hospital." His accusing tone made it clear he wondered where the father of the baby had been during the delivery.

Was there even the slimmest chance that Holly's memories could be real? That their baby was still alive somewhere? He tried to hold down the surge of hope, but it was impossible. However, he reminded himself, this still didn't rule out the possibility that Holly had given birth alone for whatever reason. She would have been frightened and in a great deal of pain and then when the baby was stillborn, she would have had a monstrous amount of guilt—as well as tearing.

"This Good Samaritan, do you know where we can find him?" Slade asked.

"You would have to ask the admitting nurse. I was called in just to check them both and pronounce…" He glanced at Holly, a practiced look of sympathy coming to his gaze. "…the baby stillborn."

"You're sure it was hers?" Slade said.

The doctor blinked. "Who else's baby would it have been? Both mother and child were covered in blood and it was obvious she'd just given birth."

"Then the umbilical cord was still attached?" Slade asked.

Dr. Wiltse looked uncomfortable. "The cord had been severed, but I assumed the mother had done that herself before she passed out."

"Is that normal—to pass out after a delivery?"

The doctor shrugged. "It's possible. It was also cold that night. She was experiencing some hypothermia."

"Could she have been drugged?"

Dr. Wiltse blinked. "I wouldn't know. We don't routinely check for drug use."

"Is there any way to find out?"

The doctor seemed to consider this for a moment. "We always do blood typing on both mother and baby, but we only keep the samples for seven days after the birth."

Blood typing. "Would the blood typing confirm the baby was hers?"

"Possibly. It would depend on the blood type of the mother and father compared to that of the baby."

Slade glanced over at Holly. She looked pale and scared. "Where do we find the admitting nurse from that night?" he asked Wiltse. "Also we'll need a copy of the blood typing."

"You might try the front desk," the doctor said, straightening his clothing as he brought himself up to his full height. "It's the novel way we do things around here, rather than in supply closets." He glanced past Slade to Holly. "I'm sorry about your loss."

She nodded, and Slade pushed open the door to let the doctor pass. "Thanks."

At the front desk, Holly asked for a copy of the blood typing on her and the stillborn baby. She filled out a written request form and was told to check back the next day since that office was closed for Christmas.

The nurse on duty didn't want to, but finally agreed to take a look at the admittance sheet from Halloween.

"I remember that night. It was pretty slow early, but then as usual we got real busy," the nurse said, checking the schedule. "Carolyn Gray was the admitting nurse." She checked the admittance sheet. "Nope. It doesn't say anything about who brought in Holly Barrows or her infant. Sorry."

"Is Carolyn Gray working today?" Slade asked.

"Called in sick." There was suspicion in the nurse's tone. But anyone who called in sick for work on Christmas would be suspect.

"It's urgent we speak with her."

It took a little coaxing but they finally got Carolyn Gray's address and phone number. She lived in an apartment house on Cedar and Spruce streets called The

West Gate. The nurse at the desk tried Carolyn's home phone number but there was no answer.

"She probably has it unplugged," the nurse said, obviously not believing that any more than Slade did. Except he was hoping for Carolyn Gray's sake that she really was sick.

On the way to The West Gate, he tried Holly's midwife again on his cell phone. He'd been trying all morning with the same result. No answer. He was ready to hang up when a female voice came on the line.

"Maria Perez?"

"No, I'm the caretaker," the woman said.

"The caretaker? Has Ms. Perez left town?"

After a long silence, the woman said, "I'm sorry, but Maria Perez was killed in a car wreck."

He sucked in a breath. "When was that?"

"October. I'm just taking care of the place until the estate is settled."

"Can you tell me when exactly she was killed? Was it on Halloween?"

"No, the day before. Would you like a member of her family to call you?"

"No, that won't be necessary." He clicked off the phone and glanced over at Holly, who was waiting expectantly. "Maria Perez was killed in an automobile accident the day *before* Halloween."

"Then she couldn't have been one of the monsters," she said.

"No." But had someone seen to it that Maria Perez wasn't at the birth?

Holly stared out at the passing town, visibly shaken by the news. He didn't have the heart to tell her what he feared they'd find at Carolyn Gray's apartment.

Chapter Four

The West Gate was about as upscale as Dry Creek got. A half-dozen two-story apartment buildings with bay windows and balconies painted the recent color of choice: tan. Slade idly wondered what kind of money nurses made these days as he and Holly found Carolyn Gray's unit, knocked at the door and waited. To neither of their surprises, Carolyn Gray didn't open the door.

"Keep an eye out," he told Holly as he pulled out his lock-pick kit and went to work on the door. It was a simple lock and Carolyn hadn't set her dead bolt.

"Are you sure about this?" Holly asked with obvious apprehension as he opened the door.

"Carolyn?" he called softly.

No answer.

Holly followed him deeper into the apartment.

He had a bad feeling that Carolyn Gray was probably the only one who'd seen the person who'd brought Holly and the baby to the hospital, especially if most everyone else had been busy that night. If Holly was right about her baby being born alive and then stolen, that person wouldn't want to be identified.

By the time he pushed open the bedroom door, he'd pretty well convinced himself that they'd find Carolyn

Gray murdered. Holly's paranoia was definitely catching. And quite possibly with good reason.

Instead of finding a body, though, he found the place had been cleaned out. And in a hurry! Empty drawers hung open, abandoned clothes hangers were piled like pick-up-sticks on the closet floor. Carolyn Gray was gone and it didn't look as if she'd be back. But had she left on her own?

After finding nothing of interest in the apartment, they left.

"There's a chance I'm not crazy, isn't there?" Holly said quietly as she climbed back into his pickup.

"Yeah." A slim chance at this point. But a chance. The same chance that he might now be looking for his own very-alive baby. He didn't want to think what had happened to Carolyn Gray.

"Did you have any tests done while you were pregnant?" he asked, hoping for at least one that might prove the stillborn wasn't hers.

Holly shook her head. "Maria, my midwife, didn't feel it was necessary."

"So you didn't know the sex of your baby?"

"No."

And there were no tests anywhere as proof. How convenient. Other than the blood tests taken at the hospital.

He drove back to Dr. Delaney's office, where they'd left her SUV. "I want to talk to your sister-in-law," he said as he pulled into the parking lot next to her car. "She was there, you said, when you woke up at the hospital. Did you call her? Or did one of the nurses?"

Holly seemed startled by the question. "I don't know. I never even thought to ask."

"I'd like to see your sister-in-law alone, if that's all right with you." He could feel her gaze on him.

"I should tell you that Inez might be difficult."

"You told her you were hiring me?" he asked, wondering if this Inez person was the one who the Santa bell-ringer had been talking to last night.

She shook her head. "I just mentioned to her that I didn't believe the stillborn baby was mine, and that I was concerned about the blanks in my memory. I didn't mention hiring you because I didn't even know myself that I was going to until I did."

"You didn't mention the…monsters?"

She shook her head and looked appalled at the idea. "Can you imagine what Inez would do?"

He couldn't, but obviously she could and it wasn't good.

"I was thinking about your painting," he said. "One of the monsters seemed smaller than the other two. Do you think it's possible it could have been a woman?" He could feel her gaze.

"Yes, that's true, one is smaller." She sounded surprised that he'd noticed. Or surprised that she hadn't.

"But the painting doesn't prove anything. I mean, how can I be sure it's even a real memory?"

She had a point there. But he found it hard to believe anyone could conjure up something like that.

"You aren't thinking it could be Inez, are you?" she asked suddenly. She seemed to find the idea laughable. "When you meet her you'll see why that isn't possible. She can barely get around."

He'd have to take her word for it. Until he met the woman.

"But I do wish now that I'd never said anything to her

about any of this." She let out a sigh and he wondered why she'd confided in him about monster memories—and not her sister-in-law. "You have to understand," she said slowly, "Inez is from an older generation and a very conservative family. My getting pregnant only a month after Allan died was considered a family scandal. Inez doesn't want me making it any worse by pursuing what she sees as lunacy brought on by guilt, grief and postpartum depression."

A possible explanation, one Slade himself had definitely considered. But so far they had no idea where Holly had given birth. Or if the baby taken to the hospital with her was actually hers. And the only other person who might know anything had left town in a hurry. Or had been taken out of town. It was enough to make him definitely suspicious.

Holly's story was crazy. It was a leap to think that some other woman had given birth that night at about the same time and close by in order to make the baby switch. Quite the coincidence. Or maybe not. Just like the midwife getting killed in an auto accident the day before Holly gave birth.

"I hope the blood typing will prove that the baby isn't...yours." He'd almost said *ours*. "Otherwise, we might have to have the body exhumed for DNA testing."

She looked shocked—and scared. "Inez will never allow it. She had the infant buried in the family plot. She even named the little boy after her brother, Allan Wellington."

The sister-in-law had named the baby? "Wellington? Not Barrows?"

"Barrows was my maiden name. I never took Allan's name," she said, and looked away from him out the side window at the passing houses. "We were married less than a week. He was older than I was."

Whoa. She married some old guy who died only a week into the marriage? That didn't sound at all like the woman he'd known. But he reminded himself, he'd never expected her to steal his money and files and skip out on him either. So he couldn't rule out the possibility that Holly had married Allan Wellington for his money. He just hoped he didn't find out that she'd offed the guy.

She fell silent as if she wished she hadn't offered as much information as she had. He wondered if she was worried about what he thought—or suspected. Or if the concern he saw in her expression was over the possibility of riling her sister-in-law.

"You always do what your sister-in-law wants?" he had to ask, studying her. The Holly Barrows he'd known before wouldn't have let some old biddy boss her around.

She seemed surprised by the question. "Inez has a way of wearing you down," she admitted, a sadness to her tone as she opened her side of the pickup to get out.

He glanced around to make sure there was no one around her vehicle, not sure who he was looking for. He doubted he'd recognize the Santa bell-ringer without his beard and hat. But there were few people on the streets with most of the stores closed for the day.

"I'll call you later," he said as she got out. He waited until she drove away, his mind racing. Who was this Inez Wellington that she had so much power over Holly? And Allan Wellington, this man Holly had married, why did his name sound familiar? Something told him the marriage hadn't been a happy one. Or maybe he just wanted to believe that.

He picked up his cell phone and dialed Chief L. T. Curtis.

"What do I need to get a body exhumed?"

"This isn't about your—"

"No." Slade had put his mother's murder on the back burner, but hadn't forgotten about it by any means. "It's for a client of mine. She gave birth recently. There is some question as to whether the baby might have been switched and the wrong baby buried."

Curtis was silent for a moment. "It's happened before. Were these babies born at County Hospital?"

"No, it's complicated," Slade said, not really wanting to get into the details or to involve the police at this point. "What would I need for an exhumation?"

"Enough information to talk a judge into giving me a court order."

In other words, proof. The one thing Slade was real short on.

"I assume this is about that plate you needed run?" the chief asked.

"Yeah. I'm getting the blood typing from the hospital tomorrow and I hope it's questionable enough for a court order."

"I thought she didn't give birth at the hospital," Curtis asked.

"No, but she did go there right after the birth and they routinely take both the mother's and baby's blood."

"This is one hell of a time to ask for an exhumation," Curtis noted.

"Yeah," Slade agreed. "I'll check back with you, but meanwhile I'll be at Shelley's. I'm house-sitting until she gets back from her trip to Tobago." Shelley'd had the chance to spend the rest of the holiday with some friends on the Caribbean island, and Slade had insisted she go. He felt better having her out of town right now.

"Too bad you didn't go with her," the chief said, and hung up.

Slade shook his head as he clicked off his cell phone, started his pickup and headed for Paradise.

INEZ WELLINGTON LIVED some thirty miles from Dry Creek in a condominium in a fancy gated community known as Paradise West. Slade had been born and raised in Montana in a time when only a jackleg log fence—and often not even that—separated the men from the cows. Because of that, he was contemptuous of gated communities and pitied the frightened people who lived behind the bars.

A stoop-shouldered thin woman with a shock of white hair and small dark eyes opened the door. Inez looked to be in her early seventies and had the pinched face of a woman who hadn't got what she wanted out of life. She leaned on a gold-handled cane and eyed him suspiciously.

"Yes?" she said, even though she knew who he was and why he'd come because he'd had to call even to get in the gate.

"I'm Slade Rawlins, the private investigator Holly Barrows hired," he said again, just so there was no misunderstanding.

But from the look of obvious contempt in her gaze, it was clear she knew exactly who he was and why he was there.

"Yes," she said, motioning him in and triple-locking the door behind him. "The only reason I'm bothering to see you at all is for Holly."

Somehow he didn't believe this woman did anything for Holly's benefit. He stood in the small stone foyer. From what he could see of the rest of the condo, the decor was as severe and cold as the woman herself. A few plaques hung on the wall, tributes to one Wellington or another. Obviously a bunch of overachievers.

He couldn't see the Holly Barrows he knew from the two months they'd spent together last year marrying into this family. He couldn't help but be suspicious and wondered just how old Allan Wellington had been.

"I need to ask you a few questions," he said, hoping the old bat would at least offer him a drink.

She pursed her lips as she shuffled past him and into a sitting room, the tip of the cane tapping the floor. She didn't head for the ornate mirrored bar, but took a straight-backed chair and offered him one that looked equally uncomfortable. It was.

"This is such a waste of time and money," she complained as she brushed at her spotless slacks.

"How long have you known Holly Barrows?" he asked, getting right to it. He didn't want to stay here any longer than he had to.

Inez lifted a thin, veined, pale hand from the arm of her chair. "About two years."

"Did you meet her before or after your brother Allan met her?"

She pursed her thin colorless lips, her hand dropping to the arm of the chair. "We met her at a party, I believe, the same night. Did she also tell you they had hoped to have children? Unfortunately, Allan succumbed to a weak heart before he could produce an heir."

An heir. Slade made a mental note to see how much money Holly Barrows had come into after her husband's rather quick demise and was disgusted with himself for his suspicious nature.

"And how old was Allan?" he asked, unable to contain his curiosity any longer.

The old woman stiffened. "Fifty-one."

"You had the same mother and father?"

Her eyes narrowed. "Of course, we did. I was the firstborn. My mother had trouble conceiving. It's one of the reasons Allan dedicated his life to infertility. He was a change-of-life baby, a miracle. Not that it is any of your business."

"I just want to get the lay of the land, so to speak. Holly, is what, twenty-eight? That's quite the age difference."

Inez raised her nose a little higher. "Allan was a very vital fifty-one. Age doesn't always matter if two people are right for each other." She seemed to choke up. "We had no idea there was anything wrong with his heart."

He wondered if Holly had known and mentally kicked himself for suspecting she had. He dropped the subject of age difference, more convinced than ever that Allan and Holly had been anything but "right" for each other. "I take it Allan didn't have any children from an earlier marriage?"

She made a face as if suddenly smelling something unpleasant. "Allan's first love was his career. He was much too busy to even consider marriage, then he met Holly." She made it sound as if Holly had hexed her poor unsuspecting brother. A definite possibility, he thought, as a man who too had been hexed by her.

"You say Allan and Holly met at a party? What party was that?" he asked.

"I can't see what any of this could possibly have to

do with your…investigation into the death of Holly's baby," Inez said. "That *is* what this is about, isn't it?"

"Yes," he admitted. "I was just curious."

And it appeared Inez wasn't about to satisfy any more of that curiosity.

"On Halloween night you got a call to go to the hospital," he said. "Who placed that call to you?"

"One of the nurses, I assume. She said she was calling from County Hospital and that Holly had delivered her baby."

"Then she led you to believe Holly had had the baby at the hospital," Slade asked.

"Well, of course she did," Inez snapped. "Where else would she have had the baby?"

"Well, that's the question isn't it? The doctor says she didn't deliver at the hospital. Someone dropped her and the baby off."

"That's ridiculous."

He could see Inez was the type of woman who believed what she wanted and nothing was going to change her mind.

"Did you see Holly the day she had the baby?"

"No, I hadn't seen her for a couple days. But the baby wasn't due for another week or so."

"The baby came early then?" Was it possible the people who had delivered Holly's baby had induced the labor? Especially if they'd planned to take her baby and had known another woman who was about to deliver a stillborn baby?

He knew that sort of thinking was way out there. But until he found out where Holly had given birth, he had to wonder if anything wasn't possible.

"What difference does any of this make?" Inez demanded. "The baby didn't live. Allan Junior is buried next to his father. There is nothing more to be said about this."

"His father? Allan Junior? But the baby isn't his, right?"

"Playing up to Holly's delusions isn't helping her," Inez continued as if he'd never spoken. "She's come up with this fantasy about another baby out of guilt. She had another man's offspring when she knew how badly poor Allan wanted a child. Of course, she feels guilty."

Slade could see that Inez was doing her best to make Holly feel that way. But as much as he didn't want this old witch to be right, he was also smart enough to know that the other baby, the one Holly thought she remembered, might be nothing more than a guilt-induced fantasy.

But the mystery still remained as to *where* Holly had given birth.

The elderly woman got to her feet with no small effort, signaling that their "meeting" was over. "It's just a case of guilt, grief and postpartum depression for the dearly loved husband she lost and the child she conceived only to appease that loss."

Slade didn't move. *Guilt, grief and postpartum depression.* The exact words Holly had used and in the same order. The words echoed, making his skin crawl.

"What if Holly's right?" he asked quietly. "What if that baby in the ground isn't hers? What if someone has her child?"

"Then good riddance," the old woman snapped, her face contorting into a mask of meanness. "That baby should never have been conceived in the first place. As far as I'm concerned, it's dead and gone and Holly's licentiousness is buried with it." She took a ragged breath, anger putting two slashes of scarlet into her otherwise gray face. "Nor will I hear of this so-called investigation of yours going any farther. Holly gave birth to a stillborn baby. That's the end of it."

It surprised him, not how she felt about Holly's baby, but that she'd bury the child as Allan Junior in the family plot.

"I'm afraid it isn't up to you," he said, slowly getting to his feet. He could see that she wasn't going to take the exhumation well, if it came to that. "If Holly wants to keep looking for her baby then she has that right."

Inez Wellington narrowed her gaze to pinpoints of darkness as she glowered up at him. "I won't see my brother's memory derogated any more than it has been. If Holly continues to behave irrationally, I shall see that she goes back to the sanitarium." She smiled at his surprise. "So she didn't tell you about her breakdown after Allan's death?" She leaned on her cane, a triumphant, self-satisfied look on her pinched face. "Holly committed *herself.* Since she left the doctor's care without a proper release, those commitment papers are still valid." She smiled. "Let me show you out, Mr. Rawlins. Unless you want to see your client locked up indefinitely, you and I won't be crossing paths again."

The intercom buzzed. He saw her glance at her watch, frown, then look at him. The intercom buzzed again. Someone was at the gate.

She walked to the front door, the intercom continuing to buzz, and waited for him. He could see the irritating sound was wearing on her and wondered why she didn't answer it.

Then it struck him: she didn't want him to know who it was!

He stopped to admire one of the commendations on the Wellington wall of fame. Dr. August Wellington had been honored for his work during World War II. How nice.

"Good day, Mr. Rawlins," Inez said pointedly as she opened the door.

"Shouldn't you get that?" The buzzing was getting to him as well. But now he really wanted to know who was at the gate. He waited, pretending to admire another one of the awards.

Glaring, she reached over and hit the intercom. That was the problem with gated communities. The damned guard at the gate.

"Yes?" she demanded.

The loud voice of the overweight guard who'd let Slade in echoed through the entryway. "Dr. O'Brien from Evergreen Institute is down here. He says it's of utmost importance." It was obvious Dr. O'Brien had been giving the guard a hard time from the tone of the man's voice.

"Let him in," Inez snapped, then spun around, no doubt ready to do battle with Slade.

He didn't give her the pleasure. "Good day, *Ms.* Wellington," he said, smiling as he stepped past her through the open doorway.

She slammed the door with a force that knocked the dogwood wreath from the door. Slade didn't bother to pick it up. Let Dr. O'Brien do it. Whoever he was. And what was so urgent? Slade wondered.

As he drove out through Paradise West, he passed a silver BMW coming up the hill too fast. He only glimpsed the man behind the wheel, but he got the impression the good doctor was very upset about something. Was the Evergreen Institute where Holly had been locked up?

Chapter Five

Slade left, thinking how much he'd like to see Inez Wellington locked up indefinitely. But he couldn't shake the terrible feeling that Inez might be right. Holly had been institutionalized? That had to have been right before he met her. Right before she told him she believed someone was trying to kill her.

He felt sick. He'd had doubts before about Holly, about her story, about the two of them. But now…

How could he believe anything Holly had ever told him? Or worse, anything that had happened between them? He felt like a fool. And on top of that, they'd had a baby together. A baby that was now probably buried under another man's name.

Why hadn't Holly mentioned she'd been institutionalized?

All the doubts he'd had about her, along with half a million new ones, flooded him, drowning him. He hadn't realized how badly he'd wanted to believe her. To believe they'd shared a baby and that that baby was alive.

He felt torn and guilty. He'd dropped investigating his mother's murder, not because of the chief's threat, but because of Holly. He'd promised his mother he'd find her killer. It was a promise that had weighed heavily on him all these years. And now he'd discovered a lead, one he wasn't sure he trusted Chief Curtis to follow up on, and he'd bailed out on it to help a woman he couldn't trust, a woman he wasn't sure he'd ever known.

He stopped at the edge of town, trying to think, his head aching. He didn't know who to turn to, who he could trust. Curtis had been like a father to him, but right now Slade didn't trust even him. He couldn't shake the feeling that the chief knew more about Marcella Rawlins's infidelity than he was willing to tell him.

He put his face in his hands, eyes closed, head aching, trying not to think about Holly. But that was like telling himself not to breathe. He knew he should just wash his hands of this case. It was only bound to bring him heartache. It already had.

But if there was even a remote chance that Holly might not be crazy, might be telling the truth— The truth was, he admitted with a curse, he still loved the woman he'd met last Christmas, and, if possible, he wanted to find her again. If she still existed. If she'd ever existed.

He rubbed his hands over his face and sat up. Impulsively, he picked up his cell phone and dialed, determined not to let anything stop him. Dr. Delaney answered on the third ring.

"I'm sorry to bother you again," Slade quickly apologized. "It's about my mother." He could hear Christmas music in the background and faint voices and wished for a moment that he'd had the good sense to wait until after the holidays.

"Yes?" Fred Delaney asked, a slight impatience in his tone.

"I found a new lead in her murder," he said charging ahead blindly. "I think she was seeing someone. A man."

The last words hung in the air for a long moment.

"Marcella?" Delaney asked sounding surprised. "You don't mean having an affair?"

Slade took a breath. "Exactly."

The voices in the background quieted as if whoever was at the house with the doctor was also listening to that end of the conversation. Or maybe Slade just imagined it. The same way he'd imagined the Christmas music playing more softly in the background as if someone had turned it down.

"That doesn't even dignify an answer," Delaney said heatedly. "Obviously you didn't know your mother. Is that all?"

"Yes." It was the only thing he could think to say, surprised by how adamant Delaney had been.

The doctor hung up, the thud of the receiver echoing in Slade's ear.

So much for Dr. Delaney.

He started to put the cell phone down and changed his mind. He'd put this off long enough. He dialed Norma Curtis. She was home, but the chief wasn't. Just as he'd hoped.

"I'm so glad to see you," Norma said when she opened the door. She was a petite woman with snow-white hair, warm brown eyes that always seemed to twinkle, and a round, full face that belied her years.

"I hope you don't mind me stopping by," he said, stomping the snow from his boots.

"You know better than that. I have a pot of coffee on and I just baked sugar cookies. Would you like some?"

He smiled in answer. He'd never been able to turn down her sugar cookies. She'd gotten the recipe from his mother, and he was pretty sure she purposely always kept a batch around for him and Shelley during the holidays for that very reason.

She poured them each a cup of coffee, then motioned to a chair at the kitchen table. He took the cups of hot coffee over, placed them on the table and pulled out a chair for each of them. She followed with a plate of just-iced cookies.

"I suspect this isn't a social call," she said after he'd downed several cookies and sipped politely at his coffee rather than just jump right in with what he'd come for. "What's on your mind?"

He smiled his thanks. With Norma and the chief, he didn't have to beat around the bush. He appreciated that, since patience wasn't his long suit.

He pulled out his mother's letter and handed it to her. "I would imagine the chief already told you about this."

Norma opened the letter, taking note of who it was from, then read it slowly. When she finished, she carefully folded it and put it back in the envelope, avoiding his gaze.

"You knew," he said, surprised almost beyond words.

"Yes," she said. "I knew."

He could see she had no intention of telling him anything. "I've never believed that Roy Vogel killed my mother."

She nodded.

"This man, whoever he was, I feel it in my gut, he's

the one who killed her. And all these years, he's gotten away with it."

She swallowed, tears filled her eyes as she looked away.

"If there is even a chance this man did it, don't you want to see him brought to justice? Please, help me. You were my mother's best friend."

"Oh, Slade."

He felt as if his heart would burst. "Then she *was* having an affair?"

Norma looked at him, her gaze full of compassion and pain. "I don't know that it was an 'affair.'" But the look in her eyes told him otherwise. "I only saw them once. I stopped by the house. Through the window, I saw her in the arms of a man. I only got a glimpse of him before she spotted me. I hurriedly left."

Definitely inconclusive evidence, even to him, that his mother had been having an affair. "That's it?"

"Your mother caught up to me as I was leaving and begged me not to tell anyone." She stopped, the words obviously coming hard. "Especially not your father."

"You never asked her about him?"

"Never. All I knew was that she met him on Tuesday and Thursday afternoons."

Tuesdays and Thursdays? The two days of the week that he and Shelley walked to the police station to meet their father and ride home with him. The two days of the week they all came home late.

Slade felt numb. "Does the chief know?"

She shook her head. "He wouldn't have believed it anyway."

"Then he didn't mention this letter to you?" Slade asked in surprise.

"No, did you expect him to?"

As a matter-of-fact, Slade had. He'd always thought there were no secrets between the chief and Norma.

"Do you have any idea who he might have been?" he asked her. "Any idea at all?"

She shook her head. "I never asked. Your mother never told me. It was better that way."

He wondered if he knew anyone, really *knew* them. "How could my mother live with that sort of deception?" He met Norma's gaze. "How could you?"

She didn't even flinch. He'd expected to see guilt, regret. Instead, her eyes blazed with something he couldn't understand.

"Your mother was happy, happier than I had ever seen her," Norma said with a rush of feeling. "I loved your mother like a sister. I wanted to see her happy."

He couldn't believe what he was hearing. "What about my dad and us kids?"

"I knew she would never leave your father or you kids."

"How do you know that?" Slade demanded.

"She loved him, loved you and Shelley, too much."

He snorted at that. "You don't have an affair if you love your husband."

"Don't you?" she challenged. "Whatever she got from this man, she wasn't getting at home."

He stared at her, shocked by her attitude as much as her words.

"Sometimes a woman needs more than her husband can give her," Norma said. "And I'm not talking about sex."

Slade could only stare at her. "You sound as if you—"

"As if I know firsthand?" She looked away. "It was

a long time ago. I was very young. I wanted children. L.T. was working all the time—"

"I don't want to hear this," Slade said, suddenly getting to his feet, sloshing coffee from his cup onto the tablecloth.

"Maybe you *should* hear this. You are so quick to judge your mother."

He felt as if she'd slapped him. "I'm trying to find my mother's killer. That's all." But he knew she'd struck a chord. He'd seen his mother as perfect. Just as he had Norma. He swore under his breath as he sat back down, took a paper napkin and began to sop up the spilled coffee. "It's just such a shock. You think you know someone…"

Norma nodded. "People are human. Sometimes they make mistakes."

"Was *your* affair a mistake?"

"No," she said flatly.

He stared at her. Was she saying marrying L.T. had been her mistake? "Did you ever think about leaving the chief?" he had to ask.

She dropped her gaze in answer.

He was almost too shocked to ask. "What happened to the man?"

"He was in love with someone else."

He shook his head, beyond disillusioned. "You have no idea what my mother would have done. Maybe she was planning to leave us and the man didn't want that." A thought struck him. "Or maybe he was married and my mother threatened to tell his wife. Whatever happened between my mother and this man, it got her killed. I'd stake my life on it."

He looked at Norma, the last person he would have

expected to have an affair. No, he thought, his mother was the last person. Norma sat with her hands wrapped around her coffee cup, huddled over the hot dark liquid as if needing the heat. He could see the weight of the deception in her shoulders, the weight of keeping her best friend's secret, of keeping her own. "You never told the chief?"

She shook her head, not looking up. "It would have killed him."

Slade nodded. "I think it killed my father."

AS HE DROVE AWAY, Slade thought back to his childhood. His mother always at the stove when he and Shelley came home from school. She seemed always to be cooking. His father was usually late because being a cop wasn't like a desk job.

Had his mother been different on Tuesdays and Thursdays? Not that he could remember. He'd always thought his mother was happy. Had everything been a lie?

Another thought wormed its way in as he drove through town. His father had been a cop. If Joe Rawlins had suspected something, wouldn't he have investigated? What would his father have done if he found out his wife was having an affair?

The thought shook him as he pulled into the visitors parking lot of the Dry Creek Police Department.

"WHY DIDN'T YOU tell me before this just whose family plot you wanted to dig up?" Curtis demanded after Slade told him.

Slade stared dumbly at the chief as he closed the door to the cop's office. "You knew Wellington?"

"Dr. Allan Wellington? Damnation, Slade."

"The baby isn't Allan's. Allan's been dead for over a year," Slade snapped. He didn't want to talk about Allan Wellington. He didn't even want to think about him. Not now. "And who the hell cares about Allan Wellington anyway?"

"I see," Curtis said in his so-that's-the-way-it-is voice. "Judge Koran will care. And Inez Wellington will care a whole hell of a lot."

"Inez doesn't have to find out," Slade said.

"Judge Koran is a good friend of Inez Wellington's. Need I say more?"

No, Slade thought. It seemed Inez had powerful connections.

Curtis let out a loud sigh as he sat back down behind his desk. "Only you would take a client who was married to Allan Damn Wellington, of all people."

He wondered how Curtis knew who Wellington was when Slade had only a vague feeling he'd heard of him.

"Holly was only married to him for a matter of days. And what did he do anyway, invent a cure for cancer or something?" Slade demanded, taking a seat across from the chief. Why hadn't he even thought to ask Holly what kind of doctor her husband had been? He knew the answer to that one. He didn't like the man. Didn't even have to know anything about him to know that.

"He was just one of *the* top infertility doctors in the U.S.," Curtis said. "He made it possible for *thousands* of couples to have children."

Something in the way he'd added the last— "You and Norma went to him."

The expression on the cop's face hardened. Curtis

wouldn't like his wife confiding their secrets. "We were one of the couples he couldn't help. It seems I'm sterile."

Slade heard the bitterness, the disappointment. "I'm sorry."

"I don't want your sympathy," Curtis snapped. "At least I'm not responsible for bringing you into the world."

Slade pulled up a chair and sat down, feeling tired and lost.

"Look, the sister-in-law had the baby named Allan Junior and buried the body in the Wellington family plot."

Curtis lifted a brow. "How did that happen if it wasn't his kid?"

"You'll know when you meet Inez—if you haven't already. Anyway, it turns out that there is a good chance the baby isn't even my client's. But the infant definitely wasn't Allan Wellington's."

"You know that for a fact?"

"For a fact," Slade said meeting his gaze.

The chief let out a long sigh. "The Wellington name means a lot in this country, let alone this area. The doc was like a god. He was on talk shows!"

Slade had heard enough. "Are you saying there isn't any chance of an exhumation if we find we need it to prove the paternity of the baby?"

"We?"

He ignored that. "Well?"

"Wellington's sister will raise holy hell. It won't be easy to get an exhumation. You're going to have to have a damned good reason."

"The baby in that grave could be mine," Slade said. That was the bottom line. "If it's not, then the infant I sired is more than likely on the black market right now. If it hasn't already been sold. Or worse."

Curtis actually seemed at a loss for words. He shook his head. "Well, I'll be damned. This must be that woman you had staying with you this time last year, the one who couldn't remember who she was."

Slade had forgotten that the chief had met Holly. "Yeah." But he hadn't come here to talk about Holly Barrows. He took a breath and let it out slowly. "I just spoke with Norma. She knew about my mother's secret."

The chief looked as if all the wind had been knocked out of him. He got up from behind his desk and went to the window, his back to Slade.

"Norma knew?" he asked, shock and disbelief in his voice. "Does she know who the man was?"

Slade studied the older man from the back, unsure why the cop was taking this so badly. From the beginning, Slade had had a bad feeling that Curtis knew more about this than he was willing to tell him, but never more than at this moment. "She says she doesn't. But I think *you* do."

"Why would you think that?" Curtis asked, his back still to him.

"Gut instinct. Isn't that what you said made a good cop? Isn't that what you told my father all the time?"

The chief didn't answer as he turned slowly around. His face had grayed. He looked older than his years. He moved to his chair and gripped the back, his knuckles white.

"When were you planning to tell me?" Slade asked, fear making his voice sound strangled.

Curtis blinked, then seemed to focus again as if, for

a moment, he'd forgotten Slade was there. "You don't think that I was her— Good Lord, don't you know me better than that?"

"I thought I knew my mother better than that," Slade snapped. "Now I'm not sure I know anyone. Even you."

"I'm going to say this once and then you and I are never going to have this conversation again, is that understood? I wasn't her lover."

Slade wanted desperately to believe him. Anyone but Chief L. T. Curtis. And yet he'd seen the cop's reaction to the news. If, God forbid, it had been L.T., then what did that do to his theory about his mother's lover being the killer? "Why do I get the feeling that you know who was?"

Curtis shook his head. "Your father was like a brother to me. I would have killed for him."

"Did you?" Slade asked.

"I think you'd better go."

Slade didn't move. "It crossed my mind that one of you could have found out that she was seeing someone every Tuesday and Thursday afternoon. One of you could have been waiting. Or both of you. If you found him with her at the house—" He shook his head. "The two of you—"

"I don't have time for this," the chief snapped as he came around his desk, hitting it with his leg, sending several files showering to the floor. He didn't seem to notice as he started past Slade for the door.

Slade grabbed his sleeve. "L.T.," he said, his voice softening at the name he used to call the chief back when Slade was just a boy. "I have to know the truth. No matter what." The words echoed. So close to what Holly had said.

L. T. Curtis jerked his arm free. His eyes hardened to stone, making it clear he was the chief of police, not the man who'd finished raising Slade. "I've reopened your mother's murder investigation based on the new evidence. It's out of your hands now. Don't butt heads with me on this. I could have your license pulled. And I will." He strode to his office door, jerked it open and stomped out.

Slade stared after the man, shaken. The chief had reopened the investigation? Because he now believed that the killer could have been Marcella Rawlins's lover? Or because he wanted to keep Slade from finding out the truth by making the case off-limits?

He started to leave, but bent to pick up the files first. He couldn't miss the photos that had fallen out of one of the files. A half-dozen snapshots of a murder scene. The chief must have been looking at Slade's mother's file when he came in. No wonder the man was worked up.

Agonized, he flipped through the photos, stopping on the last one. A close-up of his mother's hand holding the Christmas ornament she'd pulled from the tree, the last act of her life.

He stared at the tiny golden twin angels. He'd forgotten which ornament she'd grabbed. He'd always just thought she'd been clutching at the tree. But as he looked at the ornament he wondered if she could have possibly been trying to leave them a message.

Twin angels. Wasn't that what she'd always called him and Shelley? Maybe she *had* been trying to tell them something. That she was thinking of him and Shelley, that they were her last thought.

Or maybe she'd just been clutching at anything she could get her hands on—just as he was now.

Chapter Six

As Slade drove toward Pinedale and Holly's studio, the afternoon sun cast long gray shadows across the snow. He could feel the temperature dropping outside the pickup, the windows trying to frost up. He kicked up the heat, his heart heavy, mind racing.

He didn't know what to think. Or who to believe. Nothing had been as it appeared. And now he was doubting people he'd known his whole life.

He pulled up in front of Holly's place, cut the engine and stared up at the apartment, the dying light shining on the window like a two-way mirror. He felt sick with worry and couldn't tell which case had filled him with such dread. Maybe both. His mother's murder pulled at him. Just as everything Inez had told him about Holly did. He feared what Holly would tell him when he confronted her. Feared what he'd find out about his mother.

But, like Holly, he had to know the truth. No matter what. And there was no turning back now for either of them.

For a few minutes, he sat in his pickup, immobilized by a terrible foreboding. Then, slowly, he opened the door and stepped out, not bothering to zip his ski jacket against the bite of the icy breeze. The sun had set, leaving the eastern sky a cold, clear blue. By morning, everything would be covered in thick frost. Or snow. Again.

He thought about the fireplace at Shelley's and about sitting in front of it drinking a glass of Scotch, just staring into the flames. He wanted to forget about everything, just for a little while.

But he couldn't. Not until he talked to Holly. He tried not to think about the baby. The one buried in the Wellington family plot as Allan Junior. Or the one Holly claimed was alive and taken by three monsters in masks.

His steps heavy as he climbed the stairs to her apartment, he felt a weight, like a premonition of bad things to come. For the first time, he wondered if the chief wasn't right. Maybe he didn't want to know who'd killed his mother. Or the truth about Holly Barrows, either.

But he'd opened Pandora's box, and he couldn't close it until he knew what was inside. It was a character flaw, his inability to leave things unfinished. His mother's murder was one of them. Holly Barrows was the other.

Holly gave him a faint worried smile as she let him in. "So you met Inez."

He wanted to ask her what had possessed her to marry into a family like that. But he feared he already knew. "I need you to tell me about your husband's insurance policy. And your breakdown."

She winced and turned back toward the living room. "I would imagine you could use a drink."

He watched her sort through the bottles of liquor in a small bar against the wall, passing up several different Scotches to pull out a bottle of Glenlivet and pour him a couple of inches. Straight. No ice. She poured herself a cola on ice.

"How did you know I drink Glenlivet?" he asked when she handed him his drink.

She seemed startled by the question. "I'm sorry, I should have asked. I just assumed—"

"—that all private eyes drink that brand?"

She dropped into one of the wingback chairs, the glass in her hand shaking. She looked scared. He knew the feeling.

"I don't know why I do half the things I do, if you want to know the truth." Her voice broke as she glanced up at him, tears in her eyes. "I'm sure you wonder why I married a man twenty-three years my senior. I wish I could tell you." She dropped her gaze, took a drink and licked her lips before looking at him again.

"I wish I could tell you a lot of things." This time she met his gaze unflinchingly, reminding him of the woman he'd known a year ago, making him remember the feel of her lips on his mouth, on his skin. Holly had been scared last year, convinced someone was trying to kill her. But there had been a strength of will about her that he'd admired. She'd had no intention of giving up without a fight.

This was the first time he'd seen it in this Holly. It stirred all the old feelings and some new ones. This was the kind of woman he could fall in love with. *Had* fallen in love with.

"I have blank spaces in my memory," she said, even her voice sounded stronger, more determined. "Some are only for a few hours. Others…are for…longer. I married Allan after one of those blanks. To answer your question, my husband left me well-off financially. But that wasn't the reason I married him."

"Inez said you and Allan were trying to have a baby, an heir."

She jerked back, startled, her gaze nothing short of shocked. "She told you that?"

"Was it a secret?" he asked.

"No, it's just…not…true. Allan and I never—" She waved a hand through the air. "—consummated the marriage. Allan had no interest in…any of that."

Slade stared at her, more than a little confused. "Then why did he marry you? I mean—"

"I know what you mean. To be truthful, I have no idea how we got together or why." She smiled ruefully. "I've never admitted that before. At least not aloud. I can't explain why I've done a lot of things I've done in the last year."

He held her gaze, debating whether to tell her he was one of the "things" she'd done.

"I didn't marry him for his money, if that's what you're thinking," she said.

"How long have you had these…lapses in memory?" he asked, not about to touch the other.

She looked as if she wasn't quite ready to drop the other subject, but then sighed and said, "They started a little over a year ago."

"About the time you met Allan?" he guessed.

"Yes," she said, frowning. "I guess it was."

He could think of a variety of causes for memory loss. Epilepsy. Alcohol blackouts. Multiple personality disorder. Head trauma. Psychosomatic amnesia.

But he'd always been suspicious of coincidence. And it was one hell of a coincidence that Holly's memory loss had started about the time she'd met Allan and his sister, Inez.

"Have you seen a doctor about it?"

She nodded. "Dozens of specialists, including Dr. Parris at Evergreen Institute. They all say the same thing. There is nothing *physically* wrong with me. That leaves Inez's theory that I make up the memory losses to cover things I've done that I'm ashamed of."

He wondered if she was ashamed of what she'd done with him. "Evergreen Institute?" Where the upset Dr. O'Brien visiting Inez earlier had been from. "Is that the sanitarium you were committed to?"

"Yes, Inez talked me into it." She let out a humorless laugh. "My so-called breakdown was nothing more than relief. And regret that I'd ever married Allan in the first place. And, of course, confusion because of the memory loss."

"Did you ever see a Dr. O'Brien at Evergreen?"

"No," she said. "He must be new."

Slade had hoped for a tie-in. No such luck. Other than the one common denominator: Evergreen.

Holly seemed upset. "Inez believed Allan and I were trying to have an heir?"

He nodded, watching her closely.

"Well, he got his heir, didn't he?" she said.

"But it's not his baby."

"No. But it also doesn't seem to make any difference to her. Does that make any sense at all?"

"No." He was glad she'd noticed. If she'd been crazy, she wouldn't have noticed, right? He studied her, wondering if she didn't seem a little less blank this evening. "You told Dr. Parris at Evergreen Institute about your memory loss?"

"Of course. It had only just begun then, and Dr. Parris assured me it was probably caused by the trauma of losing my husband so soon after the marriage." She looked up at Slade. "I knew it wasn't that. But I had lost my mother just six months before that. My father died when I was nineteen, so my mother was the only family I had."

"I know what it's like to lose your parents," he said. "I lost my mother when I was twelve, and my father not quite a year later."

"I'm sorry." She looked down at her hands clutched in her lap.

"Did the stay at Evergreen help?" he asked, suspecting he'd met her last year about the time she'd left the place—and according to Inez, without properly signing herself out. Interesting.

"Not really."

"Why did you leave without checking out of the place?" Slade asked.

She frowned. "I don't know. It's odd that I would run away from there. Evergreen Institute is really more like a fancy spa than a sanitarium. I mostly just slept and read and rested."

He was glad to hear that. He'd been imagining an asylum with padded cells and straitjackets and screams in the night. He worried that when Holly found out about their past, it might send her back there.

"But I don't remember leaving Evergreen—or how or why."

"Inez made it pretty clear how she felt about your pregnancy," he said, still wondering what hold the older woman had over Holly.

"My pregnancy was none of her business," Holly

replied hotly. "I'm not ashamed of anything. Least of all that. I should never have told her that I didn't think that baby at the hospital was mine. Or about the memory loss. She's afraid people will think I'm crazy. But maybe I am crazy."

"Do *you* think you're crazy?"

She hesitated, but only for a second. "No. I think... I don't know what to think."

He doubted that. She had a theory, she just wasn't ready to voice it, probably because it was so off-the-wall. Nor was he sure he was ready to hear it.

"Has your memory ever come back after one of these blanks before?"

She shook her head. "Only the birth of my baby. If it's really a memory."

But she had remembered something else. She'd remembered that he drank Glenlivet Scotch straight. It was a small thing, but it made him wonder if her memory wasn't coming back and that was why she'd come to him. Again. He hoped to hell he was right.

But the question was, what had caused her memory loss in the first place?

"How long do these memory lapses last?" he asked.

She shrugged. "They vary. Usually I just sense holes in my memory. Time has passed but I can't remember what happened during that time—obviously something when you realize you're pregnant and yet can't remember even meeting a man, let alone..." She looked away, seeming embarrassed. "That's why it's so hard for me to believe that the memories of the birth were real. I'd never remembered anything, not even vaguely."

"Maybe it was the trauma that caused you to remember," he suggested, wanting to believe something was spurring the return of her memory.

"Or maybe it was love? I wanted this baby more than anything. I'm sure that seems odd to you, considering that I don't know who the baby's father is. But while I can remember nothing of those missing months, I have a good feeling about the man who—" She broke off and took a drink of her cola.

She had a good feeling about him? Was that why subconsciously she'd known to hire him to find the baby? Their baby?

Or was she pulling his string? The thought had crossed his mind, especially in light of the day he'd had. He didn't trust anyone. He was even beginning to question his own instincts.

"I don't know what is real anymore," she said, sounding close to tears as she got up to refill his glass. He hadn't even realized he'd drained it. "Just that I have to find my baby. And save her."

He watched her go to the bar again, wondering what she had to save her baby from. And knew she had to be wondering the same thing. He started. "Her?"

Holly didn't respond.

He watched her turn. Her eyes were vacant, her face ashen. "Holly?"

He'd known a boy in school who was epileptic. Rather than seizures, he had lapses where he would just zone out for short periods of time. Looking at Holly now, he was reminded of that boy.

"Holly?"

She blinked, her eyes luminous and filled with fear as her gaze came back into focus. "I said her," she whispered, sounding scared. "Oh, I remember her."

He waited, almost afraid of what she'd say.

"During the delivery, something was wrong. They were rushing around, frantic. I tried to see what was going on. I thought something was wrong with my baby." Tears welled in her eyes. "One of them left the room. When the door opened, I heard another woman, another patient. She sounded as if she was in labor."

She looked down at the glass of Glenlivet in her hand as if she couldn't remember how it got there, then handed it to him. But instead of returning to her chair and her cola, she walked into the studio.

He sat for a moment, not sure if he should follow her. To his surprise, she returned a moment later, carrying a large canvas. He knew without seeing the painted side what it was. He could tell by the way she held it, the way she frowned down at the work in her hands.

"That's why I believed the room was soundproofed," she said more to herself than to him as she propped the painting against the wall and moved back to stare at it.

The light cast an eerie glow over the acrylic monsters huddled around the delivery-room scene. He was filled with even more dread each time he saw the work. There was something so raw about the paint slashes, so chilling. He felt a cold draft move through the room.

The three monsters were huddled together, hunched over, waiting with obvious anticipation, making it hard to distinguish their shapes beneath the garb they wore. They could have been men. Or women. Or just figments of Holly Barrows's nightmarish imagination.

"I remember being scared," she continued in a hushed voice as if the walls might be listening, her gaze on that damned painting. "Something was wrong with my delivery. Or my baby." She glanced back at him, no doubt knowing what he was thinking. That all of these images could amount to nothing more than what Inez Wellington believed they did.

"I must have blanked out again. I woke to the sound of a baby crying," she said slowly as if the memory was playing out in her head. "I opened my eyes. My baby was lying on a small table near my bed. She was kicking her legs." Holly turned back to him. If she was putting all of this on, she was one damned good actress. She must have seen his skepticism, though.

"I *saw* her," she whispered fiercely. "She was close enough I could see her birthmark."

He felt a chill. "A birthmark?"

She nodded, her gaze still glazed as if focusing inward. "It was heart-shaped and on the calf of her right leg and…she had this little dimple in her cheek." She blinked. "How could I remember something like that if it wasn't real?" There was a pleading in her tone. "How is that possible to see something so clearly, if it never happened? My baby was a little girl—not a boy—and she was alive. I saw her!"

A heart-shaped birthmark and dimples. He stared at her, his pulse pounding in his ears. The dimples were genetic; he knew that well enough. But a birthmark?

Shivering, he reached up to rub the back of his neck, suddenly anxious to leave. But he couldn't leave without Holly. He wasn't sure what was going on. And he had no proof that anyone was after her. No more than he'd had this time last year. All he knew was that he didn't feel safe. And neither should she.

"I don't think you should stay here alone," he said, wondering how he could convince her.

She looked at him in surprise. "You're starting to believe me, aren't you?"

What did he believe? That she'd given birth to their baby? That monsters had stolen the baby? That the baby had dimples and a birthmark just like his twin sister Shelley's? And that Holly Barrows was starting to remember, not only the delivery but—him?

"Yeah," he said as he got to his feet and walked to the window. Parting the curtains, he looked out into the empty street. He believed that the Santa on the street below his office on Christmas Eve had reported to someone that Holly Barrows's memory was returning. That meant he also believed that someone had tried to get Holly to forget.

Not that what he believed mattered in the least. Because what the hell did he know? But he wanted to help her. How much assistance she needed was still debatable. All he knew was that he'd have a better chance of helping her if the monsters in the painting were real than if they were in her head. And if the monsters were real, then he had to find their baby—and fast. Too much time had already been lost.

He tried not to think about it. The whole thing scared the hell out of him. Because it was so far out there. And because it didn't make any sense. If the specialists couldn't find any physical reason for her memory lapses, then that left psychological causes.

And that opened up a whole new can of worms. The woman he'd met a year ago certainly had been different from this one. But a whole different personality? He didn't buy it.

"Look, let's say you're right and these...monsters stole your baby," he said carefully. "If they find out you're starting to remember the delivery—and them—well, I'd just feel better if you weren't alone right now."

She seemed to study him. "You think I should go stay with my sister-in-law?"

God, no. That couldn't be good for anyone. He didn't like the fact that Inez had talked her into committing herself. Holly seemed too smart for that. He wondered again what hold Inez had over her. "No. I think you should come stay with me."

He had so many questions, but he figured she didn't have any more answers than he did. And the questions could wait until he got her to Shelley's. He parted the curtains again, taking one last look out the window. The street was still empty, the sky clear and cold, making the fallen snow glow.

As he turned from the window, he heard a sound. "What are you doing?" he demanded, surprised by the intensity in his voice.

She jumped and almost dropped the glass of cola in her hand, the small plastic container in the other. "I was just going to take my pill."

He stepped to her and took the container. "Where did you get these?"

"It's an old prescription that Allan wrote for me. Inez had it refilled…"

He read the label. Xanax. The name of the drug meant nothing to him. No big surprise considering he never took anything stronger than aspirin and was unfamiliar with prescription drugs. "What are they for?"

"They relax me and make me feel better."

"What happens if you don't take them?"

She stared at him in obvious surprise. "I don't know. I—" She looked at the pill she'd spilled into her hand just before he'd stopped her. "Yesterday, I forgot the pills here at the house. Obviously they don't help my memory." She tried to laugh at her joke but instead tears welled up in her eyes.

He removed the baby-blue oblong pill from her hand, putting it back into the container and snapping the lid shut again. "I'd like to have a pharmacist take a look at these before you take any more."

She nodded, her eyes large and scared. "You don't think the pills—?" She picked up her cola and took a drink, her hands trembling.

"I don't know. Maybe I'm just being paranoid but I'd feel better if you didn't take them until I can have someone check them out—" He stopped. She was crying softly. "I'm sorry if I upset you."

"No," she said, hurriedly wiping at her tears. "You haven't upset me. Just the opposite. I can't tell you what it means to have someone believe me." She forced a smile. "Your paranoia is such a comfort, since for so long all I've had is my own."

He started to reach for her, to drag her from her chair and into his arms to hold her and comfort her as he would have a year ago. But he stopped himself, reminded that she didn't know him. Didn't remember the intimacies they'd shared. He was a stranger to her. A stranger who knew every curve, every hollow, every inch of her.

But she didn't know that either.

And it was that secret between them that made him walk to the window instead and look out again rather than try to comfort her. He could more easily have comforted a total stranger than he could have Holly Barrows at that moment.

"Your gallery is closed for the holiday, right?" he asked, his back to her.

"Yes?"

"We'll go to my sister's. She has a large house with lots of room. She's going to be out of town until after the New Year." He wouldn't be putting Shelley in danger. The house had a good security system, unlike his apartment. And Shelley kept the freezer stocked.

He turned when she didn't answer and saw her look around her home, her studio, as if assessing how she could leave it, let alone go with a man she had only met a night before. A man she had little reason to trust.

He followed her gaze to the painting again. If anything, it was more frightening—and convincing—than when he'd first seen it.

"I think you'd better bring that along." He didn't want anyone else seeing the canvas. Especially the ghouls in the painting. If they existed. If she was really remembering them, it was best they didn't know to what extent.

Holly still hadn't moved, he realized. She sat, holding her glass in both hands, her gaze finally coming back to it and the dark liquid. "I have to ask you something. I don't mean to sound ungrateful. Or suspicious, but why *do* you believe me?"

It was obvious she was having some doubts about coming with him. He'd hoped she would remember the two of them on her own. But he didn't have the time to wait for that now. He wanted out of here. He wanted her out of here.

"Do you recall where you were this time last year?" he asked. "From Christmas Eve through February twenty-sixth?"

Her head jerked up. She said nothing as her surprised gaze locked with his, but her face paled, and she gripped the glass, her hands shaking.

"My twin sister, Shelley, has a birthmark exactly like the one you described." He reached down and pulled up his pant leg. "So do I. And we both have the Rawlinses' dimples."

She dropped the glass. It hit the hardwood floor, shattering like a gunshot, ice shooting out across the hardwood floor, the last of the cola puddling at her feet. But she didn't move. She stared at him as if seeing a ghost. No doubt the ghost of Christmas past.

Chapter Seven

Holly stared at him dumbstruck. *"You?"* she cried, all the ramifications coming at mach-two speed.

He nodded.

"The baby?" If she'd really been with this man from Christmas Eve through February twenty-sixth then— "It's *ours?*"

"So it seems." He didn't sound pleased about that. But who could blame him?

Her head swam. She gripped the arms of the chair trying to still the trembling in her hands, in her body. "I hired you not knowing you were the man who— How is that possible?" she asked, her voice barely a whisper.

"I'd like to think you remembered me. Remembered…us."

Her gaze flew up to meet his. Heat rushed through her. This man *knew* her. Intimately. Her face flamed and she dropped her gaze. "I don't know what to say to you."

"You don't have to say anything," he said easily, his voice deep and almost familiar.

She felt a chill as something like a memory skittered across her bare skin. Fingers, warm, soothing, searching. Bodies welded together with desire and sweat—

She looked away, shocked. It couldn't have been a memory. Couldn't have been her.

"How did we meet?" she asked, almost afraid to hear it for fear he'd picked her up in some bar. Or worse.

She stole a glance at him and reminded herself that she'd had a good feeling about the man who'd fathered her baby. Then she listened as he recounted a story about a woman coming out of a storm on Christmas Eve a year ago, how his pickup had almost hit her, and when he'd jumped out of his truck, he'd found her lying in the snow with no knowledge of who she was—just the conviction that someone was trying to kill her.

Holly closed her eyes. How could she have spent all that time with him and not remember? "And I was with you from Christmas Eve through February twenty-sixth?"

"Yes."

She took a breath. "We slept together."

"We were lovers," he said softly.

She opened her eyes. "Then it wasn't…"

"A one-night stand? Hardly." His gaze hardened. "We were in love."

The words reverberated through her. In love? She couldn't have been more surprised if he'd said he'd bought her from a wagonload of roving gypsies.

He must have seen her surprise. His jaw tightened, eyes narrowing, and she realized she'd hurt him. "I was trying to find out who you were, but you seemed to have been dropped from the sky. Then I turned my back one day and you were gone with two hundred dollars of my money and some files from my office."

She stared at him, horrified. First she'd fallen into bed with this man, convinced him she loved him, then stolen from him like a common thief? Tears burned her eyes. Maybe Inez was right. Maybe she forgot because of the horrible things she'd done. Or maybe none of this was true. Just as the baby the nurse had handed her at the hospital hadn't been hers.

"Excuse me if I find this hard to believe...." She wouldn't have believed anything he'd told her and would have called him a liar to his face, but he knew the exact dates of the days she'd lost. And there was the baby. Not to mention that flash, that image of the two of them, bodies locked in passion. It had felt like more than a memory as if the image was somehow branded not only in her brain, but on her skin. And there was the birth-mark, the dimples.

And yet, she trusted none of it. "If we were in love, why would I steal from you and leave?" she challenged.

He shook his head, his gaze never leaving her face. "I was hoping you'd tell *me* that."

She heard the bitterness in his voice. It was obvious he didn't trust her. Why should he? She'd hurt him. No, not her. "I don't know this other woman you say you met this time last year."

"Unless you have a twin sister..."

"I'm sure you know I don't," she said, then continued with her train of thought. "Nor can I imagine doing the things you say I've done."

"Can't you?" he asked, his gaze refuting her claim. She felt herself blush under the heat of it.

"Then explain why you came to me again on Christmas Eve," he demanded. "Why you came to me for help a second time."

"I can't explain it," she said. "I just had this feeling I *had* to hire you. I'm not sure anymore what decisions are mine and which are—" She stopped, afraid to voice the fear that had haunted her for so long.

He was watching her, waiting.

She swallowed, realizing she had nothing to lose at this point. "I feel as if someone is…making me do things, things I normally wouldn't do, things I can't even imagine doing, and then wiping the memory from my mind."

"Things you regret?"

"Yes," she said, then added quickly, "Not everything. Not the baby. Not—" She waved a hand through the air. "I just need to remember, to understand what has been happening to me." She fought back tears, hating the need to cry. Crying had done nothing to relieve the pain. Or to help.

She rubbed at her eyes and looked away from him, the doubts haunting her. She needed her pill. The thought surprised her. "The thing is, why would anyone go to the trouble of…making me do *anything?*" she asked, more to herself than him. "What could they possibly have to gain?"

"A baby."

She turned to blink at him. "All of this for a baby?" she asked, incredulous.

He shrugged. "What else have they gained? It wouldn't be the first time somebody wanted a baby so desperately that they did something…heinous."

"Why my…our baby?" Her voice broke.

He shook his head. "It doesn't make any more sense to me than it does you. If someone wanted a baby that badly, they could hire a surrogate. Or adopt. Or just steal an infant from a shopping cart at the grocery store."

She shuddered at the thought. And yet her baby had

been stolen by monsters and she'd seen it happen. Or had she?

"You think it's possible then?" she asked.

"That someone is manipulating you?"

She nodded.

"I think anything is possible at this point."

She felt a wave of relief wash over her. Followed by a jolt of sudden fear. "But what if—" She stopped, realizing what she was going to say as she remembered the feeling she'd had driving by his office Christmas Eve. She'd felt as if she *had* to stop and hire him. Did that mean that she trusted him? That subconsciously, she'd known to go to him again because he was the one person who would help her?

Or had the feeling been *too* strong? Almost as if she didn't have a mind of her own? Almost as if someone had sent her to him?

The thought hit too close to what she'd come to suspect.

"Did anyone try to kill me while I was with you?" she asked, afraid she already knew the answer.

"No."

"Or try to find me?"

He frowned. "No."

"Didn't you find that strange?"

He seemed to study her. "Not at the time. I'm pretty good at what I do."

She suspected he was. But maybe he didn't realize who he was dealing with. Possibly, *what* he was dealing with.

"What if you were set up?" she asked. "*We* were set up? I could have been sent to you. Just as I might have been again this Christmas Eve."

"Nice present," he said with a lift of his brow.

"I'm serious. I felt as if I *had* to contact you." She swallowed, the words sounding ludicrous even to her ears and yet they'd been words she'd said over and over again in her mind. "I'm not sure they aren't controlling me right now and there is nothing I can do to stop them."

"I think you're wrong about that," he said, surprising her. "I think you're starting to remember." He sounded so calm and rational. "First you remembered our baby. Then that Scotch you served me tonight. You picked the brand I drink. You had no way of knowing that except to have remembered it."

She stared at him, wanting desperately to grab hold of any line of hope he threw her.

"I think you're starting to remember me," he continued, his gaze as soft as his voice. "Remembering us. And that's why you came to me. Again."

She smiled in spite of herself. "I like your theory better than mine."

He returned her smile. He had a nice smile. Oh, how she wished she could remember him. Desperately wished it. Because he was asking her to put her trust in him, to put her life in his hands. And she knew if he was the enemy, then he was the worst possible one she could imagine. The father of her baby. A man who knew her better than she knew herself.

"Why didn't you tell me yesterday who you were?" She hadn't meant to make it sound so much like an accusation.

"You weren't ready to hear it yet," he said matter-of-factly.

She watched him go to the window to pull back the

curtain a fraction of an inch and look out, wondering what he was looking for, worse, what he was thinking.

"I hate to imagine what you must think of me," she said. "I stole from you." She knew that was the least of it.

"You and I spent over two months together," he said without turning around. "I got to know you pretty well."

Even without the flashes of possible memory, she could well imagine, since their liaison had ended in a pregnancy. "How is that possible when *I* didn't even know me?"

He turned to look at her, his gaze softening. "The woman I knew was kind, generous, funny, smart, strong, brave, and…very…" The intensity of his gaze could have burned her. "…passionate."

He'd just described a stranger. In her twenty-eight years, she'd never known passion. And yet when she looked into his eyes, she felt something. Just as she had when she'd thought she'd envisioned the two of them locked in each other's arms.

She watched his features soften, a hint of a smile turning up the corners of his lips. "I liked you a lot, all things considered," he said, lightening his tone.

"All things considered?"

"Considering you had no past and thought someone was trying to kill you."

She let out a rueful laugh, still not sure she dared believe him. "I must have made for a fun date."

"Yeah, you were," he said. "Come on. Let's get your things together. Whatever is going on, I'll feel a whole lot safer away from here."

Unsteadily, she got to her feet, avoiding the broken glass and spilled cola. Was he just being protective? Or did he really believe her? "The more I learn, the more I think I *am* crazy."

"Well, I'm becoming more convinced that you aren't," he said. "Here, let me get that." He went to the kitchen and came back with a broom, dustpan and towel. "Once we get the blood typing results from the hospital lab—"

"We might not have to exhume the body?" she asked, her voice full of hope.

He nodded as he finished cleaning up her spilled cola.

Then Inez might not have to know. Otherwise…otherwise, what would Inez do? What could she do? And why did the thought scare Holly so much?

"Inez can't stop the exhumation if it comes to that," he said, as if reading her mind. "This baby isn't related to her either way." He glanced up. "You should know, your sister-in-law has threatened to see you institutionalized again if you don't drop this."

"I guess I shouldn't be surprised. I warned you about her."

"Inez doesn't scare me."

But she should, Holly thought with a shudder.

"I guess we'll find out just how powerful your sister-in-law is," he said. "Hurry and pack. I want to get out of here."

She went to her bedroom and pulled out her suitcase, her mind racing. Doubts overwhelmed her as she packed. But she thought of her baby. If she hoped to get her little girl back, she knew she needed all the help she could get. And she *had* to believe in someone. Mostly, she was sick of being scared. She wanted to be that woman Slade had described, strong and brave.

She took a deep breath. Maybe she *was* starting to remember. Maybe Slade Rawlins was proof of it. He had the same birthmark—and the dimples. He drank Glenlivet and somehow she'd known that. And, more important, he seemed to believe her.

She realized how desperately she wanted to trust him. He gave her hope that they would find their baby and finally still the ache inside her. Hope that they would stop whoever was behind this and end the lapses in her memory, the fear for her sanity.

And yet, she knew it could all be a trap. If she was right, if someone had been messing with her mind— If that were true, couldn't they have programmed her to do exactly what she was doing at this moment—packing to go with Slade?

She fought that horrible thought. No, she'd started to remember, and that's why the monsters had had the Santa bell-ringer outside Slade's office. They were afraid her memory was coming back, and that when that happened, she would go to Slade.

But now the monsters knew she'd done just that. They would try to stop her. And what better way than to use Slade to do it? a voice inside her head taunted. To pretend her baby had been his? To pretend they had been lovers? To pretend he was taking her some place safe?

She froze at the thought, a silk blouse in her hands. She brought the cool cloth to her face, fighting back tears. What if Slade was one of them? Wasn't that her greatest fear? That he would give her hope, then snatch it away?

"Are you all right?" he asked from the doorway.

She turned, startled, and nodded slowly.

He moved to her in two long strides and, taking the blouse from her fingers, folded it into the suitcase. "We can buy you more clothes if you need them," he said, snapping the case closed.

She nodded, feeling her eyes burn. She willed herself not to cry. She'd shed a million tears since the "lapses" in memory had begun, all wasted. Another million since the loss of her baby.

He touched her arm and she turned into him, stepping into his arms as naturally as if she'd done it dozens of times before. Maybe she had.

He held her, his arms strong and yet gentle around her. "We're going to find them," he breathed against her hair. "Find our baby if she's out there. And bring down those bastards. I promise."

The heat in his voice matched the warmth of his body. She leaned into his strength, soaking it in, telling herself she had to trust the instinct that had told her the father of her baby had been a good man.

And if it turned out her instincts were wrong about Slade Rawlins?

Chapter Eight

Her heart quickened as her body responded to being in his arms, the scent and feel of him teasing her memory. Taunting her with flashes of the two of them, naked as jaybirds, sweating and panting and—

She pulled back, stunned by the images. Even more stunned by the wanton desire she'd felt. But could she trust any of it? She looked at him, intensely aware just how dangerous this man could be if her instincts were wrong about him.

"I'm ready to go," she said, the break in her voice betraying her.

"Good," he said, but didn't move as he reached to thumb a tear from her cheek, the pad of his thumb rough against her skin, both comforting and disturbing.

His look told of an intimacy between them that frightened—and fascinated—her. Her heart drummed, her pulse a roar in her ears as his gaze moved slowly, deliberately to her lips.

He was going to kiss her! The thought sent a bolt of panic through her. Panic. And a stirring inside her that made her weak. She stared, hypnotized as his full, sensual mouth hovered only a breath over hers, afraid he would kiss her, afraid he wouldn't.

She waited, time suspended, her heart pounding as if to escape her chest. Would his kiss ignite that passion? Would it prove she was the woman he'd told her she'd been? The passionate, loving, blissfully satisfied woman she yearned to be? But mostly, would his kiss prove that he was telling her the truth, not only about him, but them?

Or would it only confirm that it had all been a lie, including a passion they had never shared.

His gaze rose again to her eyes and she knew. He wasn't going to kiss her. She felt a stab of disappointment and turned away, groping for her suitcase.

His hand brushed hers as he reached around her to take the case from her. She thought she felt a tremor course through him as they touched.

"Come on," he said, his voice as rough as his thumb had been. He dragged the suitcase from the bed and carried it into the living room.

Shaken and weak, her blood a dull thrum in her ears, she remembered her cosmetic case in the bathroom and went to get it, needing a few moments to herself.

When she came back out, he had the suitcase and the painting by the door. The broken glass was all cleared up.

The phone rang. Her gaze sprang to his. "Should I answer it?" she asked in a whisper, the apartment suddenly too quiet, the ringing too loud.

He seemed to hesitate. "Do you have caller ID?"

She nodded and stepped into the studio. "It's Inez."

"Wait." The phone rang again. "Do you have an extension?" he asked so close behind her he startled her.

"In the bedroom."

She let it ring once more, then picked up, watching

through the bedroom door as he did the same. "Hello?" Her voice sounded strange even to her.

"Holly?" Inez demanded in a tone that belied her years. "What's wrong?"

She wanted to laugh. Everything was wrong. Inez, of all people, should know that. But Inez put anything unpleasant from her mind, ordering the world to be the way she wanted it, come hell or high water.

That rankled Holly and shocked her. She usually had more patience with Inez. And yet part of her wondered why it hadn't rankled long before now.

"What could be wrong?" she asked unable to hide the sarcasm, which, of course, was wasted on Inez.

"You sound…strange."

She felt strange.

Slade gave her a warning look.

"I must have dozed off," she improvised.

He nodded his approval.

"I was worried about you," Inez said. Holly heard the clear, sharp tap of the elderly woman's cane on stone. "I was concerned that you might have gone off on another one of your…escapades."

Escapades? Was she referring to the pregnancy? Or the loss of the baby? Or was the "escapade" the hiring of Slade Rawlins? She felt a hot coal of resentment burning deep in her as she looked over at Slade. Why had she put up with Inez's interference in her life for so long?

"I want to talk to you about the private detective you hired," Inez said.

"This really isn't a good time," Holly said.

Inez continued as if she hadn't heard. Or didn't care. "I know this last year has been hard on you, losing Allan, then the baby."

"The baby had nothing to do with Allan," she heard herself say. "Or you." She'd never talked to Inez like this and she heard the shock in the older woman's tone.

"I beg your pardon?"

"I'm sorry, I'm just tired," Holly said, backing off just as quickly, just as she'd always done. Only this time it had been a sudden fear that had stopped her. A fear that upsetting Inez was…dangerous. Where had that come from?

She met Slade's gaze. He was frowning, watching her intently.

"Of course you're tired," Inez agreed, sounding wary. "You're just distraught. You always are when you do something foolish. I have tried to weather these episodes with you, dear, but this last one…. I know you haven't been yourself and I try to make allowances for you. Obviously, dear Allan's death hit you much harder than even you want to admit. That really is when this all started."

No, Holly thought. It all started about the time she met Allan. And Inez.

"But hiring a private investigator," Inez was saying. "It's so…common and…seedy."

Holly started to speak but Inez cut her off.

"Let's not discuss it further. It will only upset you to realize you've had yet another one of those embarrassing and tragic lapses in judgment. You're blaming yourself for the death of that baby, and Lord knows the guilt over that unfortunate pregnancy had to have contributed to the stillbirth. How could it not? But hiring a detective…?"

Holly thought she'd scream if she heard another word. Her head ached and she felt sick to her stomach.

"Hiring Slade Rawlins wasn't a mistake." She didn't sound convincing even to her own ears, and she didn't dare look at Slade.

"There is no need to try to justify it," Inez said. "We all have made mistakes. Certainly none as extraordinary as yours," she added with a sniff, "but still, just look at the decisions you've made since Allan's death. They speak for themselves. I know Dr. Parris discussed your guilt over Allan's death with you at the sanitarium."

Holly shot a look at Slade again, embarrassed. Inez seemed intent on reminding her of the sanitarium and her mental instability, but now she was insinuating that Holly was responsible for Allan's death. Hadn't Slade already questioned the same thing?

"Dr. Parris never said anything to me about my having guilt over Allan's death," she said defensively.

Silence. "I was there on several occasions during your sessions when he discussed this very thing with you, Holly. Are you telling me you don't...remember?"

Panic raced through her, making her limbs weak with fear. She gripped the phone tighter, her hand trembling. That wasn't possible. She would have remembered. Or would she have?

Even more panicked, she suddenly realized that she couldn't remember *any* sessions with Dr. Parris when Inez had been there.

"Holly?" Inez asked. She sounded too cheerful as if she had Holly right where she wanted her. Scared. Unsure. Beaten back. Holly was shocked even to think it. Inez was her only family now.

A bubble of hope floated up from inside her as a clear, strong thought surfaced: Dr. Parris had seen her during these blanks in her memory. A sense of relief swept over her. First Slade. And now Dr. Parris. Only, Dr. Parris was a trained psychiatrist. He could make sense of this.

"Holly, are you still there?"

"Yes," she finally managed to say. She couldn't wait to tell Slade about Dr. Parris, about her lack of memory of the sessions with Inez and what it might mean.

"I had just forgotten those sessions with you and Dr. Parris," she lied, not sure why.

Inez was silent for a moment. "You mustn't castigate yourself. Once you're well… In the meantime, I've taken care of it. I'll have my lawyer pay off that private detective so he won't be bothering you anymore and I've spoken with Dr. O'Brien. He agrees rest is probably the best thing for you now especially since—"

"Dr. O'Brien?"

"Yes, he feels he can be much more beneficial to you than Dr. Parris. You need help, Holly, and please don't argue—"

"I think you're right," Holly interrupted.

"You do?!"

Even from this distance she could see the tightening of the muscles in Slade's jaw, the hard anger in his gaze and his manner. He, too, seemed to be clutching the phone.

"Yes," Holly said, suddenly feeling better. Her head still ached and her stomach was still upset, but her mind felt clearer than it had in a long time.

"Well, that's good that you agree." Inez sounded off balance, even a little disappointed, as if she'd expected a fight and had been ready for it. "You don't even have to recommit yourself since your old commitment papers are still in force. I think you should return to Evergreen at once. For your own good. Dr. O'Brien said he would make arrangements to have you picked up tonight."

Slade was shaking his head.

"I'm really too tired tonight," Holly said.

"That's exactly why you need to—"

"Why don't I call you in the morning?" Holly said, getting a nod from Slade. "I just want to go to bed now."

"You're sure?" Inez said, an edge to her voice. She wasn't pleased. "You *are* taking your pills, aren't you?"

"Yes," she said, shooting a glanced at Slade. He had that hard angry expression on his face again. Was he right about the pills?

"They've made me very drowsy for some reason," she said. She softened her tone. "I really do appreciate your concern, and I think you're right about me needing help."

Inez seemed hesitant to hang up as if not convinced. "Well, then, get a good night's sleep. I'll talk to you first thing in the morning."

"Yes, I'll do that." She hung up, feeling worn-out by the encounter with her sister-in-law, and she realized it was always like this. So much easier to give in to Inez than to fight her. Just as it had been with Allan.

Only this time, she hadn't given in. The thought buoyed her spirits.

"No wonder you think someone has been manipulating you," Slade said as he came into the living room. "But what the hell was that about recommitting yourself?"

"I agreed I needed help—not recommitting. I remembered something," she said excitedly. "When Inez was talking about Dr. Parris and Evergreen I realized

I couldn't recall *any* discussions I had with him while Inez was there."

Slade lifted a brow. "That's a memory?"

"Don't you see, I must have been in one of my… blanks. But that means Dr. Parris would have observed this. He might know what was wrong with me based on the way I was acting." She saw Slade's expression. "I know what you're thinking. That I have some sort of personality disorder." It certainly sounded as though that was the case to her.

"You don't have a split personality," he said, sounding more convinced than she had expected. "I don't know much about personality disorders, I'll admit. And you're different from the Holly Barrows I knew this time last year. But not *that* much different. In fact, you seem to be becoming more and more like her all the time. With the kind of stress you've been under, I think it would be just the opposite. Once all your memory returns—" He broke off and shrugged, his gaze gliding over her face as gentle and warm as a caress.

She felt a rush of gratitude. Whether he was right or not, he was trying to reassure her and she appreciated that more than he could know.

And she did feel…different. Stronger. Just standing up to Inez— "Dr. Parris should be able to help us," she said again, hoping it were true.

He smiled at her, making her wonder if he thought her naive. "Maybe he does have some answers," he agreed, perhaps a little too easily. "Or this Dr. O'Brien your sister-in-law was so anxious for you to see might have."

She watched him walk to the door and pick up her suitcase and the painting, his words echoing in her ears.

"Let's get out of here." He seemed even more anxious to get away from her apartment now. Because of Inez's call? Was he worried Inez and Dr. O'Brien wouldn't wait until morning to come get her?

She realized why Slade had wanted her to take the call. He suspected Inez was somehow involved. And now, it seemed, he was even more suspicious.

Holly quickly followed after him, not so sure he wasn't right. Just before he turned out the light, the glare caught on her painting, highlighting the monsters huddled at the end of the bed. She had a flash of realization so strong it stunned her. Not a memory. But a feeling. Almost a warning. Something *had* been controlling her life. Something much more malevolent than Inez Wellington.

But the question was: Was it still in control?

Chapter Nine

Slade stepped out into the night, Holly right behind
him. The top of the stairs were dark, the sky overhead
a deep cold midnight blue, the December air frosty
and wet with the promise of snow. Slade descended
the steps, the day-old snow crunchy under his feet. He
stopped at the bottom of the stairs to search the street,
knowing that what he feared most wasn't waiting for
them in the dark.

He took Holly's hand as they crossed the street to
his pickup. He shivered, but he knew it wasn't from the
cold. He was scared as hell.

Once behind the wheel, he started the truck and
pulled away, watching in his rearview mirror.

"You're scaring me," she whispered, turning to look
back.

"Sorry," he said. "Just force of habit."

But he couldn't help checking his rearview mirror
as they left Pinedale, couldn't help feeling as though
something was after them, because deep inside he believed something was.

No car lights flashed on behind them. But then he
didn't think Dr. O'Brien had had time to round up a
couple of orderlies and a straitjacket and drive to Pine-

dale. There was no doubt in Slade's mind though, that the doctor was on his way.

Nor did he think they were being followed. At least not in the usual way. What was after them was too high-tech to use something as primitive as a tail.

Pinedale seemed hunkered down for the night as he drove through the deserted streets. After all, it was cold and late and Christmas Day.

Hard as it was to admit, he knew the fear he felt had nothing to do with Dr. O'Brien, Inez or even monsters dressed like Halloween ghouls. It was the fear he was in over his head. That Holly didn't need a private investigator. That she needed a shrink. That he was dead wrong and that, by getting her hopes up, he was only going to make things worse.

But he'd heard Inez on the phone. He had the pills in his pocket. Even if the pills didn't prove what he suspected they would, any fool could see that Holly was in trouble.

Selfishly he wanted the Holly he'd known—and who'd known him—back. And he wanted their baby. If Holly's memory of the little girl with dimples was real.

Unfortunately, he was smart enough to know that once whoever was behind this found out Holly was starting to remember, they might decide to get rid of the evidence. And that had him running scared.

He couldn't wait to get to Shelley's and build a fire. He needed the warmth of his sister's house tonight. A hard cold block of ice had settled inside him. He'd never felt so cold.

But he had one stop he had to make first. He glanced over at Holly. She sat huddled against the door staring out at the darkness, her face pale in the glow of the dash lights. He wondered what it must be like, having huge chunks of time you couldn't account for. Doing things that you wouldn't normally do. And waking up not knowing what you'd done. Or why.

The worst of it was, he didn't want to believe what was staring him dead in the face. He was one of those missing chunks of time. He wasn't sure who or what had kept him hidden inside her. And that had him worried. He hoped it would be as simple as the bottle of prescription drugs now snug in his pocket. But he doubted he could get that lucky.

"WHY ARE WE HERE?" Holly asked, unable to hide her sudden irrational fear, as he pulled into the hospital parking lot.

He glanced over at her in surprise. "Sorry, I should have told you. I want to find out if anyone has heard from the admitting nurse who was on duty Halloween night."

"Carolyn Gray." Holly had a bad feeling about the nurse. One she couldn't shake. "Do you think—" She hated to even voice her fear. "—that they would actually…kill someone to keep them quiet about this?"

"They stole our child, Holly. That's kidnapping, a federal offense. But still a step down from murder." He seemed to be studying her. "Are you afraid to go in the hospital? Because of the commitment papers?"

She shook her head. "Just bad memories." She'd been fine earlier in the day when they'd come here. She couldn't explain what had her scared now. She'd never been afraid of the dark. Or hospitals. Or monsters. But she was now.

"Don't worry," he said, his voice as soft as his gaze

in the semidarkness of the pickup cab. "I won't let them take you back to the Institute. No matter what I have to do."

Impulsively she reached over to give his gloved hand lying on the seat between them a gentle squeeze. "Thank you. For everything."

"Thank me when this is all over," he said, looking uncomfortable. "I haven't done much to protect you so far."

They found the head nurse in the break room, sitting at one of a half-dozen round tables, reading. Mrs. Lander, according to her name tag, was a small woman dressed in an immaculate white uniform. Just the way she was sitting, her back ramrod straight and a no-|nonsense aura about her, told Holly she would not be easy to work for.

"Yes?" Mrs. Lander inquired, as she looked up from her reading.

Slade showed her his identification. "Carolyn Gray is a key witness in a case I'm involved in. Have you heard from her?"

"Yes," Mrs. Lander said, a great deal of disapproval in that one word. "She called yesterday to say she had taken another job and wouldn't be coming back."

The same day Holly and Slade had gone to Carolyn's apartment to find it hastily cleaned out.

"You spoke to her yourself?" he asked.

"No, the receptionist took a message."

"But the receptionist was sure it was Carolyn Gray?" he persisted.

Mrs. Lander looked from Slade to Holly. "The receptionist is new, but the woman called herself Carolyn Gray. Why would she lie?"

Holly wandered over to a bulletin board full of photos, afraid Carolyn Gray might have had an accident like the midwife, Maria Perez.

"You don't seem surprised Carolyn Gray would leave without giving proper notice," Slade was saying.

"No."

"Why is that?"

"Why the interest, Mr. Rawlins?"

"I think she might be in trouble."

"I think with Carolyn that goes without saying," the nurse retorted. "Carolyn didn't take her job seriously. There were times she would leave her post without telling anyone. We often had a hard time finding her when we needed her."

Interesting. Holly moved along the bulletin board, wondering if Carolyn Gray was one of the nurses in the candid snapshots tacked up there. The snapshots made the hospital look like a fun place to work.

"What do you think the problem was?" Slade asked.

"Men. She liked men, especially doctors. I caught her once coming out of an empty room with one of the doctors."

"Which doctor?" he asked.

"I really can't say." Holly heard the scrape of a chair and turned to see the nurse on her feet. She closed the book she'd been reading. "I really need to get back to work."

"Can you tell us what Carolyn Gray looks like?" Holly asked. "Maybe there's a photo of her over here?" She motioned to the bulletin board.

The nurse seemed to hesitate, but walked over to the snapshots. She lifted several that had been tacked over older ones. "This one wouldn't help you. She's wearing a costume."

Holly felt her heart leap in her chest. "May I see it?"

The nurse removed the photo and handed it to her. "It was taken during the Halloween party."

Holly almost dropped the photograph. In between two other people dressed as monsters was the exact costumed monster Holly had painted.

"Which one is Carolyn?" she managed to ask, surprised her voice didn't betray her.

Nurse Lander pointed to the monster in the middle—the one from Holly's painting. "That's Carolyn. For what it's worth."

It was worth a lot. Holly handed the photo to Slade. He looked as taken aback as she was.

The nurse rummaged through the other snapshots on the board, grumbling about what a mess the bulletin board was. "Here's one of Carolyn. It's a fair likeness."

Holly took the photo the nurse handed her. It was of a woman in a nurse's uniform standing behind the admitting desk. Carolyn Gray was a buxom woman, tall and broad-shouldered. In her costume, Holly could have mistaken her for a man.

She handed the photo to Slade.

"Why monsters?" he asked.

"Actually, I think it was Carolyn's idea," Nurse Lander said. "She was in charge of the party. She *made* her costume, which goes to show she has some talent— at least for the hideous. I think she won Most Frightening for it."

Holly could believe that. She searched the rest of the photos from the party on the bulletin board for the other two monsters, but unlike Carolyn's costume, the rest were pretty uninspired—and none of them familiar.

"Do you mind if we take these two with us?" Slade asked Lander. "I'd be happy to return them."

The nurse shook her head. "They're all yours," she said with a wave of her hand. She glanced at her watch. "If there is nothing else—"

"Just one thing, Carolyn would have had a check coming so I'm sure she gave you a forwarding address when she called, or at least her new place of work, so you could send it. If she really was the person who called."

The nurse pursed her lips. "She asked that her check be sent to Evergreen Institute. That's all I can tell you." Mrs. Lander swept past him and out the door.

"Sweet heaven," he breathed, after the nurse left, his gaze coming to Holly.

She nodded, still shaking. "Carolyn Gray was one of the monsters and now she's working at Evergreen."

"Do you recognize any of the other masks?" he asked.

She shook her head. The photos had been taken at random and probably not everyone had ended up on the bulletin board—even if they'd all been photographed. Or maybe all the monsters hadn't been part of the hospital crew that night.

"Anyone dressed as a monster would have had the run of the hospital Halloween night," she said. "All they would have had to do was dress as monsters."

"My thought exactly. They could have brought you in and no one would have been the wiser."

"Except Carolyn. She was at the birth, Slade."

He nodded. "The always-disappearing-from-her-post

Carolyn Gray. You had to have given birth close to the hospital then. Close enough that Carolyn could slip out and slip back in without causing too much notice."

"And even if she did get noticed, everyone would just think she was meeting one of the doctors," Holly added. "Too bad we don't know which doctor."

ONE MONSTER DOWN, Slade thought as he drove to his sister's. Two to go.

All he needed now was to find out where Holly had given birth. He still didn't have squat for proof, but there was no doubt in his mind it was all true.

Carolyn Gray was working at Evergreen. Or at least having her check sent there.

He felt even more jumpy, more anxious, after seeing the photos at the hospital. *Don't think there are no crocodiles just because the water is calm,* his father used to say.

And the water was anything but calm.

He got out and opened the garage door, then drove inside and waited until the door closed solidly behind them before he felt safe.

"Holly?" She hadn't moved. Hadn't said a word since they'd left the hospital. And now she sat staring blindly at the front wall of Shelley's garage as if... "Holly?"

"I knew one of them," she whispered.

He didn't have to ask who she meant. The monsters.

"I remember thinking, 'My God, I recognize that voice.'"

Sweet heaven. "A man's or a woman's voice?" he asked quietly.

She shook her head slowly. "I just remember feeling disbelief. Like, how can this be? Not this person?" She glanced over at him. "Someone I know took our baby. Someone I...trusted."

Like a doctor, he thought.

As he got out of the truck and led Holly into Shelley's house, he realized that this monster she'd recognized might also be someone *he* knew.

He got Holly settled in the spare bedroom, then went downstairs to scare up some dinner. He'd just put one of Shelley's casseroles in the microwave to defrost, when the phone rang. For just a moment, he thought it might be Inez. But Inez couldn't have found him that quickly.

He and Shelley didn't share the same last name. Shelley had been married for a very short time. Her husband had been killed in a motorcycle accident. She'd kept his last name, Baxter.

"Hello?"

Silence.

"Hello?" He felt the hair rise on the back of his neck. His heart pounded even though he told himself there was nothing to fear about a wrong number. Right.

The person at the other end of the line hung up. He stood holding the phone, trying to rationalize his sudden fear. It could have been anyone. It even could have been a real wrong number. Or a bad connection at the other end. It could have been Shelley calling from Tobago.

He started to put the phone down, but changed his mind. He dialed Chief L. T. Curtis, uncomfortable with the way he and the chief had left it earlier and needing someone sane to talk to. That is, if Curtis was still talking to him.

"What do you know about Evergreen Institute?" he asked when Curtis answered, keeping things pretty much as they'd been for years.

If the chief was surprised to hear from him, it didn't show in his voice. "You finally decided to see a shrink?" the cop asked. "Probably not such a bad idea."

The defrost timer went off on the microwave. "I'm serious," Slade said as he hit the Reheat button.

"You're always serious. Do you have any understanding of the word *holiday?*" Curtis asked with a sigh.

"Not really," Slade said, realizing how true that was. "My client spent some time at Evergreen Institute."

"The case involving the alleged switched babies?"

"Yeah. What do you know about the place?"

"Why don't you ask your client?" the chief said. "Her late husband started Evergreen Institute."

"Dr. Allan Wellington?" He couldn't have been more surprised. Why hadn't Holly mentioned that to him?

"We're talking about the same place, right? That place that looks like a fortress off the old road to Butte?" Fenced and gated. Like the condos where Inez lived.

"The place with the stone spires sticking up out of the pines," Curtis said. "It was once a high-dollar private residence, built by some out-of-stater with more money than good sense—or taste. Dr. Allan Wellington bought it and started the first infertility clinic of its kind in this part of Montana."

Dr. Allan Wellington. Everywhere Slade turned, he kept running into the doctor. He didn't believe it was a coincidence. And to make matters worse, Curtis even sounded in awe of the good doctor. Sweet heaven.

"It's not an infertility clinic anymore, right?"

"No, it's a funny farm. More like a mountain resort than Warm Springs though," Curtis said. Warm Springs was where the state mental hospital was located.

"What about a Dr. Parris? Or a Dr. O'Brien?"

"Why the sudden interest in Evergreen?" the chief asked. "What does it have to do with your baby-switching case?"

"Maybe nothing," Slade said truthfully. He didn't want to talk about the case. Not yet. "Anything new on my mother?"

"No," Curtis said too quickly.

Not that he thought the chief would tell him until it was official anyway.

He tried to think of something else to say. "Happy New Year" just didn't quite cut it. "Well, thanks." He replaced the receiver, suddenly tired, mentally shot.

He wondered if there *was* something new on his mother's case. He knew the chief's threat was a good one and the last thing he wanted to do was lose his P.I. license. He'd have to be very careful when he started looking for his mother's lover again.

But right now all he could think about was Holly and their baby. First thing in the morning they'd drive up to Evergreen and see Dr. Parris. No, first thing, Slade thought, he'd have Holly's pills checked out by a pharmacist to see exactly what they were—and what they were capable of doing to her.

He didn't relish the idea of going to Evergreen to see Dr. Parris. He was scared about what the doctor would tell him about Holly. But what really had him worried was that Parris or O'Brien might try to recommit Holly. And Slade wasn't about to let that happen.

The phone rang, making him jump.

"I had some spare time, so I dug out the blood typing the lab did on Holly Barrows and her baby," a woman said, keeping her voice down as if she didn't want any-

one to hear her. "I'm not supposed to do this but you
seemed so worried…."

It took him a moment to realize it was the hospital
admitting nurse he and Holly had met earlier. "What
did you find out?" he asked, his heart in his throat.

"Mother and baby aren't related."

Slade felt his legs give under him. He sat down
heavily at the breakfast bar, closed his eyes and took a
deep breath. "You're sure?"

"Well, it's not as accurate as DNA testing, but hey,
it's what they used to use before all these fancy-pants
tests. You see, the way it works is this. If the mother
has— Look, just trust me. The baby isn't hers. I've got
to go. You did *not* hear this from me. When you pick
up the report tomorrow, act surprised."

"One more question. Were there any other births on
Halloween?" He could hear her rustling papers. "That's
odd. No other births."

"Thank you. You didn't happen to call earlier, did
you?"

"No," she said. "This was the first chance I got."

He hung up, shaken to the soles of his boots. The
stillborn male infant wasn't Holly's. Wasn't theirs. Their
baby could be alive! And now, he had enough evidence
to get a court order to open the casket if it came to that.

He took a couple more deep breaths, just trying to
deal with the fact that the baby buried in the Wellington family plot wasn't his. He felt weak with relief,
weak with fear.

Knowing didn't help them find their baby. It just
proved Holly had been right.

He turned at the sound of footsteps behind him.
Holly appeared in the kitchen doorway, her wild mane

of dark hair pulled back into a ponytail, her face looking freshly washed and shiny clean sans any makeup.

He felt as if struck by lightning. For just a moment he let himself hope— But when his gaze locked with hers, he could see that there was still no recognition of what had been between them. No memory.

He tried to hide his disappointment. "Dinner's almost ready," he said brightly. "I hope you're hungry."

She nodded, looking uncomfortable. "I heard the phone."

He tried to think of a way to tell her without just blurting it out. "The hospital called. One of the nurses decided to check the blood typing for us."

She paled, one hand reaching out to grip the countertop.

"The baby wasn't yours."

Her face relaxed in a swell of relief, her eyes filling. "I was right."

He nodded, desperately wanting to hold her and comfort her in some way. While it was a relief to know that the stillborn baby hadn't been theirs, it was almost more frightening not to know what had happened to their baby.

"Our baby is alive," she whispered. He prayed she was right. "Dr. Parris will help me get my memory back. I know at least one of the monsters. Once we find him…"

Or Carolyn, Slade thought. *If* Dr. Parris could get Holly's memory back. *If* they could find the monsters. *If* the monsters knew what happened to the baby. Way too many ifs, Slade thought miserably.

The timer went off on the microwave. "Let's try to eat something now and not talk about it." He knew she probably wasn't any more hungry than he was, but they both had to eat. He turned to pull the casserole out, burning his fingers. Grabbing up two pot holders, he took the casserole to the table.

She didn't argue. "I like your sister's house," she said, as if trying to make conversation, as she wandered around Shelley's kitchen. "Where do you live?"

"In an apartment next to my office. It's pretty basic." The truth was he wasn't much of a nester. He liked his sparsely furnished apartment just fine, no matter what Chief Curtis had said. Or Shelley. "I think you have a fear of domesticity," the chief had said the first time he'd seen the place. "Either that or no taste."

"It's fear of commitment," Shelley had said.

"I happen to like simplicity," Slade had argued. "If I want homey, I can always go to Shelley's."

Curtis and Shelley had looked at each other knowingly. "It's fear," they'd both said in unison.

Holly leaned against the breakfast counter. "Where did we…"

"Make love? Here. At my place. And a variety of other places—in- and outdoors."

Holly seemed shocked by that information. "Outdoors this time of the year?"

"You didn't know you had it in you?" Obviously not.

She blushed and looked away, and he could have bitten his tongue.

"I just can't imagine—"

But he'd seen the answer in her eyes. She *had* imagined. Imagined the two of them.

She turned away as if to inspect Shelley's cookie-cutter collection on the kitchen wall. His mother and sister had been collectors. Maybe that's why Slade didn't collect. At least not "things."

Her hair was still wet from a shower. As he moved back into the kitchen, he picked up the scent of her. She smelled like spring, fresh and new as the first bright blades of green grass. He felt starved for an end to the winter—that had only just begun—and her.

As she started to step past him toward the table, he caught her arm. She stopped, motionless. He turned her slowly to him, her blue eyes as clear and deep as a mountain lake.

She wore jeans and a T-shirt. Both accentuated a full, rounded body he knew intimately.

The kiss was inevitable. He needed her in his arms, needed to hold her and feel her warmth, needed that reassurance that they would somehow get through this. Together. No matter what happened. He needed that more than his next breath.

He lost himself in her eyes, in all that blue as if untethered from earth and suddenly airborne. Her lips parted, the tiniest of sighs escaping.

His mouth lowered slowly, achingly to hers. A light brush. Their eyes locked as his lips again hovered over hers.

Her breath quickened, her heart answering the feverish beat of his own as he pulled her closer. He grazed her mouth again, heard her intake of breath, then her lips parted, opening to him. He dropped his mouth over hers, losing himself in the familiar touch and taste of her, finding in her the sanctuary he so desperately needed right now.

But he knew the kiss was more than finding sanctuary. It could possibly bring him back the woman he loved.

He was startled when she suddenly pulled away, her palms on his chest as she pushed back from him.

He looked down at her in surprise. Her face flamed and she lowered her lashes as if embarrassed. He cursed himself, backing up against the kitchen counter. She looked shaken, her cheeks flushed, her hands trembling.

"I'm sorry," he said, silently cursing himself again. "I told myself I wouldn't do that."

She shook her head, biting at her lower lip.

"You don't remember me, let alone us," he said in a rush. "You hired me to find out about the baby, not—" He slashed the air with his hand. "I'm sorry."

"It wasn't your fault. I wanted—" She looked away. "I was hoping the kiss would make me remember—"

Obviously it hadn't. "I guess I was hoping that, too." Hoping they could find comfort in each other's arms. He wouldn't admit it to her, but he was afraid, afraid that no matter what they did it would be too late for their baby.

"We should eat," he said.

She nodded and he moved aside to let her go to the table.

They ate, picking at their food, trying to make small talk, the kiss between them.

"You didn't mention that Dr. Allan Wellington started Evergreen Institute."

She looked up from her plate. "I just assumed you knew. Is it a problem?"

He shook his head. Dr. Allan Wellington was a thorn in his side that just kept needling at him.

She insisted on helping clean up the dishes. He caught her yawning and could see how drained she was.

"Go on up to bed. I can finish this."

She glanced toward the stairs.

"Don't worry, I'll be right down the hall if you need me. You're safe. Get a good night's sleep. Tomorrow we'll go see Dr. Parris. That is, if you want me to go with you?"

"Oh, yes," she said quickly. "Please."

He nodded, wanting to reassure her in some way, but feeling unable to. At least not with simple words. "Good night."

He watched her ascend the stairs, feeling anxious, antsy. He desperately needed to do something, something more than he had so far, something more than talk to a shrink.

She stopped part way up and turned to look back at him. "Thank you."

He had done so little, felt so confused, so frustrated. But at least he didn't have blank spaces in his life. Except for the last year when he hadn't been able to find her.

"Good night."

"Good night," he said again, knowing it would be anything but.

She disappeared up the stairs, him watching after her, longing in every cell of his body. He yearned for the Holly Barrows he'd known. For a moment during the kiss, he'd thought he'd felt the old Holly struggling to get out. But he could have imagined it, he'd wanted it so badly.

He swore, desperate to destroy whoever, whatever had done this to her. To them. Something or someone had brought her back into his life. Either her memory…

or something dark and malignant could have sent her to him, setting them both up for a terrible fall.

What scared him was that if someone really had been controlling Holly, couldn't that person snatch her away again? Only this time, Holly might not be able to find her way back to him. This time, she might be as lost to him as their baby was to them at this moment.

With a chill, he thought of Inez's call and her insistence that Holly check herself back into Evergreen. Why had Inez been so adamant? Did she truly believe Holly was sick? Or did she know that Holly had begun to remember and was now a liability?

Slade stood in the kitchen, scared of his own thoughts. Did he really believe someone had…brainwashed Holly? He went into Shelley's office, booted up the computer and found the phone number on a web page under Government Conspiracies.

He hadn't seen Charley Watts in years, not since Charley told him he thought the government was controlling Montana's weather. Slade didn't think the government was that organized.

Charley, a good twenty years older than Slade, had been the hippie janitor at the high school until—as locals called it—"Charley went off the deep end."

The deep end was government conspiracies.

But right now Charley was the only person Slade could think of to dare even mention the words *mind control* to.

"Hey!" Charley said when he answered. "Sure I remember you! What's going on?"

"What do you know about mind control?" Slade said, diving right in.

Charley laughed. "What don't I know? Hey, man,

I've spent years researching it." He rattled off some code names. "What do you want to know?"

Slade was afraid he'd made a mistake calling Charley, but asked, "What are those?"

"Government research projects, man. You can't believe it."

No, Slade thought, he couldn't.

"We're talking using LSD on civilians to see if they would tell their darkest secrets, brainwashing with radiation, low frequency and ultrasonics, hypnosis—"

"Hypnosis?" Slade heard himself ask.

"Oh, yeah, man. Hypnosis and all kinds of drugs trying to come up with a hypnotic resistance to torture. They implanted secrets with special codes, turned regular men into killing machines and then erased their memories, man."

"They can erase memory? Give someone a drug, then hypnotize them and make them do things they normally wouldn't do, then erase their memory?"

"Dude, they can do a lot more than that!"

"But I always heard that a person wouldn't do anything under hypnosis that he wouldn't do under normal circumstances," Slade said.

"Yeah? Well, here's how it works," Charley said. "Say a guy who would never commit murder is drafted into a war. He'll kill on the battlefield, right? Well, with hypnosis, the mind becomes the battlefield. If we're told under hypnosis that it's a battlefield, then we believe it and will kill. It's all a matter of perception."

Slade frowned. Was it really possible? "But I thought with hypnosis you went into an—" He parroted the words he'd found in the dictionary. "—altered state of focused awareness. I've always heard that you're awake, you know what's going on and you can stop it at any time."

"You've been talking to shrinks, man," Charley said. "If they can tell you you can't lift your damned arm during hypnosis, and, no kiddin', you try and you can't lift your arm, then why can't they make you do just about anything? It's all about mind control."

"It sounds so…crazy."

"Listen, governments have been doing this kind of research for years and lying about the outcome. They can program a guy to kill, they can get him to keep government secrets because he doesn't really 'know' anything on a conscious level—"

"Like the movie with Frank Sinatra, *The Manchurian Candidate?*" Except that was fiction. Pure fiction, right?

"Kinda. Problem with hypnotically induced amnesia, there's memory leaks and that's how we've found out so much about what they've been doing. Guys are remembering."

Slade gripped the phone. "Memory leaks?"

"Bits and pieces of repressed stuff that suddenly pops up in dreams, flashbacks, you know…memories. So the government came up with screen memory. They fed 'em false stories to recall, like seeing spaceships and stuff like that, so no one will believe them."

Slade shook his head, not sure how much of this he was buying. "You mean the memories may not be real?"

"Not if the guy who programmed 'em did screen memories on 'em."

Slade let out a sigh as he moved over to the kitchen window and looked out into the night. He felt exposed. He turned off the light. Something whipped by the window, startling him. Just snow blowing off the roof. He moved into the dark living room where the drapes were drawn.

"Okay, let's say someone was programmed? How do you get them unprogrammed?"

"Could use hypnotic regression. Depends on how deeply the dude's been programmed. Sometimes just getting off the drugs and away from the programmer…"

"But if they get around the programmer?" Slade asked.

"Oh, man, then they can be zapped into another state with just one word. There was this one case of this woman who got involved with this military man. She didn't even remember how they'd met. Missing-time experiences are common. So are personality changes."

Slade felt his heart begin to pound. It sounded too much like Holly. Too much like her experience with Allan Wellington. "Charley, you remember that place outside of town, Evergreen Institute?" He could hear Charley scrambling for a pen and paper. "I'm not saying anything is going on out there."

"Yeah, I got ya. I'll do some checking. I've got friends in low places." He laughed.

"Well, be careful. It could be dangerous," Slade said, realizing that that *was* something he did believe.

Charley let out a low whistle. "Man, not even Dry Creek is safe. Whoa, that blows me away."

"I don't have anything definite," Slade protested.

"No problem, man. If there's something to get, I'll get it."

Slade started to give Charley his phone number.

"Caller ID, man. There are no secrets anymore." Charley hung up.

Chapter Ten

December 26

A swollen gray sky spat snow as Slade and Holly drove through town early the next morning. With stores not yet open, the town felt abandoned.

Holly stared out the side window, watching the buildings sweep past, lost in thought. Last night when Slade had kissed her, she'd believed it would open up her memory like a floodgate. Instead, she'd felt confused and…afraid.

Now, she tried not to think about the kiss or Slade. All she could think about was the blood typing results in her purse. Inconclusive. The baby could have been hers.

So why did someone call from the hospital last night to say the blood typing proved the baby wasn't hers? She wanted to believe someone had "fixed" the results. But what was left of her rational mind knew that the young nurse who'd called Slade last night might not have understood the report.

She realized she was beginning to question her own sanity. What if they found out that she'd given birth somewhere near the hospital, alone? What if she'd been the person who'd brought the baby—and herself—to the hospital? Maybe there was no mystery at all. Just that she was very, very sick.

She tried to concentrate on what she would say to Dr. Parris. Thinking herself crazy wasn't helping. It was too close to what she suspected was the truth.

"Do you trust this Dr. Parris?" Slade had asked this morning at breakfast.

"Yes." The answer had come so quickly, she'd had to stop to think why. "He doesn't like Inez."

"He told you that?"

She recalled only one time Inez had come up to Evergreen. "There was a row," Holly told Slade. "I heard it from the sunroom. I didn't even know it was Inez, although I probably should have. I saw Dr. Parris rush by in the hall and I stuck my head out to see what was going on. That's when I saw Inez. She was giving the staff hell over something. I never did find out what. But Dr. Parris took her aside and spoke with her and she left, obviously angry. I caught the expression on his face before he saw me. He definitely didn't like her."

Now, as Holly stared out the side window at the passing town, she wondered what Inez had been so upset about. Inez hadn't stayed that time, but she must have come back if she'd sat in on sessions with Dr. Parris when he'd discussed Holly's possible guilt over Allan's death.

That seemed strange—that Dr. Parris would let Inez attend sessions, especially after their initial meeting. Or *had* that been the first time they'd met?

She rubbed her temples. Why could she remember Inez's first visit and not the others? Her head ached too much to think. She reached for her purse. *It's time for me to take my pill.* Her hand wavered just over her purse. Slade had taken the pills.

But that wasn't what stopped her. It was the thought: *It's time for me to take my pill.*

Where had that come from?

She felt a rush of panic as another thought rear-ended the first. *Take your pill. You need that pill. The pill is the only thing that helps you.*

But she *didn't* have to have the pills. She'd forgotten on Christmas Eve and hadn't taken one yesterday. It wasn't as if she was addicted to them. Suddenly she wasn't so sure about that. She definitely couldn't remember feeling better after taking them. What she remembered, though, was Inez insisting they helped.

She'd never been one to take pills. Not even aspirin. Except when she had a headache, which was rare. How had she come to depend on pills? Because since she'd met Allan and his sister, she seemed to have headaches all the time.

No, she realized, that wasn't fair. The headaches had started before then. When her mother'd died. Holly'd had a headache the night she met Allan. Was that when he'd suggested the pills? Had it started that far back?

She shook her head, amazed that she'd been taking the pills for so long. Desperation. She realized she'd been desperate to believe *something* would help her memory loss, her mental confusion, her...fear that she was losing her mind. And she was still desperate, she reminded herself as she glanced over at Slade.

She noticed his hands and was fascinated by their size and shape and strength on the wheel. Long fingers. Strong, masculine hands. Hands that had touched her most private places. Shocked, she looked away.

Hadn't she just substituted him for the pills? Put her faith in him, convincing herself that he would help her, just as she had the pills? Only she was clear enough now to know that he might not be any better for her than the drugs.

She closed her eyes for a moment. When she opened them, Slade was driving past the cemetery. Through the chain-link fence, past the towering stands of pine trees and the snow-cold tombstones, her eye caught the huge marble monument that was a memorial to Allan and Inez's father. Next to it stood the godlike statue Inez had erected over Allan's grave and next to that—

Her heart leapt, and she sat up with a start. "Stop the truck!"

"What?"

"Go back to the cemetery. I saw someone. A woman. She was at the baby's grave." She didn't have to add at the bogus Allan Junior's grave.

Slade immediately swung the pickup around in a U-turn and sped back down the road to the cemetery turn-in. Through the pines, she could get only glimpses of the Wellington monument now. The hard-packed snow crunched under the truck's tires as Slade wound the pickup through the maze of narrow roads, turning at Holly's directions until she told him to stop.

The snowflakes grew larger, falling from the low, sullen clouds, silent as goose down. A magpie put up a ruckus in a nearby pine. The woman was gone.

"You're sure you saw someone?" he asked.

Without answering him, Holly opened her door, the cold morning air making her catch her breath. She pulled her coat around her as she walked toward the newest grave in the Wellington family plot. She hadn't been here since the funeral, not that she remembered much about that day. While it wasn't a complete blank, it felt surreal, just real enough to hurt.

"It could have been Inez you saw," Slade suggested as he joined her.

"It wasn't Inez," she said without looking at him. "There was no car." They both knew Inez couldn't have gotten away that quickly on foot. Whoever had been here had walked into the cemetery—not driven. As she neared the grave, she spotted the woman's footprints in the crusted snow near the grave. Beside an ostentatious sympathy spray was a tiny bouquet of blue silk forget-me-nots tied loosely with a blue ribbon.

"It was his mother," Holly said, knowing that to be true, the way she was starting to know herself again. She looked over at Slade. He was staring down at the tiny bouquet—and the footprints in the snow.

She followed his gaze as it chased the tracks through an empty part of the cemetery to the border of pines and the road on the other side.

Did the woman come here everyday? Or was this the first time? Would she be back? Holly felt her heart jump at the thought.

"It would be dangerous for her to visit the grave," she said, more to herself than to Slade. "That's why she came so early, why she parked over on the road and walked through the pines. She didn't want to be seen."

She turned to look at him then, blinking as if suddenly blinded by the sun. "If she knows that her baby was buried as my child—" A thought stopped her. Why would a woman agree to let her child be buried as someone else's? "Oh, my God!" Urgently she grabbed for Slade, getting a handful of his jacket in her fist. "She has our baby!"

SLADE FELT THE hairs stand on the back of his neck as her words echoed through the frozen cemetery.

"She traded her stillborn for our child!" Holly cried. She jerked on his jacket as if she could physically convince him by shaking the truth into him. "Why else would she agree to this? Don't you see?"

He placed his gloved hand over hers and gently pried her fingers open, freeing his jacket to hold her hand in both of his. Her eyes shone too brightly. She tried to pull her hand away as if too nervous to hold still. He turned her palm up, sandwiching it between his hands as if to warm it, when the truth was he didn't want to let go of her, afraid she'd fly off in a dozen different directions in a thousand different pieces.

"Holly," he said quietly, hoping to stop her before she let her hopes run so high he couldn't get them back down without doing permanent damage. "Why would these…people go to that kind of trouble simply to replace this woman's child?"

She stopped, the light dimming a little in her eyes. "Maybe she's someone. She has a lot of money or—"

"Not by the looks of the flowers she brought," he broke in, hating to disappoint her.

"She just didn't want anyone to know she'd been here," Holly said.

"Then a spray like the one already on the grave would have been less conspicuous, don't you think? Or none at all."

He watched Holly's breath come out in frosty white

puffs. Tiny specks of snow floated down to land in her dark hair, to catch on her lashes. She frowned, fighting what he was saying.

"Another thing," he said, motioning to the footprints in the snow. "Look at what she was wearing. An old pair of sneakers, the tread nearly gone on the heels. The snow is deep on the way in from the road. Her feet had to be cold. Why didn't she wear snow boots? Unless she didn't have any."

"Maybe she was in too much of a hurry," Holly said. "Or was too upset."

He shrugged, giving her that.

Holly pulled her hand free of his, but didn't move away from him. He watched her blink, the tears making all that blue seem endless. "If she doesn't have our baby, then she has to know who does, right?"

He couldn't take that away, too. "I would think she'd have to know at least one of the players." He didn't want to tell her that the woman might have just been paid to give up her baby. Especially if she'd known just before the birth that the baby would be stillborn. But that would mean that some local doctor was in on the switch. How else could the people behind this have found her— and made some deal for her baby?

"She knows where her baby is buried," Holly said. "She has to know about me."

Maybe. If she really was the mother. The county was small. Dry Creek even smaller. All the woman had to do was check the obits in the paper to find her baby. He didn't believe this woman would know much. Just as he didn't believe she had their baby.

He took Holly's arm and turned her away from the grave, away from the towering Wellington monuments to the dead and back toward his pickup, managing to step squarely on Allan Wellington's grave in the process. It was a childish show of disrespect. He didn't like Allan Wellington. Nor could he entirely justify his animosity toward a dead man. But he planned to be able to soon. He fervently believed Allan was somehow involved in all this—even though the man had been dead for months. Slade felt it as surely as the winter cold around him.

"How do we find her?" Holly asked when they'd reached the pickup.

He'd already been thinking about that. The other mother, if that's really who she'd been, could be added proof that the babies had been switched. Plus that mother would have given birth at the same place Holly had. She might be able to help them with that as well.

"I'm not sure," he said as he climbed behind the wheel. He didn't have a clue how to find her. She wouldn't have gone for medical help even if she'd needed it. Too many questions would have been asked.

"You know, something's been bothering me," he said. "If these…monsters who delivered your baby, if they were doctors, why didn't they do an episiotomy? Why were you suffering from hypothermia when you arrived at the hospital?"

"Maybe they wanted it to look as if I'd given birth alone, without any help," she suggested as he started the truck.

"Maybe." He thought about her memory of the three ghouls appearing frantic, the feeling that something was wrong. "That seems a little too cruel, even for monsters. Maybe they didn't know what they were doing because they lacked the medical expertise. Maybe they weren't doctors at all." He didn't like that theory because it opened up too many possibilities. "Have you remembered anything more about the room? It wasn't just a bedroom in some house?"

She shook her head as she squinted out at the gloomy day. "The bed made me think it was a hospital because of the rails."

Hospital-type beds could be rented. Or purchased.

"I don't know," she said with a sigh. "I can't be positive it wasn't just a bedroom but— Wait a minute. The ceiling." Her voice had dropped to a whisper.

He looked over at her.

Her eyes were closed. "The ceiling seemed too high for a regular house. And…there was something on it."

He waited, afraid to speak for fear of making the memory—if that's what it was—slip away.

"A mark." She opened her eyes and frowned.

"You mean like the roof leaked?" he asked when she didn't continue. "Or the plaster cracked?"

She nodded. "It was in the shape of something large and scaly."

He stared at her for a moment, then looked back to his driving. "Like a dragon?"

"Or some kind of monster," she said with a sigh. "Obviously, I saw monsters everywhere I looked," she added, her tone dismissing the ceiling design and the memory as useless.

He wanted to assure her that every possible memory was important. But three monsters at the end of the bed and another on the ceiling?

He shifted down at the edge of town, the pills he'd taken from her rattling softly in his coat pocket. Who knew what those pills could have made her see? he thought as he pulled into the drugstore parking lot, anxious to find out.

"Do you mind if I wait here?" she asked.

He would much rather have had her with him, but the pharmacy was near the front of the store and he knew he would be able to keep her in sight. "I'll get you something for your headache."

"How did you know I had a headache?" she asked in obvious surprise.

He shrugged. "You get this little ridge between your brows when your head hurts," he said, feeling strangely shy about revealing the things he knew about her.

She studied him openly for a moment. "You do know me, don't you?"

He nodded, his gaze brushing hers, sparking like flint on granite. He opened his door, breaking the connection, telling himself to let her take the time she needed, hoping she had the time to take.

Last night, unable to sleep, he'd stayed up going through old photo albums from when he and Shelley were kids. This morning he'd put in a call to her, just wanting to hear her voice. But she hadn't been in her room. He'd left a message asking her about the twin-angel Christmas ornament, asking her to call him. The moment he hung up, he wished he hadn't said anything about the ornament. He hadn't meant to.

He felt disconnected, dreading what he might find out, knowing somewhere deep inside himself that the news on neither case would be good, and wondering how he would be able to tell Holly. And Shelley.

"Slade Rawlins?" Jerry Dunn said when he saw him. "I haven't seen you in a month of Sundays."

Jerry and Slade had gone to school together. They

were two of a handful of classmates who still lived in Dry Creek. The difference was, Jerry had left long enough to become a pharmacist. Slade felt anchored here by the past.

He reached across the counter to shake Jerry's outstretched hand. For a pharmacist, Jerry had a hell of a grip. He'd played fullback on the football team and looked as if he still worked out. Jerry had married his high-school sweetheart and started a family. Slade knew why Jerry had stayed in Dry Creek. Jerry had inherited his father's drugstore and pharmacy when his father'd retired.

"So how's business?" Slade asked, although the drugstore was empty except for a young clerk at the front.

"Crazy before Christmas. Fortunately it's slowed down, but hey, flu season is coming." Jerry grinned. "It will pick up."

Slade pulled the container of pills from his pocket. "I need to know what these are."

"Sure." The former fullback took the bottle, checked the prescription, then shook a couple of the pills out into a small plastic tray. "Looks like a generic of Xanax. A common anxiety medication," he added when he saw that the name rang no bells for Slade.

"Strong?"

"Not really."

Slade glanced toward the truck and Holly. She'd leaned back against the seat, her eyes closed. He'd hoped Jerry was going to tell him that the pills were something strong enough to cause memory loss. But Slade knew it had been a long shot. What pill was strong enough to cause a woman to forget months out of her life?

"Is there any way to test these pills?" he asked. "A lab, somewhere I can take them?"

"What about the Butte hospital's computer?" the young clerk asked. "Can't they run the number on the pill?"

Slade hadn't heard her approach. She was young, college-age, blonde and with a look of intelligence. Her name tag said she was Penny.

"I was just getting ready to suggest that," Jerry said, obviously not happy about the interruption. "Want me to call for you?" he said to Slade.

"I can do it," Penny said. "I've been going to pharmaceutical school and I need the practice," she told Slade. "Isn't that what you always tell me when it comes to your grunt work, Jerry?" She grinned as she picked up the phone, reaching over to take the tray and pills from Jerry.

"See this," she said to Slade as she waited for the hospital to answer. She pointed to a small indentation that appeared to be a letter and a number. "The hospital computer database can tell you what generic it is."

"How long does it take?" he asked.

"Not long."

"Anything else you need?" Jerry asked, sounding a little testy.

"Yeah, something for a headache."

"I know what you mean," Jerry said, coming out from behind the counter to help him. While they moved through the drugstore, Slade kept an eye on Holly. Jerry asked about Shelley and made polite conversation. He and Jerry never had had much in common, Slade realized.

Armed with a bottle of painkillers for Holly's headache and a pop out of the cooler, he and Jerry returned to the pharmacy counter. The clerk was just getting off the phone.

"Wow," she said, eyeing one of the pills as she hung up the phone. "I don't think I've ever seen one of these. They're the same color, size and shape as Xanax, but they're Halcion."

"Are you sure?" Jerry said in surprise.

"What's Halcion?" Slade asked.

Jerry let out a low whistle. "Halcion is an oldie, been around literally for years. It's a sedative hypnotic," he said, obviously stealing the young clerk's thunder.

Slade felt his breath rush from his lungs. "A hypnotic?"

"There was this big case in Utah," the clerk said enthusiastically. "A woman was taking Halcion and killed her mother. Got off too."

"Side effects?" Slade managed to ask.

"Oh, yeah," she said before Jerry could. "Disorientation, light-headedness, mental confusion, loss of memory, paranoia."

He felt a little light-headed himself. "Addictive?"

"Highly," Penny said. "This stuff is dangerous. I can't imagine a pharmacist making a mistake like this." She eyed the prescription. "The bottle's so old it's hard to read where the prescription was first filled. Halcion isn't easy to come by. It's so dangerous that you can only get ten pills at a time."

Unless you knew someone who could get you the stuff without raising suspicion. The question was, who had put the Halcion in the Xanax bottle? Inez was the obvious choice.

Jerry picked up the bottle, frowning at the prescription. "Dr. Allan Wellington?"

"It's an old prescription."

"I guess. He's been a dead a while, hasn't he?"

Not long enough, it seemed.

"Holly Barrows?" Jerry said, still reading the prescription.

"A client of mine. Don't worry, I won't let her take any more of them."

"Good thinking. You want me to throw out the pills for you?"

"No," Slade said quickly. "I'd like to hang on to them for a while."

Jerry put the pills back in the container. "I'd throw them out if I were you."

Not likely. They were evidence.

Jerry glanced toward Slade's pickup and the woman sitting inside it, openly curious.

Slade wasn't interested in satisfying his curiosity. He thanked Jerry and his assistant for their help and paid for the headache pills and the soda. Behind Jerry on the wall was a family photograph of Jerry and his wife Patty and a couple of towheaded little boys about six and four.

Slade felt a tug at the sight of the kids and the happy family. He tried to imagine a photo of him and Holly and their little girl—and couldn't.

"You should see the latest photos of the kids," the clerk said, noting what he'd been staring at. "They are *the* cutest things."

He thanked Jerry and Penny again and left, the Halcion safe in his pocket.

GRATEFULLY, HOLLY took the bottle of tablets and the drink Slade handed her as he climbed into the pickup.

"Thanks."

He was right. She had a blinding headache. After she tried unsuccessfully to unscrew the cap on the pill bottle, he took it from her, opened it and shook two tablets into her outstretched palm.

She fumbled to pop the top on the soda can, downing both pills in a swallow of throat-tingling cold liquid. She closed her eyes for a moment, knowing why he'd gone into the pharmacy, afraid of what he'd found out.

"The pills?" she said after a moment.

"They're probably responsible not only for your headache, but also your memory loss," he said as he started the truck and pulled back out onto the highway.

"What are they?" she asked, shocked.

"They aren't what they say on the prescription."

That shouldn't have come as a surprise to her since Slade had already suspected as much. She listened while he told her about the hypnotic drug and its side effects.

She was too stunned to speak. "Then it was just the drug. Someone must have mixed up the prescription—"

"Not likely," Slade said. "I think there is more to this than just the drug. Did anyone besides Inez have access to the prescription?"

All she could do was stare at him. Inez. "You think she was the one who—?"

"It could depend on where she got the prescription filled."

Holly looked out the window at the passing town, remembering how Inez had asked last night if she'd taken her pill. How Inez had insisted she go back to Evergreen. How Inez had planned to fire Slade.

"The other day when I was at your sister-in-law's, someone buzzed at the gate," Slade said, not looking at her as he drove. "It was obvious Inez didn't want me to know who it was. But eventually, she answered the intercom. It was a Dr. O'Brien from Evergreen."

Holly felt sick to her stomach. She had to fight back tears of anger—and pain. For the last year, Inez had been her only family. As difficult as Inez had been, Holly had trusted her.

"I feel like a fool."

"You shouldn't," Slade said. "The pills are identical to Xanax. You had no reason to believe they were anything but what they said they were on the bottle."

"Still…"

"I think your memory started coming back when you came to Dry Creek and forgot the pills in Pinedale," he said. "Maybe you did that on purpose."

Was it possible that on some subconscious level she'd suspected the pills weren't really helping her?

"I talked to a friend of mine last night," Slade was saying. "He said these kinds of drugs are used in conjunction with hypnosis."

Hypnosis?

"You said you felt as if someone was manipulating you," he reminded her. "Drugs and hypnosis have been used in mind-control experiments."

Hypnosis. She tried to grasp it, her thoughts scattering like bits of paper in the wind. She'd seen a hypnotist once in a bar in Butte. He'd made grown men hop around and cluck and flap their arms like chickens. No, not *like* chickens. The men had appeared to believe they *were* chickens.

"Did Dr. Parris use hypnotism on you at Evergreen?" Slade asked.

"I don't remember ever being hypnotized." She did remember, however, that a hypnotist, through hypnotic suggestion, could wipe out all recollection of a person ever being hypnotized. Case in point: the chicken/men at the bar. They'd gone back to their stools, confused by the laughter and applause, believing the hypnotist had failed to put big, strong men like them "under."

At the time, it had seemed silly. Now it was disturbing. "This drug I've been taking, would it make it easier for me to be hypnotized?"

Slade nodded, his gaze seeming to access how hard she was taking this. "I have a feeling you were also programmed to take the pills."

The words she'd heard in her head this morning echoed now. *It's time for me to take my pill.* Dear God. "So it is possible someone *has* been controlling me?"

"I'd say it's a whole hell of a lot more than possible."

Still, Holly hadn't really accepted the ramifications. Inez had given her the pills. Inez thrived on control. But Allan had written the original prescription. And when she'd met Allan, that's when it had all begun.

"But why? It has to be more than just the baby," she said, watching the dense snowcapped pines blur by as the pickup snaked up the narrow old two-lane road toward the summit of the pass—and Evergreen Institute. She hadn't seen another car for miles and had forgotten how isolated it was out here. "My memory lapses go back a whole year," she pointed out.

"I wish I knew," Slade said. "Unless they'd had something planned for you that far back."

"You mean—" She glanced over at him. "You don't think they purposely got you and me together?"

"No. For what purpose?"

"The baby?" she said. "Like you said, that's all they appear to have gained."

He drove in silence for a moment. "How could they know we would have a baby together?"

She stared at him. "Because they know everything about us. Once they were in control of my mind…they could control you as well."

He smiled over at her. "They couldn't make me fall in love with you."

"Maybe they hadn't planned on that." Hadn't planned on her going back to him this Christmas Eve for help. Hadn't planned on the bond that had drawn her to him. She wanted desperately to believe that. To believe she and Slade had the upper hand. It gave her hope that they could find their baby and get her back. "Just as they hadn't planned on my memory coming back and me coming to you for help," she said, hoping he'd agree.

He looked over at her and smiled. "I'd like to think we're one step ahead of them."

His smile warmed her to her toes. "Thanks," she said, feeling almost shy. She was changing, wasn't she? She felt stronger. Just knowing that she wasn't losing her mind helped. That it had been the pills making her feel that way and that someone had been unconsciously forcing her to keep taking the pills. All of it made her angry—and more intent on foiling their plans.

A thought struck her. "No one knows I've quit taking the pills or how much of my memory is coming back." The thought pleased her immensely. "How long do you think we have before they know?"

Slade slowed the pickup, turned into a paved, pine-lined driveway, bringing the pickup to a stop before an ornate locked steel gate.

"That all depends on whether Dr. Parris is in on it," he said as he rolled down his window and reached out to buzz the intercom of the Evergreen Institute.

Chapter Eleven

Dr. Parris seemed genuinely pleased to see Holly. He came from one of the long hallways, his footsteps echoing through the massive stone foyer as he moved toward the reception desk, a tall man with graying hair and long arms and legs that appeared almost disjointed. He reminded Slade of a marionette.

"Holly," Parris said, greeting her with a smile. "How are you?"

"That's what I hope to talk to you about," she said. "I'm sorry I didn't call for an appointment."

Parris waved that off, then looked to Slade, his smile still firmly in place. On closer inspection, Slade could see that the doctor seemed disheveled. His pale blue smock was stained from the leaky pen stuck in the breast pocket and his name tag was askew. He didn't look like a man who could control anything—certainly not Holly's mind.

"This is a…friend of mine," Holly said. "Slade Rawlins."

The doctor offered his hand. "Pleased to meet you," he said, sounding as if he meant it. "Rawlins? Why does that name sound so familiar?" he commented more to himself than to Slade. "Come on down to my office."

Slade and Holly followed him down a long, wide marble hallway. The place looked like a palace. Outside, Slade had glimpsed a horse barn, a covered pool and indoor tennis courts. He had seen no patients and hardly any staff. He figured it had something to do with that wonderful scent of food he kept picking up. Not school-cafeteria-type food. A gourmet lunch from the smell of it, served somewhere deep in all this luxury.

The doctor's office was large but filled. The huge desk had long disappeared beneath an avalanche of papers and books. He had begun to stack books on the floor around his desk like a wall.

Slade watched him close the door behind them, then rush to uncover two chairs for them. "I usually don't use my office for therapy sessions, as Holly knows," he said by way of explanation to Slade.

"I have been concerned about you," he said to Holly when they were all seated. "I heard about your recent loss. I'm so sorry."

Slade found himself listening to the doctor's words and watching Holly's reaction. If she'd been hypnotized, hadn't Charley said that a catchword or phrase could be used to control her? But to his relief Holly seemed to have no reaction to Dr. Parris or his words other than gratitude.

"Thank you," she said and looked over at Slade.

"That's partly why we're here," Slade said, introducing himself as a private investigator. The doctor seemed a little surprised but not overly. "Holly has been experiencing some memory loss. I'm looking into the missing parts for her."

Dr. Parris swung his gaze to her. "You mentioned that before when you were here."

"That's just it," Holly said. "When Inez told me about the sessions she sat in on with you and me where—"

"Inez?" Dr. Parris interrupted, frowning. "She never sat in on any sessions with the two of us."

Holly stared at the doctor. "Are you sure?"

"Holly," he said, concern in his voice, in his expression. "You and I never *had* any sessions with Inez in attendance."

Slade watched her let out a long breath before she looked over at him, relief in her gaze and something more. Anger and an even stronger determination.

Not wanting Parris to know just how important that information was, Slade jumped in, "Did you ever hypnotize Holly during any of her sessions with you?"

Parris frowned. "No."

"Or prescribe Xanax?"

The doctor shook his head, his frown deepening.

"How about Halcion?"

"Halcion?" Parris said, sounding shocked. "Of course not. That's a hypnotic. Very dangerous."

"So no doctor you know here at the Institute uses Halcion in conjunction with hypnosis?"

The doctor looked horrified. "Perhaps you should tell me what this is about."

Slade looked at Holly, unsure how much they wanted to confide in Dr. Parris. "Were you aware Holly was taking Halcion?"

The doctor shook his head. "Not while she was an inpatient here."

"How can you be so sure?" Holly asked.

"Because it would have shown up in your blood work," Parris said.

Slade rubbed his eyes. "What about a nurse named

Carolyn Gray? I understand she just started to work here?"

Parris shook his head. "We have made no new hires."

Another dead end. But why did someone want Carolyn Gray's check to come here? "When was Holly released from the Institute?" he asked, remembering the commitment papers.

"I'm afraid she wasn't," Parris said. "It was a most unfortunate incident. We aren't used to losing patients around here."

Slade glanced at Holly. She looked as confused as he did. "What incident was that?"

"Holly leaving the way she did," the doctor said. He glanced at each of them and frowned. "She just took off one afternoon during a huge snowstorm."

"Christmas Eve," Holly said.

"Yes, that's right, Christmas Eve," Dr. Parris agreed and shook his head. "Fortunately, your sister-in-law called to say you were safe, and we didn't need to continue looking for you."

Slade felt his heart drop like a stone.

"Inez called you?" Holly said, her voice cracking. "When was that?"

"That afternoon just before we were going to start a full-scale search," the doctor said.

Inez had stopped the search. Because she didn't want Holly found in the state she was in? Or because Inez knew that Holly was with Slade—as per plan?

Slade raked a hand through his hair, fighting every instinct in him that told him to get the hell out of this place as fast as possible. When Holly had run in front of his pickup on Christmas Eve a year ago, convinced someone was trying to kill her, she'd been running from this place, it seemed. And at the same time, Inez Wellington was calling Evergreen Institute to say that Holly was safe.

"What exactly is it the Institute does?" Slade asked, surprised that his voice sounded calm, in control, when he was more convinced than ever that something had happened to Holly *here*, something that had frightened her and made her leave on Christmas Eve in a blizzard, something that had her believing that someone was trying to kill her. And Slade no longer believed it was all in her mind.

"What goes on here?" Dr. Parris parroted as if he thought everyone knew. "Well, originally Dr. Wellington opened it to continue his research in infertility. After his death, it became more of a medical retreat. We now specialize in the needs of today's clients."

Clients, not patients. People with money, Slade thought. It would take a lot of money to run a place like this.

"Our clients often need a quiet, out-of-the-way sanctuary where they can relax and work on health-related issues such as weight loss, better nutrition, stress management, smoking cessation, insomnia, drug and alcohol addiction. These are stressful times wrought with social problems. Sometimes, as in Holly's case—" the doctor smiled over at her "—our clients just need a place to rest."

It sounded so benign. "Kind of like a health club where you can decide if you want to work on your abs or your fear of heights."

Dr. Parris smiled as if relieved. "Exactly." No mind control here, his smile said.

"What about Inez Wellington?"

Parris looked confused.

"How is she involved with the Institute?"

"She isn't."

"Even when her brother ran the place?" Slade asked, not believing it.

"Not even then, that I was aware of," Parris said, seeming actually to believe it.

Slade didn't, not for a moment. Inez had some power either over the place or at least over one of the doctors— in particular Dr. O'Brien, the impatient man who'd been at her gate yesterday afternoon.

"Well, thank you for your help," Slade said, getting to his feet, relieved to be leaving.

"I'm not sure what help I've been, Mr. Rawlins," the doctor said as he got up to see them out. "Rawlins?" he said thoughtfully as he shook Slade's hand. "Marcella Rawlins?"

Slade felt himself tense. "She was my mother."

Dr. Parris nodded. "I thought so. A fine woman. I was so sorry to hear about…what happened. A terrible tragedy for everyone involved. I had wished there was something I could have done."

Slade stared at him. "Done?"

"For Lorraine. Obviously, there wasn't anything I could have done for your mother or Lorraine's son Roy at that point. But Lorraine…"

Lorraine Vogel. The mother of the young man who'd allegedly killed Slade's mother.

The doctor must have seen Slade's confusion. "I was afraid Lorraine wouldn't complete her training after everything that happened. She was training to be a nurse here at the Institute. But she did finish. Now she works part-time here—and part-time at the hospital."

It took Slade a moment to find his voice. Lorraine worked at the Institute? And Slade's mother— "You knew my mother?"

Dr. Parris seemed surprised by the question. "Only to say hello in the hall really."

"Here at the Institute?" Slade asked.

Parris realized he'd made a mistake, but it was clear he didn't know how. "Yes."

"She was a patient here," Slade said.

Dr. Parris smiled and looked relieved. "Yes."

His mother was a patient here? How was it possible that he and his sister and his father hadn't known that? He couldn't remember even one day his mother hadn't been at the stove on his return from school or from playing in the neighborhood with friends.

"Back when Evergreen was a fertility clinic," Slade said, trying to put it together. "Back when Dr. Allan Wellington was running the place." He felt something like a flash go off in his head and wondered if it was like this for Holly. A thought. A memory? A piece of knowledge just appearing in a bolt of crystal clear bright thought. "I was pretty young then, but, that's right, she came up here every Tuesday and Thursday."

Dr. Parris beamed. "That's right. She always had a kind word and a smile."

Stunned, Slade was still trying to make sense of it. His mother had come up here every Tuesday and Thursday afternoon. No affair? But what had she come up here for? It couldn't have had to do with infertility— and his mother didn't drive. She'd been in a near-fatal car accident and had a deathly fear of driving. Norma always drove her wherever she wanted to go. Or Slade's father, Joe.

Who had driven her to Evergreen twice a week? Not Joe, the person she'd said in her letter she didn't want to know about her afternoons away from home. So who had driven her? Not Norma. Dr. Wellington? Was he also the man who'd had Marcella Rawlins in his arms the day Norma had seen the two of them at the house?

Slade felt sick, all of it coming too close to home. "You have a very good memory, Dr. Parris. You probably remember that my mother didn't drive," Slade said as they moved out of the office and into the empty hall.

"Why, that's right," Parris exclaimed. "I think that's why she came up on Tuesdays and Thursdays, so she could ride with Lorraine on Tuesdays and Dr. Delaney on Thursdays. My, but that has been years ago. My memory serves me well."

Slade fought to breathe. Dr. Delaney?

"Give yourself some time," Parris was saying to Holly. "You're a strong young woman. You're going to be just fine."

"Thank you, Doctor," she said.

"I didn't realize that Dr. Delaney worked here," Slade said, interrupting Holly.

"Only on special projects anymore. A fine man and a wonderfully compassionate doctor," Parris said. "Let me know if there is anything else you need. It is always nice to see you, Holly, and nice meeting you," he said again to Slade, then turned and disappeared back into his office.

Slade took Holly's arm as they started down the hall toward the exit. "Are you all right?"

"Yes. No. Inez lied about the sessions."

He nodded, wondering why Inez had done that. Unless it had been a test. A test to see if Holly was remembering.

"*And* she lied about where I was last Christmas Eve," Holly said, sounding angry and scared. "Unless she knew I was with you."

"Yes," Slade said. "I thought of that. Or maybe she just didn't want the staff up here looking for you. Any idea why you left here in such a hurry? You didn't even have a coat on when I found you."

She shook her head. "You said I thought someone was trying to kill me. Do you think it was just the pills?"

"Dr. Parris swears you weren't taking them while you were here," he pointed out. "Nor were you taking them when you were with me."

A door opened off to the right ahead of them. A woman in a business suit and heels came out carrying a large cinnamon bun and a mug of something hot. She headed down the hallway in front of them without looking back, her high heels clicking on the hardwood floor, turning off one of the many hallways.

Through the glass window in the office door, Slade spotted a desk and computer. Seeing no one else around, he quickly pushed the door open before it could shut completely. He pulled Holly into the office and closed the door behind them.

"What are you doing?" she whispered in obvious horror as he grabbed a straight-back chair from in front of the desk and stuck it under the door so it couldn't be opened from the outside.

"Buying time." He hurried around to sit down at the computer. "I want to see your file. And my mother's."

"Here, let me do that," she said after a moment of watching him try to call up files.

He moved to let her sit down and, standing behind her with his hands on the back of her chair, watched in awe as she quickly maneuvered her way through the system. "I didn't know you knew anything about computers."

She let out a quiet chuckle. "So, there is at least a little something about me that's still a mystery."

Her joking tone stirred old memories deep within him of the way it had been between them. "You will always be a mystery to me," he said softly.

She leaned back, waiting for the computer to respond, her scent filling him. Her hair brushed the tops of his hands, reminding him only too well of the feel of it against his bare skin.

He could see her reflection in the computer screen as her eyes came up to meet his. For the first time, he didn't see fear, but something just as familiar. A look that made him ache inside.

His hands slipped from the chair back to her shoulders. She pressed against the pressure of his fingers and closed her eyes. Slowly he moved his hands down her arms to her elbows as he bent over her, breathing her in, wanting to envelop her. She felt warm and solid, strong.

Her eyes opened and her gaze met his in the screen. Her lips parted, her look softening, deepening. He would have kissed her. The chance of getting caught be damned.

But just then the computer screen flashed. No Holly Barrows found.

He straightened, releasing her.

She typed in Holly Wellington. "Look at this," she said. Under Medications, it read, None. "And this." She pointed to a notation at the top of the file: Genesis Project. When she clicked on it, the screen flashed: Enter Security Code. She tried several. None of them worked.

He heard the sound of high heels tapping down the hallway. They grew louder as they approached. "See if you can get Marcella Rawlins's file."

Holly typed in the name. "I can't find her. How long ago was it?"

"More than twenty years ago," he whispered, watching over her shoulder.

"Let me try something else." She hurriedly clicked at the keys. "Wait, I've got it." He watched her type in Keyword: Inez. What came up on the screen was a list of patients under Genesis Project. She scrolled down to Wellington, Holly. File: Current.

"What is the Genesis Project?" Slade asked.

"I have no idea." She moved the cursor through the list. Norma Curtis. Genesis Project. File: In storage.

He spotted another name. Patty Dunn. Genesis Project. File: Current.

Pharmacist Jerry Dunn's wife.

He wasn't surprised when Holly stopped the cursor on Marcella Rawlins. Genesis Project. File: In storage.

"What do we all have in common?" Holly whispered, turning to look at him.

"I wish I knew. My first guess would be infertility if I didn't know better."

Outside in the hall, the footsteps grew closer.

Slade put his hand over Holly's on the mouse and scrolled on down to the end of the list, stopping just once. On the name Lorraine Vogel. Genesis Project. File: In storage.

"Clear the screen," he said next to her ear, then quietly stepped to the door to remove the chair blocking it, hoping the woman he'd seen leaving the office hadn't forgotten something. But the sound of the footfalls went on past the door as Holly joined him.

He waited for a few moments to make sure the hallway was clear, then opened the door.

"You looked as if you'd seen a ghost when Dr. Parris mentioned your mother," she whispered as they headed for the exit again. "What happened to her?"

He kept his voice down even though it appeared everyone had gone to lunch—even the woman who'd been at the front reception desk earlier.

"She was murdered twenty years ago by the son of the woman who supposedly drove her up here on Tuesdays. Lorraine Vogel."

"The woman who was also in the Genesis Project file," Holly said.

He nodded at Holly's thoughtful expression. "The thing is, my mother kept all of this a secret. Why is that? And why would she be coming to a fertility clinic in the first place? She had two twelve-year-olds."

"Twenty years ago. And she was a Genesis Project patient," Holly noted. "Like me."

"Yeah," he said. "That's what has me worried." What was the Genesis Project? And what did any of this have to do with their baby? Probably nothing. They were just wasting time here. All he wanted was to get out of this place. It felt even more dangerous than he'd first suspected—and he had no idea what there was to fear here.

They were almost to the exit, crossing the great expanse of marble that made up the massive foyer, when an older man in a white lab coat over an expensive gray suit stepped from a doorway, almost colliding with them. Behind him was Inez Wellington.

"Holly," the man said, a reprimand in his voice.

"Holly, you remember Dr. O'Brien," Inez said, not seeming that happy to see them, or at least not Slade.

"Inez." Holly sounded scared, and when she looked at Dr. O'Brien it was clear to Slade that she had never seen him before—that she could remember anyway.

A tall man with thick dark hair, a square face and small, dark eyes behind wire-rimmed glasses, the doctor ignored Slade and turned all of his attention on Holly.

"I thought you were checking in?" O'Brien said, his voice low and rough as sandpaper and about as warm.

Holly shook her head. "I've changed my mind."

"Let's discuss this in my office. Alone," he said pointedly.

"There is nothing to discuss," Holly insisted.

"From what Inez has told me, I'm not sure you're capable of a reasonable decision at this point."

"I disagree," Slade said stepping between O'Brien and Holly. "I think she is more than capable of making a reasonable decision, and that decision is that she doesn't need your…help."

Slade heard Inez say something about commitment papers and court orders, but he'd already swept Holly past the doctor and Inez. He hit the massive front door, half afraid he'd find it locked. It flung open, the cold and snow hitting him in the face as he grabbed Holly's hand and bolted.

He could hear both O'Brien and Inez call after them. And another voice. Female. He glanced over his shoulder, thought he glimpsed Carolyn Gray step behind a column on the outside edge of the building entrance, but his attention was quickly drawn back to Dr. O'Brien. The doctor reached for something. An alarm went off.

"Run!" he yelled to Holly over the clamor.

The sky had darkened to gunmetal gray, huge floating snowflakes fell around them like confetti.

He and Holly reached the pickup before he let himself look back again. To his surprise no white-coated bodybuilder types had come exploding out of the Institute.

Holly jumped into the cab and he slid in after her. The pickup started, almost to his amazement. He wasn't sure what lengths these people would go to. He told himself they needed Holly back under their control. She was starting to remember too much, and by now they had to know that.

He spun the pickup out of the parking lot, snow flying off the hood and windshield, and headed for the gate, expecting that would be where the doctor planned to stop them. Pushing down the gas pedal, he increased his speed as he raced down the narrow evergreen-lined road, pretty sure he could ram through the gate if it came to that.

One glance at Holly told him she was braced for just that. She was buckled in, both hands on the dash, a look of incredulity on her face.

But to his amazement, the gate was open when he came around the bend. No guard tried to block his exit. No big orderlies tried to jump them.

Slade cruised out of the Institute's grounds and onto the highway, putting his foot to the metal as he watched in his rearview mirror, unable to believe their luck. No, not luck, he thought as the pickup put distance between them and Evergreen Institute. Dr. O'Brien had let them go. But why?

He glanced over at Holly. She too was looking back,

obviously just as surprised. Then her gaze shifted to him and he had such a feeling of dèjá vu he almost drove off the highway. She was staring at him as if she'd never seen him before.

Chapter Twelve

"Holly?" Slade let out a curse as he met her gaze. They'd gotten to her. But how? The alarm? Or something O'Brien or someone else had said or done?

"Holly, you remember who I am, right?" Wrong.

She was gripping the door handle. He kept the speed up on the pickup, pretty sure she wouldn't be foolish enough to leap out, but not really sure *what* she'd do.

In his rearview mirror, he spotted a car coming up fast and swore.

She glanced back at the winding two-lane highway, then back at him. "What's going on?" She sounded only a little scared. "Rawlins?"

He shot her a look. "You called me Rawlins."

"Yeah," she said, still eyeing him strangely. "I've always called you Rawlins."

His heart hammered so hard in his chest he couldn't breathe. He stole another look at her. What he saw almost floored him. He let out a laugh. "Everything's just…fine now." He stole another look at her. Wasn't it?

She gave him a tentative smile. "Did you just call me Holly?"

The car was gaining on them, its cornering abilities far exceeding the pickup's, especially in the middle of a snowstorm. He didn't dare go any faster. He was having enough trouble keeping his eyes on the road in this storm—and on the rearview mirror and Holly.

"You like the name?" he asked, praying he was right about who was sitting in the passenger seat next to him.

She smiled. God, but he'd missed that sexy, teasing, full-of-life smile. "It had better be your new name for me—and not just a slip of the tongue. Holly? I guess it's appropriate since you found me on Christmas Eve. Does have a nicer ring than Janie Doe."

He shook his head, grinning like a fool. Holly was back. His Holly. All he wanted to do was stop the pickup and take her in his arms. But that wasn't an option at the moment. The car was right behind them now. Something silver and sporty, like the BMW Dr. O'Brien drove.

"You know, I feel as though I've missed something here," she said, glancing nervously back at the car, then at him. "You sure everything is all right?"

"Yeah, what's the last thing you remember?" The car was trying to come around him on a solid yellow line.

"You in the shower."

He almost drove off the road.

"Don't tell me *you* don't remember?"

"Oh, yeah." His heart was threatening to burst from his chest. "*Where* were we getting ready to go?"

"As if you don't remember. Your sister Shelley's. Dinner with Norma and the chief. You'd been grousing about going all day."

My God. She thought it was February 26 of last year, the day he came out of the shower not only to find her long gone, but his money and the files from his office gone as well.

"Right," he said, trying to keep the shock from his voice and his eyes on the road and the car behind them. The car made another attempt to pass, but backed off. A straightaway was coming up and Slade knew he wouldn't be able to keep the car from coming alongside him.

"You left the shower to dry your hair. The phone rang." He looked over at her, realizing now that was when someone had gotten to her. "By the way, who was that on the phone?"

She frowned. "That's funny. I can't remember."

The straightaway was just ahead. He reached across to the glove box and pulled out his weapon.

"Okay, now you're scaring me," she said. She bit at her lower lip. "Rawlins, are those the people who are trying to kill me?"

"Maybe, sweetheart. I need you to get down and stay down, okay?" He couldn't help but take another look at her, afraid it might be his last. The irony of it poleaxed him. He'd finally gotten her back, and, in the blink of an eye, he could lose her again.

He rolled down his window, snow pelting him. He squinted, one hand on the wheel, the other holding his weapon, as he watched the car come up his side of the pickup like a bullet, the driver hidden behind tinted windows. His trigger finger twitched. They weren't taking Holly from him. He'd kill them all if that's what it took.

He started to raise the gun, but then realized it wasn't Dr. O'Brien's car. His car hadn't had tinted windows.

The car seemed to hesitate for one heart-thundering moment next to the pickup, then sped on past, disappearing into the snowstorm. He watched it go and slowed the pickup, realizing he was shaking all over.

Whoever was behind this hadn't come after them because obviously they'd accomplished what they'd set out to do. Zap Holly. Take away her memory. Again.

But that meant they didn't see him as a threat. Probably because basically, he had nothing. Some pills that Inez could say she knew nothing about. A blood typing that proved nothing. And a woman with a shaky mental history and no memory. He had zip and they knew it.

But he had Holly. Or did he?

"Holly?"

Her head popped up from where she'd hunkered down in the seat.

He pulled off onto the first side road, cut the lights and turned to her. She flew into his arms and he hugged her to him as if there were no tomorrow. The way things were going, there might not be.

"Rawlins, you act as if you haven't seen me in weeks," she laughed, drawing back a little to look into his face. It felt as if they were in a cocoon, the snow falling silently around them, covering the pickup in white.

"Feels more like months," he said, touching his fingers to her lips. "God, I've missed you."

"Rawlins." She laughed, then sobered. "You're serious."

He nodded. "There's something I need to tell you."

"It's bad, isn't it?" She braced herself for the worst. "What did you find out about me?"

"We can't stay here," he said starting the pickup.

"Rawlins, tell me what it is."

"I'll tell you on the way."

She listened, watching the snow fall hypnotically down from the heavens as he drove down the mountain.

At first it felt as if he was talking about someone else. She would never steal files from him, let alone money. Nor could months have gone by. It was impossible.

But on the outskirts of Dry Creek, she began to see the Christmas lights. Too many of them for February. And this was Slade Rawlins, a man she trusted with her life. With her love.

"We had a baby together?" she asked in awe, her voice breaking. "A little girl?"

He pulled over at the edge of town as if suddenly realizing he didn't know where to go or what to do. "We can't go back to Shelley's. Or to my office or apartment. They'll probably be waiting for us. We can catch a flight from Butte." He started to turn the truck around.

She stopped him, shocked that he'd think she would run away. "We have to find her. We can't leave until we do."

"Holly," he said, killing the engine to turn to her. "You don't know what these people are capable of."

"Don't I, Rawlins? They stole our baby. They drugged me. They made me marry some crazed scientist. They messed with my mind and memory. I'm not about to let them keep my baby."

"Holly, they could have already—"

"They wouldn't hurt her," she said, believing it. "They went to too much trouble to get her."

She could see he wasn't so sure about that, but she couldn't doubt it. She had to believe their daughter was alive. "I have to remember the birth—the voice you said I recognized. Take me to this Dr. Delaney. You said he worked for Evergreen. If they took my memory away, then he should know how to bring it back."

"Or completely erase it. Do you realize what you're

asking me?" he demanded. "I just got you back after all these months. Holly, we can't be sure our baby is still alive. You're asking me to jeopardize your life, your sanity. I can't do that."

"Rawlins, listen to me," she said, reaching over to grasp his upper arm. "I know you, remember? You're not the kind of guy who runs away. It's just not in you."

"Holly." His voice cracked, his eyes filled with pain. "I'm not the same guy, not after a year without you. I want our baby as much as you do. But just the thought of never being able to hold you, to make love with you—" He was shaking his head, but she knew he could no more run from this than she could.

She cupped his face in her hands and kissed him tenderly on the lips. "Trust me, Rawlins. We will make love again," she whispered. "I promise you that."

He closed his eyes and pulled her to him with a groan.

"God help us," he whispered.

Silently, she echoed his words, more afraid than she would ever let him know. But equally determined never to be the woman Rawlins had described to her, the woman it seemed she'd been for almost the entire last year.

SLADE WOULD RATHER have cut off his right arm than do it, but he started the truck and headed for Dr. Delaney's house.

"Why would someone want to brainwash me?" Holly said beside him. "I'm an artist, right? Who in their right mind would want to brainwash an *artist?* That would be even more useless than brainwashing a private detective."

He knew what she was trying to do. She'd always joked when she was scared. And she had to be running scared as hell right now. "You're a great artist."

He wanted to argue that they should drive to Butte, find a hypnotherapist, see if the guy could get her memory back. But he knew he'd be wasting his breath. Holly was too smart not to know that time was of the essence. And Dr. Delaney might be the one person who knew how to get her memory back quickly. But would he? Even at gunpoint.

"So you've seen my work?" she asked, looking nervously at the road ahead.

He thought of the painting she'd done of the birth. "You have real talent, trust me."

"Sounds like you're not the first man to say that to me," she said. "Tell me about Dr. Allan Wellington."

He was saved by the ringing of his cell phone. "Rawlins."

"Slade, man, have I got news for you," Charley said. "Dude, don't go near this Evergreen place."

"Too late for that. What have you got?"

"The place was started by a guy named Dr. Allan Wellington as a fertility clinic—"

"Got that."

"Then you already know about Dr. August Wellington, the headshrinker?"

Slade frowned, trying to remember where he'd seen that name. Inez's. A plaque on the wall. Some award. "No."

"Man, he was just one of leaders in mind control during World War II, *and* he was Allan Wellington's *father*."

Slade looked over at Holly. "That makes a lot of sense. Was the old man connected with Evergreen?"

"You bet your best sneakers he was," Charley crowed. "But unofficially, of course."

So Allan could have learned the techniques from his father. "Did you find out anything on a Dr. O'Brien?"

"Not yet. Still checking. But if he's bad news, I'll get the dirt, man. You can count on me."

"What about Inez Wellington?"

"The headshrinker's daughter?" Charley asked. "Word I got, she's an old maid with an attitude." That about covered it. "Flunked out of medical school. But she *did* work with her father and brother, unofficially. Not much on her. Still digging."

"Listen, be careful. At least one person is dead and another missing and I suspect it's all connected."

"Always careful, man. That's the name of the game. Later, dude."

"Who's dead?" Holly asked the moment he clicked the phone off. "You haven't told me everything, have you?"

"Your midwife. She was killed in a car wreck just before you gave birth. Supposedly, it was an accident."

"So she wasn't one of the monsters," Holly said thoughtfully.

"No. But it's quite the coincidence she died before she was to assist your birth."

Holly nodded, still looking stunned by the news, but stronger than the Holly who'd stumbled up to his office on Christmas Eve.

And Carolyn Gray was missing, it seemed, but he suspected she hadn't gone far. In fact, he'd have sworn he saw her outside the Institute just minutes ago.

Dr. Delaney, it appeared as they neared the house, was home, and with luck, the doctor would be alone. Dr. Delaney lived just outside of town on a small hobby ranch. As Slade pulled into the drive, he noted that only one vehicle was parked out front. The doc's black Suburban.

A mongrel dog came out to meet them, barking as it ran alongside the pickup. Slade parked behind the doctor's car and asked, "You're sure about this?"

"Positive," she said and gave him a smile. "After everything you told me, Dr. Delaney must realize Evergreen's house of cards is falling fast. He'll want to help us."

"Yeah," Slade said checking the clip on his weapon. "Or kill us." Or kill him and zap Holly into another state of mind.

And yet, he still had no proof that anything was going on. Nor was he ready to involve the police. But he wasn't fool enough to go to Dr. Delaney without letting at least someone know where he was.

He dialed Chief Curtis's private number and got his answering machine. "I'm at Dr. Delaney's house. He has some tie-in with Evergreen and might be one of the people who has been using mind control on Holly. We're about to find out. Just want you to know in case you don't hear from me again."

Dr. Delaney opened the door before they reached it as if he'd been expecting them. Not a good sign. He didn't seem surprised to see them—or the weapon Slade held in his hand.

"Are you alone?" Slade asked.

Delaney nodded.

"You knew we were coming?"

"Heard all about it on the police scanner." Delaney pointed into his den.

Slade could hear the chatter, turned low. "Why would we be on the police scanner?"

"Someone broke into Evergreen Institute, stole confidential information and destroyed the lab. You were seen leaving the Institute. There's a warrant out for your arrest and a court order for Holly Barrows's recommitment. I just had a feeling I'd be seeing you."

Slade couldn't believe what he was hearing. And now Chief Curtis knew exactly where to find the two of them.

"We took nothing from Evergreen, and we certainly didn't destroy any lab," he said. "It's a lie."

"That's why you're waving a gun around." Delaney didn't seem upset though. Or worried that Slade would shoot him. The doctor looked questioningly at Holly.

"I understand we've already met," she said, extending her hand. "I'm one of the casualties of Evergreen Institute's mind-control program, the Genesis Project, but I have a feeling you already know that as well."

The words had the effect Holly had obviously been shooting for. Delaney looked more than surprised.

"Look, we know you're involved with the Evergreen Institute and the Genesis Project," Slade said.

Delaney didn't bother to deny it.

"To make a long story short," Slade said. "We were just at Evergreen. Someone zapped her. She can't remember the past year. Convenient, huh?" He waved the weapon in his hand. "Now you're going to help her remember the birth of her baby and the monsters who stole it. Then you can tell us about the Genesis Project and why you used to take my mother to Evergreen."

Delaney looked at Holly. "What do you mean by 'zapped'?"

"Mind control. It seems I've been taking Halcion mixed with equal parts hypnosis," she said.

"Halcion? Unless it was a very low dosage, you wouldn't have even been able to function."

"It sounds as if I just barely could," she said. "But then someone else was controlling me so I didn't need to think much."

"How do you know this?" Delaney asked, turning to Slade.

He shook his head. "It doesn't matter. As long as you undo it. I know you've worked with hypnosis and deprogramming."

Delaney let out a sigh. "This isn't the same thing. If Holly's memory loss wasn't hypnotically induced, putting her under will do no good."

"I guess there is only one way to find out," Slade said, "but first let's search the house," he said motioning with the weapon.

The house did appear to be empty, just as Delaney said.

When they returned to the main floor, Delaney motioned to the den. "Come on in here," he said to Holly.

"I'm coming too," Slade reminded him.

"I never doubted it. But put the gun away. It won't be necessary."

"I hope not."

Delaney stepped over to the police scanner and turned it off, then closed and locked the door behind them.

"Why do you have a scanner?" Slade asked.

The doctor gave him a pitying look and said sarcastically, "I secretly work for the police." Delaney shook his head in disgust. "Have you always been so paranoid?"

"More so lately," Slade admitted.

"You can sit here," the doctor said to Holly. "This might surprise you Slade, but even though I'm trying to retire, if there is an accident or some reason the hospital might need assistance, I still go in to see if I can be of help."

"I was just wondering," Slade said. "The bell-ringer, the one you had outside my office, did he call you on Christmas Eve? Or Carolyn Gray?"

Delaney shook his head. "I don't know what you're talking about."

Slade narrowed his gaze at the doctor. "And why didn't you just lie when I brought Holly to you to be examined? If you'd told me she hadn't had a baby, I might have just dropped the case."

"I had no reason to lie," Delaney said. "I'd never seen her before and knew nothing about any of this, but I don't expect you to believe that." Delaney looked at him, obviously irritated. "I suppose it would be too much to ask you to sit over there." He pointed to a spot off to Holly's right. "If I stand any chance of helping, you can't distract her in any way."

Slade nodded and took the seat Delaney suggested, but kept the revolver out, resting on his thigh, ready. He listened for any sound beyond the room, recalling how the doctor had locked the door behind them and the dog was outside. It would bark if anyone came around, warn them in time.

Delaney dimmed the lights, put on some soft music and took a chair facing them. Slade watched the doctor take Holly's hands in his. "Try to relax. Hypnosis is a state of increased suggestibility and concentration," he began, his voice low and soft.

"Under hypnosis you never relinquish your free will," he said, then looked over at Slade. "Hypnosis works on suggestion, but as with its use in weight loss or quitting smoking, it takes repeated attempts, and even then it is only viable if the patient accepts the suggestion. Although it is widely used, the success rate over a long period of time is poor."

Got the message, Slade said with a look.

Dr. Delaney turned his attention back to Holly. "Relax. Try to clear your mind. Make your mind peaceful. Quiet. Serene."

Slade rubbed the back of his neck. The room was almost too warm. He tried to focus outside the room, listening for the dog to bark, listening for any sound that might mean they were no longer alone.

"Holly," Delaney continued softly, as melodic as the faint music he had playing. "Hear only the sound of my voice, the sound of your own breathing. In and out. In and out. That's it. I'm going to help you to remember everything. You do want to remember, don't you?"

She nodded slowly.

Remember.

Slade shifted in his seat, still holding the weapon on his thigh, wondering if he hadn't heard the dog bark. Delaney shot him a look of warning and motioned for him to be quiet.

"Concentrate," Delaney said. "Hear only the sound of my voice. Nothing else matters. Just the sound of my voice and what I am going to tell you."

Slade let his attention shift back to Holly and Dr. Delaney's voice, the music now almost part of the room.

He watched Delaney, spellbound, as the doctor's voice dropped in the darkened room. Slower and slower, softer and softer came the flow of words until the beat of the words seemed to match the beat of his heart.

Remember.

Remember.

The weapon slipped from his hand, fell in slow motion to the floor, hitting, but without sound. Slade thought about picking it up. Then lost the thought.

Chapter Thirteen

Remember.

Remember.

At the sound of Dr. Delaney's voice, Holly came awake in an instant, but she didn't move, barely breathed. With her eyes still closed, she tried to remember. Some of last year came to her as if it had never been missing.

But not the birth of her baby. It was just as elusive as it had been before, she realized with aching disappointment.

She started to open her eyes, but stopped at the sound of Delaney's voice again.

"You probably won't believe this, but I'm doing you a favor," Delaney said, off to her left.

She held her breath, wondering who he was talking to, afraid to open her eyes and find out. She realized she was sitting on something hard and cold and damp. From the air around her, she was no longer in the doctor's warm den and she knew without looking that that was a very bad sign.

"You really made a mess of things this time," Delaney said.

She could hear him moving around on the concrete

floor, the scrape of his soles. He stopped directly in front of her. Her heart thundered so loudly in her chest she thought for sure he would hear it. She waited, afraid he knew she was awake.

"This is the best I can do for you," Delaney said.

She felt more than heard something drop beside her. Whatever it was hardly made a sound when it hit, but kicked up the cool, damp musty air. She felt her hair move. Her eyes flickered. She tried desperately to breathe slowly and not move. Not blink.

Then she heard him move away. She opened her eyes to slits and peered through her lashes, willing herself not to move another muscle.

She saw Slade sitting directly across from her and her breath caught in her throat. His eyes were open. He was staring at her, but it was clear he wasn't seeing anything! Oh, my God! A scream rose up her throat—

Then she saw his chest rise and fall, rise and fall. He was alive. She closed her eyes for a moment, trying to dam the tears of relief.

She could hear Delaney off to her left working on something metallic. It clicked as he moved.

Cracking her eyes open a little, she tried to see where she was and what Delaney was doing without moving her head. She and Slade were in a small concrete room with no windows. It would have felt like a basement if it wasn't for the battery-operated lamp overhead and the massive steel door that Delaney was standing by. In the middle of the door was a mechanism that looked like the lock on a vault. Only the dial was on the *inside!* And Delaney was turning it.

He stopped, as if sensing her watching, and started to turn in her direction. She closed her eyes and willed herself not to move. Instinctively, she knew he was looking at her, watching her closely. It was all she could do not to hold her breath. Not to twitch.

Her mind raced. She'd seen a place like this before when she was a kid. Panic filled her. It was a bomb shelter—like the one her grandparents had built in the nineteen-fifties. Why would Delaney put them—

She heard the metallic *click, click, click* and opened her eyes. He was planning to seal them up in here! She frantically looked around for a weapon, seeing only the pile of blankets Delaney had dropped next to her earlier, as she scrambled to her feet and rushed at him.

Dr. Delaney looked back in surprise, his hand on the door.

"No!" She threw herself at him, but he'd seen her coming. He slammed the door. It clanged shut, a deafening, final sound, just as she hit it. "No!" she screamed, her cry echoing in the tiny room.

She pounded on the door, knowing it was senseless. Pressing her palms and her cheek against the cold steel, she listened, thinking she might be able to hear if Delaney was still out there. As if from that, she could determine whether or not he'd ever be back.

She tried to turn the knob, but it wouldn't move. She leaned against the door and closed her eyes. No one knew they were down here. No one knew what Dr. Delaney and the rest of them had been doing to her mind for over a year. And no one knew about her baby. Her—and Slade's—baby girl.

And now Slade was gone into that other world. And she had no idea how to reach him. She'd never felt so alone. Or so defeated.

REMEMBER.

Remember.

Slade woke to a loud clang. He blinked, instantly aware that he was no longer in Dr. Delaney's den and that he no longer had his weapon.

Remember.

Remember.

He sat up, cobwebs of confusion clouding his thoughts. A voice inside his head kept repeating: *remember.* And yet he could remember little of what had happened in Delaney's den.

He blinked again, taking in the concrete room, the steel door and the woman standing in front of it.

"Holly?" he asked, his heart in his throat at just the thought that he might have lost her. Again.

She spun around, her eyes flying open. "Rawlins!" And then she was on the floor and in his arms.

He cupped her head in his hand as she pressed her face to his chest, his arm crushing her to him.

"I thought you were gone." She was crying, her head against his chest. "I thought I'd lost you the way we'd lost each other last year."

He rocked her, turning his face up to the heavens, a silent prayer of thanks on his lips. Wherever they were, whatever they were locked inside, however much time they had, they had each other right now.

He lifted her face, wiped her tears with the pads of his thumbs, as she stared at him, her eyes wide and dark. She seemed to hold her breath. He imagined that he could hear her heart pounding beneath her breast, but he knew he couldn't have heard it over his own.

"Holly." He said her name like a prayer. Like a promise. "Holly." He gently touched her face, cupping her cheek in the palm of his hand, thumbing away her tears, then trailing across the silken skin to her lips, her full, lush lips. She kissed the pad of his thumb, her eyes locking with his.

He felt a stab of desire so sharp it cut to the heart of him. The heat moved through him, a hot lava flow that ignited him. Drawing her onto his lap, he dropped his mouth to hers, opening her, entering her as her lips parted in invitation. He cradled her head in his hands, deepening the kiss, feeling the aroused throb of her pulse through his fingers, the sudden spurred quickness of her breath against his mouth, her small gasp as he drew her lower lip into his mouth, caught it between his teeth.

Her eyes filled with liquid fire, lighting up like stars. Or sparks. He thought his heart would burst from his chest.

"I've missed you, Rawlins," she whispered breathlessly against his mouth. "I'd forgotten how much."

HOLLY TREMBLED AT the look in his eyes. He buried his hand in her hair and pulled her down onto the blankets for his kiss. His mouth, his wonderful mouth, moved from her lips down her throat, leaving a trail of fire across her skin. "Rawlins," she whispered, feeling an urgency.

He opened her blouse, baring her breasts, his breath warm, as he moved down her, pushing aside her clothing to make way for his mouth as if he too couldn't bear them being apart another moment. His lips found her breast, provoked her nipple to a hard, pulsing point.

She arched against his mouth, her body melting against him. Then she drew him back up to her. His gaze locked with hers. They needed no words. Only this coupling of bodies, of hearts. A bonding that affirmed life.

She fumbled to free the buttons on his shirt in a desperate demand to feel his warm bare skin against hers. Pushing back the cloth, she flattened her palms again the solid heat of his chest, breathing in the scent of him, the feel of him. He groaned and pulled her down, surrendering to her touch as his mouth took hers again, and they struggled out of their clothing, their lips never parting. She tore at his clothing, needing nothing between them. Needing him.

And then they were naked. Her body melded with his, heat to heat, her skin alive from his touch, wet from his kisses. He lifted his mouth from hers, his gaze connecting with hers, then he entered her, filling her, fulfilling her, finally bringing her home.

SLADE ROLLED HER onto her back on the thick pile of blankets when it was over and looked down into her eyes, a smile on his lips. "You are the most desirable, beautiful, enchanting woman I have ever met."

She smiled up at him. "Rawlins," she said with a satisfied sigh, "you don't get out enough."

He lay down beside her, holding her in his arms. "I'm just so glad you're back."

"Rawlins, we're locked in a bomb shelter," she said.

"I see that." But all he saw was her, her wonderful face and eyes and lips, and her silken body next to his. He took her hand and kissed the tips of her fingers.

"It appears there's a timer built into the door."

"I understand the concept," he said. He didn't dare let himself think about the fact that they were trapped,

powerless to do anything about their baby or the world
outside that steel door. He didn't know how much time
they had. Only that they had it together. He didn't plan
to spend that time worrying about what could have been
or losing his mind over something he could do nothing about.

"The door isn't going to open until that timer goes
off," she said. "And maybe not even then."

"Uh-huh." He ran his fingers from her palm up the
inside of her arm to her elbow.

"You don't seem too upset about that."

"Holly, I'd break down that door for you if I could.
Since I can't..." He spooned her against him as he ran
his fingers from her shoulder, down the long slope of
her waist and up over her hip. "I spent the last year
dreaming about having you in my arms again. Now
that I do...I just want to make love to you until that
door opens."

"What if it never opens?" she asked, sounding a little breathless as she turned in his arms to met his gaze.

He grinned. "I think you know the answer to that
one." He drew her to him again.

HE WOKE WITH a start, not sure at first what had roused
him from a sated sleep. The first thing he felt was
Holly's warm body curled in his arms. Before that, he'd
thought he'd only been dreaming. But it all came back
in a flash and instinctively, he pulled her closer as he
looked around to see what had awakened him.

He'd forgotten they were locked in a bomb shelter.
He'd even forgotten to worry whether or not there was
sufficient air. His plan had been to make love to Holly
until hell froze over. Or until they completely ran out

of air in this steel-lined concrete box. Or until the door opened.

He sat up.

"What is it?" Holly asked sleepily.

"The door," he whispered. "It's open."

Chapter Fourteen

December 27

Holly sat up, drawing the blanket over her nakedness as she stared out into the dark beyond the open door. Without a word, Rawlins handed her her clothes and motioned for her to follow him. She half expected Dr. Delaney to appear at any moment in the opening. Or that the door would suddenly slam shut before they could reach it.

Neither happened. She hurried out of the bomb shelter to find a set of stairs leading up. Slade was pulling on his jeans. She quickly dressed and, taking the hand he offered her, let him lead her up the stairs, tiptoeing, quiet as mice.

The house seemed too quiet as Slade pushed open a door and they came out in the laundry room.

They stood for a moment, Slade obviously listening, his gaze warm on hers as if reminded of what they'd just shared. As if she could ever forget it.

She could see her own emotions mirrored in his eyes. Disbelief that they had found each other again. Fear that they might lose everything in the next few minutes. And hope, hope that they would still find their baby.

"My gun might still be in the den," he whispered.

She nodded, unsettled by the quiet of the house.

Up here, they could hear the howl of the wind outside, but nothing more. Where were the cops? Surely whoever Slade had called had gotten the message by now.

He motioned for her to follow him. As if she'd let him out of her sight for an instant if she could help it.

They moved through the darkness of the house, the white of the snowstorm giving them enough light through the undrawn drapes to navigate around the furniture and realized that it was a new day.

As they drew near the den, Holly felt a chill, as if there was a draft. The door to the den was partially open. Slade gave it a little shove, keeping back as though he thought he'd find Dr. Delaney waiting there with a weapon trained on them.

But Dr. Delaney wasn't sitting in the big chair by the fireplace. Nor behind the massive desk. Nor in the chairs she and Slade had occupied before.

Holly looked down and saw something at her feet that set her heart hammering. "Rawlins," she whispered, terror in her voice. She pointed to the floor and the bloody partial footprint on the hardwood.

He quickly found another print, then another. They led down the hall toward the front door. She followed him and the prints, the air growing colder, the bloody footprints more distinct.

The front door was ajar. Dr. Delaney lay sprawled in a pool of blood at its base, his left arm caught in the door as if he'd tried to keep it from closing behind his killer.

"Oh, God," Holly cried as Slade knelt beside the doctor's inert body.

"Is he...?"

"Yeah, he's dead. He's been shot. I would suspect with my gun." Slade stood and turned to look at her.

"Why kill Delaney?" she whispered. "He was one of them, right?" A thought hung suspended between them. "Why didn't he tell them we were in the bomb shelter?"

She watched Slade open the door with the sleeve of his shirt, hesitate, then close it again. "My pickup's gone."

He checked Delaney's pockets, then moved past her, headed back toward the den.

She followed him, not saying the one thing she knew they both were thinking. If these people would kill Dr. Delaney, what would they do to the little baby girl Holly had given birth to? "Rawlins, we have to call the police," she said as she followed him into the den.

"We can't, Holly," he said as he began to go through the desk drawers. "Even if they believed that we were locked in the bomb shelter at the time Delaney was killed, they'd hold us for questioning. It could take hours."

And they didn't have hours. That's what he was thinking.

"What are you looking for?" she asked.

"Keys to Delaney's Suburban, my weapon, any weapon," he answered, not looking up.

He slammed the drawers and headed for a set of cabinets on the opposite wall. She grabbed his sleeve as he started past. He cupped her cheek in his hand and she leaned into it, grasping his wrist, needing to feel the steady beat of his pulse, to assure herself they were still alive and there was still hope of finding their baby alive as well.

"I'll help you look," she said, letting him go. She could hear the police scanner now, turned so low the sound was like a moan. The room was warm, but she hugged herself for a moment to chase off the chill, then began to look around on top of the desk for Delaney's keys to keep from thinking about who had killed him and what those people would do next. Or why they hadn't come down to the bomb shelter and killed her and Slade. Several answers presented themselves. Either the killers hadn't known the two of them were down there. Or they couldn't get the door open.

If it was the latter, then they might be back to finish the job. She watched Slade search the drawers of the desk, noticing the way he used his shirtsleeve, leaving no prints, realizing they were both wanted now. Him by the law. Her by monsters and mad psychiatrists.

Her gaze was drawn to another sound in the room. The computer. It was on. Using her sleeve to cover her fingers, she touched the mouse.

The screen flashed on. She stared at the words typed there and said, "Rawlins, you'd better come here."

He was at her side in an instant.

"Look. I think it's a confession." It appeared Delaney had started to type it before he was killed. Whoever had murdered him must not have realized it because the computer had gone into standby mode, the screen dark.

"What the—" Slade read the words aloud.

To Whom It May Concern: In 1935, Hitler established a semisecret breeding program called *Lebensborn* meaning the Fountain of Life. The main function of *Lebensborn* was to provide racially ideal women for breeding to members of the SS and other selected men. Women were kidnapped and children were separated from parents. Some children were rejected. Some were placed with other families and were brainwashed to believe they were the offspring of these parents.

Slade stopped reading to glance over at Holly, his eyes dark and troubled.

She nodded and swallowed as he continued,

Hitler's programs put the government in the position of controlling people's sex lives. "We regulate relations between the sexes. We form the child," Hitler proclaimed. Selection, breeding and elimination was the key.

For more than thirty years, there has been a modern-day *Lebensborn* operating right here, only its methods are much more efficient, much more covert and insidious. Using the brainwashing techniques his father had initiated, Dr. Allan Wellington started his own superior breed. He formed a microcosm of what could be if babies were born only to the best possible couples. His sights were on the future of mankind. It wasn't until I became involved with Carolyn Gray that I learned the extent of Dr. Welling—

The cursor blinked. The rest of the screen was blank.

"Sweet heaven," Slade whispered.

All Holly could do was stare at the screen. She wanted to scream, to cry. "What does this mean? Is he saying our child was part of some experiment to create a master race? Or one of the ones rejected?" Eliminated?

Slade shook his head as he pulled her to him and stroked her hair.

"But Allan is dead! How could he…"

"I don't know, Holly."

She pulled back to look at him. Of course, he was as stunned and scared as she was—and just as shocked by the possible ramifications. For more than thirty years? Slade's mother had been part of the Genesis Project. So had Holly. But at least his mother hadn't married the crazy doctor. But Holly had! Even if it had only been for a few days. She realized how lucky she was that he'd died when he had. How *had* she gotten that lucky? It seemed almost too convenient. She shivered.

"I'm not sure what any of this means," Slade said, "But let's not jump to conclusions, all right?"

She wished that were possible. She watched him move back to the cabinets he hadn't searched yet, unable to keep from thinking of babies that were deemed unacceptable.

Slade opened a cabinet and froze.

"What is it?" she asked, deathly afraid to find out.

He turned slowly, and she saw the mask he held in his hand. She recognized the monster face from the night of her delivery. "Delaney was one of them."

He threw down the mask. "Let's get out of here. If I have to, I'll hot-wire Delaney's Suburban." He stopped and turned to look back at her, realizing she wasn't following him.

She was still standing behind the desk staring at the words Delaney had written. Her movements seemed jerky as if she'd been somewhere cold for too long as she hit Print, then Save, and waited. When the machine finished printing, she folded the sheet and stuck it in her coat pocket and turned off the computer.

Only then did she look at him. "I'm ready."

SLADE WATCHED HER movements. Cold, calculating, a hardness in her expression. An anger. A resolve. He recognized it because he felt it just as strongly as she did. Holly was a fighter, and he was thankful for that. A weaker woman wouldn't have made it this far.

He couldn't even comprehend the extent of the Genesis Project. For thirty years these people had been playing God. He concentrated on only one thought: stopping them. He held little hope of getting their baby girl back. He couldn't shake the horrible feeling that if it wasn't already too late—it would be soon.

Hadn't somebody once stated that the world will be saved by one or two people? He hoped he and Holly were enough. Then he realized, Allan Wellington had thought he was saving the world. Delaney and Carolyn Gray probably had thought they were, too.

Slade took Holly's hand as they passed Dr. Delaney's body and stepped out into what had become a raging blizzard. Wind whirled the falling snow, pelting them with stinging ice crystals that felt more like sand. Ice-cold sand.

"The garage," Holly yelled over the wind. She motioned to the detached garage and the disappearing tracks that led from it.

Why would Delaney have put a vehicle in the garage?

Slade took Holly's hand and ran through the drifting snow and cold to the side door of the garage. He felt around, found the light switch and flicked on the garage lamp. His pickup was sitting there, ice and snow melting beneath it, the keys in the ignition.

"Maybe Delaney really did put us into the bomb shelter for our own good," Holly said. "Maybe he was trying to protect us. Hide us, just like he did the truck. But if he wanted to help us, why didn't he just call the police?" she said, echoing his very thought.

"Because he was guilty as hell," Slade said, realizing Delaney might have been planning to confess on the computer, then skip the country—leaving him and Holly the pickup and the confession.

He doubted they would ever know what Delaney really had planned for them. Holly climbed into the front seat of the pickup, and he hit the garage-door opener. He climbed behind the wheel. Delaney was dead. Carolyn Gray was out there somewhere. That still left one monster unmasked. Slade knew they had to find him—before the two remaining monsters found them.

He put the pickup in four-wheel drive and backed out into the storm.

Snow had drifted across the road, but he could still see distinct tracks where someone had broken a trail in—and out again. The elusive Carolyn Gray? Or the third monster? And what if there were others involved in this? How could there not be? And yet, he knew something like this couldn't have been kept a secret for more than thirty years unless only a select few knew.

"Rawlins?"

"Yeah?" He burst through the last drift and hit the snow-packed highway, headed for Evergreen Institute. That's where the answers had to be. Someone had destroyed the lab. Trying to destroy evidence?

He glanced over at Holly when she didn't say any

more, half afraid that he might have lost her again. "Holly?"

"I just remembered something. I was thinking about the bomb shelter…cold, damp, concrete places…" Her gaze swung to his in the glow of the dash lights. "I know where I delivered our baby!"

Chapter Fifteen

It was late enough that the hospital parking lot was almost empty. Slade put his arm around Holly's shoulders as they hurried through the snowstorm to the front door.

The admitting nurse wasn't at her desk. As a matter-of-fact, all hell seemed to be breaking loose. Holly saw Head Nurse Lander rush by, a grimace on her face. From down the hall came a familiar braying voice.

"Inez," Holly said, immediately moving toward the sound.

The door to Inez's room was open. Nurse Lander had pushed her way in and was trying to raise her voice higher than Inez's.

"What seems to be the problem here?" Nurse Lander was demanding.

Inez began telling her, but stopped abruptly at the sight of Holly and Slade.

"I'd like to see my sister-in-law alone, please," Holly said to Nurse Lander.

The head nurse looked so grateful that Inez Wellington had finally shut up, she just gave a curt nod and motioned for the other nurses to leave with her.

The moment the door closed, Inez said to Slade, "I thought I fired you."

Slade was moving around the bed to the side opposite Holly, who calmly demanded, "I want to know where my baby is."

Inez rolled her eyes. "Oh, you aren't going to start—"

Slade laid a hand on the older woman's shoulder. "She asked you where her baby was."

Inez's eyes glittered maliciously. "Dead. Just like my brother, the man you killed!"

"He died of a heart attack!" Holly said, trying to keep her voice down.

"There was nothing wrong with his heart. Nothing!" Inez spat. "Until he married *you.*"

Holly shook her head. "He had to drug me to get me to marry him. What about that?" She waved away the question. "Evergreen. Tell me about his Genesis Project. Tell me about the babies. What did he do with the babies he stole from the mothers?"

Inez looked at her blankly.

"Dr. Delaney told us. I know what Allan was doing, using mind control to build what he considered a superior future generation." Inez started to protest, but Holly cut her off again. "Dr. Delaney is dead, but he left a confession."

Inez paled. The monitor beside her bed started to beep loudly. Slade reached over and unplugged it. "Whoever took over for your brother stole our baby. I don't think I have to tell you to what extremes we will go to get the truth."

Inez's eyes widened. She tried to ring for the nurse, but Holly grabbed the call button and moved it out of her reach.

A nurse stuck her head in the doorway, obviously alerted by the monitor suddenly going off.

"Everything's fine in here," Slade said, keeping a restraining hand on Inez's shoulder.

"Help me, you stupid bitch," Inez yelled at the nurse.

"My sister-in-law is a little distraught," Holly said. "Just give us a few moments to calm her down."

Inez started to protest, but the nurse shot Inez a call-*me*-a-bitch look and left, closing the door firmly behind her.

"You're going to kill me," Inez whined. "I'm a sick old woman."

"Yes, you are," Holly agreed.

Inez narrowed her eyes, anger making her nostrils flare. "My brother saw what was happening in the world. Stupid, lazy, ill-equipped people having child after child, children who would do nothing but become burdens on society, dependents of dependents, multiplying at staggering rates, the useless conceiving more of the useless."

Holly stared at her. "Who did he think he was that he got to decide who had children and who didn't? No wonder Delaney compared him to Hitler."

Inez looked shocked. "Allan was a brilliant doctor who was trying to save this planet. How dare you compare him to Hitler? My brother wasn't a racist. He was a realist."

"What did he do with the children?" Slade asked, his voice deadly low.

Inez turned her head to look at him. "The desirable ones got good homes with desirable parents who would provide the right kind of environment. It was the Wellington legacy to the future world," she said proudly.

"And the undesirable babies?" Holly asked, her voice barely a whisper.

Inez slowly turned to look at Holly again. "They were disposed of."

Holly felt her heart crush under the weight of the words. "Slade's and my baby? Which was it?"

"Do you even have to ask?" Inez said, seeming to have trouble breathing. She reached again for the call button to ring the nurse, looking small and weak in the large hospital bed.

Holly buzzed the nurse for her and dropped the call button on the bed beside Inez as she turned and walked away, afraid of what she'd do if she stayed a moment longer.

"Tell me who took over after Allan died," Slade demanded. "Tell me who is responsible for our baby's... theft."

"Go...to...hell," Inez wheezed.

"I will destroy the Wellington name, yours, your brother's and your father's," Holly heard Slade say to Inez. "The Wellington legacy will be a disgrace, dishonor and disgust."

"You won't live that long," Inez managed to utter. "And neither will Holly."

Then the hospital-room door closed, and Slade joined Holly in the hall. Holly could hear the clatter of a code-blue cart and the scurry of nurses. She didn't look back.

"We need to find the basement," she said, no longer sure she wanted to see where their baby had been born, but realizing she had to. She prayed it would make her remember something that would help them find their baby. If nothing else, she had to prove what the monsters had done and stop every last one of them once and for all.

SLADE FOLLOWED HOLLY down the hall, too shaken to speak. He'd wanted to throttle the truth out of the old woman, but he knew Inez would take it to her grave.

Holly had told him about her memory of the birth room. "It had to be close to the hospital, right? A room that was virtually soundproof, accessible and yet close enough that if something went wrong, they could get the mothers to the hospital quickly." He'd agreed. "What about under the hospital? My father was a bricklayer. He helped build the new hospital. I remember him telling me that they built the new one over the old one. Just like Seattle built over the city below it. It wasn't all that unusual back in those days."

Now all they had to do was find a way to access the old part because he believed Holly was onto something.

"I'm sure there is an outside entrance somewhere," she said now. "But there also has to be a way to access it from inside the hospital. A way to make it easy to bring patients in and out."

They found the door to the basement. It was locked. Of course. He pulled out his lock-pick kit. It only took a few moments while Holly stood guard. The door swung open and he pulled her onto the landing at the top of the concrete steps. Below them was nothing but darkness and cold.

Cold. Holly had been suffering from hypothermia, as if she had been outside.

"Carolyn Gray probably had a key," Holly said next to him.

"Yeah," he agreed as he fumbled around for a light switch. A long line of lights blinked on, illuminating a short set of stairs. With Holly right behind him, he descended the steps to find a long hallway running north. At the end of the hall was another door.

It too was locked—but only temporarily. As it swung open, Holly let out a gasp. "This is it. The hallway I remember from my dream." She started down it, passing up several doors.

He hurried after her, passing rooms stuffed with boxes and old furniture.

"This part of the hospital isn't directly under the other," he said more to himself than Holly.

"Soundproof," Holly said. "No one would be able to hear a woman scream."

Her words sent a chill through him. He ached at the thought that Holly had given birth down here.

"Rawlins?"

They were almost at the end of the hall. He heard only that one word and the sound of Holly's voice breaking and knew she'd found something.

She stood in one of the doorways, her body rigid, her face pale.

He moved to look past her into the room. It was bare except for the large hospital bed at its center—and a hospital bassinet. It was obvious that the room had recently been cleaned.

She stepped in, then stopped. "This isn't the room," she said, turning to look at him, then her gaze moved past him to the last room, the one across the hall.

He could see from her expression that she was thinking the same thing he was. This would have been the room the other woman gave birth in. Holly moved past him, out into the hall. Slowly, she opened the last door. He heard her let out a small cry.

The room looked exactly like the other one, and he

realized it too had been cleaned. There would be no evidence that Holly had given birth here. Nor any proof that the other woman had either.

"Is this the room?"

She nodded, but he couldn't see how she could be sure. The rooms looked identical to him.

He stood just inside the door, almost afraid to move, his heart pounding wildly as he watched Holly walk to the bassinet as though in a trance. He tried not to imagine what she must be reliving. The room was so cold, so remote. As he stared at the bassinet, he fought hard not to think about what had happened here. Or would happen again if they didn't stop it.

"Oh damn, Rawlins," he heard her say. He swung his gaze from the bassinet to her. She was standing beside the bed, staring up at the ceiling.

Slowly, he followed her gaze. The paint had cracked at the corner of the ceiling just above the bed, leaving dark lines in the shape of something unimaginable. A monster.

Behind him, he heard the distinct scuff of footsteps on concrete. He spun around, realizing he had no weapon.

Holly turned at the sound as well. A figure stood in the door. "Rawlins, that's the woman! The one from the cemetery!" The woman wore a blue housekeeper's uniform, her face ashen, her hands clutched over her chest as if in prayer. "Where is my baby?" Holly cried, lunging toward her.

The woman's eyes widened, then rolled back into her head. Slade barely reached her before she hit the floor. He caught her in his arms and carried her over to the hospital bed.

"That's her," Holly said, staring down at her. "She's not…dead is she?"

"No, she just passed out." The woman's name tag read Gwen Monroe. She appeared to be in her early thirties, but she could have been much younger. She was one of those women who had a lot of miles on her, and it showed in her face. Her hands were rough and red, the nails chewed to the quick. "Do you know her?"

Holly shook her head. "The first time I saw her was at the cemetery. That is, as far as I can remember."

Gwen Monroe. A housekeeper at the hospital. The hospital where both Holly and Gwen had given birth— only in an old deserted underground part of it.

The housekeeper's lashes flickered. She came fully awake and, with obvious fear, pushed herself up, backing across the bed away from them until she reached the wall. "Who are you?"

"Don't you know?" Holly said. "You gave me your baby."

The woman blanched, and, for a moment, Holly thought she would faint again.

"Where is my daughter?" Holly demanded.

Slade touched her arm. "Easy," he warned. "Ms. Monroe?" he coaxed. "We aren't going to hurt you," Slade continued in that same soothing voice. "We're looking for our baby, the one Holly gave birth to the same night you gave birth to your son down here."

What were they doing—good cop, bad cop?

"I don't know nothin'!" Gwen Monroe said.

"Would you rather talk to the police?" Holly asked.

Panic washed over Gwen's features. "You can't prove nothin'."

"You're wrong about that," Slade said calmly. "The

doctors upstairs took blood from both Holly and your baby Halloween night. That blood will prove that the infant is yours."

"Blood's not conclusive evidence," Gwen said, obviously just repeating what someone had told her.

"But DNA is," Holly said.

The woman blinked.

Holly continued, "It would mean digging up the baby's grave, but we are prepared to do that if you don't—"

"No," Gwen Monroe cried. "I don't want him dug up."

"Who contacted you about giving up your baby?" Slade asked.

It had to have been nurse Carolyn Gray, but Holly knew Slade just wanted to confirm it.

"She said I better not say nothin'." The woman's face crumbled. "My baby, he quit movin'. She checked and said he was dead and would have to come out. That I'd have to bury him." Tears streamed down her face. "I don't have no money. I got two other kids, no husband. She said she would help me. Get him a decent burial. Let him be somebody and that I would get money to help my other kids." She looked up at them, her gaze pleading with them to understand.

"Who was she, this woman who helped you?" he asked.

"Lorraine. Lorraine Vogel," she said, her voice barely audible.

Holly stared in shock. The woman Dr. Parris had talked about. The mother of the young man who'd killed Slade's mother.

"How do you know Lorraine?" Slade asked with obvious shock.

"She works here as a nurse," Gwen said.

"What did they do with *my* baby?" Holly asked.

Gwen shook her head. "I don't know. I was real sick."

"But you knew they'd switched your baby with mine," Holly persisted. "That's why you were at the grave."

Gwen looked scared. "Not till later. She told me not to think about it. Not to go there. But I had to. Just that one time, really."

"Who delivered your baby?" Slade asked.

She shook her head. "They had on masks. Lorraine said it was better that way, then I couldn't get in no trouble." She looked up at Slade. "I can't give the money back. I ain't got it no more."

"How much did they pay you?" he asked.

"Two thousand dollars." There was awe in her voice.

"You don't have to give the money back," he assured her. "What were you doing down here today?"

"Sometimes I just come down here. I can't go to the cemetery. So I just come down here."

THE WIND HOWLED on the outskirts of town, rocking the pickup and blowing snow into deep drifts. After her son's confession and suicide, Lorraine Vogel had moved from Slade's old neighborhood to a run-down stretch of windblown, low-rent space behind an old motel and gas station on the edge of town.

"*This* is where she lives?" Holly asked in surprise as she stared through the blowing snow.

According to the address in the phone book—and the rusted, dented mailbox—Lorraine lived in an ancient small trailer at the back, with old tires holding down the roof to keep it from blowing off.

Slade pulled behind the abandoned motel and they got out, fighting the wind and the airborne snow as they waded out to the trailer. He pounded on the rusted metal, the wind whistling through the tread-bare tires on the roof, the air thick with snow.

Lorraine Vogel opened the door, a gray sweater wrapped around her bony shoulders. She didn't seem surprised to see him.

"I'm Slade Rawlins—"

"I know who you are." Her voice was hoarse, her body was small and thin. She looked eighty but would have been closer to sixty by his estimation. He could see her in a Halloween monster mask at the foot of Holly's bed. As frightening as the other two monsters even for her age and frailty.

"I'm here about Gwen Monroe," he said and realized she must have known that as well.

She nodded, unhappiness stamped in a lifetime of lines on her face. He wondered if the woman had ever known peace. He'd heard that Roy's father had taken off on her long before the boy was born, long before her real problems with Roy had begun.

She stepped aside to let them in. "What other reason would you have for being here?" she asked, sounding a little drunk.

The trailer was dark and cold, a woodstove working futilely in one corner. Slade spotted an almost-empty bottle of cheap bourbon sitting on the kitchen counter with an empty glass next to it.

"This is Holly Barrows," he said.

Lorraine gave her the once-over and dismissed her.

If the name rang any bells, Lorraine's expression didn't give it away. But maybe the older woman had already recognized her.

Lorraine motioned to the couch, a lumpy, discolored blob slumped against the wall of the living room. He and Holly chose to stand as Lorraine took the chair in front of the woodstove, her thin form molded into the cushions of the chair from the long hours she must spend in it in front of the fire.

"Gwen told us about the deal you got her for her baby," Slade said, wasting no time.

Lorraine made no sign that she'd heard him. She seemed to be watching the fire through the cracks in the old cast-iron woodstove as if lost in thoughts of her own.

"I need to know about the other baby, the one Holly gave birth to," he continued. "Whoever else helped you deliver those babies, I think they're the same people who killed my mother. I believe they killed your son too. But you probably know more about that than I do."

Still she didn't move, didn't respond, as if she'd lost interest years ago in her son's guilt or innocence or her own.

"Dammit, Lorraine, these people have Holly's baby. My baby."

Her head turned slowly, her eyes narrowing as she looked at him. "Your baby?" She seemed confused and he saw that she was drunker than he'd first thought.

"Please, help us, Mrs. Vogel," Holly pleaded. "I was told I had given birth to Gwen Monroe's stillborn—but you know I had a baby girl. What happened to her?" Holly's voice broke, and Slade could see her fighting tears. "Please, we don't care about anything but getting our baby back."

Lorraine was staring at Holly, her eyes rheumy and moist in the firelight. "I never know where the babies go."

"Who does?" Slade asked.

She wagged her head, her neck seeming too weak to hold it anymore.

"Lorraine, I don't want to have to call the police—"

Her look was pitying. "As if anyone can keep history from repeating itself. I was there the night you and your sister were born. That's when he got the idea."

"Wellington?" Slade guessed.

She nodded, and tears filled her eyes and splashed down her cheeks seemingly without her notice.

"I know you and my mother were part of a special project at Evergreen Institute, Genesis," Slade prodded. "What is it?"

"Through Genesis he will live forever," she said and smiled. "You probably thought Allan was dead."

Slade was trying to decide if Lorraine was drunk. Or nuts.

Holly knelt at the old woman's feet and took Lorraine's hands in her own. "Tell me about my baby, please."

Lorraine shook her head; it wobbled, then drooped to her chest.

"Slade, I think she's taken something!" Holly was on her feet, moving to the liquor bottle. He heard the rattle of an almost-empty pill bottle as he moved to Lorraine's side.

The older woman seemed to rally for a moment. He could hear Holly on the phone calling 911, but he doubted the paramedics would be able to get here in time.

"Lorraine, for God's sake tell me how I can find my baby," he said, not sure she could even still hear him.

Her eyes glazed over, opaque as cataracts, her mouth opened, the words that fell out almost undistinguishable. But he heard enough to make him lurch back in shocked horror.

He stared at the woman, wanting to cry out his frustration. His rage. But it would have been a waste of words. Lorraine Vogel was gone.

"The paramedics are on their way," Holly said. "Rawlins, this prescription is today's date. I think she took almost the entire bottle."

He felt for a pulse and shook his head.

"My God, no!" Holly cried. "She was our last hope."

"No," he said, refusing to believe that as he rose. He was still shaking from what Lorraine had told him. It was worse than he'd first expected. So much worse.

"Why would she kill herself? She couldn't have known we were coming here," Holly said.

"Maybe Dr. Delaney warned her. Or Carolyn Gray. Or maybe she knew Carolyn would be coming after her."

He could feel Holly's gaze on him. "What did she tell you? Please, you have to tell me."

He tried to find the words. "She told me my mother was infertile and that my life, my sister's and my children's lives would always be in danger because of my genes." He swallowed, his mouth tasting of bile.

"Your genes?" Holly said.

"It seems Allan was fathering babies at Evergreen Institute by using artificial insemination and mind control on unsuspecting women who believed they were infertile."

"Rawlins, what are you saying?"

"The program didn't end with his death."

Her eyes widened in obvious confusion and shock.

"He froze his own sperm and whoever took over his 'master plan' took over the baby-making and the baby elimination."

"But not our baby," she whispered, fear making her look like a deer caught in headlights. "Our baby had a dimple. Tell me between that and the birthmark there is no way—"

"There is no way," he said. "But at first I thought, if my mother was part of the Genesis Project—"

"But then you remembered the Rawlinses' dimples," she said.

"Yeah. Joe Rawlins was my father, and I'm the father of your baby." So what did the Genesis Project have to do with him? And his and Holly's baby? It all came back to his mother. If she really was infertile… What bothered him was that he couldn't remember any photos of his mother pregnant. He'd looked at all the albums last night and right now, he couldn't remember even one of his mother pregnant with him and Shelley.

He shook his head, trying to shake off the horror of what the old woman had told him. "Lorraine said my mother was too smart for her own good."

"You think she figured out what Allan was doing?" Holly asked in a hushed whisper.

"Maybe. I don't believe she wanted more children. But she might have pretended she did if she'd discovered something odd going on up at Evergreen."

"But why wouldn't she tell your father?"

He shook his head. "Maybe because she knew he'd try to stop her."

He glanced around the trailer. They had to search it before the paramedics arrived, because he and Holly had to be gone by then. He began going through drawers while Holly dumped out the contents of Lorraine's purse on the couch and started sifting through them.

He found the photograph of Roy Vogel first. It was a shot of the boy at about five. He was standing beside his mother, both Roy and Lorraine were smiling into the camera, although even then Roy looked too intent.

There was another photograph in the drawer; this one rubber-banded to a worn bankbook.

Carefully, Slade slipped the photo from beneath the rubber band, his fingers shaking with revulsion. It was a photograph of Roy, again at about age five. The boy was sitting on a man's lap, the man holding him the way a man would hold his son. The man in the photo was Dr. Allan Wellington. "Sweet heaven."

"Slade?" Holly said behind him. She held up a mask, exactly like the third one from her painting. "She was there."

The three monsters. Dr. Delaney. Carolyn Gray. Lorraine Vogel. And now two of them were dead. He thought he should feel something. Relief. Something. He just felt sick.

He handed her the photo without a word and opened the bankbook, shocked by the amount. Lorraine Vogel was a rich woman, and Slade had a pretty good idea how she'd come by most of the money.

He turned to look at Holly. She had paled, her hand trembling as it held the picture. She glanced at the bankbook. "Why would she live like this if she had all that money?"

Slade shook his head. He could hear the whine of

an ambulance in the distance. Hurriedly, he stuffed the photos and the bankbook into his coat pocket.

"I found these." Holly held up a large ring of keys. "She still works at Evergreen. Wanna bet there's a key on here?"

He took the key ring from her, his gaze meeting hers.

"Don't even think about trying to talk me out of it, Rawlins," Holly said. "I'm going with you to Evergreen. These people drugged me, made me think I was losing my mind, they stole my memory and they stole my baby before I even got to hold her—" Holly's voice broke, but a steely resolve honed among the tears in her eyes. "No matter how this ends, I plan to be there. That is where Carolyn Gray has to be—where the Genesis Project began."

One look at her and he knew arguing would be a waste of time. "We have to make one stop on the way."

As they left he glanced at Lorraine. He hoped she was with Dr. Allan Wellington again, someplace real hot.

Chapter Sixteen

Slade drove past Chief L. T. Curtis's home, not surprised to see that the cop's car wasn't there. He parked down the street and looked over at Holly.

"Rawlins?" Holly asked, sounding worried. "You aren't thinking you're going to leave me here, are you?"

His gaze met hers, all their hopes and dreams captured in that one look. He had thought about having the chief lock her up. That's the only way Slade knew he wouldn't worry about her. The truth was, however, he feared Curtis would put them both behind bars. For leaving the scene of a murder, if nothing else. By now the chief would have been out to Dr. Delaney's.

That was one reason Slade had no intention of going near the police station. If there hadn't been a warrant out for his arrest earlier, he was pretty sure there would be now, if he knew the chief.

"With Carolyn Gray still on the loose, I'm not about to go out to Evergreen Institute without some sort of backup," he assured her. "We'll tell Norma. She can contact the chief after we've left."

"Our baby girl's alive," Holly said. "There has to be something at Evergreen, some record of where we can find her. I feel it." She placed her hand over her heart, her eyes shining.

He nodded. He couldn't argue with a woman's heart—even if he'd wanted to.

"YOU JUST MISSED L.T.," Norma said when she opened the door, obviously surprised to see them. "He's worried to death about the two of you."

"I figured as much," Slade said. "You remember Holly?" Norma nodded and smiled, holding out her hand. "We met last year."

"Yes, I remember," Holly said.

Norma ushered them into the living room. "Can I get you something to drink? I still have a few of those sugar cookies left, Slade."

"No. We don't have time for that. There's something I need to tell you."

She offered them a seat and Slade poured out everything they knew, from Holly's mind control to the monsters stealing her baby to Dr. Allan Wellington's superbabies and Dr. Delaney's and Lorraine's involvement and subsequent deaths.

Norma stared at him. "It's all so…unbelievable."

"What is the Genesis Project that you and my mother and Lorraine Vogel were involved in at Evergreen Institute?" he asked. "I know you were a patient there."

"I told you that. L.T. and I were trying to have children."

"But Dr. Allan Wellington couldn't help you?" he asked.

"You know that, too. But I don't know anything about a Genesis Project. Nor did I know about Dr. Wellington's…superbabies."

"So you were infertile?" Slade asked, remembering what Lorraine had said about his mother.

"No." She seemed to hesitate, looking at him as if trying to gauge how much he knew. "I came close once, but the babies were stillborn."

Babies? "Twins?"

She must have realized her slip. While she must have known that it would have been common knowledge she had been pregnant, not everyone knew it had been twins.

He stared at her, hearing the echo of Lorraine's words about history repeating itself, hearing the chief say he was sterile, hearing his own heart banging against his rib cage. "Do you have a photo of my mother when she was pregnant?"

Norma turned white, all the color bleaching from her face in an instant, and he knew. Should have always known. It had been right there in front of him the whole time.

"Who was the father of your babies?" he asked, his tone as cold and hard as the look he gave her. "I know it wasn't L.T. because he told me he was sterile."

She opened her mouth, then closed it. Tears filled her eyes. He watched her fight the inevitable. "Your father."

Slade squeezed his eyes shut. He wanted to put his fist through the wall. "And I was afraid my *mother* was having an affair," he ground out. He opened his eyes, fighting hard not to lose his temper. Lose his sanity. He felt Holly behind him, felt her hand squeeze his shoulder as she moved to stand behind his chair.

"You don't understand," Norma pleaded. "I did it for your mother. It was her idea."

"For you to have children by my father?" Slade

glared at her. "He was the man you were in love with, wasn't he? Did my mother know *that?*"

Norma said nothing, dropping her gaze in answer.

He shook his head, trying hard to make sense of all of it. So many lies. So many deceptions. But what did it have to do with his and Holly's baby? "What do you know about Holly's and my baby?"

"Slade, I swear to you on your father's grave that I didn't even know the two of you had a child together," Norma cried.

"Where were Shelley and I born?" he asked.

"In the hospital. The old underground part."

He felt Holly's hand tense on his shoulder.

"Dr. Wellington and Lorraine delivered you," Norma was saying. "Your mother was there. She pretended to be pregnant during the nine months. It wasn't that unusual back then for a woman to fake a pregnancy. There was a stigma to adoption. And infertility."

"That's why there weren't any photos of my mother pregnant, because everyone close to her knew it was a lie," he said, more to himself than to her. Was that the secret his mother had begged Aunt Ethel not to tell? Not about an affair. Not about Evergreen. But about the biggest lie of all. Except Joe Rawlins was in on this, he realized. It had to be another lie, this one his mother's own.

He felt Holly's hand, warm and reassuring. "My father agreed to this?"

"Not at first. But yes. He would have given your mother anything."

"Shelley doesn't know, does she?"

"No. How could she?"

"What about the chief?" Slade asked.

Norma seemed to hesitate again. "He knew."

"He was against it?" Slade guessed. "But you did it anyway, and we both know why. Obviously, the chief did, too. How does my mother's murder fit into all this?"

"It doesn't," she looked shocked.

He couldn't help thinking about what Lorraine had said about his mother being too smart for her own good.

"I loved your mother," Norma said angrily. "I would have done anything for her."

"Even sleep with my father." He got up. "Why did you tell me my mother was having an affair?"

"I thought she was." Norma's gaze dropped. "Maybe I just wanted to believe it. It would have made things more...even."

"L.T. keeps an extra service revolver in the house," he said. "I need it and a box of cartridges."

Norma got to her feet, looking old and tired.

"We're going out to Evergreen," he said when she handed him the weapon and cartridges. "Carolyn Gray is still at large," he said, loading the weapon, then dumping a handful of extra cartridges into his coat pocket before slipping the gun in the other pocket. Without looking at Norma, he turned, taking Holly's hand, and headed for the door. "Give us twenty minutes to get out there, then call the chief. Tell him everything we've told you."

"Slade?"

He kept his back to her but stopped, knowing she wasn't going to ask him not to go to Evergreen. She knew him better than that. After all, she'd been like a mother to him.

"I'm sorry. But if I hadn't done what I did, you wouldn't be here."

"No," he said. "And, right now, that would be a blessing."

Holly didn't say a word as they climbed into the pickup and started toward Evergreen. She laid her hand on his thigh and seemed to watch the road ahead.

"Thanks," he said after a few miles, thankful that she hadn't asked a lot of questions or tried to offer him sympathy or even comfort right now.

"Rawlins, when this is all over I want us to take the baby to someplace warm," she said. "Have you ever been to Arizona?"

He glanced over at her, wondering if she felt as cold as he did inside. "No, but I'd go there with you."

She smiled. "Good." After a few minutes, she said, "Did I tell you I remembered the first time I met Dr. Allan Wellington? It was at a party right before Thanksgiving. I hate parties, but I went because Dr. Wellington supposedly wanted to buy some of my art. I had a splitting headache. He offered me a little something for it."

Slade glanced at her in the glow of the dash lights. She was staring out the window.

"Once he had control of my mind, he didn't need the pills anymore. I guess I should feel lucky that at least I wasn't taking the Halcion when I met you, when I got pregnant with our baby and during my pregnancy. Inez insisted I start taking the pills again right after I came home from the hospital because of the weird dreams I started having. Memories."

He drove for a few miles in the falling snow, silence between them.

"I guess he wanted a legitimate heir," Holly continued as if there hadn't been a break. "That's why he married me. I was lucky he died when he did. I guess he planned to impregnate me the way he had all his other 'mothers.'" She paused for a moment. "You thought I might have killed him for his *money.*"

The pickup's lights cut through the snow and darkness. Ahead, Slade spotted the turnoff for Evergreen. He slowed the truck. He glanced over at her and frowned. "You think someone killed Dr. Wellington and made it look like a heart attack?"

"It's possible. Especially now that we know that Dr. Delaney was a friend of Allan's and part of all this."

"Sweet heaven." He couldn't help thinking of his father's heart attack.

He brought the pickup to a stop at the entrance to Evergreen Institute, the headlights shining through the snow to illuminate the gate. Only this time, he wasn't going to buzz in and let them know he was coming. He took the key ring Holly had found at Lorraine's and climbed out of the truck, leaving the pickup running, the headlights on, and, walked over to the lock.

It took him a few minutes. The snow fell around him silent as death. No wind up here. No sound but the hum of the pickup's engine behind him and the glow of the headlights.

He finally found the key that activated the gate. It swung open. Holly drove the pickup through, the gate closing soundlessly behind the truck.

She slid over as he got back in. He turned off the headlights and waited for his eyes to adjust. He could make out the pines along the edge of the road.

Slowly, he drove through the falling snow toward Evergreen. He'd noticed an employees' entrance road yesterday. It wound behind the Institute. Slade took it now. Through the snow, he saw a light glowing in the employees' parking lot. He followed it, stopping at the edge of the late afternoon darkness.

"We'll have to walk from here," he told Holly as he cut the engine. He wanted to tell her how he felt, all the emotions roiling inside him, one clear. He loved her. He loved their baby. "If something happens—"

She laughed softly. "What could *possibly* happen?" Then she touched his face, leaning toward him to kiss his lips. A soft, tender kiss.

Then he heard the click of her door opening as she slipped out. He followed her.

One of the keys on Lorraine's ring opened the employees' entrance. He'd half expected an alarm to go off. Or a dozen guys in white coats to appear the moment they stepped inside.

But no alarm sounded. No team of white coats. The door closed behind them. Slade stood with Holly in the silence, tense as a spring. Holly pointed down the dimly lit hallway, away from the section of Evergreen that resembled a country club to the part without the pool or tennis courts, without the spa and the gym. Toward the part that she said was closed to "clients."

The gun he'd taken from Norma's felt cold and heavy as a rock in his coat pocket. In his other pocket was the key ring and the extra cartridges.

He was counting on Dr. Allan Wellington's ego. The man couldn't have helped himself; he would have kept track of his babies just to feed that incredible ego. Slade was also counting on the person who'd taken over for Wellington to have the same type of egocentric character. So there would be a record of what had happened to their baby.

The problem was, Slade wasn't sure how much access Lorraine would have had. He didn't think she'd have had a key to the files. He'd probably have to break in. And Carolyn Gray was still at large. And, as far as Slade knew, armed and dangerous.

They reached a caged door with a sign announcing it Off Limits. Only authorized personnel. As quietly as he could, he tried one key, then another until almost the last one. The lock opened. Again, no alarm sounded. At least not one he and Holly could hear.

He glanced over at her. She looked scared but not about to stop now. That was his Holly.

They moved quickly, stepping through the door, closing it firmly behind them. This section looked like a hospital. Smelled like one, too. It was the smell that worried Slade. He pulled the weapon from his pocket and edged down the hallway. There were only four doors, the second one on the right standing open. He moved cautiously, motioning for Holly to stay behind him. The first two were examining rooms, the third, on the left, appeared to be an operating room.

He stopped just before the open doorway, took a breath, gripped the weapon in both hands, then started to step around it, ready to fire.

"Adding another breaking and entering charge to your record?" Chief L. T. Curtis asked as he stepped from what was obviously the lab. "I figured you'd show up here." He wagged his head at him. "Have you lost your mind, Slade?"

"Not yet. But the night is young." He assumed Curtis had spoken with Norma or he wouldn't already be here. Obviously Norma hadn't waited twenty minutes to call him.

"I thought you had more sense than to jeopardize your client's life as well as your own," the chief said.

"It's my baby who's missing," Holly snapped.

"I understand that," Curtis said, sounding almost compassionate, a stretch for him even on one of his good days. "But you have no business here. Neither of you do."

Slade looked past him. The lab had been vandalized, just as Delaney had told them. Slade felt his heart drop. "I think whoever took our baby kept records. I need to look in those files." He motioned to a huge set of file cabinets against the right-hand wall of the lab.

"You aren't searching anything," Curtis snapped. "I can have you both thrown in jail, and it appears that's what it's going to take."

"You should be out looking for Carolyn Gray, not busting my chops," Slade snapped back.

"We *are* looking for her. She was last seen inside the Institute. We've searched the entire place. We haven't found her, but that doesn't mean she isn't here. Now you listen to me," the chief continued. "I have a couple of police officers in the main office upstairs. I can either call them down here to remove you bodily. Or you can do this my way."

Slade glanced toward the file cabinets. They didn't look as if they'd been broken into. Yet. "You'd better go ahead and call your officers down here." He started to step past the cop.

The chief swore at he grabbed Slade's arm. "You want to add resisting arrest to all the other charges against you?"

They glared at each other for a long moment. Slade wondered if Norma had told the chief everything? It didn't seem the time to bring up her confession. Slade suspected her liaison with his father was one of the reasons the chief had never let himself get too close to Slade and Shelley. Or maybe it was just the cop's nature.

Curtis let out a sigh. "Well, at least don't jeopardize Holly's life with your damned foolishness. Until Carolyn Gray is found, I want Holly with those two policemen upstairs—no argument," he snapped when Holly started to protest. "I'll take her up myself. When I get back down, I'll let you be present while I search the lab. That's the deal and believe me, it's a better deal than you deserve."

Slade saw his chance to be left alone here to search on his own. "He's right, Hol," he said quickly. "I'll feel much better knowing you're safe." Hurriedly, he pulled her to him and whispered, "I have a better chance of finding something without the chief here."

She kissed him and nodded, obviously not liking it but realizing if she didn't go along with it, the cop would force them both to go with him. "Be careful."

"Always."

"Come on," the chief said. "Wait right here," he ordered Slade. "You touch anything and it will be inadmissible as evidence."

He was no longer looking for evidence. He just wanted his baby. "Got it."

Curtis shot him a look. "I mean it, Slade. I'll put your ass behind bars so fast your head will swim."

Slade waited until Curtis and Holly disappeared through the locked doors and around the corner before he hurried into the lab.

The room was large with ceiling-high cabinets along the left wall, what looked like a huge walk-in cooler at the rear and a lab setup and office off to the right. Someone had broken a lot of the glassware and smashed some of the equipment. Strange, it looked more like vandalism than anything else. Certainly not the kind of thing he thought Carolyn Gray would do to cover her trail.

Slade moved to the desk and quickly checked the drawers. Nothing of interest. But on the wall over the desk was a plaque that read:

> The question of genetic quality of the coming generations is a hundred times more important than the conflict between capitalism and socialism and a thousand times more important than the struggle between Germany and other countries.
> > Fritz Lenz, leading German eugenicist.

Next to it was another:

> Eugenics: the movement devoted to improving the human species through the control of hereditary factors in mating.

Sweet heaven.

He turned to the row of steel file cabinets. This time, he doubted he'd find a key on Lorraine's ring. He was right. No key.

He glanced around for something to try to pry open the cabinets with. He found a metal letter opener in the top desk drawer, broke each of the locks and drew out one drawer after another.

They were all empty.

Whoever had cleaned them out had a key. So why bother to make it look like the place had been vandalized? Unless whoever had done it was in a hurry and didn't have the time or patience to break the locks on the files.

Had Carolyn had the key all along? Slade doubted it. She must have taken it from Dr. Delaney. No wonder they hadn't been able to find the keys to his Suburban.

He glanced over at the cabinets lining the wall across the room, doubting Carolyn had left anything. She'd known exactly what she was looking for, it seemed.

And yet, his only hope was that she might have missed something. He started toward the cabinets, slowing as he spotted something dark pooling beneath one of the far cabinets.

He pulled the weapon from his pocket and moved cautiously toward the cabinet.

HOLLY BARELY HEARD what Chief L. T. Curtis said as she walked beside him down the hall. All she could think about was Slade back there alone in the lab. She hadn't wanted to leave him, but she knew that if she hadn't, Curtis would have forced them both to go. Selfishly, all she could hope was that Slade would find what they needed. A lead to their daughter.

Let Curtis bring down Carolyn Gray and see that she got her proper punishment. Holly just wanted her daughter—and Slade.

The chief was talking about Slade, how stubborn he'd always been, telling stories about Slade as a teenager. "He's been obsessed with his mother's murder for as long as I can remember."

So the cop didn't know that Norma had told Slade the truth. "That seems pretty normal," she said, only half listening. This part of the Institute seemed completely abandoned. She could hear nothing but the sound of their footsteps and the cop's voice. Her mind, however, was on Slade and what he would find. He had to find *something*.

"Shelley doesn't just look like her brother," Curtis was saying. "Smart as a whip, that one. Always had to be careful around her. She never missed a trick."

"I'm sure you and Norma love them like your own children," she said. Somewhere deep in the bowels of this place she could hear what sounded like water running. Or maybe it was the heating system cranking out warm air, trying to heat this monstrosity. "I'm a little confused about where we are." They'd been walking, it seemed, for some time and yet she hadn't seen the entrance she and Slade had come in. Nor any elevator or stairs.

"This place is much larger than you would think from looking at it on the outside," he said. "The guy who had this place built thought the world was going to come to an end, so he had this part put in separately from the main house. The walls are made of reinforced concrete four feet thick. You could drop a bomb on this place and it would stay standing." He seemed to realize she wasn't listening. "So fill me in on what you know about this baby thing."

"I'm sure Norma told you most of it."

"Norma was too upset, she wasn't making much sense."

Holly told him about the three monsters huddled at the end of her bed during her delivery in the abandoned part of the hospital.

"So you think they were Dr. Delaney, Lorraine Vogel and this nurse, Carolyn Gray?" he said.

"Yes, except..."

"What's wrong?" he asked.

She frowned as she remembered something. "I have this memory of one of them talking to me and this distinct feeling that I knew the person. I remember being shocked because it was the last person I would have suspected. But I didn't know Lorraine or Dr. Delaney or Carolyn Gray."

"That is odd. Maybe you'd just heard one of them somewhere and thought you recognized the voice," he suggested.

Out of the corner of her eye, she saw him clutch his side. "Are you all right?"

"Just a little indigestion. Slade gives it to me all the time."

She spotted both stairs and elevator down the hall. She was anxious to get off this level. The echo of their steps along the concrete hallway was giving her a headache. The halls seemed to wind like a maze down here. She felt turned around, but then she hadn't been paying attention.

Unconsciously, now that she could see the elevator ahead, she slowed her steps, trying to give Slade as much time alone as possible in the lab.

"I wouldn't worry if I were you," the chief was saying. "We have a warrant out on Carolyn Gray, the crime lab is sending someone down from Missoula to help us with the investigation of Dr. Delaney's murder, and we'll continue to look for your baby." He ran his beefy hand over his face. "One way or the other, it will be over soon," he said, his hand muffling his voice. "So don't you worry."

They had almost reached the end of the hallway and

the elevator. Her heart slammed against her chest. She stumbled, losing her balance.

Curtis grabbed her to steady her. "Are you all right?"

This time she saw him flinch. Something was definitely wrong with him, but her mind was on the flash of memory. It moved through her mind like a wisp of cloud. She could feel him staring at her oddly. Just get to the elevator, she told herself. "I think I'd like to sit down once we get to the main office."

"No problem," the chief said as he took her arm. "Let's get you taken care of as quickly as possible so I can get back to your...boyfriend."

SLADE COULD SMELL the blood pooling in front of the cabinet as he drew near. He reached out cautiously for the knob, half expecting the cabinet door to be locked. He pulled. The door swung open.

Carolyn Gray tumbled out.

One good look at her, and Slade knew there was no reason to check for a pulse. She'd been shot and shoved into the cabinet as if her killer had been in a hurry. He could see now where the blood that had splattered on the white tile floor had been hastily wiped up.

He stumbled back, confused. Three monsters. All dead. If Carolyn had killed Dr. Delaney, then who had killed her? Not Lorraine. Carolyn's body was still warm and Lorraine—

He jumped at the sudden sound of his cell phone ringing. Hurriedly, he dug the phone out of his shirt pocket before it could ring again. "Rawlins." He'd expected it to be Holly warning him that the cop was on his way back down.

"Slade?" It was Shelley. "Is everything all right?"

Not a chance. "Yeah."

"I got your message. Sorry I didn't get back to you sooner. I was farther up island."

He started to cut her off, to tell her this really wasn't a good time, but then she said, "You asked about the Christmas ornament. The twin golden angels?"

He'd almost forgotten, so much had been going on. He moved away from Carolyn's body, toward the door.

"I *do* remember it," Shelley was saying. "You know who made it? Francie Dunn. You know, Jerry Dunn's mom. That was back when we were kids and played together."

He'd forgotten that Jerry had lived down the street from them back then. When he'd called Shelley, he'd hoped maybe the ornament had meant something to their mother—their adoptive mother, he mentally corrected himself.

"So Francie Dunn gave it to Mom," he said.

"No, Francie *made* it. L.T. gave it to Mom that Christmas, right before…"

He stopped in midstep, freezing. That Christmas, right before she was murdered? "You're sure L.T. gave it to her?"

"Positive. I remember because she looked at him and burst into tears. That was so unlike Mom. Slade, what's going on? Why ask about the ornament now?"

He was trying to understand his mother's reaction and why the chief would have given her the twin angels. Norma said he'd been against the pregnancy. He'd never been close to either Slade or Shelley—and he definitely wasn't an angel kind of guy. Unless there was some special meaning other than the fact that the angels were twins that had made his mother cry.

"Slade, what's going on?" Shelley asked, sounding worried. "Has something happened?"

"You know me, I just get sentimental this time of year."

"Oh yeah, right. You're sure everything is all right?"

"It's fine. Shel, I've got to go. I love you." He snapped off the phone before she could question him further and turned to find Chief L. T. Curtis framed in the lab doorway.

Chapter Seventeen

Holly woke in total blackness, dazed, head aching. The last thing she remembered was reaching for the elevator button.

She tried to get up and bumped into a wall in the dark. She could hear the sound of water and heat pipes but couldn't tell if they were over her head—or just one misstep below her. Carefully, she got to her feet, afraid of falling into an abyss.

Once on her feet, she discovered the knot on the side of her head. She half expected to find no memory of anything. But not only could she remember being hit, she remembered the voice and the muffled familiar words. "It will be over soon." The same words she'd heard the night she delivered her baby. And she realized now why she'd known the person speaking the words even through his mask. Why she'd been so shocked. Because she'd met Chief L. T. Curtis last February with Slade, right before someone had wiped Slade from her mind—but not from her heart, she thought.

No wonder the monsters had found her soon after she met Chief Curtis.

But at least now she knew she'd gone to Slade this

Christmas Eve of her own free will, because she was in trouble and instinctively she'd known to go to him.

And now she had her memory back, for all the good it did her. Slade was waiting at the lab. And Curtis had told him he'd be back as soon as he took care of Holly. Well, he'd taken care of her all right!

Gingerly, she reached out her arms, fearing what she might feel in the dark, but desperately needing to escape this prison—and get to Slade. He would trust Chief Curtis. He would believe that she was safe with the two police officers she'd bet weren't waiting upstairs in the main office. Slade would be a sitting duck.

Her fingertips touched a wall directly in front of her. And another off to her left and right. A closet? Or a coffin stood on end? The thought sent a chill through her. She felt for a doorknob, desperate to find one.

Her hand found the handle of a broom or mop and shoved it aside, only to have it hit something over her head. A large container tumbled down, striking her shoulder, almost knocking her to her knees.

She grabbed her shoulder in the blackness of the closet and felt something wet and sticky. Blood? She leaned against the wall, holding her shoulder, waiting for the pain to subside a little. The closet smelled strongly of floor cleaner. She crouched down and found a large plastic bottle and something wet and sticky spilled on the floor. Not blood. Floor cleaner.

She wasn't bleeding. That was a relief anyway.

She wiped her hands on her jeans and went back to looking for a doorknob. Nor was she in a coffin, she thought counting her meager blessings.

Her hand banged against metal. Smooth, round metal. She'd never been so happy to find a doorknob in her life. She tried to turn it, not terribly surprised to find the door locked—and obviously with a key—from the outside.

She considered throwing herself against the door, but knew that breaking it down was out of the question even if she'd had enough room to get a run at it. Banging on the door for help seemed just as ridiculous. She hadn't seen a soul on her walk with the chief down the labyrinth of hallways. Wherever she was, it wasn't on a main floor and she would never be heard over the sound of the water and heating system now roaring in her ears.

She was trapped. In the dark. And Slade was out there with at least two crazy armed people—Carolyn Gray and Chief L. T. Curtis.

She fought the desire to scream. Or cry. *Think.* She felt around for the broom or mop handle she'd discovered earlier. Mop, she decided, when she found it and ran her fingers the length of it.

Maybe she could use it as leverage to break off the doorknob. She wasn't sure the door would open even if she managed such a feat, but she had to try. She couldn't just stand here in the broom closet, unable to warn Slade, just waiting for the chief of police or Carolyn Gray to come back and kill her.

She got the mop handle between the wall and the knob and pulled down with all her strength. She thought she felt it give a little. If only she had a little more room. Or more weight. The mop handle broke. She fell, slamming into the closet wall.

She felt tears rush her eyes and a sob catch in her throat, just waiting to be let loose. She threw down the piece of broken mop handle, hurt and scared and frustrated. And angry. But she wasn't going to cry.

Bracing herself against the wall, she put her foot against the doorknob. She would break the thing even if it killed her!

She kicked, then kicked harder, ignoring the pain in her arch. The doorknob gave way on the ninth kick. It clattered to the floor. She leaned against the wall, realizing she was crying, but not sure how long she had been.

She wiped the tears from her face with her sleeve and turned her back to the wall opposite the door, figuring she'd have to kick her way out, but determined she would, come hell or high water.

The moment her boot touched the door, the door swung open and she slipped on the floor cleaner and fell to the floor. Crying and laughing and closet-blind, she scrambled to her feet and burst out into the dim light of the hallway.

Once out, she realized she had no idea how to get back to the lab.

SLADE HADN'T HEARD the chief open the door because he'd been on the phone. Curtis stood filling the doorway, his service revolver in his beefy hand. He was looking at Carolyn Gray's body, his expression one of regret rather than surprise.

"Who was on the phone?" the cop asked.

"Wrong number."

"You always were a bad liar, Slade. I figured Shelley would remember the ornament incident. She always paid more attention to the little things than you did."

Slade stared at him, trying to get control of his fury, his fear, his repulsion, trying to understand with his mind something his heart just refused to believe. "What did you do with Holly?" he demanded, fear making his blood run cold as he advanced on the cop.

Curtis lifted the revolver in his hand, the threat too clear.

Slade stopped, his own weapon in his coat pocket, where he'd put it when he'd found Carolyn dead. He knew he couldn't get it out, aim and pull the trigger before Curtis fired and killed him, so he didn't even consider it. He wouldn't do Holly any good dead.

"I locked her in a closet until we could get some things sorted out," the cop said.

He didn't know why, but he believed Curtis. "Why?" he asked, his heart breaking. "Why would you get involved with someone like Allan Wellington?"

"Allan was a genius," Curtis said.

"All madmen think they're geniuses."

"Do they? You think I'm mad and yet I'm no genius. If I were I wouldn't be here right now." The cop glanced toward Carolyn Gray's body. "I wish you'd left this alone, Slade. I told you Marcella would never have had an affair."

Slade eyed the contents of the lab, looking for something he could use for a weapon. A small microscope lay on its side on the lab table in a pile of broken glass. If he could get to it—

"Marcella must have found out what Wellington was doing when she was getting the fertility treatments," Slade said, edging slowly toward the lab table. "She would have come to you, because for some reason she didn't want my father to know she was getting treatments? Or trying to expose Dr. Wellington." He frowned as he glanced at Curtis. "And she would have trusted you." A thought struck him. "She found out about your involvement."

The cop was nodding thoughtfully. "I didn't want to hurt Marcella, but she wouldn't listen to reason."

Slade swore. "She was trying to tell us who her murderer was. You gave her that ornament as a warning. If she talked you'd do something to her kids. No, not her kids, Norma and Joe's kids."

"So Norma told you," Curtis said disgustedly. "I figured eventually she would." His gaze hardened. "They betrayed me. Especially Marcella. She's the one who talked Norma into having Joe's children, and Norma—" he shook his head angrily "—jumped at the chance to be with your father."

"That's why you stole Holly's and my baby," Slade said with a start. "You couldn't stand the thought of Norma having a grandchild."

"You always were a bright kid," the cop said. "Must have gotten that from your father."

His father. Slade looked into Curtis's eyes and knew. "You made it look like a heart attack." *He never had a bad heart.* Inez's words seem to echo. Sweet heaven. "You killed my father—and Dr. Wellington." It was everything he could do not to launch himself at the man and take his chances. If he could just get his hands around the cop's throat— "Dad must have found out that you were the one who killed Marcella."

"Your father was one hell of a cop," Curtis said almost sadly. "He wanted to blow me away himself, but he had too much honor. It was just one of the things Norma loved about him. He gave me until the next morning to turn myself in. Wellington told me what I needed to make the death look like a heart attack. Ironically, I used the same drug on the good doctor when the time came."

"But why kill Wellington if he was such a genuis?" Slade asked, trying to put it all together, knowing somewhere in it all was the key to what had happened to his baby girl.

"He was getting out of control and I was getting tired of cleaning up after him. And I didn't need him anymore."

"Holly," Slade guessed, inching toward the lab table. He moved so slowly. Too slowly. But he didn't dare make a misstep. He had to think of Holly. Finding Holly. "You were afraid of him marrying a woman so much younger and controlling her mind through the use of drugs."

"Wellington had taken her off the drug so he could get her pregnant, but he was having trouble controlling her."

"It was you she was running from when she left the Institute last Christmas Eve," Slade said. It all made sense now. The way Holly had disappeared right after she'd met the chief and Norma. "You could have killed her after you used the mind control to make her forget me," he said, wondering if there wasn't some human compassion in the man.

"You were already obsessed over your mother's murder," Curtis snapped. "If I'd killed Holly, you would never have let up until you found out the truth."

Slade was almost within reach of the table—and the microscope. Suddenly he saw something that stopped him dead. He watched a drop of blood fall from the cop's left side and splat on the floor, bright red, at the man's feet. Slade's glaze leapt to Curtis's zipped jacket.

The knit band around the bottom on the left was soaked with blood. He'd been wounded! Had Carolyn Gray fought back? But how badly was the cop hurt? "You had to know she was carrying my baby, Norma's grandbaby."

"Inez convinced me that the baby was Wellington's."

Slade saw it now, all of the pieces finally falling into place. Except one large empty hole that he had to have filled no matter what happened in this room tonight.

HOLLY STOOD IN the middle of the hallway, lost. She had no idea where she was or where the lab was. She felt tears blur her vision. She swiped at them angrily. Which way? Back down the hall away from the elevator? But then the halls made a junction and—

She saw something on the floor and knew before she reached down to touch the bright red spot what had been wrong with Chief Curtis. Blood. He'd been wounded. It made no sense, but she didn't question it as she looked down the hallway for another drop of blood, then another. Better than a bread-crumb trail, she thought.

She took off her boots, not wanting to make a sound, then began to follow the bloody trail back to the lab. As she drew closer, she began to run, fear and anger coursing through her veins like blood, a hot cauldron of fury. "Dammit, Rawlins, don't you dare let that psychopath kill you!"

"WHAT IS IT YOU WANT, SLADE?" The way Curtis said it he could have been asking him what he wanted for lunch. The cop sounded tired and old and Slade found himself wondering how well he'd ever known him.

"My baby and Holly."

Curtis cocked his head to the side. "Why don't I believe that's all you want?"

"That's it. I don't give a damn about the rest of this." It surprised him, but it was true.

The cop grabbed a shelf on the wall next to him and flung its contents to the floor. "Not you, Slade. You have to have truth *and* justice. You couldn't live with yourself otherwise."

"You might be surprised," Slade said.

Curtis wagged his bald head as he pulled a second gun from his coat.

Slade recognized it as his own—the one he couldn't find at Dr. Delaney's. "Dr. Delaney was telling the truth. He wasn't at the birth of Holly's and my baby. It was you. You put the mask in Delaney's closet to frame him." He could reach the microscope now. All he needed was the right moment and a hell of a lot of luck. "There is one thing I don't understand. Why not let Holly keep the baby? All Inez wanted was an heir for her brother—even a dead one. Why not let Inez have a live family heir? No one would be the wiser."

"Holly was too unstable," Curtis said with a sigh. "I figured after her baby was born dead, she'd probably end up committing suicide."

He'd planned to kill Holly. No doubt still did. Sweet heaven. "What part did Dr. Delaney and Dr. O'Brien play in all this?"

The question seemed to take Curtis by surprise. He frowned. "Dr. O'Brien has nothing to do with this. Why would you ask about him?"

Slade spotted Holly out of the corner of his eye and couldn't believe it for a moment. She peeked around the edge of the door frame and winked at him. He'd never been so glad to see anyone in his life.

"I saw O'Brien at Inez's," Slade said.

The cop's frown deepened. "Inez and Dr. O'Brien? She told me she was just trying to get Holly recommitted, and Dr. O'Brien had offered to help."

It was obvious Curtis wasn't so sure about Inez now. "You know there is something that bothers me," Slade said, motioning to the lab, actually motioning to the microscope on the lab table, hoping that Holly would see what he had planned. "You don't give a damn about superbabies or changing the world to meet some master plan. What were you really doing here?"

Holly nodded. She had her boots off. One in each hand. She motioned that she could throw them.

"Haven't you already guessed? At first, I was just angry that Norma and I couldn't have children when all the wrong couples were having babies. Then I realized there was money to be made with the babies that didn't quite stack up. Allan thought I…disposed of them. But babies, I found, are worth much more alive, either in hard cash or to pay off a debt."

Slade wanted to kill the man with his bare hands, but instead he nodded at Holly as if answering Curtis. "Was my baby cash or payment of a debt?"

"A debt. I was shutting down. Wellington had needed someone to clean up his messes, so we had a pretty good thing going until he became too much of a liability. Your baby was going to be my last…deal. Had a good run, no reason to push my luck."

"But then Holly began to remember," Slade said.

The cop nodded. "Having your baby be stillborn, it's really made you crazy. And when it all comes out about

Dr. Wellington and his mind control…well, everyone involved will be dead. I think I'll retire, too broken up about your death to continue law enforcement. Holly will commit suicide. That shouldn't surprise anyone. Once I get her back under my control again. My old method doesn't work, thanks to Dr. Delaney. I knew the day would come when his conscience would get to him. But he's gone now. All I have to worry about is Shelley. I'm sorry, Slade, but I think all of Norma's children and grandchildren are going to have to die."

A thought lodged itself in Slade's brain like a splinter. The three monsters in Holly's painting. He'd thought they were Carolyn Gray, Lorraine Vogel and Dr. Delaney. Why hadn't he remembered that the monsters didn't seem to know what they were doing? Delaney had delivered thousands of babies. He wouldn't have panicked. But Delaney hadn't been there—Curtis had.

"What went wrong during Holly's delivery?" he asked the cop, positioning himself to grab the microscope the moment Holly threw the boots.

"Nothing," Curtis said, momentarily distracted by the question. "Just a little surprise. We were expecting one baby—not two!"

"Twins?" Slade shot a look to Holly. Curtis caught the look and started to turn. "Now!" Slade yelled.

Holly threw the boots and ducked back out of the doorway. Slade grabbed the microscope and lunged at the cop.

But Curtis was in good shape and quick for a man of his age. He swung back around, realizing Slade was the greatest threat. The microscope hit the cop's hand, the gun went clattering across the floor, and then Curtis was on him, the second gun, Slade's own, in the big man's hand.

They fell to the floor, wrestling for the weapon.

"Get the other gun!" Slade cried to Holly as he and Curtis fought, Slade's pistol between them, Curtis strong as a bull.

She ran into the lab. Curtis's service revolver had slid under one of the cabinets near Carolyn's body. Slade saw Holly cringe at the sight of the dead woman, then flatten herself to the floor to reach back under the cabinet. Everything was happening so fast, and yet it seemed in slow motion, each detail so clear. He could see that she'd cut her bare foot on some glass, blood soaking through her sock, but she seemed oblivious of the wound as she dug for the weapon, unable to reach it.

Slade struggled for the gun between them, Curtis rolling so he was on top.

The blast surprised Slade when the gun went off.

For a moment he didn't know which of them had been hit. Maybe neither. Then he felt something wet and hot across his chest. Curtis was still fighting for the gun, not appearing harmed in anyway.

Slade didn't think he'd been hit, but he knew gunshot victims often went into shock, unaware for a few minutes that they'd been injured. He got an elbow up to Curtis's throat and with effort shoved the man off him. Curtis tumbled backward, coming down hard, but the cop still had Slade's gun in his hand.

"I've got it!" Slade heard Holly yell. She sent the cop's revolver skidding across the floor to Slade. Out of the corner of his eye, he saw Curtis swing his arm up to fire, the barrel of the gun pointed at Holly.

Slade grabbed the skidding revolver, knowing he wasn't going to make it in time.

Another gunshot echoed through the lab. Slade had the revolver and was bringing it up to fire at Curtis, but he didn't get a shot off. He heard Holly gasp, heard someone enter the lab. He swung the barrel of the gun toward the door as Dr. O'Brien filled the doorway, a gun in his hand.

"FBI, drop your weapon!" O'Brien yelled, just before Slade could squeeze off a shot.

"FBI?" Slade dropped his gun.

Holly was screaming at O'Brien. "You killed him! You killed him before he told us where our babies are!"

Slade took her in his arms. "It's okay, Hol, I think I know where our babies are," he whispered. He looked over her shoulder at O'Brien. FBI? "Where the hell have you been?"

"Right behind you, following the trail of death and destruction you left in your wake," the FBI agent snapped. He turned to Holly. "I tried to get you into protective custody by having you readmit yourself to Evergreen, then I could have protected you."

"Could you have?" she challenged. "Then you knew it was Chief Curtis?"

"No," O'Brien admitted. "That I didn't know. But I've been working this case undercover since Dr. Parris called me in on it. He'd discovered the Genesis Project and contacted my office."

"It would have helped if you'd told us who you were," Slade said as he helped Holly to her feet, keeping his arm around her, never planning to let her go ever again.

"I couldn't be sure just what your involvement was," O'Brien said. "From the information I was getting from

Inez Wellington... That day I passed you on the road to her place, I'd just found out that she'd been leading me on a wild-goose chase." He shook his head. "Where do you think you're going?" he said as Slade and Holly moved toward the door.

"To see my pharmacist," Slade said.

"Jerry Dunn?" O'Brien asked. "We have a warrant for his arrest on interstate trafficking of drugs."

"Add kidnapping to the charge," Slade said. "We're going to go get our babies. I hope you aren't going to try to stop us."

The FBI agent backed off. "I'll need statements from both of you later."

Slade nodded, then he and Holly headed for town.

"Rawlins, how can you be so sure Jerry Dunn has our babies?" Holly asked as they neared town.

"Curtis said he used them to pay a debt. It dawned on me. Who else had to be involved? Someone who could supply the drugs. Patty Dunn was one of the names I saw on the list of Genesis Project patients. Jerry's father was also a pharmacist. He did so well in a little town like Dry Creek that he retired and gave Jerry the drugstore."

"You think Jerry's father was involved with Allan?"

"Yeah." Delaney had said this had been going on for more than thirty years. It just finally made sense.

JERRY DUNN ANSWERED the door. Behind him, Slade could hear the sound of babies crying. He pushed his way in. "Chief Curtis is dead. The FBI are on their way."

Patty Dunn sat on the couch, rocking the two infants in the double baby carrier. "If one cries, the other one does," she said and looked up, obviously surprised to see Slade and Holly.

"That's how my sister and I were," Slade said as he moved to the carrier and looked down at the identical twins. They had the Rawlinses' dimples and Holly's blue eyes.

"Oh, God," Holly said and dropped to her knees beside the babies.

Patty Dunn looked from her babies to her husband. "Jerry?" Jerry said nothing. Behind him, FBI agent O'Brien appeared in the doorway with several police officers.

Slade picked up one of the babies and handed her to Holly. Holly began to cry as she held her baby for the first time. He picked up the other infant and cradled her in his arms. The one Holly held stopped crying, and a moment later the one in Slade's arms did as well. He smiled down at the infant in his arms and couldn't hold back his own tears.

Behind him he could hear Jerry being arrested and read his rights along with his wife, Patty. A female officer said Patty's other two children, the two boys Slade had seen in the photograph at the pharmacy, would be taken into police custody.

Slade looked over at Holly. "I was just thinking. You know what you said about going someplace warm? I think we should head south. Someplace tropical, maybe. Someplace we could get married."

She had been gazing in awe back and forth at the two identical baby girls they held. Now she looked up with a start. "Rawlins, are you asking me to marry Ωyou?"

"What do you think?" he asked, his heart in his throat.

"I think it's about time!"

Epilogue

The following Christmas Eve

Holly sat on the couch smiling. Christmas music played on the stereo while Slade and Shelley and her new husband, John, helped the twins decorate the tree.

"How are you feeling?" Norma asked as she came into the room and handed Holly a cup of hot cocoa.

"Better."

Norma sat down beside her. "I never thought I'd see this day."

Holly reached over to take her hand and gave it a squeeze. The last year seemed like a blur now. She and Slade and the twins had flown to Tobago to join Shelley. They'd gotten married there, on a white sand beach, the sound of the turquoise surf in the background and the twins watching from the shade of the cabana.

Back home, Jerry Dunn had told the FBI everything he knew, including how his father had worked with Dr. Allan Wellington and how he'd taken his father's place. Jerry had been the bell-ringer outside on Christmas Eve. He'd called Carolyn Gray to warn her at that point. Curtis hadn't known yet. Inez was arrested in the hospital, but didn't live long enough to see jail. She took an overdose of Halcion. Jerry's wife, Patty, cleared of charges, filed for divorce, took her sons and left town.

It had taken the FBI a while to sort everything out. But following in the footsteps of egomaniac Dr. Allan Wellington, L. T. Curtis had kept a record not only of the births he'd "manipulated" but the lives he'd taken, starting with Roy Vogel's twenty years ago. Dr. Wellington hadn't been happy with his first son's development and decided it was time to terminate that "experiment" and provide a killer for Marcella Rawlins's murder.

From there, Curtis had killed as needed, always able to cover it easily as police chief. His next victim had been Joe Rawlins when Joe discovered the truth about Marcella's death.

Along with the cop's records of events were Wellington's accounts of using mind control on Holly. It seemed the doctor had been taken with her and decided he should have a child with her, but was killed by Curtis before he could artificially inseminate Holly. Wellington had always been incapable of conceiving in any other way but through artificial insemination.

Unfortunately for Curtis, Holly had seen him inject Dr. Wellington with the drug that caused his heart attack. The cop tried to control Holly through mind control and drugs with Inez's help but he feared it was just a matter of time before Holly remembered Wellington's death and told Inez. Curtis had tried to kill her the Christmas Eve she ran away from Evergreen Institute and into Slade's headlights.

For two months, the cop had searched for her. Then to his delight, she'd turned up with Slade. The cop reprogrammed her that evening on the phone and had her steal some files—including the one on Slade's mother—and some money, hoping that would be the end of it.

But of course it wasn't.

It all made sense now. Why Holly hadn't wanted Slade to go to the police when he'd found her in the snowstorm. Why she'd been afraid for her life.

After a few weeks in Tobago, waiting for everything to die down, Slade and Holly and the twins returned home to Montana.

"You know we don't have to stay in Dry Creek," Slade had said.

"No, Rawlins, we don't. But we will," she said, smiling as she'd leaned over to kiss him. "Because it's home."

His eyes had widened. "We're going to have to buy a house!"

She'd laughed. "One with an art studio and a big backyard."

They'd found a house—right next door to Shelley's and closed on it the same day Shelley announced her engagement to John, the wonderful man she'd met while vacationing in Tobago.

It had taken time for Slade to forgive Norma. Then, one day when Norma had stopped over, Holly heard him tell the twins, "This is your gramma." Holly felt tears come to her eyes even now, just remembering the look on Norma's face.

Norma had been a part of their family ever since. The family was growing too; Shelley and John were expecting in March.

"You've been through a lot," Holly said now to Norma as the Christmas tree started taking shape to the sound of "Jingle Bells" and laughter.

"Pish," Norma said. "I've been through nothing compared to you and Slade and the twins. No, I mean Slade. I never thought I'd see the day that he would actually be enjoying Christmas again."

Holly tried not to cry. She was so emotional these days. Just the sight of Slade and the twins made her close to tears of happiness. "I can't tell you how thankful I am to have him and our little angels."

"You don't have to," Norma said. "Believe me, I know."

Courtney toddled over with one of the ornaments cradled in her small hands. "Oook," she said smiling up at her grandmother.

Carmen toddled over to take a look at her twin's ornament, then showed her grandmother hers. "Look, angels, Gramma."

"They're beautiful," Norma said of the ornaments. "Just like the two of you!"

"Are you ready?" Shelley called out. She nodded to John to do the honors. He plugged in the lights.

The tree lit up, a warm glow of bright colored ornaments and twinkling lights.

"It's beautiful," Holly breathed, unable this time to hold back the tears. The twins climbed up onto the couch, one on each side of her, their eyes huge with surprise and excitement.

Slade sat down on the floor at her feet. "How are you feeling?" he asked, putting his hand on Holly's swollen belly. He smiled up at her as he felt a small foot kick.

"Rawlins, what would you think about having Christmas babies?" she asked as she felt another contraction coming.

"Are you serious?" he cried, getting onto his knees in front of her. "You don't mean…*now?*"

In an instant, he was on his feet. "She's going to have the babies!"

Shelley was at his side. "Take it easy. Go get her suitcase and start the pickup. Mom and I and Johnny can take care of Courtney and Carmen. But who's going to take care of Slade?"

Slade hadn't moved. He was looking down at Holly, his eyes so filled with love Holly thought she would burst.

"I just want this time to be…different," he said quietly.

"It will be, Rawlins," she said, smiling up at him. "This time I'm having twin boys!"

* * * * *

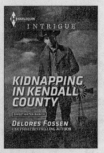

"The woman in Greenleaf Bar was you?"

"You don't remember?"

"Vaguely."

He struggled to put things in perspective. That had been a hell of a night. He'd stopped at the first bar he'd come to after leaving the rodeo. A blonde had sat down next to him. As best he remembered, he'd given her an earful about the rodeo, life and death as he'd become more and more inebriated.

She must have offered him a ride back to his hotel since his truck had still been at the bar when he'd gone looking for it the next morning. If Brit was telling the truth, the woman must have gone into the motel with him and they'd ended up doing the deed.

If so, he'd been a total jerk. She'd been as drunk as him and driven or she'd willingly taken a huge risk.

Hard to imagine the woman staring at him now ever

being that careless or impulsive.

"Is that your normal pattern, Mr. Dalton?" Brit asked. "Use a woman to satisfy your physical needs and then ride off to the next rodeo?"

"That's a little like the armadillo calling the squirrel roadkill, isn't it? I'm sure I didn't coerce you into my bed if I was so drunk I can't remember the experience."

"I can assure you that you're nowhere near that irresistible. I have never been in your bed."

"Whew. That's a relief. I'd have probably died of frostbite."

"This isn't a joking matter."

"I'm well aware. But I'm not the enemy here, so you can quit talking to me like I just climbed out from under a slimy rock. If you're not Kimmie's mother, who is?"

"My twin sister, Sylvie Hamm."

Twin sisters. That explained Brit's attitude. Probably considered her sister a victim of the drunken sex urges he didn't remember. It also explained why Brit Garner looked familiar.

"So why is it I'm not having this conversation with Sylvie?"

"She's dead."

Find out what happens next in
MIDNIGHT RIDER
by Joanna Wayne,
available January 2015 wherever
Harlequin Intrigue® books and ebooks are sold.